MW00790657

Wedding at Sea

A MUIR HARBOR NOVEL

3

MELISSA TAGG

BOOKS BY MELISSA TAGG

MUIR HARBOR SERIES

Autumn by the Sea

A Seaside Wonder

Wedding at Sea

MAPLE VALLEY SERIES

Now and Then and Always

Some Bright Someday

In the Sweet Ever After (coming soon)

WALKER FAMILY SERIES

Three Little Words (prequel e-novella)

From the Start

Like Never Before

Keep Holding On

All This Time

ENCHANTED CHRISTMAS COLLECTION

One Enchanted Christmas

One Enchanted Eve

One Enchanted Noël

WHERE LOVE BEGINS SERIES

Made to Last

Here to Stay

To my coworkers-turned-friends at Hope Ministries

There's a spot in this story where Lil talks with her brother about how much she loves her job. I'm so glad I can say the same. It's a joy to serve, pray, and laugh with you!

And thanks for putting up with my frequent rambling about my "other life." :)

*T*he houseboat bobbed on choppy waters, little more than an inky shadow against the faintest shards of moonlight.

Storm clouds had gathered and groaned all evening—as if dragged into place with the same foreboding reluctance that weighed Lilian's every step on the wobbling dock. A lone raindrop landed on her cheek, accompanied by the midnight sky's distant growl. *Stupid. This is so, so incredibly stupid.*

Worse, it was reckless.

And if there was one thing Lilian Muir had never been a day in her life, it was reckless.

Well, except, perhaps, for that singular day so many years ago when she'd made this same seaside walk to this same rickety-looking houseboat. Only it hadn't looked so rickety then. And the summer sky had beamed with golden color. On that bright Sunday afternoon she'd been all hope and no hint of hesitance.

She'd also been all of ten years old. A reckless mission at ten wasn't at all the same thing as a reckless and most likely futile one at thirty.

But stubbornness, or maybe desperation, pushed her on. If

1

she hurried, she could make it in and out of Wilder's house-boat before the coming squall took the harbor captive. Shouldn't be too difficult to find the file. Of course, whether she'd discover anything helpful inside it, who knew. But she had to at least try.

Because after a lifetime of pushing the unknowns away, every speck of resistance had dissolved earlier today. One simple question from a doctor who already knew the answer. One scribbled sentence in his uneven handwriting.

Family medical history unknown.

Not even a full sentence. But it was enough.

Scattered drops of rain tapped on the dock as she reached the houseboat that belonged to her older brother's best friend. Wilder Monroe, the bane of her existence, lived on the boat part-time. He spent the rest of his time squatting at Muir Farm—sleeping on the couch in the living room or claiming the guest room upstairs when no one else needed it, just down the hall from Lilian's own bedroom. The man mooched off their family at mealtimes, took advantage of Maggie's kindness at every turn, and had the unbearable nerve to practically consider himself part of the family.

Maggie. What would she think if she knew what her adopted daughter was up to just now?

Humidity hung heavy in the late-spring Maine air, smelling of the brackish sea and curling around Lilian as she stepped onto the houseboat. *Maggie would understand.*

Yes. Because Maggie carried her own burden of unanswered questions.

Anyway, it was too late to rethink any of this now. Lilian had come this far. She'd made the drive from the farm into town, parked at the harbor front, walked the veritable plank. Now it was time to jump, as it were.

And maybe, if she was lucky, some minor trespassing and a search of Wilder's boat would keep her from obsessing over the rest of the neurologist's words from earlier in the day. Or the small card stuffed in her jacket pocket with the date and time of her next appointment. The MRI that might explain everything or nothing.

"It can take a while to pinpoint a diagnosis, Lilian. We're going to take this one step at a time. Meanwhile, if the symptoms return—"

She shook her head, dislodging Dr. Cho's voice. *Focus.* The boat rollicked underfoot and a chugging wind billowed her raincoat. *Get in, get out, get home before the storm picks up.*

At the narrow door that led into the houseboat's living quarters, she pulled a key ring from her raincoat. Another thing it was too late to reconsider—swiping Wilder's keys from the pocket of his leather jacket after everyone else back home had called it a night. But he was the one who'd left the thing slung over the farmhouse's stairway banister. He was the one who'd been infringing on her family's residence for years. All she was doing now was returning the favor.

Hopefully quickly. And without him ever knowing. Because the last thing she needed was a repeat of the past. Wilder's crushing words from the last time she'd stepped on this boat still echoed, even all these years later. She didn't need to hear them again.

"It's impossible, Lil. You'll probably never know. You need to accept it."

With a determined huff, she tried the first key on the ring. No luck. But the second slid in easily, and a moment later, she turned the paint-chipped knob and padded her way in.

Instantly, a scent she wished she didn't recognize washed over her. An irritatingly good one—the same cedar-and-spice aftershave aroma that lingered in the upstairs bathroom on the mornings after Wilder stayed over at the house.

Except, come to think of it, the man hadn't been shaving these days. Or sleeping much either, according to the telltale circles under his eyes. He hadn't cut his hair in months, and the other day when she'd scowled at him over some inane comment he'd made that she couldn't even remember now, for once, he'd scowled back. He hadn't joined the Muir family for nearly as many meals lately either, for that matter.

Something was up with him. But this wasn't the time and definitely not the place to wonder about whatever had Wilder Monroe tied up in knots. She had her own tangles to unravel.

And if she had any hope of succeeding, it started with finding the file she prayed still existed. The one Wilder's P.I. dad would've first opened almost exactly twenty-eight years ago.

Possibly on the very day Maggie had found Lilian on her porch. A toddler. Alone.

Jagged lightning cut through the small horizontal window of Wilder's living space, casting just enough light to briefly make out the avocado-green couch along one edge of the room, a beige afghan Maggie had probably crocheted draped over the back, and a pair of work boots sitting outside what she assumed was a bedroom door.

His father's boots. If ever Lilian could dredge up anything besides annoyance toward Wilder, it was at the thought of Harry Monroe and his death three years ago. The memory of the shattered look in Wilder's eyes during the funeral.

Another rumble of thunder cut through the tense silence. *Hurry up.* She plucked her cell phone from the pocket of her raincoat and tapped its flashlight to life. Bold light budged into the dark, and she moved it in a slow circle, scanning the crowded space. Where would Wilder keep his father's old files? He wouldn't have thrown any of them out, not considering he'd taken over Harry Monroe's private investigation agency.

Her gaze caught on the fridge, on a Polaroid snapshot held in place by a *Smokey the Bear* magnet. Must've been taken five or six years ago, on a Christmas when Wilder and his father had spent the day at Muir Farm. The two of them were squished into the photo with Lilian's whole family.

They were all haphazardly posed in front of the Christmas tree: Neil, her older brother, born in Scotland, taken in by Maggie when he was fourteen. Lilian's little sister, Indi, adopted as a newborn. And Maggie herself, the incredible woman who'd brought them together, made them a family.

Her focus scooted to Wilder. He stood behind her in the photo and, of course, he was giving her bunny ears, wearing a smirk. *So very mature.*

But then, she'd stolen the man's keys and was currently traipsing around his houseboat. So maybe she wasn't one to talk. And she needed to get on with it, find what she was looking for.

Bingo. Her phone's light caught on a glint of metal. A rusty filing cabinet was shoved against one wall, wedged in between a worn recliner and the edge of the kitchenette counter.

She skirted around a trunk positioned as a coffee table, raindrops now steadily pattering on the metal roof, and reached the cabinet. She yanked on the top drawer, but it stuck. Locked. As were the two below.

Keys. Right. She pulled the key ring from her pocket once more and held it up to the light of her phone. Shoot, none of these keys looked small enough for the filing cabinet lock. So where—

Every skittish nerve inside her froze at the sudden jostling of the boat. Another crash of thunder. A thump.

Someone's here.

Wilder's keys dropped to the floor as she fumbled to tap off her phone's flashlight. But what good did that do? Now she couldn't see to make her escape. *What escape?* Only one door led out of this space and that thudding she was hearing now was most definitely footsteps that were most definitely growing closer and—

At the exact moment the door pitched open, she dove into the sliver of space behind the recliner, her heart battering her rib cage. The boat's floor quivered underneath her. *Now what?* Maybe she'd get lucky and Wilder would skulk right to his bedroom and crash into bed. And then she could pick her way to the door and tiptoe free.

But why was he even here? Hadn't she heard Wilder's snores from the couch in the living room before she'd left the farmhouse? She'd figured he'd once again decided to spend the night at his "second home," as he liked to call the Muir family home—*her* home—rather than risk a stormy night on this ridiculous boat.

How would he have even gotten here? The keys to his Jeep were on the same ring as his boat key, currently in her possession.

But if it wasn't Wilder, then who . . . ?

Rain must be falling in sheets now, the noisy cadence on the roof making it difficult to track the scraping of the floorboards as whoever it was moved farther into the living quarters. Her lungs pinched as she held her breath. *Stupid, stupid, stupid . . .*

The chair in front of her lurched, coils creaking, as someone sat, the chair's cloth back shoving purposefully into her. Wilder. Definitely Wilder. And he obviously knew exactly where she was. But he might not know exactly *who* she was. What were the chances she could scooch out of here and race for the door without him seeing her face?

"You know, if you were hankering for a tour of the place, Lil, you could've just asked."

Pressed into the wall, she let out her breath, humiliation shooting its way through her. She didn't have to see the man's face to know he wore a smirk. She'd never hear the end of this, would she? He'd badger her for the rest of their lives.

Worse, he'd tell everyone in her family how he'd found her

here and, sure, they'd laugh, but eventually, at some point, they'd all ask the same thing. *Why?* And she couldn't tell them. She just . . . she couldn't. Not yet. Not until she knew . . .

"You ever going to come out, Ms. Muir?"

It was all she could do to swallow her groan. "No. I think I'll just stay here."

Wilder rocked back in the chair, nudging her closer to the corner. "Be my guest. Except, wait, you already did. Broke into my boat and made yourself right at home, didn't you? Never really took you for the lawbreaking type, but—"

Before he could finish his sentence, she shoved her weight against the back of the chair, fast and hard. Hard enough to send Wilder sprawling forward as she scrambled from her hiding place.

"Didn't break in." She ducked past the chair, past Wilder heaving himself upright after having tumbled to the floor. Lightning crackled outside, rain pounded. If she could just make it to the door—

"Not so fast." Wilder's tall form budged in front of her so quickly she knocked into his cotton tee. Probably would've gone flying backward if not for his arms reaching out to steady her. Laughter rumbled from his chest as his low voice rose above the noise of the storm. "Haven't given you that tour yet."

She wrenched free. "I don't need a tour of your dumb boat."

"Then explain to me what you're doing here. Did you have your heart set on a late-night rendezvous with yours truly? That could've happened just as easily back at the farm. You know, where it's nice and warm and dry."

She couldn't have stopped her retort if she'd wanted to, never mind the lethal mix of mortification and frustration mangling her nerves. "Rendezvous? I didn't know you knew such fancy words."

With another baritone laugh, he slapped one palm against the wall and a flood of light filled the room. She winced at the brightness—and then, after her eyes adjusted, again at the sight of his charcoal gaze pinned on her. His too-long dark hair was rain-dampened and disheveled, his T-shirt rumpled underneath his open leather jacket. Stubble shadowed his cheeks and chin.

And yet, behind the sleepiness that clung to him, beyond the smug half-grin, hovered something else. Something serious and direct.

"I-I'm sorry, Wild." A feeling a little too close to guilt pricked her. "I shouldn't be here."

"You really shouldn't. You know how people in this town talk. The two of us alone. Together on my boat. This late at night. We might as well send out wedding invitations."

"I'd rather jump in the ocean. Lightning and all."

His grin only widened. But there was still that something in his near-black eyes. Stalwart curiosity. Stubborn determination. Twenty years she'd known this man, since long before the word *man* applied, but this might be the first time she'd found Wilder Monroe almost . . . intimidating.

"Anyway, I'll be going—"

He shot one arm out in front of her, barring her from the door. "Out with it. What're you doing here?"

Thunder pealed through the air and the wind moaned, hurling itself against the boat, rocking it once more. And miracle of miracles, it was enough to make Wilder lose his balance. Only for a moment, but a moment was all she needed. She charged underneath his outstretched arm and pushed through the door.

"Guess you stayed at our house one too many times, Monroe," she called over her shoulder as she escaped onto the houseboat's deck. Rain pelted her, slicking down her cheeks and over her raincoat. "You've lost your sea legs."

"Lil, be careful. The rain—the deck—it's slippery."

A jagged flash lit up the sky on the heels of Wilder's warning. Too late. The wet deck caught her off guard, set her feet into a slide she couldn't escape from. She careened toward the edge of the boat, where a low railing wasn't enough to catch her. To stop what happened next.

Her shriek was lost to a thunderous bellow. And then a splash.

And then an ice-cold darkness that pulled her under.

For just a moment there, right around the time he'd witnessed poised, practical Lilian Muir dive behind Dad's ratty old recliner, Wilder had almost felt like himself.

Like the Wilder of three years ago. The one who'd worn his amused curiosity as if it were tailor-made instead of tattered and tired.

And after the day he'd had today, a moment like that, unburdened and wildly unexpected, was a gift. He'd needed a reason to laugh, and watching Neil's little sister go into full-on panic-and-hide mode had done the trick.

But then the woman had gone and fallen off his boat. In the middle of a storm, no less. One growing nastier by the second.

With a grumble that rivaled the thunder, he shrugged out of his leather coat and shucked off his Nikes. Lil could swim, of course—she'd grown up on a farm perched right at the edge of the Atlantic, after all—but that raincoat she'd been wearing reached nearly to her knees. Waterlogged, it might drag her down or snag on something underneath the stormy waves. What choice did he have but to play the hero?

Even if that was the last thing he felt like anymore.

He charged from the shelter of the houseboat's living quarters, only scant seconds having passed since the ominous splash and the sight of a flailing Lilian disappearing over the railing. But terrible things could happen in mere seconds.

Terrible, life-changing things . . .

A dangerous wind pummeled him, sheets of rain making it nearly impossible to see. Any of the day's earlier warmth was lost now to a chill that seeped past his instantly soaked clothing and coated his skin. With another groan, he paused just long enough to pluck his phone and wallet from his pocket and toss them back inside, then crossed to the boat's edge and looked out over the opaque water. No sign of Lilian. Only angry breakers—frigid, surely. This . . . wasn't going to be pleasant. But there was nothing for it.

He pulled in a breath and plunged into the sea.

The surging cold engulfed him, but instinct took over the second his head went under. He kicked, moved his arms with force, refused to let the water bully him. *Okay, where are you, stubborn woman?* He felt around, his fingers brushing over wood—probably one of the dock's mooring poles.

He pushed his head to the surface, flinging his gaze from side to side as needling rain pricked his cheeks. *Where . . . ?*

"What the heck are you doing?"

Lil? He jerked his focus to the sound of her voice behind him, twisting his body in the merciless sea. *There.* The barest outline of a form hovering beside the houseboat. He squinted, made out the white flotation device attached to the side of the boat, Lilian with one arm hooked through it.

Relief warred with irritation. Or maybe that was just exhaustion. The ever-present fatigue that had lurked at the borders of his brain for too long battled with his limbs as he fought to keep afloat. "Lil?"

"Why'd you jump in?" she called. "What were you thinking?"

He pushed his way toward her. "Oh, I don't know, maybe that I'd save your life."

"Do I look like I need saving?"

Rain slapped against the water's surface, against his face. They had to get out of this before the lightning found a new target. He reached Lilian's huddled position beside the houseboat and joined her in looping one arm through the life ring. The boat rocked against the storm. "You just had to fall in. You just couldn't wait out the storm inside like a rational person." Were his teeth chattering?

Hers definitely were. "You d-didn't have to come in after m-me."

"You got some brilliant plan for hefting yourself up onto the boat?" A peal of thunder boomed overhead.

Rivers streaking down her cheeks, Lilian glanced upward. She was a tall woman and obviously a strong swimmer, but no way were her arms long enough to reach the railing above. "I-I guess I'll swim to the dock. C-climb the pole."

He grasped her forearm before she could set herself free. "Don't be ridiculous." It took him less than a second to feel around for the cable holding the life ring to the boat, then another to give it a tug to make sure it was secure before hoisting himself upward. The muscles in his arms, already tired, strained as he climbed, but it didn't take long to reach the edge of the deck, grip the metal railing, lug himself over.

He dropped to his knees on the drenched deck and flung one arm toward Lilian. "Grab on."

"I don't think—"

"For once in your life, Lil, don't be obstinate. Just take my hand and let me pull you up."

If not for the rain pounding his back and the thrashing back-and-forth of thunder and lightning, he might let himself sink into awe at Lilian's instant obedience. *So unlike her.* He closed his palm around her cold fingers and pulled, towing her up and then over . . .

And then rocking backward as she collided into him. His back hit the floor, Lilian landing on top of him, her nose knocking against his chin and a piece of her wet hair winding up in his mouth. He sputtered and coughed, half-dazed, half-amused. Fully conscious of the knee jabbing into his side.

"Lil, could you maybe—"

She gasped as she jerked her head up, eyes wide. "Sorry." Her palms were on either side of his head, her knee pressing into him even harder as she tried to get up. But her coat was tangled around her—or maybe him. Her foot stabbed his shin as she attempted to get free.

He winced, but he couldn't help a strangled laugh at the same time. This night, this whole thing, him flat on his back and Lilian grappling to get away . . . absurd. But somehow, he'd needed it. He'd really, really needed it. "I sure hope Old Bob a dock over is watching this through his binoculars. It's got to be more entertaining than those Westerns he loves." Even this close, he had to shout to be heard over the storm.

Lilian stopped moving for one blessed moment, drilled him with a glare from above, raindrops—and seawater, too—spilling from her face and hair and landing on his cheeks. "Sometimes I really can't stand you, Wilder Monroe."

"Only sometimes?" He pushed up and she toppled to the floor beside him. "And I think the words you're looking for are 'thank you.' You'd still be glued to a life ring if I hadn't helped you up." He hauled himself to his feet, then reached for her hand.

She slapped it away just like he knew she would and rose on her own, fists finding her hips the moment she stood. "Fine. Thank you. And good night."

She whirled, but not quickly enough. He nabbed her palm

and didn't give her the choice of yanking away. "Lil, you can't drive in this storm. It's raining way too hard. And we're both being idiots at the moment, just standing here asking to get hit by lightning. We're going inside."

He didn't let her argue, tugging her toward the narrow door and nudging her into his living quarters. He shoved the door closed behind him before marching past Lilian, into his bedroom, then the tiny attached bathroom, returning with two towels seconds later. He thrust one at his guest. "Here. Dry off. You should probably get out of your wet—"

She interrupted him with an indignant huff. "I am not *undressing*. I don't even want to be here."

"I was going to say *coat*. And you can stop scowling at me. I didn't ask you to come here. If it were up to me, I'd still be asleep on the couch back at the house." He wiped his towel across his face, then over his hair. "If it were up to me, I never would've woken up to see you playing thief with my keys and sneaking off to do who-knows-what."

"You didn't have to follow me." She peeled her coat free, revealing a gray sweater molded to her skin just like the black jeans below. Water puddled around her feet.

"You took my keys. You broke into my boat."

"I didn't break—"

"Close enough. And if you didn't owe me an explanation before, you certainly do now after what you just put me through."

She whipped the towel around her shoulders like a blanket. "Again, you didn't have to jump in."

"Chivalry, Lil. I've got it in spades."

For just a moment there, it seemed like she might crack. Let a smile slip free. A laugh. But then the boat rocked and she wobbled. And this time, his instincts weren't quick enough to catch her. She tripped over the trunk behind her and landed on the couch with an *oomph*.

14

Wilder snickered. "Gotta admit, I like this clumsy midnight version of you. You've always got that poised and graceful thing going on during the day. It gets old."

"Can it, Wilder." She jolted to her feet but kept one hand on the back of the sofa for balance as the boat continued to sway. "Is this thing even safe?"

He shrugged. "Probably. Maybe. Hopefully."

"H-hopefully? That's not quite good enough for me."

"Yeah, well, your failure to explain yourself definitely isn't good enough for me. So tell you what?" He stepped toward her, the last of his patience evaporating. "I'm going to go into my bedroom. I'm going to change into different clothes. Warm, dry, comfortable clothes that'll make you seethe with jealousy." He closed the final inches between them and glowered down at her. "And when I come back out here, you're going to talk. You're going to stop stalling and tell me exactly what possessed you to come here tonight."

Her crystal-blue eyes went wide again. Bluest eyes he'd ever seen. He'd said as much to Neil once. Got a look of warning in return that'd made him burst into laughter.

"You have nothing to worry about, man. Your sister can't stand me."

She'd acknowledged it outright tonight—and not for the first time. But instead of the vexation that usually filled her expression when she was in his presence, right now Lil actually looked a little nervous. Well, good. He could take her ire and her scowls and her unwavering dislike most days—found it all comical, to be honest.

But apparently, right in this moment, he'd reached his limit. He brushed past Lilian toward his bedroom. Today had been too much. Too disappointing. Another roadblock. Another dead end.

And the nagging, battering conviction that he was going to fail. He was going to let down Maggie Muir. Again. The woman who'd loved him like a son. Who'd done her best to comfort him after Dad . . .

He was going to fail her.

He whipped around just outside the bedroom, realization wriggling through him as he faced Lilian once more. "That's why you're here, isn't it?"

She cinched the towel over her collarbone. "What?"

"Maggie's case." *The* case. Inherited from Dad. Impossible to solve. "Cynthia Muir."

The name of Maggie's missing granddaughter had begun to haunt him. Had it done the same to Dad in the twenty-five years he'd spent looking for her?

One corner of Lilian's towel slipped free of her hold and dipped down her shoulder. "Wilder—"

"You came here looking for notes, for all the files, didn't you? You're losing patience." He raked his fingers through his wet hair. Tough luck for her. The files weren't in the cabinet she'd clearly set her sights on when he'd found her here. "You're probably thinking you can put that lawyer brain of yours to work and discover something I missed. Something Dad missed."

"That's not—"

"The thing is, I can't even blame you." Especially not after today. His one lead, the best he'd had since taking on the case . . . gone. Just like that.

All the steam left him then, and he trudged into his bedroom, leaving Lilian alone, closing the door quietly behind him.

At the sight of the bed he'd left unmade whenever he'd last slept here, he almost gave in to the urge to let himself flop onto the navy blue sheets. Instead, he opened the chest of drawers lodged into the corner, pulled out a pair of track pants and a sweatshirt, then dragged himself into the bathroom. One look in the mirror was enough to send a chill through him. Good grief, he looked terrible. Hair matted, skin pale under unshaven cheeks.

Give yourself a break. You just dove into the ocean.

Yeah, well, that didn't explain the bluish half-circles under his eyes.

He shed his soaked clothing. Dressed. Avoided looking into the mirror again. He ran the towel through his hair once more, then ducked into the bedroom.

And halted.

Something's not right.

The feeling slammed into him. Hard enough he had to gulp to catch his breath. To blink—once, twice—before shooting his gaze around the room, focused in a way he hadn't been when he'd first come in. The framed photo atop his dresser, him and Dad, was just slightly out of place. One of his pillows was on the floor. And there, near the foot of the bed . . . the edge of a slim, plastic tub, just visible from underneath the bed frame. Maggie's case files.

Someone had been in here.

Lil?

No, he'd tracked her from the farmhouse in Neil's truck and arrived at the houseboat within minutes of her. She hadn't made it farther than the living room by the time he'd caught her, he was sure of it.

Still. He angled around the bed and charged from the room, knowing what he'd find even as he burst into the living space. *Empty.* Of course she'd left. He'd known as soon as he'd closed his bedroom door that he was granting her a reprieve. One she'd clearly pounced on.

But she'd left something behind. On the floor, beside the keys she'd "borrowed." Brow furrowing, he bent to pick up the small rectangle of paper. Held it out in front of him. A couple lines of tiny print. A handwritten date and time. He turned it over.

Dr. Gordon Cho. Mercy Hospital, Department of Neurology

Had Lilian dropped this? If so . . .

His eyes traced the path of wet footprints to the door she'd fled through.

Lilian Muir, why do you have an appointment with a neurologist?

And who else had been in his houseboat tonight?

3

The voice found her as it always did. Deep and distant. A fleeting, velvet murmur. Whispered words she could never quite make out, save three.

Sweet little Lily.

And then there was the familiar, swaddling warmth. Strong arms and the feel of cotton. Soothing and sure. *Sweet little . . .*

"Lil, wake up!"

It was snatched away from her—the voice, the warmth, the dream she knew so well. Inhabited by a stranger she knew not at all.

Lilian's bed frame creaked as she rolled to her side, pulling her comforter over her head with a moan. "Not now, Indi. Whatever it is, it can wait." It was too early and she was too tired and her pillow was far too comfortable. If she was lucky, she might fall back asleep, right into the same dream and maybe this time, finally, she'd see a face.

His face.

The mattress sank as her sister plopped next to her. "Fine. But if you were going to pick today to go into the office late for the first time ever, you could've given the rest of us some warning. And by *the rest of us*, I mean me. I about went into shock when I took a shower this morning. A *warm* shower. I'm so used to you and Neil using up all the hot water."

What?" Lilian lurched upward, flinging her comforter to the side. "What time—"

"It's eight forty-five, my friend." Amusement flared in Indi's grin. "Did you go to bed with wet hair? It's looking a little wild."

Eight forty-five? She should've been at the law office an hour ago. Should've woken up at least an hour before that. She clambered over Indi and scuttled into action, reaching for her phone the second her bare feet landed on the hardwood floor. She was halfway across the room, phone up to her ear, mind scrambling, when Morris's voice sounded on the other end.

"Well, if it isn't my truant partner, calling to make her excuses, I assume."

Lilian riffled through her closet. Pitch-black blazer. White button-down. Hmm, pencil skirt or starched slacks today? "I'm sorry, Morris. I-I don't know what happened. I guess I forgot to set my alarm." Which shouldn't matter because she usually woke up long before the thing went off. But on the one morning she'd needed it, it hadn't come through for her. Her own fault since apparently last night she hadn't remembered to—

Last night.

It came cascading in then, every humiliating fragment. Her midnight trek to the harbor. Her accidental dunk in the Atlantic. An unnecessary rescue, a cowardly escape.

Wilder Monroe, peering at her through eyes like black orbs, as dark as they were weary.

And yes, she had gone to bed with wet hair last night. After her harrowing, stormy drive back to the farmhouse, she'd tried to warm herself up with a shower, hoping the sound of water trickling through old pipes wouldn't wake up anyone else. Because there was no way she could've explained her rash and nonsensical decision to go snooping through Wilder's houseboat.

Not without telling her family about that consultation with Dr. Cho yesterday. All that Googling she'd done after her appointment, trying to predict what her upcoming MRI might reveal.

Nothing. Please let it reveal nothing.

But maybe that was the wrong thing to hope for. What about her symptoms? They might've gone away weeks ago, but what if they came back?

"You really don't have to apologize, Lilian." The sound of clinking accompanied Morris's voice. She could picture him stirring one spoonful of sugar after another into his morning tea. "Your hours are your own to set," he went on. "I'm your partner, not your boss."

Maybe so, but it was hard to think of the older man who'd mentored her all the way through law school so casually. She'd never quite outgrown her need to impress him. "Still—"

"Still," he cut in and echoed her, "I appreciate the call. I was starting to worry one of your bike tires had gone flat or something."

She tapped to turn on her speakerphone and set the phone on her dresser, then began changing, vaguely aware that Indi was still camped out on her bed. "Well, I'll be there soon. I'll skip the bike today and drive—"

"No need for that. Just get here by nine thirty-ish, okay? Nine forty-five, at the latest. Because, well . . ." He cleared his throat. "I might've taken the liberty of adding a couple appointments to your schedule today. Three, actually. The first is at ten."

"What?" She was supposed to have a beautifully empty calendar today—no meetings or phone calls with clients, no depositions or court dates. Just a lovely little pile of paper-work in the peace of her office. Her favorite kind of workday.

"I'll explain when you get in."

"But—"

"See you soon."

The phone went silent.

Lilian shoved her arms into her shirt with a groan. Since when did Morris schedule appointments for her? And why today of all days? When yesterday had left her mind a churning, sleepy mess?

"You're off a button."

Lilian met Indi's eyes in the mirror over her dresser. Her sister was sitting cross-legged, chin propped on her elbows. If Indi was trying to hide her grin, she was doing a miserable job. It pinched her cheeks and sparkled in her green eyes.

"You're enjoying this too much." Lilian yanked a string of mismatched buttons free and started over, moving her fingers up her shirt as fast as she could.

"Can you blame me? Years of you being ready for school eons before me, telling me to hurry up or we'd be late. A whole childhood of running behind while my prompt and dependable big sister ran on ahead." She let out a light laugh, the bracelets on her wrist jangling. "So yes, I am definitely enjoying this."

"Glad I can provide some morning entertainment," Lilian muttered. She zipped up her skirt, then shrugged into her blazer before glancing in her oval mirror and wincing.

Indi hadn't been wrong about her hair. *Wild* was an under-statement. *Try chaotic.* But it was finally long enough that with the help of a few bobby pins, she could manage a ponytail. That and a quick swipe of makeup and she'd be plenty presentable for whoever she was supposedly meeting with today.

"I like the blazer." Indi shifted, scooting to the foot of the

22

bed and letting her legs dangle over. "But have you ever thought about branching out from blacks and neutrals once in a while?"

"Hey, I throw in a nice blue every now and then. Besides, I'm a lawyer. This is how we dress." Unlike Indi the artist, who could make just about any color choice come off as picture-perfect. From her wavy hair to her assortment of jewelry, she had a lively, bohemian flair to her.

Whereas Lilian had always felt like she was all angles and sharp edges by comparison. Short, straight blond hair. Ice-blue eyes. Tall and long-limbed. Great for those couple years she'd played basketball in junior high, but not so much for filling out a dress.

Lilian reached for the simple gold studs she wore most days and turned to Indi. "Thanks for waking me up by the way."

"It wasn't entirely a mission of mercy." Indi tapped her heels against the bed frame. "I've actually been waiting to pounce on you all morning."

Lilian felt her forehead wrinkle as she poked first one earring and then the other into place. "Why?"

"Because I know about you and Wilder."

"Um . . . what?"

"I have every creak of every floorboard in our old house memorized. I heard you leave last night. And Wilder only a few minutes later." Indi rose from the bed, lips quirked, one eyebrow cocked.

Oh, a whole world of possibilities hovered in that sugges-tive expression. Hilarious, impossible, *ludicrous* possibilities. "And you assume that means . . ."

"Well, isn't it obvious?"

"You think . . . me and Wilder . . . you actually think . . . " She burst out laughing.

Indi's eyes narrowed. "It's not the craziest thought."

"No, it's so far past crazy, I don't even have a word for it. And I've got a terrific vocabulary." Lilian spun back to her dresser, reaching for the plain gold necklace that matched her earrings and lifting it to her neck. But she didn't have a hope of clasping it, not with a second round of giggles spilling over.

"Oh brother, let me help you." Indi moved behind her and tugged the necklace from Lilian's fingers.

"It's just the thought . . . You know he drives me insane."

Indi hooked the necklace and stepped back. "Which is how some of the best romances begin."

She gave an exaggerated shudder even as a straggling chuckle slipped out. "I'm going to pretend I didn't hear that." She turned back to her mirror and reached for a hair tie, then gathered up her hair

But in the next moment, she let the strands fall around her face once more as her gaze hooked on the frayed corner of an index card sticking out from behind the mirror. Why had she never found a better resting place for the thing?

Not that hiding it away would change any of its impact on her life. Or erase its scrawled words from her memory.

Lilian. Birth date 9/12/88. Allergic to bananas.

The entirety of her past, pre–Muir Farm, summed up in faded scribbles. The note had been pinned to her corduroy overalls on the day she'd been found. The day Maggie had walked out of the house to water her rosebushes only to discover Lilian sitting on her porch swing. It was all the authorities had had to go on when they'd tried to determine who Lilian was and where she'd come from. It was all Harry Monroe had had to go on when he'd begun his own investigation.

And when Lilian was older, it was all *she* had had to go on when the questions came speeding toward her. From a child psychologist. From the kids at school. Questions, so many of them. And she could never answer . . .

With a sharp inhale, she reached out to straighten her mirror, covering the corner of the card.

"Wow, you *really* don't like him."

Her gaze shot up to meet Indi's in the mirror once more.

"The way you just flinched . . ." Indi shook her head. "I was so sure you were hiding a relationship with Neil's bestie, but you really, really don't like the guy."

"Not exactly news, Indiana." She slipped her hair tie around her wrist and brushed past her sister. She'd finish getting ready in the bathroom—and quickly. By now it was almost nine, and if she didn't hurry up, she'd definitely need to skip her usual bike ride to the office.

Indi followed her from the room. "Yeah, but I've never really figured out what you've got against him."

Lilian started down the hallway, past Indi's bedroom door and toward the bathroom. On the other side of her own bedroom, the room that'd once housed Neil had been vacant for months, ever since he'd married Sydney and moved up to the attic. He'd renovated the space into a master suite for him and his new wife.

Lilian had a feeling it wouldn't be long now before Indi also moved out of her childhood bedroom. She'd been dating Philip, a professor from Augusta, for four or five months now and they were probably on a fast track to engagement, one she doubted would drag on all that long.

Which meant, with Maggie's bedroom downstairs, Lilian might end up the sole occupant of the farmhouse's second floor in the not-so-distant future. The thought was strangely discomfiting.

Not that she wasn't happy for all the changes in her siblings' lives. In addition to getting married, Neil had recently built a luxury treehouse, the first of several he planned to complete for his new Airbnb business. Indi had recently been on a remarkable healing journey, which had included meeting the daughter she'd given up for adoption over a decade ago.

"Wilder's charming and congenial."

Lilian stopped at the bathroom doorway. They were still talking about this? "He's grating and galling."

Indi crossed her arms. "He's nearly as smart as you, and that's saying something."

"He's smug and excessively self-assured."

"Let's stop with the alliteration."

Lilian shrugged. "I was having fun with it, but okay."

"I'm just saying, I don't get what you have against him. It can't just be a grudge from that time he gave you a bloody nose during dodgeball in elementary school."

Of course it wasn't. But she'd gone twenty years without telling anyone about what had happened at the houseboat the first time she'd made a futile trip there. About how kind Harry Monroe had been when he'd let her down so gently.

Then how blunt the man's teenage son had been in the aftermath. Wilder had eavesdropped, heard the whole pitiful thing, then wounded her with the truth.

"It's impossible, Lil."

He probably didn't even remember . . .

"Look, Indi, if I tried listing all the reasons Wilder Monroe is in my black books, I'd never make it into the office." And if she finally shared the one reason above all others there was a cavern between them as deep and wide as anything Mother Nature could produce, the memory might just drive her back to her bed and under the covers.

She'd made a fool of herself back then. And again last night.

"It's a shame, really." Indi gave a long, embellished sigh. "You two would make adorable babies."

"Oh, Indi, gross." She pushed into the bathroom. "Excuse me while I go throw up." She closed the door in her sister's face and whirled to the mirror, her expression caught somewhere between repulsion and hilarity. She and Wilder. *Ridiculous.*

Even more ridiculous after the previous night. The man probably thought she was a lunatic.

The man deserves an apology.

The unwelcome conviction swept over her in a flurry. She *had* swiped his keys and trespassed on his boat.

Well, okay. She'd text him later. Or maybe get especially stalwart and call him. But she'd keep it short and to the point. And if all went well, she'd get through it with Wilder being none the wiser about why she'd really—

A knock interrupted, and she grabbed the doorknob. "We're done with this conversation, Indi. The day I have Wilder Monroe's baby is the day—"

"Please don't say *the day pigs fly.*" Maggie grinned at her from the other side of the door. "You're too much of a wordsmith to settle for a cliché like that."

Maggie clutched a metal travel mug, her usual snow-white braid hanging over one shoulder. The once-vibrant red of her hair had faded before its time, but strangely, the change hadn't done much to age her. At sixty-five, thanks to the energetic light in her hazel eyes, she could probably pass for someone a decade younger.

Except that wasn't only light in her eyes just now. It was laughter. "What's this about Wilder?"

"Nothing. Nothing at all."

Maggie held out the covered mug. "Coffee for the road. But before I give it to you, I need a promise in return. Promise me you'll be home for dinner tonight. You've worked late every night this week and I'm missing my daughter."

For a moment, her harried morning and all the lingering effects of last night faded into the background as she looked to the woman who'd raised her. Who'd taken her in when she was two, legally adopted her when she was eight. Lilian might call her Maggie instead of Mom—they all did—but Maggie was her mother in all the ways that counted most.

This . . . this right here was why she never should've followed a wayward whim to Wilder's houseboat last night, thinking she might find some scrap of information in his father's old files about where she'd come from.

She already knew where she belonged. Right here with the people she loved most. In the place she loved most. Maggie and Indi and Neil and this creaking old house by the sea.

"I'll make it to dinner. Promise."

And she'd put all the rest of it out of her mind. Just like she'd been doing for most of her life.

———•———   ———•———

There were times Wilder could swear the Muir family lived inside a fairy tale.

Just look at the scene on the other side of his windshield. Well, Neil's windshield.

That big yellow farmhouse with its gingerbread eaves and sprawling white porch, the lawn a blanket of vivid green, dotted with budding trees and reaching toward the rocky shore. And beyond the shore, foam-tipped swirls of turquoise and blue, tussling with the rugged coastline.

Wilder tapped his thumbs on the truck's steering wheel. A darn fairy tale. And he was about to waltz into the place and announce that the happy ending Maggie had been waiting on for so long wasn't nearly as close as he'd thought just days ago.

At a knock on the passenger-side window, he jerked his head to the side. "What're you doing with my truck?" Neil's muted voice called through the window.

Wilder pulled Neil's keys from the ignition and opened his door. "Returning it."

The morning air smelled of rocks and brine and soil, the distant barking of Neil's dog colliding with the whoosh of the waves.

"I thought you stayed here last night. You left?" Neil's Scottish accent had faded some in the twenty years since he'd crossed the Atlantic to live with Maggie, but it was still plenty noticeable. "And why'd you take my truck instead of your Jeep?"

Wilder met Neil by the truck bed just as Captain, Neil's collie, loped to his best friend's side. "Little issue locating my keys."

Not entirely the truth. He'd known exactly where his keys were when he'd left the farmhouse the previous night. But he hadn't decided just yet whether to blab about Lilian's little adventure at his houseboat to Neil or anyone else in the family.

Just as he hadn't decided what to do with the knowledge that someone besides Lil had rifled through his boat last night.

Or how to tell Maggie about the latest setback in his search for her granddaughter.

Neil leaned over to scratch Captain's head, eyeing Wilder as he did. There was always just a little too much knowing in the man's steady gaze. Everyone liked to talk about Wilder's infernal gut instincts—it's what he was known for, it's why he'd followed in Dad's footsteps to become a P.I.—but Neil had a way all his own of reading people.

His friend straightened and smoothed one palm over the front of his plaid shirt. "Got chores. Let's walk."

"I'm here to see Maggie, actually."

"You just missed her. She's spending the day with her fiancé. He picked her up ten minutes ago and—"

"Wait, did you just say *chores?*" Wilder stopped at the corner of the farmhouse porch. "Dude, it's like nine thirty. You're usually out at the barn three hours before now."

Neil kept walking, rounding the house and heading toward the back. "Married man now, Wild," he called over his shoulder. "Got a persuasive wife."

He hurried to catch up to his friend. "Nope, can't make myself believe it. Not even Sydney could talk Farmer Neil into sleeping in."

"Who said anything about sleeping?"

"Actually, I don't really think we need to continue this conversation."

Neil snorted. "She brought me breakfast in bed, if you must know."

"See? Total fairy tale."

Neil gave him a sidelong glance as they crossed through the backyard toward the grove that separated the house from the main farm grounds. It wasn't entirely fair to sum up his best friend's life so simply. Truthfully, the man had been through a lot, starting with being orphaned as a kid in Edinburgh. Really, none of the Muirs had had it that easy, Maggie most of all.

Decades ago, she'd lost a fiancé in Vietnam. Years later, the first child she'd adopted, long before Neil or any of the rest of them had come along, had died in a tragic car accident at only nineteen years old. And then there was her granddaughter, Cynthia Muir . . . who may or may not still be out there somewhere.

And yet, despite all the hurt in her past, Maggie Muir had cobbled together an awfully loving and close-knit family.

Never once had Wilder regretted his own unique childhood—just him and Dad on their old houseboat—but he'd be lying if he said he never imagined growing up in a regular house with a passel of siblings running around.

Or that there weren't days, even now, when he envied Neil.

He followed his friend into the shade of the grove, the ground still damp from last night's rain, mud slurping at his boots. Captain wove through the thicket ahead of them.

"I hit another dead end, Neil. The case . . . we're talking really dead. Literally. Dead. He's *dead*."

Neil didn't have to bother asking who. For months now, Wilder had been intent on tracking down one person and one person alone. The last and only link he knew of to long-lost Cynthia Muir.

Neil didn't break his stride. "Feels a little morbid for first thing in the morning."

First thing? Wilder had been awake for hours, tossing restlessly in his bed amid the houseboat's sway and, later, pacing the too-small confines of the living room. Finding Lilian Muir in his place last night had been a nice interlude for a while. A blessed distraction. But this morning, not even the memory of Lil's drenched and defiant appearance was enough to subdue his churning thoughts.

At what point did a man simply throw in the towel? Just . . . give up?

The question was a punch in the gut. Sharp, bruising. A bitter unearthing of his worst day, the one horrible what-if he'd worked so hard to bury . . .

Dad.

"Wild?"

Neil had paused up ahead, turned, Captain going on without him. When had Wilder stopped walking?

"You just see a ghost or something? You look . . ." Neil didn't finish.

Didn't have to. Hadn't Wilder caught a glimpse of his own reflection last night? It was as if he was deteriorating right in front of everyone's eyes. All because of this case. This never-ending, hopeless case.

It's not only the case, and you know it.

And it *wasn't* hopeless. He couldn't let himself believe that.

Twigs and leaves crunched underfoot as Neil retraced his steps before coming to a stop in front of Wilder. Steady, solid-as-a-rock Neil. The day Maggie Muir had taken him in, she'd unknowingly done Wilder Monroe one of the greatest favors of his life. Given him a friend as close as a brother.

It was just another in a long list of reasons why he owed it to her to put this blasted case to rest once and for all. But with the news he'd received yesterday, the last breath of wind had seeped from his sails.

And he didn't know what to do next. He honestly just . . . didn't know.

"Keep asking questions, son. That's the key in this work. Keep asking." Dad.

Neil stuffed both hands in the pockets of his Levi's. "You don't have to do this, you know." Neil's brogue always deepened when he was concerned about something. Or someone.

Which was why Wilder forced the closest thing he had to nonchalance into his voice. "What? Help you with chores? But you know how much Melba loves me."

Neil should've laughed at the mention of his cow. Especially considering the old thing definitely *didn't* like Wilder. Instead, he only fixed Wilder with that too-knowing stare of his. "Maggie will understand. If you need to stop looking, if it's time—"

"It's not." The wind shuffled through his hair and he resisted the urge to flatten his palms over his cheeks, rub the exhaustion from his eyes. "I've hit dead ends before. This probably won't be the last one before it's all over." *God, please let it be the last one.*

If that was a prayer, it was his first one in a long time.

"Just needed to vent," he added. "That's all."

He knew Neil well enough to know the man wanted to argue. But he also knew he wouldn't. Because that was Neil. His silences tended to say as much as his words.

Instead, Neil started walking again, picking his way through the trees that separated the Muir family home from the cluster of outbuildings that made up the farm's main grounds. Wilder matched his friend's long strides.

"So how'd he die?" Neil finally asked.

"Plane crash. A private jet, actually. Details are fuzzy." But the reporter from Atlanta who'd called Wilder yesterday hadn't left any room for doubt in his words. Nicholas Cornish was dead.

Nicholas Cornish.

At one time, the name wouldn't have meant anything to Wilder. But he'd finally cracked a major piece of the investigation earlier this year when he'd identified the man as the father of Cynthia Muir.

For literal decades, no one, Dad included, had been able to hunt down that information. All they'd ever known was that Diana Muir, Maggie's oldest daughter, had run away from home thirty years ago after high school, only to return to Muir Harbor two years later with a toddler in tow. It was the first and only time Maggie ever saw her granddaughter. The accident that had killed Diana happened that same weekend, not far from where he and Neil walked now.

Supposedly, Cynthia had been in the car with Diana. But her body had never been found, which meant Maggie had never stopped hoping she might still be alive. Somehow, somewhere.

But there'd never been much to go on. They'd known Diana had been in Atlanta during her years away from Muir Harbor, but not who she'd been with.

Until earlier this year, when it'd seemed like the investigation had well and truly cracked open. When he'd learned the name Nicholas Cornish. When he'd finally had something concrete to sink his teeth into.

Except that in the months that followed, he'd never been able to track down the man. His boots sank into the ground now as he kept pace with Neil. "If only I'd pieced things together sooner. I could've gotten to Nicholas earlier. Before—"

"Wilder—"

"He was a criminal, Neil. Involved in all kinds of shady business dealings. That's why he was on a plane. Apparently he was trying to get out of the country." They emerged from the grove into the morning light. "What if he came to Muir Harbor with Diana the weekend she died? What if he was there, at the accident? We know there was a second vehicle involved. For all we know, it was his and he whisked Cynthia away just like he did Diana and she's been alive this whole time and now—"

"Wilder." Neil's voice was firmer this time and he stopped again, clamping one hand on Wilder's shoulder. "Did you sleep last night?"

Sunlight assaulted his eyes. He pulled his sunglasses from his shirt collar. "Yes. I slept." Two hours. Possibly three. He shoved his sunglasses in place.

"You don't look like it."

"You keep talking about my appearance. And not in a very flattering way. Trying to give me a complex?"

Neil rolled his eyes. "I'm trying to be a good friend. This isn't what Maggie would want for you. You've become obsessive about this case. Frankly, it's freaking me out a little. And I'm not the only one who's noticing."

Behind Neil, the farm grounds were hushed and mostly still. Wilder's gaze traveled from the smaller barn that housed the animals to the larger one that was always a bustle of activity around harvest time. It contained the air blower and packing equipment that made Muir Farm's direct-to-consumer blueberry harvest possible each fall. Then there was the cooling room, the machine shed, the henhouse.

Wilder knew this farm as well as he knew the houseboat. Sometimes this place felt even more like home than the boat, no matter all its good memories.

Good memories that were far too often, far too easily drowned out by the one bad memory. By the wondering, the not-knowing . . .

Maggie's missing granddaughter wasn't the only mystery that kept him awake at night.

But it was the one he still had hope of solving. A feeble, fragile hope. But hope nonetheless.

"So what's next, then? If Cornish is gone, what's your next step?" Neil stepped into the barn and freed his milking pail from a nail.

"Keep asking questions, I guess," Wilder said, following Neil to a stall. "It's what Dad would do. He always said to keep asking questions." He let out a sigh. "By the way, who else has noticed?"

"Huh?"

"You said you're not the only one who's noticed how obsessive I've become—a term I reject, for the record. I'm being thorough and focused about this case. That's a far cry from obsessive. Is it Maggie you're talking about?"

Neil only grunted and opened Melba's stall.

"I just don't like the thought that she might be worrying about me or anything. She already feeds me half the time and lets me hang around as if I'm one of the family. She shouldn't have to worry about me, too." He took a step toward the stall, but Melba let out a low mewl of warning. Wilder halted.

Neil snickered. "Easy, lassie. I won't let him get too close."

"What does she have against me?" Wilder eyed the black-and-white beast.

"She's tight with Lil."

Of course. Lilian Muir *would* turn a cow against him. Well, he could get her back easily enough if he wanted to. All he had to do was open his mouth and fill her big brother in on her surprise escapade last night.

If not for that hospital appointment card he'd found, the one in his pocket right now, he just might. He could think of about a hundred reasons why Lilian might be meeting with a neurologist and none of them were good. Was she sick? Had she told anyone in her family about whatever was going on? Somehow, he doubted it. Lilian was the hold-things-close-to-her-chest type.

"Wilder?"

He glanced over to where Neil now sat on an overturned bucket beside his grumpy cow. Sunlight squeezed through wooden slats and reached down from the rafters. "Yeah?"

"If you don't want Maggie to worry, come to dinner tonight. She likes having you around. We all do."

Wilder combed his fingers through his shaggy hair. "With one glaring exception." Two, if they counted the cow.

"You never know. Lil might just warm up to you one of these days."

"And Melba here might just run for president."

Neil chuckled, then stilled. "You are one of the family. Always have been." He held Wilder's gaze only for a moment before patting Melba's side and looking away.

———•—— ——•———

"I don't understand, Morris. How could you do this without telling me?"

Morris Groves turned away from the expansive picture window at the front of what used to be a dining room. The little cottage the older man had long ago transformed into a workplace sat right at the edge of Muir Harbor's town center, where the quaint downtown with its cobblestone street, decorative storefronts, and glossy black lampposts ended and a residential neighborhood began.

No longer a dining room, this space was now Morris's office, sprawling and comfortable, with leather furniture and bookcases lining the walls.

The familiar creases in his face deepened as he let out a throaty chuckle. "Goodness gracious, you make it sound as if I sold off the practice. I'm trying to help you, Lilian."

Lilian perched on the arm of a wingback chair, still wearing the tennis shoes that looked comical with her slick blazer and skirt. But they were a practical necessity anytime she biked into town, which was most days spring through fall, even the occasional unseasonably warm winter day.

She had a pair of wedges waiting for her in the leather messenger bag at her feet, but she hadn't gotten as far as swapping out her footwear yet. Hadn't even made it to her own office. The moment she'd arrived, propping her bike underneath one of the cottage's dormer windows, its whitewashed cedar shake shingles gleaming in the bright morning, Morris had popped his head out the front door and told her to hurry up.

So much for her hours being her own. *"You said to be here by nine forty-five at the latest. I made it with six minutes to spare."*

"No time for congratulations. You're conducting a job interview in twenty minutes."

"But I don't need—" she began now.

"I know, I know." Morris reached under his polished desk and came up with a spray bottle, then moved to the overflowing potted ivy on a plant stand in the corner. "Who cares that you've been working sixty- or seventy-hour weeks for going on three years now? You're capable of keeping up." He spritzed the plant.

Lilian straightened. "Not to sound arrogant, but yes, I am. I don't need a paralegal." Especially one Morris had advertised for without telling her.

Not just advertised. Apparently, as she'd learned in the past few minutes since she'd come into Morris's office and walked straight to the electric teapot he kept on a corner shelf, the man had looked at more than two dozen résumés and cover letters over the past week. He'd invited not just one but three applicants to come in today for interviews.

So much for a quiet day of paperwork.

She fiddled with her tea bag string, steam lifting from the mug she'd filled. What she wouldn't give to be guzzling that travel mug full of coffee Maggie had given her earlier instead. She probably should've told Maggie she'd gone off caffeine weeks ago. "Morris, if you want a paralegal, that's great. But—"

"No, we're hiring someone for you. That is, *you're* hiring someone for you. I just pared down your options some." Morris moved on to his next plant. "I am sorry I didn't give you longer to prepare, though. I meant to tell you yesterday afternoon after the Lansing deposition—"

She stood. "To warn me, you mean."

"—but Jemima gave out on me three blocks from the courthouse." He didn't miss a beat, spraying another plant as he shook his head.

"Really? Blaming your beloved station wagon?"

"Had to get her to the shop, and by the time I got back here, you were gone."

Yes, because of that appointment with Dr. Cho. "I suppose Jemima's also the reason you couldn't tell me *before* the deposition or the day before or the day before that."

With a huff, Morris finally set down his spray bottle on the side table between the two wingback chairs in front of his desk. "Sit, Lil."

"But—"

"Sit." It was his stern voice. The one he hardly ever used. Certainly not the same tone he employed whenever reminding her that he wasn't her boss anymore.

Today, clearly, he *was* her boss.

Her gaze drifted past Morris's desk to the picture window and out into the front yard, where a dangling bronze sign glinted in the sunlight.

Groves & Muir Law

The day two years ago when Morris Groves had replaced the old sign with this one, her last name joining his, she'd straight-up burst into tears. And then just about died of embarrassment. But the older man had been delighted by her show of emotion.

"You've been cool as a cucumber 'long as I've known you, Lilian Muir. Nice to know you're capable of cracking once in a while." He'd chuckled and squeezed her shoulder, then nudged her inside and warned her not to get a big head.

Morris lowered into the chair next to her now, rubbing one palm over what was left of his frizzy gray hair. "I *am* sorry about the way I went about this. But I knew this would be your reaction. That's why I went behind your back to advertise. That's why I had Danine help me sort through the résumés and call our best prospects."

So their receptionist had been in on it, too? That explained Danine's chagrined expression when Lilian had passed her desk minutes ago. "Am I dropping the ball somehow? Did I forget to file a brief or miss a court date or something?"

"Of course not." Morris's kind brown eyes settled on her. "You're a good lawyer, Lilian. But you *have* been working crazy hours. You can't deny it. And you're in a hurry so much of the time. Appointments that would take me ninety minutes, you get through in thirty."

"Isn't efficiency a good thing?" She abandoned her mug on a coaster on the side table, yet to take a drink.

"Yes and no. I think sometimes you forget it's people we serve, not paperwork or items on a to-do list." There was a gentleness in his tone now, and yet, every sentence felt like a dart. An accusation.

"I'm trying to do a good job, Morris. I-I guess I didn't realize I was missing the mark."

"I never said you were." He laced his fingers over one knee. "I just want to free you up a little so you can remember why you became a lawyer. Remember how to enjoy what we do. A paralegal can help you with that."

"But—"

"Plus, I'd like to retire soon. And I need to know I'm leaving this practice in good hands."

She opened her mouth, closed it again. Morris was going to retire soon? *Of course he is. He's pushing seventy.* And he'd been talking about a long-awaited RV trip with his wife to see the redwoods in California for as long as she'd known him.

But clearly he wasn't comfortable leaving her at the helm.

Because . . . because she loved paperwork too much? Because she wasn't enough of a people person? Gosh, if that didn't knock a girl down a peg or two.

"And then there's that."

She looked up, realized what Morris was looking at. She'd been massaging her right arm. Again. Never mind that she hadn't felt a tremor in weeks. She dropped her hand with a start.

But it was too late. Too much suspicion hovered in Morris's gaze. He leaned forward in his chair. "Since when do you drink tea, Lilian?"

"Since . . ." Words she wasn't ready to say jammed in her throat. *Since the symptoms came back.*

Last month, when she'd first noticed the trembling in her right hand, she'd had the bright idea that maybe laying off caffeine would help. But going cold turkey had only left her with headaches on top of everything else.

Unless the headaches, too, were connected to . . . to whatever diagnosis Dr. Cho was mulling. Whatever the MRI might reveal.

Morris was still watching her, waiting. But finally, he exhaled with a puff of his cheeks. "I didn't go about this the right way. Again, I'm sorry for that. But I really believe it's for your own good and the good of the practice." He stood. "Danine put all the résumés and cover letters on your desk. Your first candidate, Mariana, will be here soon."

Yes. For an interview Lilian wasn't even slightly prepared for. "Okay." She didn't know what else to say.

"I talked to all three candidates on the phone, and Mariana's the only one who made me laugh." Morris retrieved his spray bottle, his expression consoling and maybe a little pleading. "So I'd say she already has a leg up on the others, but it'll be your call, of course."

"Okay," she said again, reaching for her messenger bag, slinging it over her shoulder as she stood. She was halfway to the door when Morris stopped her.

"Lilian."

She turned.

"I'm not just your partner and mentor. I'd like to think I'm your friend, too. If you ever need to talk . . ."

The temptation to tell him everything was almost too much. She hadn't wanted to unburden herself to her family. Not with so many other changes afoot, so much recent joy filling the walls of their home. Neil, still practically a newlywed. Indi's romance with Philip and reconnection with her daughter.

And Maggie—dear, sweet, deserving Maggie. She'd been through so very much in her life, but when Ray Camden, Philip's grandfather, had swept into her life earlier this year, she'd begun a whole new chapter. Lilian had never seen her so happy as when Ray had proposed a few weeks ago.

So what would've been the point in dropping her own troubles at anyone else's feet? Especially when she didn't have any answers anyway. Especially when it all might amount to nothing.

Please, God . . .

But Morris. She might be able to tell Morris.

However, Danine ducked her head into the office before Lilian could form words. "Your appointment's here, Lil. I'll show her to your office."

Lilian looked past the doorway to see a woman with honey-gold hair moving to follow Danine down the hallway, and beside her, ears perked, a dog with sleek black fur. A service dog?

Morris handed Lilian the mug of tea she'd almost forgotten about. "Give it a chance, Lil. I think you'll like her."

4

*S*he was late for dinner. Nothing new about that.

Or about the raucous cacophony of laughter and voices filling the farmhouse as Lilian dropped her work bag in the entryway and hurried down the hallway. Her stomach gurgled at the familiar aromas joining the noise in the air—Maggie's pesto chicken, buttery garlic bread. A far cry from the pitiful granola bar she'd eaten in three bites around lunchtime, in between her second and third interview of the day.

She was late and ravenous and . . .

Home. She slowed under the arched doorway that led into the crowded dining room of Muir Farm. Lavender walls. An aged table too large for the space. Almost every chair filled. Tangerine light filtered through lace curtains, and the frustration of her workday slowly slid to the back of her mind.

A little like magic—this seaside house, this makeshift family.

From her usual chair, Maggie lifted a glass, a grin tugging at her lips, the engagement ring her beau had given her glinting under the amber light of the dated brass fixture overhead. Next to her, Neil was saying something to Sydney, and across from them sat Indi. No Philip tonight? Even though he lived up in Augusta, Indi's significant other had become as much a regular around here as anyone, as had his teenage half sister, Holland.

Instead of Philip, though, Wilder sat in the chair beside Indi.

And there went Lilian's appetite.

Of course it *would* be him who spotted her lingering in the doorway before anyone else. The moment Wilder's focus landed on her, the corners of his mouth pinched and crinkles deepened around his eyes. Great, he was replaying last night in his mind, wasn't he? Picturing her looking like a drowned rat, no doubt. Rehearsing the exact words he'd use to tell everyone at this table about what she'd done.

If he hadn't already.

"Look who decided to join us." Wilder leaned back in his chair, far enough it bumped into the oak hutch behind him. "Late again, Miss Muir?"

"Freeloading again, Mr. Monroe?" She strode into the room and took the chair beside him because it was the only one left with a place setting, then turned to everyone else. "Sorry. Work."

"Is it ever anything else?"

At Wilder's snide comment, Maggie narrowed her eyes from the head of the table. "You're one to talk, young man. How many meals have you missed altogether lately?"

Lilian didn't even try to hide her smirk as she served herself a piece of chicken.

"I'm here tonight," Wilder mumbled.

Lilian reached over his plate for the basket of garlic bread, lowering her voice to a whisper. "Unfortunately." Before her fingers could close around the basket, Wilder nabbed the last piece.

"All the same," Neil piped up, "you could try to switch it up now and then, Lil. Instead of blaming work when you're late, tell us you were . . . I don't know, roller skating and you lost track of time."

She refused to look at Wilder while he demolished the garlic bread he'd stolen. "I haven't been on roller skates since I was seven."

"Fine." Neil scraped his fork on his plate. "Tell us you were spelunking. Or fishing. Or practicing your caber toss." His burr deepened at the end with his mention of the Highland game. Probably for Sydney's benefit. Lilian's sister-in-law could never quite get enough of her new husband's Scottish accent, and Neil knew it.

"Ooh, I know." At Neil's side, Sydney leaned forward. "Instead of blaming work, she tells us she's late because she was out having a secret tryst with a secret lover." Sydney pointed her butter knife in the air. "Now that would make things interesting."

"Because you're a newlywed, Syd, with romance on the brain, I'm going to let the silliness of that slide." Lilian spread her napkin on her lap. "Except to say it wouldn't really be a secret if I told you, would it?"

Indi chuckled. "It's funny you should say that because last night I totally thought—"

Lilian choked on a too-large bite of chicken, dread pooling in her stomach as she coughed and swallowed, drawing everyone's attention. Worth it if it kept Indi from finishing that sentence. "Wow, this chicken," she sputtered, throat finally unclogged. "It's delicious. Marvelous, actually."

Maggie lowered her fork. "Well . . . thank you?"

"It's the best chicken I've ever had."

"Overdoing it a little, aren't we?" Wilder muttered.

She shifted in her chair to face him. "Are you insulting Maggie's chicken?"

"No. I'm not. But . . ." He peered at her through eyes the

color of granite, gradual understanding dawning on his face. And, oh, that grin. That stupid, slow grin she couldn't stand. With a whirl, he rotated away from her. "Indi, what was it you were saying? Last night you totally thought . . ."

Ice clinked in Indi's glass as she lifted it. "You're going to think it's hilarious. I heard Lil leave the house and then I heard you leave—"

"Is there more bread in the kitchen, Maggie?" Lilian jerked to her feet.

"To go with my delicious chicken? Yes, dear." Maggie's eyes sparkled. "But I need you to sit back down for one minute. I've been waiting to say this until you were all here and I could get a word in edgewise. Take a seat, Lil." Maggie glanced around the table. "Oh for heaven's sake, why do you all look worried all of a sudden? It's good news."

Better than good if the pure elation in Maggie's smile was any indication. Lilian lowered into her chair.

"Ray and I have set a date," she finally said, the joy in her eyes deepening. "We don't want a long engagement. Heaven knows, we've both waited for this long enough as it is. June twenty-ninth. That's our wedding date."

She barely got her last words out before Indi let out a shriek and jumped from her chair. "Oh, Maggie, this *is* good news. It's the best, most marvelous news." She threw her arms around Maggie.

Wilder dropped his napkin on his plate. "Even more marvelous than the chicken."

Any other day, Lilian would've punished him with a glare, but not even Wilder could spoil this moment. She rose and took her turn hugging Maggie. "I'm so very happy for you," she whispered in Maggie's ear. "Beyond happy."

Maggie's arms squeezed her. "You don't think six weeks is too quick to pull off a wedding?"

Neil pushed in for his turn. "Syd and I got it done in less

time than that. Or, well, Lil planned most of it, so she should get the credit."

"'Got it done'?" Sydney gave an exaggerated pout. "How utterly romantic."

Neil let out a booming laugh and the room once more erupted into noise. The best kind of noise. Excited voices and boisterous hugs. Indi was saying something about a venue and decorations and Neil was coaxing the pout from Sydney's face and Maggie was beaming. Absolutely beaming.

"You got awfully lucky, Lilian Muir." Wilder's voice was low near her ear.

She blinked and bumped into him as she turned. "What?"

"Indi was about to regale us with a little story before Maggie stole the spotlight."

He couldn't let her have one minute of unbridled enjoyment, could he? "I don't know what you're talking about." She plucked the empty bread basket from the table and whirled.

"Last night. Indi heard you leave." He followed her toward the kitchen. "She heard me leave. One plus one equals—"

"Nothing," she hissed, the warmth of the kitchen rushing over her as she entered. And something that smelled heavenly. Maggie's blueberry cobbler, no doubt. "It equals nothing."

It made no sense that Wilder's smile could widen even further. It already rivaled a Cheshire cat's. And the dumb dimple in his chin didn't help matters. "Can't really fault her for making the assumption. Everyone else is coupling up around here. She probably figured we didn't want to be left out so—"

She slapped the bread basket onto the island counter. "Oh my word, how many times in one day do I have to have this same conversation?"

"So Indi *did* think we were having a little tête-à-tête." He strode to the other side of the counter. "That's hilarious."

"No, it's ludicrous."

He leaned over the counter on both elbows. "You say potato, I say—"

"Impossible. Preposterous. Absurd."

"You done?"

She crossed her arms. But only a moment later, she dropped them and sighed. "Look, Wilder, I was going to call you today. Or text you. Or . . . something." But she hadn't gotten around to it, what with Morris hijacking her schedule, those three back-to-back interviews.

He lifted an eyebrow. "You were going to call me of your own free will? I find that . . . impossible, preposterous, absurd."

Was she frowning because of his teasing or because of what she knew she had to do now? *Both. Definitely both.* "I owe you an apology."

Across the counter, he straightened. "Say what?"

"You heard me. I said I'm sorry."

"Actually, you didn't—"

"I'm saying it now, then," she snapped. "I'm sorry. For last night, I mean. I shouldn't have taken your keys or snuck onto your boat or . . ." She cleared her throat. "Any of it. All of it. I shouldn't have and . . . I'm sorry."

He stared at her for a long moment, voices and laughter from the dining room drifting in the background. Maggie had left the window over the sink open and a cool evening breeze floated in, rustling through the leaves of the plants lining the windowsill. Buttery yellow walls wrapped around the room, along with the cabinets Neil had painted a pristine white a few years ago.

The heart of our home. That's what Maggie always called the kitchen.

Wilder finally broke his silence. "You left something last night." He tucked his hand in the pocket of his jeans, then pulled out a card, slid it across the counter, all without taking his eyes off her.

She sucked in a breath. The card from Dr. Cho's office. "Wilder, I—"

"Oh good, I was hoping I'd find you two together." Maggie swept into the room.

With a barely perceptible movement, Wilder nudged the bread basket over the card. Then, with a nod so slight she might've imagined it, he pulled his gaze off her and turned to Maggie. "You found us. Together."

"Perfect. Because I have a favor to ask."

Thoughts churning, stomach growling—had she even taken two bites of her chicken?—Lilian willed her composure to hold. But the card . . . what did Wilder know? Or think he knew? "A favor?" She moved to the stove, where half a loaf of homemade bread remained in a pan. She reached for a nearby knife and cut herself a slice. The oven's heat warmed her cheeks, the smell of blueberry cobbler pulling another gurgle from her stomach.

"Yes, and it's a big one." Maggie clasped her hands. "Really big."

"Ask away." Wilder draped an arm around Maggie. "Any of us would do anything for you. You know that."

Maggie's eyes were on Lilian. "Well, I wanted to ask if you'd plan my wedding."

Lilian spoke around a bite of bread. "Of course—"

"Both of you. As a team."

———◆——— ———◆———

Lilian Muir was hands-down the most exasperating woman Wilder had ever known.

But she was also the most entertaining. Especially when her feathers were ruffled.

He gave a sidelong glance to Maggie as Lilian sputtered on the bread she'd shoved in her mouth a moment ago. How many times was she planning to choke herself tonight? "Do you want to do the Heimlich or should I?"

How Lilian managed such a brassy glower in the midst of coughing, he had no idea. But at least it was proof there must be some air getting through her windpipe.

"Oh dear, Lil," Maggie murmured, scooting to Lilian's side and patting her back. "I didn't mean to shock you like that."

"I'm fine," Lilian rasped. She gave another cough.

Wilder stuffed his hands in his pockets. "Shoot. After saving you from drowning last night, I was thinking maybe I could go two-for-two."

"You didn't save me!"

"You saved her?"

Lilian and Maggie spoke in sync and he couldn't help a chuckle. "Story for another day. So you want the two of us to plan your wedding? I'm flattered. And a little surprised. Confused, actually. I'm not really the event-planner type."

"And I'm more than capable of doing it on my own." Lilian abandoned her slice of bread on the spoon holder at the back of the stovetop. "I would absolutely love to do this for you, Maggie. You know how much I love planning things."

He leaned against the counter behind him. "How much you like playing supervisor and bossing everyone else around, don't you mean?"

She only spared him a brief glare before directing her words back to Maggie. "But there's no reason to force Wilder to help."

Maggie let out a light laugh. "I'm hardly forcing him. I just think it'd be good for you to have some assistance. We're on a tight timeline—"

"I planned Neil and Syd's wedding with even less time."

"Yes, and they wanted a small, intimate wedding. It's probably silly of me but . . ." A faint blush rose on Maggie's face, turning her cheeks a rosy pink. "I've waited a long time for this . . . and, well, darn it, I want the whole big deal. Tons of guests and an elaborate cake and maybe even a live band. I want something . . . big. Maybe even a little flashy. A spectacle."

Somewhere in the past few seconds, Lilian's scowl had begun to dissolve and, wow, that was pure, unadulterated tenderness in her sapphire eyes now. *Must've forgotten I'm in the room.* He bit back a laugh.

"If that's the wedding you want, it's exactly the wedding you should have." Lilian leaned into Maggie's side and she suddenly looked . . . soft. Strands of white-blond hair fell over her forehead as she wove her arm through Maggie's. "We'll make it happen. Tight timeline or no."

"Good." Maggie patted Lilian's hand where it rested on her arm. "Then you'll let Wilder help."

Lilian went rigid. "I didn't say—"

"You said *we*," he interjected.

Her gaze settled on him and the softness fled. "I didn't mean you and me."

Maggie stepped away from Lilian and faced her. "Lil, I know you're perfectly capable of pulling off a wonderful event. But we're talking about planning a wedding in June, the busiest month for weddings, in just a month and a half. It's not going to be easy to find a venue and caterer and florist and musician and everything else in that short of time. Wilder can be an asset."

"Yeah, Lil, I can be an asset." He flashed a grin. And would've bet money that if Maggie hadn't been facing her daughter, Lilian would've stuck out her tongue.

As it was, her eyes were mere slits now. "I don't see how."

"By being charming, that's how," Maggie answered.

It was all he could do not to take out his phone and snap a photo of Lilian's fully aghast expression. Better yet, record the rest of this conversation for sometime in the future when he needed a pick-me-up.

"I'm serious." Maggie came up beside him. "I know it may pain you to admit this, dear daughter of mine, but Wilder Monroe is Muir Harbor's golden boy. Everyone loves him. No one is going to say no when he comes around asking to book a reception hall on short notice. Or trying to get a good price on one of Misty Sprinkle's fancy cakes."

He reached for the bowl of fruit in the middle of the kitchen table. Popped a grape in his mouth. "Oh, Misty loves me. I basically single-handedly keep the bakery open."

"A donut a day keeps the doctor away." Dad's voice stole in, a memory nowhere near hazy. Oh no, it was crisp and clear. The taste of a still-warm glazed donut. The distant sound of icecaps collapsing into the shore. The familiar tenor of his father's laughter.

He swallowed the grape with a thudding gulp. Willed away the memory. Ignored another frown from Lilian. "I'm happy to help, Maggie. Whatever I can do. I'm honored you asked."

Maggie squeezed his arm like she'd squeezed Lilian's only a moment ago, then slid a glance to her daughter. Mozart could've written an entire sonata in the time it took Lilian to exhale. But, finally, she gave the barest of nods.

Maggie clapped her hands together and pulled Lilian into another hug. "Thank you. Obviously, Ray and I will do anything and everything to help, and I'm sure Neil and Indi will, too, but I feel especially good knowing you two are at the helm."

You two. Him and Lilian. Thrust into the role of dynamic duo wedding planners. He really hadn't seen that coming. But as Maggie moved on to embrace him, he knew he would've agreed to just about anything she asked.

Because Maggie Muir had saved him. Plain and simple as that.

Three years ago, when he'd found Dad's letter, when the realization had found *him*, with his head pounding and the alcohol roiling in his stomach . . . Maggie had saved him.

So, yes, he'd plan her wedding. He'd plan a dozen weddings, if she asked, all while continuing the search for Cynthia. Forget dead ends. Forget the frustration that had dogged him yesterday and again this morning and throughout the day.

He tried to meet Lilian's eyes over Maggie's shoulder, but she turned away too quickly and walked from the room. Not before sidling past the island counter, though, surreptitiously swiping her appointment card from underneath the bread basket, and slipping it in her pocket. *Smooth, Lil.*

"She'll adjust to the idea," Maggie said as she backed away.

"Maybe. Maybe not." The sound of Lilian's padding foot-steps was lost to the din still rising from the dining room. "Just promise me one thing, Maggie. Promise me this isn't some wayward matchmaking scheme."

Laughter chimed from Maggie as she moved toward the stove and slid on two oven mitts. "That might be the funniest thing I've ever heard. Ha! No, Wilder. I'm not trying to set you up with my daughter. I value my life too much for that."

It was his turn to laugh. "Good. Glad to hear it. But I don't buy for a second that my unwavering charm is the only reason you want me helping her."

Maggie pulled a steaming pan from the oven, lowered it onto the stovetop, and angled to face him. "You and that infal-lible gut instinct of yours."

"Let me guess. Neil told you about my latest setback with the case. And you're worried about me. You're trying to give me something light and fun to focus on so I'll stop obsessing over the investigation."

Maggie pulled a stack of dessert plates from the cupboard, then opened a drawer and pulled out a spatula. "You read me like a book." She dished up a plate full of cobbler, then another.

"I'm going to solve the case, Maggie. I'm not going to give up just because of a roadblock."

She didn't say anything.

"And Lil? What are you trying to distract her from?"

Maggie held out two plates and nudged her head, motioning for him to take them. "Go on and deliver some desserts." She propped a fork atop each plate. "And don't you worry about Lil."

"I kind of have to since apparently she's going to be the Robin to my Batman for the next six weeks." He started for the doorway.

"Wilder?"

He paused and glanced over his shoulder. Maggie abandoned her perch by the stove and moved in front of him. She lifted her palms, still hidden under oven mitts, and touched both his cheeks. "You could give it up. I need you to know that."

Her head was tipped back and he could feel her gentle gaze searching his. But he couldn't quite meet her eyes.

Until she patted his cheeks. Drew him in with one more laugh. "And let's be clear. You're like a son to me and I absolutely adore you, but make no mistake—you are most definitely Robin to Lilian's Batman." She gave him a cheeky grin and moved out of his way. "Go on now. There's a rowdy crowd out there waiting for dessert."

He obeyed, leaving the kitchen and starting down the hallway. But instead of veering into the dining room, he followed a hunch. He moved toward the entryway, shifting one of the plates until he balanced both in one hand, then let himself out the front door. At the flash of color in his periphery, he knew he'd found his target.

"Dessert?"

Lilian whirled from where she stood at the corner of the wide porch.

"She just pulled it out of the oven. Here." The floorboards were cool under his socks, and twilight was little more than a sliver of gilded color in the sky now. Across the front lawn, patchy green grass gave way to pebbles and rocks and eventually, the craggy coastline. Foam-tipped waves in endless blues and deep greens brawled with the jagged shore, stretching into the infinite distance. "If the kitchen is the heart of the house, then this is definitely the soul."

Lilian's head tipped enough he could see the tiny wrinkle of confusion etched into her forehead, the question in her eyes.

"Oh, you know. Maggie always says the kitchen is the heart of the home. I'd call this right here the soul." He probably sounded like an idiot. Or overly sentimental.

"It's weird, I was just thinking . . ." Instead of finishing her sentence, Lilian shook her head and accepted the dessert plate. "Thanks."

"It's not going to be so bad, you know. Working together, I mean. You'll survive it. We both will." He took a bite of the cobbler and all but moaned in delight. Another reason he spent so much time here—Maggie's baking. He swallowed another bite. And another.

"Enjoying that, are you?"

He opened his eyes—wait, when had he closed them?—to see Lilian's half-smile. An actual almost-grin. Directed at him, of all people. "Wow, if I'd known all I had to do to get you to like me was eat with abandon—"

"Let's not push it."

He stifled a chuckle and turned his gaze back to the sea, eating in silence for a few minutes. And then, "Lil—"

"Please don't." Her fork clinked on her plate.

His chewing slowed.

"Don't ask about the card. The appointment." Lilian's voice dipped low. "I'm not ready. Please just . . . don't ask."

"Okay."

"Okay?" She turned toward him slowly. "That's . . . that's it?"

He scraped a last bite from his plate. "You asked me not to ask, Lil. Whatever else you think of me, I'm capable of respecting your privacy."

She only stared at him, and it might be the first time he'd ever seen this woman at a loss for words. Might also be the first time he'd ever noticed her pierced ears. He was an observant guy. How had he never noticed her earrings? Or the way her ears tilted outward just slightly?

Because of her eyes. You've always been distracted by her eyes.

Because they were so blue. Because they sparked with intelligence. Always had.

Except tonight instead of sparks, he was pretty sure he saw something else. A weariness he related to a little too well. He set his plate on the porch railing. "Hey. You okay?"

She shrugged, then abandoned her plate beside his. "I'm fine. My pride took a hit today, that's all. My boss doesn't think I can do my job without help. Maggie doesn't think I can pull off a wedding without help. It's just a little deflating."

The evening breeze sifted through the wind chimes in the corners. "There's something to be said for accepting help sometimes. Doesn't mean you're not competent. Just human."

"Says the man trying to solve an almost-thirty-year-old missing persons case on his own."

Oh, there were the sparks. And honestly, he was relieved to see them. "Actually, you want to talk about your pride taking a hit—in the span of one day, both Neil and Maggie subtly suggested I drop the case."

"Really?"

It was his turn to shrug.

"Listen, I hope you appreciate how difficult this is for me to say, Wilder, but you've gotten closer to finding answers about Cynthia Muir's whereabouts than anyone. If you want to drop it, drop it. But only if you want to. Not because you think you can't hack it."

All he could do was stare. Fumble for a response that refused to come. Until, finally, he found his voice underneath his shock. "I do appreciate how difficult that was for you to say. Had to have been torturous."

And then . . . then she really did smile. The dim, nearly lost light of sunset wasn't enough to hide the way it took over her whole face. It was . . . stunning, really. A look like *that*. From *her*. "Lil—"

"We should probably stop now. A brief, civil conversation is one thing but if we keep going—"

"Help me."

At his blurted words, she paused, both eyebrows shooting upward.

"With the case. I know you were looking for the files last night."

"But I wasn't—"

"And you're the smartest person I know. I could use . . ." Embarrassment flooded him, but he kept going anyway. "I could use a sounding board. Dad and I used to bounce ideas off each other, but he's not here and . . . and I could use another set of eyeballs on all his notes and files. On mine. Maybe if we put our heads together . . ." He felt ridiculous. But also strangely revived. "Maybe we could solve a case while we're planning a wedding."

She frowned and folded her arms. Classic Lilian. But

something had shifted in these past few minutes. When she'd told him about her day, expressed her frustration, she'd offered him a glimpse—the tiniest peek—into her head. Her emotions. It'd given him a shot of boldness.

And her? Maybe, just maybe, she'd looked past her irritation with him long enough to see, well, him. Asking for a sincere favor.

"Okay," she eventually said.

"Okay? That's it?"

"Didn't we just have this exact conversation?"

He wanted to snicker but didn't. Didn't want to risk spoiling whatever hesitant camaraderie they'd just discovered. He held out his palm. "Deal? In light of the fact that we now know we're capable of making it through an entire conversation without drawing swords, we work together?"

She rolled her eyes but placed her hand in his. He closed his fingers around hers, and then, because he couldn't hold it in anymore, he laughed. "Don't look so worried, Batman. We're totally going to pull this off."

"Batman?"

He released her hand, then reached around her for their plates. "Ask Maggie."

5

$\mathcal{T}$he police officer's polished shoes clacked over the cottage's hardwood floors, sunlight streaming in from the front windows and landing in splotches around the small group gathered in the entryway.

Lilian's poor new paralegal. First day in the office and this is how they welcomed her? An overnight break-in and morning visit from the local police?

"Tuesday mornings are never this exciting, I promise." Lilian moved toward Mariana, drawing a stare from the German Shepherd at the woman's side, his shiny black fur begging to be touched.

But hadn't Lilian read somewhere that you weren't supposed to interact with service dogs as if they were pets? He was a striking dog, and serious, too. The opposite of Neil's collie, who bounced from person to person, eager and easily distracted.

Reminded her a little too much of a certain P.I. she knew.

One she hadn't so much as seen a glimpse of since Friday night. Apparently Wilder had been stuck in Bar Harbor over the weekend, working some case or another, according to

Neil. Area police departments often hired him for contract work and consultation.

Because apparently he was oh-so-good at what he did. Because everyone knew about his oh-so-uncanny gut instincts.

What were the chances his talents extended to planning an elaborate wedding? Would he even remember to show up at the church for their appointment with Pastor Hastings later this morning? And what in heaven's name had induced her to make that ridiculous pact with him in the first place?

It'd been that look in his sable eyes, that's what. That hint of desperation in his gaze mixed with the faintest trace of hope when he'd blurted those two surprising words. *"Help me."*

"You sound apologetic, but you don't need to be." Mariana's voice cut into her thoughts. Her lips spread into a smile, her gaze landing somewhere over Lilian's shoulder. "I like a little intrigue in my days."

Did a break-in count as intrigue? Officer Tompkins didn't seem to think so. He'd taken the bashed-in window in the kitchen in stride. Same with the knocked-over plant holder by Danine's desk. The scuffed hallway rug. The autographed baseball missing from Morris's office.

Danine had been the first to arrive today and then the one to call the police, followed by Morris. Lilian had been perching her bike in its usual spot when the cop car had pulled up to the curb out front, and by the time Mariana had arrived a short time later, Officer Tompkins had already finished his inspection.

"I know this probably feels alarming," he said now, tucking a notebook in the pocket of his dark shirt, "but I wouldn't get too up in arms. Pretty sure we've got some harmless freshman hazing going on with the high school baseball team. Not the first incident this month. Coach Brightman's '88 state championship ring went missing last week."

Oh. Hence the missing baseball.

"You don't sound like you're taking this all that seriously." Morris crouched beside Danine's desk, righting the plant holder, then freeing the pot and tucking it under one arm as he stood. "Only a spider plant but I've kept it alive for fourteen years now." He brushed spilled dirt into a pile with his foot.

Danine appeared behind Officer Tompkins with a broom and dustpan in hand. Her stylish gray hair was cut into a bob and her open cheetah-print cardigan flounced around her. "Let me take care of that, Morris."

"We are taking it seriously," the police officer cut in. "Sorry if I implied otherwise. But I don't think you have to worry about it happening again. We'll identify the culprits and get your baseball back."

"And the window?" Danine drilled Officer Tompkins with a stare.

"I'm sure the kids' parents will make certain that's taken care of, ma'am."

Danine pointed the dustpan at the man. "Don't ma'am me, Timothy. I still remember when you and your unruly band of friends were the ones causing trouble around town. Little Timmy Tompkins and his entourage of ruffians."

The man's ears pinked. "No one's called me Timmy in years, ma—Mrs. Stone."

"It's Mrs. Rockwell now. Got remarried last summer. Keep up, Timmy."

Mariana inched closer to Lilian. "You know, I really think I'm going to like it here."

Lilian chuckled. "Come on, I'll take you to your office. That is, if . . ." She glanced to Officer Tompkins, then Morris. "Need anything from me?"

Morris was too busy inspecting his plant to answer. Officer Tompkins shook his head. So she gave Mariana's elbow a light touch, then started down the hallway, leaving the sound of Danine's annoyed broom strokes behind them. The dog's paws tapped the floor as he accompanied Mariana behind her.

"So Danine went from Mrs. Stone to Mrs. Rockwell?" Mariana asked.

"Would you believe me if I told you her maiden name was Pebble?" They passed the French doors that led into Morris's office.

"I'd desperately want to believe you just for the comedy of it, but that feels a little too far-fetched."

Lilian played up her sigh. "You got me. It was Peabody."

"Guess we could always hope for a third marriage someday. But that feels wrong somehow."

Lilian laughed, slowing her steps to let Mariana come up beside her. "I know you said I don't have to apologize, but I really do feel bad about your first day starting this way." She felt bad about Mariana even being here today. Lilian had only called to offer her the position yesterday, had figured Mariana might need a few days to make living arrangements or get settled before starting her new job.

But no, Mariana had asked if she could come in today. She'd even had a few boxes delivered to the office yesterday afternoon. She was clearly eager.

And Lilian was clearly . . . out of her depth. After a day full of meetings yesterday, the pile of paperwork she hadn't gotten to on Friday was still waiting for her in her office. She had a wedding to plan. A private investigator to help. Somehow. And someone needed to clean up the broken glass in the kitchen.

Yet here she was trying to make a new employee feel welcome when she was still halfway convinced Morris had made the wrong decision in insisting Lilian hire someone in the first place. He thought he was helping her, but hadn't he only handed her more responsibility?

Lilian stepped into the small space that had probably been a bedroom back when this cottage had functioned as a home. It left a lot to be desired as an office. Unadorned beige walls, only one narrow window. "The wall color isn't great in here, but we could always paint—"

Mariana let out a laugh. "As if I care about wall color."

Oh, for goodness' sake. Mortification coursed through her. "Oh man, I'm sorry—"

"Don't worry about it." Mariana brushed her hand over the doorframe as she moved into the room, stopping near Lilian and reaching out her palm until she found Lilian's arm. She gave it the barest squeeze. "You don't need to walk on eggshells around me—or *talk* on eggshells. Is that a thing? I'm just saying, you don't have to worry about saying the wrong thing to me. I've been blind, visually impaired, whatever term you prefer, for as long as I can remember. You won't hurt my feelings. I'm talking way too much for my first day on the job, aren't I? And squeezing your arm is probably totally unprofessional, but I feel like we might end up being friends. My partner's name is Flannel, by the way." She motioned to her dog and gave a nervous laugh.

One Lilian found herself echoing. "How about we start over completely? Welcome to Groves & Muir Law, Mariana."

Still laughing, Mariana held out her palm. "Sounds good to me. And thanks. Happy to be here."

Lilian shook the woman's hand. "I'm not that great at delegating and I've never had a paralegal before, so you might have to be a little patient with me, but I'm looking forward to getting to know you and working together and . . ." And who knew, maybe Mariana was right. Maybe she'd get a friend in the bargain. They were close to the same age, and though she might have her reservations about finding time to train a new employee, she genuinely liked Mariana.

A shoot of longing sprouted up inside of her, as surprising as it was sudden. She wouldn't have considered herself in the market for a new girlfriend, not with such a full plate. But with Indi spending so much time with Philip these days and so many of her old school friends married with kids or scattered about in other states, her social life wasn't exactly hopping lately.

What social life?

Truth be told, she'd never had an overly large circle of friends. But there wasn't anything necessarily wrong with that. Not everyone was a social butterfly. Look at Neil. He'd had one best friend for twenty years now, and he seemed completely content.

A best friend who drove her up the wall and had somehow conned her into agreeing to work together.

Who she was due to meet in—she checked her slim gold watch—two hours.

"Are you a coffee drinker, Mariana?"

The woman was moving across the room now. She'd left her dog standing near the modest mahogany desk in one corner and was currently tracing her fingers over a narrow set of bookshelves, the only other piece of furniture in the room. They needed to get her some chairs, maybe a lamp.

"Not so much a coffee drinker as a guzzler," Mariana answered.

"Then you'll want to visit Trinna's Teatime—closest thing Muir Harbor has to a coffee shop. They serve ridiculously good coffee. So good that it's the only thing anyone ever orders, much to the owner's dismay. Trinna's an anglophile who's obsessed with tea and continually aggravated at the popularity of her own coffee."

Mariana stopped by the small window, moving her gaze

toward the sound of Lilian's voice. "Like I said, I really think I'm going to like it here. Muir Harbor seems . . . quirky."

"Oh, you don't know the half of it. I will gladly fill you in sometime—as much as I can, anyway. Mostly, you just have to experience this place for yourself. We've got our spring market coming up soon. You definitely need to go to that—it's the perfect crash course into all things Muir Harbor. But for now, I'll grab you a cup of coffee from the kitchen and you can start getting settled in. The boxes you had delivered are under the desk."

"Perfect. And Lilian?"

Lilian stopped under the doorframe.

"Thank you. Again. For the interview and the job and . . . everything. I really needed a fresh start and . . . I'm just really happy to be here. I know I already said that and I'm rambling again but . . ." Mariana let out a breath. "Thank you."

"You're welcome."

There was so much warmth in the woman's grin, so much sincere gratitude in her gaze, it almost made up for the strangeness of this morning.

No, not almost. And it wasn't just Mariana's gratefulness wrapping around her as she moved toward the kitchen now. There'd been something else in her voice. Something more in her expression. Some sort of hovering need Lilian recognized.

Maybe because she'd caught a glimpse of that same need in Wilder's eyes the other night on the porch.

Maybe because she'd heard its echoes in her own soul more than she wanted to admit. More than she could even understand. Need for what?

Her steps slowed as she neared the kitchen. *Someone to notice . . .*

Her thoughts came to an abrupt end as the scene in the kitchen appeared before her. The jagged edges of the broken window. The glass shards on the laminate floor. She sucked in a breath.

And memories she'd shunned months ago came barging back in. A trespasser at the farm. Vandalism. The cliffside . . . *Peyton.*

She shook her head, refusing to go there. She marched across the room, avoiding the shattered glass, and filled a coffee mug, then turned so sharply hot liquid sloshed over its edges. She ignored the sting and hurried from the kitchen.

Then halted all over again at the sound of Wilder's voice drifting from Mariana's office.

"Flannel, though? Just doesn't seem like the right name for a . . . what is he?"

"German Shepherd." Lilian peeked around the office door in time to see Mariana shifting what looked like a printer around on her desk. "I'm into textures. Comes with the whole not-being-able-to-see thing. Plus, I had a flannel blanket I slept with as a kid that I never forgave my dad for throwing away when I was eight."

Wilder was crouched near an outlet in the corner of the sparse room, untangling a mess of cords. "For me, it was a teddy bear. And I was ten. Except my dad didn't throw it away. He just gently suggested that I might not want to have it out when a few friends came over for a birthday party. He was saving me from being teased, I guess. That's when Teddy started sleeping in a box under my bed."

Mariana pulled something from one of the boxes on her desk. "So, basically not the same situation at all."

"Guess not. Especially considering I don't have a dog named after him."

"A good thing," Lilian interjected, finally entering the room. "Your houseboat isn't big enough for a dog."

Wilder didn't so much as look up at her as he finished

unknotting the cord, then plugged it into the outlet. "Morning, Lil."

Mariana lifted her gaze from her box, cheeks rosy. There was only one window in the room, but it let in streams of sunlight that spun Mariana's hair with threads of gold. Gosh, Lilian hadn't really noticed until now just how pretty the woman was. A fact that only intensified when Mariana's smile spread as Lilian placed the coffee mug in her hands. "This smells like heaven."

"Getting settled in?"

Mariana sipped her coffee and nodded, then motioned to the printer. "This is a Braille embosser." She lowered her mug to the desk and reached for the item she'd pulled from her bag earlier. "And this is a display device. Hooks up to the computer and displays whatever's on the screen in one line of Braille at a time."

"You shouldn't have to provide your own office equipment, Mariana. We can order whatever you need."

"I'll take you up on that if my OrCam dies. It's been acting weird lately." She reached into her box and held up a small, narrow black device. "It's AI technology. Scans whatever's on a page or screen and reads it to me. You might regret your offer, though. These babies are pricey. And I totally forgot to ask earlier—you're not allergic to dogs, are you? Once I learn the layout of the place, it won't be as vital that Flannel accompany me every day, but—"

"No dog allergies, Mariana. No need to worry."

"Only bananas." Wilder rose and wandered to the desk. "Right, Lil?"

"And the occasional houseboat dweller. What are you doing here?"

He shot her one of his lazy grins. "Meeting your new paralegal. And picking you up."

"Our appointment's not until later. And I can drive myself to the church."

"I was hoping we could move it up. Mrs. Jenkins called this morning practically begging me to meet with her around lunchtime. Her cat's pregnant again, and I think she legit wants to hire me to track down the offending alley cat, and I have no idea how I'm going to let her down. But such is the life of an in-demand private-eye-slash-houseboat-dweller."

She rolled her eyes at his exaggerated sigh. "Wilder, I can't just leave—"

"Don't let me stop you," Mariana interjected. "I've got stuff to unload, an office to finish getting settled into. If there's anything I need, I can ask Morris or Danine. I'll be perfectly fine."

"But—"

"She'll be perfectly fine," Wilder echoed. "So let's go. You've got no reason to keep arguing."

No, she had about a dozen reasons to keep arguing. Namely, all the work waiting for her in her office. She wanted to refuse him, but what was the point? With Mariana looking so eager to please and Wilder looking so . . . like Wilder.

Maggie called it charm. Lilian called it coercion.

No, she called it *unnerving*, the way he stood there by Mariana's desk, tall and taunting, pinning her with his opaque gaze. Where was the halfway desperate Wilder from the porch on Friday night? Of all the people for Maggie to insist she cooperate with, why him?

"Fine."

His blasted grin widened. "Nice to meet you, Mariana. You too, Flannel."

Mariana nodded. "Good luck with that pregnant cat."

Wilder chuckled, then touched Lilian's back. "To the church we go, Miss Muir."

The interior of the church smelled just as Wilder remembered. Like Pine-Sol and old carpet. Lemon and must.

And as his practiced gaze scanned Pastor Hastings's office from the open doorway, collecting one detail after another—leatherbound books lining built-in shelves, family photos scattered in between, a humming mini-fridge in the corner—he was pretty sure everything looked exactly as he remembered, too.

Exactly as it had the only time Wilder had sat in one of those faded brown chairs in front of the pastor's desk. Three years ago.

After the funeral. Before he'd gone back to the boat.

Before the pain he'd thought couldn't get any worse had all but exploded . . .

"I thought you said you called Pastor Hastings."

Lilian's snappish tone rescued him from the memory. "I did—"

"You said he agreed to meet earlier than we planned."

"He did." He had, just an hour ago when they'd spoken on the phone. Wilder had no clue why the man wasn't here now. Which he'd tried to tell Lilian already.

Didn't do a thing to dim her glare. "I have three days' worth of work waiting for me back at the office." Lilian sifted her fingers through her hair, frustration brimming in her blue eyes. "I can't just flit off because of one of your whims."

He crossed his arms. "Not a whim. I told you—"

"Or because of Mrs. Jenkins and her knocked-up cat."

"Sheesh, we're in a church, Lil. Probably shouldn't use a phrase like 'knocked-up.'" And he probably shouldn't be fighting back a laugh just now.

"It can't be like this, Wilder." She fiddled with the buttons of her light gray blazer—unbuttoning, then buttoning, and over again. "Work is crazy busy and now I've got a new employee to train, and if we're really going to plan this wedding together, then we have to be organized and scheduled and—"

"Oh my word, you need to calm down." Without thinking, he reached for her fidgeting hands and clasped them between his own.

But she jumped back in the same second. "What are you doing?"

"Trying to make a move on you, obviously." She clearly did not appreciate his sarcasm. Nor his shift in tactics—hands going to her shoulders instead. She frowned, but at least she didn't jerk away this time. "Lilian, I'm sorry I switched things up on you. I'm sorry Pastor Hastings is late."

"He's not late. We're early."

He could've predicted the words before they were out of her mouth. "But we're here so we might as well make the most of it. Let's go take a look at the sanctuary. Try to envision Maggie's wedding or something. I know perpetual annoyance with me is your comfort zone, but if you can step out of it for a minute, we can make sure this isn't time wasted. All right?"

"You don't have to talk to me like I'm a petulant child." She whirled away from him and started toward the sanctuary.

It was all he could do not to laugh. "Well, if it walks like a duck—"

She shut him up with a scowl flung over her shoulder. But there was an accompanying glimmer of amusement in her eyes. A tiny one, but unmistakable. She could pretend otherwise all she wanted, but the woman had a sense of humor lurking somewhere in there. It came out most often when she was around her family. The fact that he'd spied a hint of it when there was only him for company floored him.

Or would've if she hadn't hefted open the oversized sanctuary door just then. If the sight and smell and hushed atmosphere of the expansive room didn't suddenly do the same thing as the pastor's office had minutes ago . . .

Reach around him with burly arms, squeeze until the memories were forced free.

Full pews and organ music. The suffocating warmth of his suit, the tightness of his collar. The open coffin. *Dad* . . .

Three years. It'd been three years. It shouldn't still do this to him.

Maybe it wouldn't if he'd never found the letter. If he'd never wondered—

"Wilder?"

Lilian was facing him from halfway down the church aisle, her silhouette framed by light from the path of lofty windows on both sides of the room. He made his legs move once more, her face coming into sharper focus as he neared. Telling him she'd seen something on *his* face moments ago. Tangled emotions he wouldn't have been able to tell from one another if he tried.

The letter had stolen any possibility of a simple grief. A peaceful healing.

But he made himself shake it off. Smile. Nudge his head toward the platform behind her. "Did you know Neil and I broke in here once? Went hot tubbing in the baptistry."

Lilian studied him for a moment. Hard to believe she wasn't Neil's biological sibling when she looked at him like that, as if she knew perfectly well he was forcing his humor. But she let him off the hook. "Can't be true. Neil would never do that."

"Ask him."

"If he did, then you peer-pressured him into it."

"How do you know he didn't talk me into it?"

She gave him a deadpan stare.

He *tsk*ed. "Neil is plenty capable of getting into trouble.

You just can't see it because you've got those loyal little sister blinders on."

She turned back to the front of the church, hands at her waist, and he stepped up beside her, glancing down to take in the sight of her vivid gaze traveling the room. Was she imagining a wedding party lined up on both sides? Decorations? Maggie and her fiancé standing face-to-face?

He looked to the carpeted platform and tried to visualize the same. Needed to. If he could replace the memory of Dad's still form in that velvet-cushioned coffin with something, anything else, maybe he'd be able to bring himself to start regularly attending this church again. Dad would hate knowing he'd ever strayed from it.

Oh, he dragged himself to services once in a while. Managed to hold on to the faith he'd grown up with. But he'd be lying if he pretended it was the same as before. His was a bruised, limping sort of belief. There, but undeniably worse for the wear.

His gaze drifted to the cross behind the pulpit. *You didn't have to take him, too. You could've stopped it.*

Or if nothing else, God could've at least kept Wilder from finding the letter. Could've reached down from heaven and plucked the note from underneath Dad's mattress before Wilder had ever discovered it. Flung it into the sea so he'd never have to wonder . . .

"Well, as long as we have the time, you might as well catch me up on the case."

He blinked. Tore his blurry gaze from the cross to the woman at his side. She wasn't even looking at him, but she knew, didn't she? Somehow she'd sensed what coming in here had done to him, what it'd dredged up.

Lilian knew.

And he knew exactly what she was doing. Throwing him a life preserver. Lilian Muir showing *him* compassion. It was unsettling. He rubbed his palm over his unshaven jaw. "You don't want to talk wedding details?"

"We don't even know yet if the church is available on the twenty-ninth. There's no point in getting ahead of ourselves. And you said you needed someone to bounce your thoughts off of. We made a pact or whatever. So talk to me about the case." She dropped into a pew and tipped her head to meet his eyes. "Catch me up as if I don't have any personal connection."

"Okay." He turned his back on the front of the church and leaned one palm on the side of a pew a couple rows ahead of where Lilian sat. He started talking.

"Thirty years ago, Maggie's daughter Diana runs away from home. She's seventeen, only a few months post–high school graduation. Two years pass—two years during which she only calls Maggie once, lets her know she's in Atlanta and nothing else—and then one weekend in September 1990, she returns to Muir Farm. She's got a daughter with her." He lifted his hand to the back of his neck. "You already know all this."

Lilian leaned back in her seat. "Keep going anyway."

"Maggie's overjoyed but Diana refuses to tell her who the baby's father is. Or what exactly she's been doing for the past two years. Diana tells her she can't stay long. On Sunday night she gets in her car, despite Maggie asking her to stay longer. She's got her suitcase. She's got Cynthia. And then . . . the car crash along the shoreline."

Lilian nodded at him again. An unspoken *go on.*

"Maggie actually hears it happen from the farmhouse. She arrives on the scene before anyone else. It's total wreckage, there's a fire . . ." He hated picturing it, thinking of the woman he cared for so deeply coming face-to-face with something so tragic. So traumatic. "There's no saving Diana. Her body is identified easily, but they can't find Cynthia. There are tracks. They know there was another vehicle . . . they think Cynthia's body might've been thrown . . ."

Why was he saying this? Lilian knew all the rest. But she was watching him intently. Completely still. Listening as if she was filing away every detail like facts in one of her cases.

He paced to the other side of the aisle and went on. "Local authorities eventually give up and declare Cynthia presumed dead. But Maggie doesn't give up. She hires my father. Dad looks into everything he can think of. The tire tracks at the scene of the accident. The rumors that when Diana originally left town, it was with someone she'd met at the local pub. But everything goes cold.

"Fast-forward twenty-eight years." To the big break. To what should've blown this thing wide open. "Peyton Cornish comes to Muir Harbor."

Lilian's rapt attention finally faltered. She winced at the name. "We can skip that part."

"We can't skip that part, Lil. It's the part where the pieces start falling into place."

She bolted from the pew. "It's the part where my whole family is in danger. The part where he almost . . . I hate thinking about it."

Of course she did. Everything that had happened earlier this year felt like something from a nightmare. "I hate thinking about it, too. The guy tried to kill Indi. He—" He clamped his lips together the second he met Lilian's eyes.

How they could look so luminous and so injured at the same time was beyond him.

"Peyton Cornish arrives in Muir Harbor," he repeated slowly. The man had come to town last fall, right around the time strange things had begun happening at Muir Farm. Headlights pointed at the farmhouse in the middle of the night. Footprints. They'd chalked it up to bored teens at the time. But . . .

"Peyton pretends to be friendly. Cozies up to your family. But eventually, we learn the truth. We learn that it was his father, Nicholas Cornish, who whisked Diana down to Georgia. We learn that at the time, Nicholas already had a family, including a wife, a son—Peyton. We learn he kept them tucked away in Savannah and set Diana up in an apartment in Atlanta, bouncing between his family and his young mistress for a time before finally leaving Peyton's mother altogether to stay with Diana and the baby they had together—Cynthia."

And Peyton, apparently, had nursed a grudge for years. Decades. He'd come to Muir Harbor intent on repaying the Muir family for what he said they'd stolen from him. He'd trespassed at Muir Farm, vandalized, his hatred so entrenched he'd eventually threatened Indi's life.

It'd happened in January. Peyton had tried to force Indi off a cliff a few miles down the shoreline from Muir Farm. They'd all been there . . . Wilder, Neil, the man Indi was dating now.

Lilian. Who was clearly remembering every moment of the incident now, the color draining from her cheeks. "I've been trying not to think about it. As soon as it was over, I told myself, don't think of what could've happened. What almost did happen. But then this morning I saw that broken window and—"

He whipped his head up. "Huh?"

Lilian hid her hands in the pockets of her blazer. "Oh, we had a break-in at the office overnight. It brought back memories."

"What? Why are you just now telling me?"

She stared at him from across the aisle. "It wasn't a big deal. Just some kids." She shook her head. "Anyway, I'm caught up now."

Not exactly. He hadn't finished the story. He hadn't recapped the part where Peyton had fallen off the cliff or reminded her the man had been comatose in a long-term care center ever since.

But clearly he didn't need to remind her. She'd begun pacing from one side of the aisle to the other, cheeks still pale. Why had he thought this was a good idea? Not the Muir family history lesson, but pulling Lilian into this? He'd been selfish, so desperate for someone to be in it with him that he hadn't thought about how it might affect her after everything she'd been through earlier this year . . . seeing her sister in danger, watching a man go over the edge of a cliff.

Sounded like something out of an Alfred Hitchcock movie. But it'd happened and it'd horrified all of them. And dragging Lilian even deeper into it now was a mistake.

"You left out some of the story."

Her voice drew his gaze once more.

"You left out the part where strangers visited Muir Farm over the years, claiming to be Cynthia Muir. Or the part where you were at one time so mistakenly convinced Sydney Rose was Cynthia that you dragged her to Muir Farm."

Was that actually a hint of a smirk on her face just now? After the things they'd both just remembered?

She's doing it again. Throwing you a life ring.

Or maybe reaching for it herself. Pulling out of one chapter of the story, the most recent, and finding solace in another. He was mixing metaphors now, but oh, how well he knew that move.

Oh, how many times he'd walked onto the houseboat and then turned around and walked right off. Choosing to crash at Muir Farm instead of confronting the ghost of that memory. The clanging *what-if*.

"Yes, well, I'd say Neil, for one, is fairly glad I made that mistake with Sydney."

"Obviously." She must be growing impatient with the pastor, the way she was tapping her bare foot on the floor.

Wait, her bare foot? He glanced to the pew where she'd

76

been sitting minutes ago, spotted her shoes abandoned on the floor.

Then his gaze slid back to her bright-red-painted toes. Lilian Muir—she of the sleek business blazers and monochromatic wardrobe . . . with cherry-red toes.

She caught him looking. "What are you staring at? You've seen my feet before. They're not a novelty."

"The color choice is."

She shrugged. "The other day Indi said I should wear bright colors more often. I dipped my toe in the water, so to speak. All my toes." She giggled at her own pun. Actually *giggled*—not the caustic laugh he was used to, the one she let out whenever he said something ridiculous and she amused herself with a zinger.

"I feel like I'm seeing a whole new side of you, Lilian Muir."

She rolled her eyes, then bent to reach under the pew and started up the aisle, shoes dangling from her fingers at her side. "Come on, for all we know, Pastor Hastings has been waiting for us in his office for ten minutes now."

He caught up to her in easy steps. "I disagree with Indi, though. Light blues and greens—those are your colors."

She slanted a look at him.

"What? I'm good with colors. Something you should be happy about considering we're going to have to talk wedding colors and decorations and all that eventually."

"Not eventually. Soon. Clock's ticking, Wilder. We've got less than six weeks. We haven't even made a task list yet. And since you disappeared all weekend—"

"I have a job just like you, Lil. Just because my hours are different—"

The sanctuary door creaked open before he could finish his sentence, before they made it up the aisle. Pastor Hastings entered, wearing those same wire-rimmed glasses he'd worn the day of Dad's funeral. Same dark hair, though maybe a little thinner.

The pastor moved toward them with a hearty grin. "Wilder Monroe, it's been a little too long since you deigned to darken our doorstep."

———•———— ——••——

What in the world had just happened in there?

Lilian hurried down the church steps, trailing Wilder, his strides so long and resolute she had to practically run to catch up to him at the curb. The sun had climbed to its highest perch while they'd been inside and now it cast brash light in every direction. "What's the rush?" He'd cut their meeting short after only fifteen minutes with the pastor, then practically bolted from the church.

"You need to get back to the office. I need to get to Mrs. Jenkins."

Right. Mrs. Jenkins and her cat. "What we need is to figure out a Plan B." Apparently the church was having all its carpets replaced at the end of June. The pastor was available to officiate the service, but it wouldn't be happening at Maggie's church. "We need a new plan."

Wilder rounded his Jeep and peered at her over its hood. "I don't know why we even came here. Maggie doesn't want a church wedding." He opened his car door and disappeared inside.

She pulled her door open and ducked her head in. "How do you know what Maggie wants? And what's wrong with a church wedding?" She tossed the blazer she'd taken off at some point inside onto the dash, then climbed into the Jeep.

"Nothing, but Maggie told us what she wants. Something flashy. A spectacle." He flipped down his visor and pulled a pair of sunglasses from behind it. He slipped them over his eyes, then turned on the vehicle and tapped the A/C button.

"Trust me, Wilder, I know Maggie. She wants a church wedding."

"Flashy. Spectacle. Those were her exact words."

"I know, I was there." More than that, while he'd been out of town over the weekend, she'd actually sat down with Maggie and talked to her about the wedding. They'd talked about a daytime versus an evening event, the size of the guest list, menu and cake and music ideas. Okay, so she hadn't specifically asked Maggie if she wanted the wedding at the church they'd attended for as long as Lilian could remember, but wasn't that a given?

"Well, you obviously weren't listening—"

"What in the world is wrong with you? I'm supposed to be the perpetually annoyed one. Isn't that what you said? I'm supposed to argue with everything you say, not the other way around." She reached for her blazer. "And why are you trying to blast us to Antarctica with the A/C?" She attempted to shrug into the blazer, but the cramped space made it difficult.

Wilder let out a sigh and reached over to help her, holding up one side so she could shove her arm in. She muttered her thanks and he leaned away from her, turning the air conditioning down a notch.

Then, finally, he spoke again. "Sorry. I just . . . don't love that church. Too many memories."

She'd gathered as much when they'd first walked into the sanctuary. No, when they'd first walked into the church altogether. She'd felt him stiffen beside her. Even when he'd joked with her outside Pastor Hastings's office, when he'd put his hands on her shoulders, there'd been something strained behind his eyes. Something that had deepened as soon as they'd entered the sanctuary.

And then returned the moment Pastor Hastings found

them. Wilder had grown increasingly more uncomfortable throughout the meeting. Was there some kind of history there she didn't know about? Or was he remembering Harry's funeral again? That's what he'd been thinking about earlier, right? When she'd caught him looking at the cross . . . had he realized he'd been clenching and unclenching his fists in those stilted moments?

It was why she'd brought up the case. It'd worked then. Maybe now . . . "So, the case. What's next?"

His palm rested on the gear shift but hadn't moved it out of park yet. "We don't need to keep talking about the case."

"But—"

"In fact, I shouldn't have asked you to help. There's not anything you really can help with."

"You said you needed a sounding board—"

"Neil said I can vent to him anytime, so I'm set. Thanks anyway." He started to shift gears, but at Lilian's huff, he switched course, twisting and yanking the key from the ignition. "What? If you've got something to say, go ahead and say it."

"All right, I will. You gave me a nice little pep talk last Friday about accepting help when you need it. Well, take your own advice. You need my help. You might be the one with the legendary instincts and intuition, but I think in puzzles and logic." She tapped the side of her head. "It's what makes me a good lawyer. Who knows, maybe I can find something in your dad's files—"

"You couldn't even *find* his files on my boat."

"I wasn't even looking for his files." She crossed her arms and flopped back in her seat, refusing to meet his gaze any longer. He was confounding. And confusing. He wasn't supposed to be the sullen one.

He's not over his father.

Of course he wasn't. Harry Monroe had been a fixture in

Muir Harbor and his cancer diagnosis three years ago, followed by his sudden death only weeks later, had shaken their little community.

But it had downright devastated Wilder. Understandable. If she ever lost Maggie, she'd never get over it either.

"You weren't looking for his files . . ." Wilder shifted in his seat to face her. "Then what were you looking for?"

Oh, she hadn't meant to reveal that.

Or maybe she had. Maybe there'd been a piece of her feeling guilty ever since last week for letting him think she'd gone snooping on his boat on Maggie's behalf instead of her own. "I-I was looking for his files . . . a file . . . just not those ones."

He pulled his sunglasses from his eyes and dropped them in the console between them. "Go on."

She angled her attention out her window, toward the church, the cherry trees on both sides of the path that led up to the sun-bathed building. Pale pink blossoms fluttered in the wind, breaking from their branches and raining to the ground.

"I had a doctor's appointment Thursday morning. He asked me about my family medical history. Obviously, well, you know I can't answer that. It . . . did something to me. Momentary loss of common sense, I guess." She braved a look at him. "Thought I could steal onto the boat and find any notes Harry might've kept back when he was investigating my . . . unknown past."

She watched the understanding play out on Wilder's face. His Adam's apple bobbed as he swallowed, his body loosening behind the steering wheel.

"Oh." He slid his palms over his jeans. "Lil, I don't think—"

"I know he never found anything. I know it was every bit as much a cold case as Cynthia. Even if there is a file, there's probably not much in it. It was total impulse. I blame Dr. Cho." She tried to laugh, but it came out strained.

And Wilder just sat there, the weight of his stare never leaving her. She was sure he'd ask. Waited . . .

She should've taken the escape for what it was. But no, now that she'd started the confession, she felt inexplicably compelled to finish it. "It was about a month ago. I started having these tremors in one arm. And I was having some numbness now and then in my legs, too. And one morning I woke up and my vision was blurry. I kept blinking but it stayed that way for a few minutes. Freaked me out a little. I went to the doctor thinking she'd tell me I was feeling the effects of stress or something. Tell me to work less, take some supplements, get more sleep. But she seemed concerned when I told her something like this has happened before—back when I was in law school. I assumed it was the same thing then—stress. They ran a few labs. Then the nurse called a few days later and said they wanted to order an MRI. I went from a little freaked out to really . . ."

She let her voice trail off as she knotted her hands in her lap. "Anyway, my insurance wouldn't cover the MRI unless a specialist ordered it, which was this whole hassle, so my doctor referred me to a neurologist and last week was the initial consultation so he could get the MRI ordered and . . ." She let out a long sigh. "I don't know anything. The symptoms all faded away after about a week. Could be something as silly as a vitamin deficiency or . . . something else. I plugged the symptoms into WebMD—"

"Bad idea, Lil."

"I know. But the fact that my doctor's first thought was to send me to a neurologist rather than some other kind of specialist makes me think she's thinking . . ." She wetted her lips. "Something with my brain. Something like . . . MS, maybe."

It was the first time she'd said it out loud. And to Wilder, of all people.

Wilder, who sat in complete silence next to her. He'd lifted his hands to grip the steering wheel at some point, but they slid down its sides now. Finally, he turned to her again. "Why did you tell me that?"

"I have absolutely no idea."

"You haven't told anybody else?"

She shook her head.

"Lil—"

"You don't need to say anything consoling, okay? I don't even know why I told you. Except I felt guilty for letting you think I went to the houseboat for one thing when it was really another. Another really ridiculous, pointless reason. I just kept hearing Dr. Cho in my head, asking about family history, and I don't know. Like I said, temporary loss of common sense."

"If it helps, that was the high point of my week last week— seeing you hide behind Dad's recliner. And then later, soaked to the bone and yelling at me for jumping in to save you."

She gave him a frown she didn't feel. "I didn't yell and you didn't save—"

"You did yell and it was hilarious. The whole thing was hilarious."

He lifted his hand from his lap and for a moment, she thought he was going to reach toward her and . . . what? Awkwardly pat her shoulder? He must've thought better of it because he leaned forward instead, propping his wrists on the steering wheel. "Well, this is all the more reason we should drop the idea of you being a part of the case. You've got enough on your plate—"

"No, it's all the more reason I want to help. I need a distraction, Wilder. This might be nothing or it might be something, but I'd prefer not to think about it at all until I have to. At least let me read your dad's files and your own notes. It'll keep me from going back to WebMD, and you never know. Maybe something will jump out at me."

"I don't want to pull you into anything dangerous. When you said there was a break-in at the office—"

"That was nothing. Officer Tompkins said it's just some teens."

"Yeah, well, Peyton isn't nothing."

"Peyton's in a coma."

"Someone else rummaging through my boat isn't nothing." She just stared at him.

"You weren't the only one on the boat that night, Lil. I think there's more going on here. I think maybe we aren't the only ones looking . . ."

"For Cynthia?"

"It's a gut feeling."

Of course. And because it was Wilder, because it was *his* gut feeling, she was supposed to just trust it. No holds barred. No questions asked. "You were wrong about Sydney. You were wrong about why I was on your boat. You don't always get it right."

"You don't have to remind me." He pushed his key into the ignition and started the engine once more.

"You're wrong about Maggie not wanting a church wedding." She was just goading him now. Suddenly in desperate need of a return to normal. Because she'd said too much earlier.

And maybe she'd seen a little too much, too. The way Wilder had looked for those few seconds in the sanctuary, staring at the cross . . . pain as raw as she'd ever seen. And it hadn't mattered then that he'd been a thorn in her side for decades, that he'd injured her with the truth all those years ago.

He'd lost the thing she'd never had. Or at least, what she didn't remember having. Except in those dreams . . .

A father. One he'd been so very close to.

She felt the Jeep jerk as he shifted into drive, but he didn't lift his foot from the brake. "You really haven't told anyone in your family?" One hand on the wheel, he retrieved his sunglasses from the console. "Not even Maggie?"

"No."

He fit his glasses over his eyes but she could feel him still watching her all the same. "Well, she knows something's up."

"I don't think—"

"Trust me, Lil." He pulled away from the curb, the engine rumbling. "She knows."

6

*W*ilder held the scanned photo only inches from his face, pinched tightly between his thumb and index finger. It was grainy and faded, creased from the number of times he'd handled it, scouring each face just as he did now.

As if by staring at an old newspaper photo of Nicholas Cornish and his business associates—something he'd dug up months ago when he'd still thought Cornish was the breakthrough he'd been waiting on all this time—he'd somehow absorb some hint of information about a man who might not have helped his case any even if he was alive.

With a groan of frustration, he tossed the paper onto the passenger seat where Lilian had sat just two days ago and spilled her secret.

It'd been enough to flummox him. And the second he'd dropped her off at her law office afterward, with the faint scent of her perfume still lingering in the Jeep, light and citrusy, he'd kicked himself for handling the whole thing like an oaf.

He should've said more. Or maybe less.

Even now, he didn't know what to say. Or what to think.

What to do with the thread of worry that'd tied a sailor's knot around his thoughts in the past forty-eight hours. *She said it might be nothing. Just a vitamin deficiency.*

But it might be something. MS. Multiple Sclerosis. It would be a serious diagnosis, but not a death sentence. But there were other things, too. Other possibilities. What if that MRI showed a tumor on her brain? Some other neurological disorder? He'd had to physically stop himself from Googling her symptoms last night. Had purposely put his phone and laptop on the opposite end of the houseboat before settling in for the night.

And frankly, he was pretty sure he'd only stayed at the boat the past two nights because he wasn't sure what he'd say to Lilian when he saw her next. She'd most likely bite his head off if he tried to show any sympathy.

Which meant maybe he should do exactly that because biting his head off would probably give her more comfort than anything else. Or maybe he should take a cue from her. They'd exchanged a flurry of texts about wedding details in the past few days and she hadn't once brought up what she'd told him. So maybe he was supposed to follow her lead, pretend she'd never said anything.

Pretend he didn't know something no one else in her family did. Well, save Maggie. He knew he wasn't wrong about Maggie knowing more than Lilian thought. She might not have the particulars, but just like she'd had her reasons for asking him to be a part of this whole wedding planning business, he'd reckoned all along Maggie had her reasons for asking Lilian, too.

He cut the engine and directed his gaze out his windshield toward Ansel Barrett's two-story farmhouse. Time to focus on said wedding business instead of his flailing investigation.

He gave the photo one more futile glance. He'd managed to identify three of the five men pictured with Nicholas

Cornish over the past few months. He'd spoken to two of them. Hadn't led him anywhere. Nor had any of his other calls to random connections and acquaintances to Cornish.

He'd even made a trek to Atlanta back in February. Mostly fruitless. He'd thought maybe he could track down some family members who might have information, but Cornish's ex-wife had died not even a year after Diana had and relatives were scattered and disconnected. There'd been another daughter, Elizabeth, Peyton's younger sister, but according to a reporter Wilder had spoken with, the same one who'd eventually called him to let him know Nicholas Cornish had died, Elizabeth had been sent to live with a distant aunt after her mother's death.

In other words, he'd had very little to add to his case files when he returned.

Another thing Lilian had been texting about in the past few days. She still wanted to see the files, read all the notes, lend a hand in a search that might have nowhere left to go.

He leaned his head against the back of his seat and closed his eyes for a second. *What would you do, Dad? What would you try next? Who would you call?*

When would you give up?

Oh, there were layers to that question that could suffocate him. He opened his eyes and jolted from the Jeep, sucking in a deep breath the moment the afternoon air hit him.

"Wilder Monroe?"

Across the dusty circle drive that framed Ansel's house, the man himself appeared, scooting out from underneath the ancient Ford truck he'd been driving as long as Wilder had been alive. Possibly much longer.

"Hey, Mr. Barrett." He barricaded the sense of defeat that had accompanied him on the drive out to Ansel's farm behind a friendly smile. He waved, remembered why he'd come here.

Lilian was convinced Maggie was all in on a church

wedding, but he'd had a notion of an entirely different sort the other day. So while Lilian busied herself calling every church in town, he figured he'd pursue his idea on his own and make sure it wasn't entirely impossible before floating it past Maggie or Lil.

Ansel wiped his hands over the grease-stained front of his coveralls. "Don't *Mr. Barrett* me, son. When you're old enough to shave, you're old enough to call another man by his first name. Not that it looks like you've bothered with a razor lately."

Wilder accepted the man's handshake and this time, his grin wasn't forced. "Neil's rubbing off on me, I guess."

Ansel's ruddy cheeks were a maze of pleasant creases, and his face a familiar one around Muir Farm. He was the Muir family's closest neighbor, operating his own small berry farm while also serving as mechanic extraordinaire to just about every farmer in the county, including Neil.

He wondered if the man had any idea how often Neil and Wilder had snuck onto his property as kids, fished at the creek that bordered the west edge? Barrett's farm didn't have the seaside view of the Muirs', but it was a picturesque piece of property all the same.

"The old rust bucket's putting up a fuss again, as you can see." Ansel rapped on the hood of his truck. "Might finally be time to lay her to rest. Besides, it's not nearly as fun to drive her without Cherise complaining about how loud she is."

How long had it been since Ansel's wife had passed away? Seven, eight years? "Parades in Muir Harbor would never be the same without you as grand marshal behind the wheel of this old thing."

Ansel chuckled. "Don't I know it. Almost didn't get her tuned up in time for last year's Fourth of July parade. Thought our esteemed Chamber of Commerce president might lose her head over it."

Patti Brighton-Smythe had been planning town events for as long as Wilder had been alive. Lilian might have a penchant for bossing everyone around, but Patti was a veritable drill sergeant. "Lose her wig, more like."

Ansel slapped his leg and cackled. "I've always liked you, Wilder. But tell me what you're doing here. Couldn't have come out here just to gossip about my truck or Patti's wigs."

"Uh, well, I'm helping with some plans for Maggie Muir's wedding and we haven't managed to pin down a venue yet. Are you still in touch with Walter Wallace?"

"Old Wally Wally? Of course. But I'm not sure how he can help you with a venue."

"It's a whim of an idea. Probably a little crazy. But I can't find a current number for the guy. I tried Googling. He doesn't show up anywhere."

Ansel pulled his cell phone from the pocket of his coveralls with a laugh. "Walter Wallace doesn't do technology. He's got a thing against Big Brother." He scrolled through his phone, then held it out to Wilder. "Here. This is Birdie's number."

"Birdie?"

"His mother. Wally visits her once a week at her retirement village. Call her and she'll have him call you next time she visits."

Hmm, not the most efficient way to reach the man. With the wedding date only five weeks and two days away, they weren't exactly swimming in time to spare here. All the same, he tapped the number into his own phone's contact list. "You don't by any chance have his address, do you? Might be faster just to track him down."

"Sorry, but no. He's a sailor without a port. Last I talked to him, he was somewhere in the Tremont area, but that was a few months ago. Your dad always kept better track of him than I did." Ansel pocketed his phone when Wilder handed it back. "Sure miss him, your dad."

Wilder looked away. "I miss him, too."

"So many memories," Ansel went on. "Harry and me and Wally, fishing at the pier as kids. Fishing at the pier as teens. Fishing at the pier as adults. We were as tight as you and Neil back in our day."

"Dad loved fishing."

Ansel lifted his hand and squeezed Wilder's arm. "He loved you, son. More than anything."

He had no choice but to look away again. To swallow hard against the emotion that would rise up to choke him if he let it. He gazed over the peeling siding of Ansel's farmhouse, the unruly hedges bordering the porch. Was that a *For Sale* sign lying on its side on the porch?

"Ansel, are you—"

The man must've followed his line of sight because he cut in before Wilder could finish the question. "Planning to sell. Yes, indeed. Both my girls are down in Florida. Reckon it's about time I retire and relocate. Haven't put it on the market yet. But soon."

Wilder returned his attention to the older man. "Wow. I want to be excited for you, but I can't help being a little sad. The Muirs will miss having you as a neighbor. The whole county will miss you."

Ansel sighed. "I'm hoping I can find a family to buy it rather than a property developer. I have half a mind to split up the parcels. Sell the house and the farmland separately, make sure the land goes to someone who will preserve it. There'd be legal details involved, no doubt. What I'd really love is to sell the land to Neil."

Oh, he had a feeling his friend would jump at the chance to expand Muir Farm if he could. Money would be an issue, though. "Lilian could help you with the legal stuff."

"Thought of that." Ansel looked around the farmyard, his gaze taking on a distant quality. "Yep, it's going to be hard to leave this place. But on the other hand, it's never really been the same since Cherise passed. Honestly, there was a while there where I didn't even want to walk through the kitchen. It was always her domain."

Wilder could understand that. Could still remember how foreign it'd felt to step on the houseboat, knowing he wouldn't find Dad waiting for him in their tiny living space. He'd struggled to sleep for months on end in the houseboat's sole bedroom without Dad in the twin bed on the opposite side of the room.

Come to think of it, that's probably when he'd started crashing on the couch at Maggie's so often. Or sometimes taking the guest room upstairs when she offered. A little pathetic, really.

But it was too painfully easy to miss Dad when he stayed at the houseboat.

Too achingly difficult to push away the memories. The day he'd discovered Dad on the floor. The night he'd found the letter.

Tell me you didn't do it, Dad. Tell me I'm imagining things. That of all my gut instincts that have ever proven right, this is the one that's blessedly wrong.

"In a way, might be nice to split up the property," Ansel added. "Might feel a little less like I'm leaving what Cherise and I had behind."

He could understand that, too. He'd finally started sleeping a little better when, six months after Dad's death, he'd forced himself to haul both Dad's and his own old lumpy mattresses off the boat. Bought himself a king-sized bed that was way too big for the cramped bedroom. But it was a peculiar comfort. An attempt at moving on.

He just wished he could convince himself he had.

"Well, Ansel, we'll all miss you. Really. And thanks again for Wally's number. Or Birdie's, I guess."

"Of course. Don't worry, she'll make sure he gets in touch with you. By the way, I don't mind if you tell the Muirs about my plans, but try not to let the cat out of the bag to anyone else. I'd rather my move not hit the gossip chain just yet or I'll have every warm-weather-loving widow in church knocking on my door. It's already been a constant merry-go-round of baked goods since Cherise passed."

Wilder started toward his Jeep. "So that's why you're really moving. To escape your inordinate amount of romantic prospects."

Ansel laughed and reached out his palm for another hand-shake, then Wilder ducked into the Jeep once more, tossed his phone to the passenger seat. He jutted his key into the ignition and the vehicle rumbled to life.

But he waited a moment before backing down the drive. Watched Ansel walk back to his rusted truck, tried to imagine this house and this land without him. How did a man pull up such deep roots? Replant himself somewhere new?

Wilder had tried once. Had chased a dream out of state, only to turn around right when it was within reach. Something he'd never regretted. Not one time.

Finally, he gripped the gear shift. But his phone trilled from the seat beside him. Eyes still on Ansel, now scooting back into place underneath his truck, he reached for the blaring device and answered without looking at the screen. "This is Wilder."

"Wilder Monroe? Agent Peter Franzen. FBI. I hear you're looking for Nicholas Cornish."

"Maggie, what are we doing here?"

It was the second time she'd asked the question since

they'd pulled into the cement lot beside the brick building Lilian had never had a desire to visit. The first time, Maggie had merely reached into the back seat of her Buick and lifted a rectangular Tupperware as if that answered the question.

Partly, it did. A delivery of homebaked goods.

But why here? Unless Lilian was mistaken, the only person Maggie knew in the long-term-care center, located in a larger town about thirty miles from Muir Harbor, was the one man Lilian hoped never to see again.

She'd spent months trying to forget Peyton Cornish. Talking about him with Wilder on Tuesday had been bad enough. But now . . .

This was absolutely not how she'd pictured spending her Thursday evening after-work hours. In a rare move, brought about by the fact that only three days into her new role, Mariana had turned out to be more helpful and efficient than Lilian could've possibly imagined, Lilian had actually left the office by four. She'd planned to go home and hopefully find Maggie. Which she had, but Maggie had been on her way out the door and had invited Lilian to come along as she "ran an errand."

Lilian had figured why not? She could tell Maggie what she needed to in the car as well as anywhere. Break the news that there wasn't a single church in town available for a June twenty-ninth wedding.

And maybe, somewhere in that conversation, she'd find a way to test the waters, too. See if there was, in fact, something to Wilder's frustrating assurance that Maggie already knew something was going on with Lilian's health.

He's wrong. He's just trying to get you to tell her.

And yet, this was the man who'd predicted Danine and Tobias Rockwell would get married months before shy, widowed Tobias had ever worked up the nerve to stop by the cottage and ask Danine to dinner. This was also the same man who'd said once when they were only teens that the white brick building on Main that'd stood empty for most of their childhood had Indi's name written all over it, and lo and behold, years after he'd made that random pronouncement, Indi had indeed purchased the building and opened her artsy shop.

Then there were the café owners, Annie and Dale. No one in Muir Harbor probably ever would've known they were millionaires if Wilder hadn't let it slip at a town meeting a few years back that they were the anonymous donors who'd paid for that summer's downtown beautification project. He'd blanched when every person within hearing distance had turned to stare at him after what he'd clearly meant as nothing more than a side comment. *"Uh, I'm . . . sorry. I thought everyone knew . . . Wasn't it an unspoken-but-we-all-know-it type of secret?"*

Everyone might joke that Muir Harbor was a small town where everyone knew everything about everyone else. But for those who'd managed to hold on to their secrets, Wilder Monroe was a constant risk factor.

Look at how easily he'd managed to coax her own secret out into the open.

"Are you coming, dear?"

A warm spring breeze skimmed over her cheeks as she blinked and realized Maggie had reached the entrance of the care center without her. They hadn't gotten around to talking about the wedding on the drive—or anything else, really. Lilian had been too caught up in her confusion when she'd realized where they were headed.

She picked up her pace now, the flip-flops she'd replaced her black heels with after work slapping against the pavement. The red polish on her toes was already chipping. *What a silly whim.*

What a silly thing for Wilder to so noticeably . . . notice.

"Seriously, Maggie, why are we here?" She slipped into the wide revolving door with Maggie and, seconds later, they were deposited into a lobby with pale walls and pale floors and little in the way of decoration.

Maggie's hair fell around her shoulders in soft waves, her bright yellow cardigan woefully out of place in this space that was all whites and grays. "Delivering scones to the staff. I come once a month or so."

"Why here? Why not the hospital in Muir Harbor? Is there someone you know here other than Peyton?"

Maggie shook her head. "Come on, we need to sign in. Then we'll head up to the third floor."

Was that Peyton's floor? She waited until they were in the elevator to speak again. "Do you actually go see him? And if so, why? After what he did?"

Just that fast, the flashback grabbed hold of her and she was there. Legs aching as she grappled up the hillside and pushed through the barrier of trees into the clearing, her harried, frightened mind fighting to make sense of what she was seeing. Peyton Cornish attacking Indi, his hands on her throat. Philip's half sister had been there, too. And the cliff . . . so close.

It'd been over in minutes. Maybe only seconds. Philip had hurled himself at Peyton. Neil and Wilder had scrambled into action, as well.

Lilian had held her sister, tears streaming down her face, trying and failing to understand.

And then, Peyton had locked gazes with her. *"Hello, Lilian."*

Even now, just the memory of his tone, baleful and taunting, could make her shudder. And what'd happened next—

The ding of the elevator wrenched her from the memory. Maggie was saying something about showing kindness to the staff, trying to keep herself from harboring resentment toward a man who had obviously been hurt deeply as a child.

But he would've killed Indi. If we hadn't gotten there in time, Maggie, he would've killed her and probably Philip's sister, too, and maybe then he would've come for the rest of us.

He'd ranted about hating their family. About how they'd stolen from him, never mind that Neil and Lilian and Indi hadn't even been a part of Maggie's family when Diana had. That it wasn't Maggie's fault Diana had run away with Nicholas Cornish. That it was Peyton's father who'd chosen to have an affair with a minor.

A distant, dutiful forgiveness was one thing. But being here now, up close to the man . . . it didn't make sense.

And yet, Lilian followed Maggie from the elevator to a nurses' station on the third floor. Smiled as Maggie chatted with several nurses who oohed and ahhed over the scones. Pretended she wasn't itching to leave. That her lungs didn't tighten when Maggie said she was going to stop in Room 306 for a moment and Lilian was welcome to wait out here without her.

Room 306. Must be Peyton's room.

She didn't know why she followed Maggie. Entered under a metal doorframe into a sterile room devoid of sunlight. Devoid, it almost felt, of life altogether.

But Peyton Cornish wasn't dead. Not with the machines around his hospital bed humming, the occasional beep cutting into the stillness. His skin was pasty, barely a shade off from the crisp white sheets coddling his immobile form. His sandy blond hair had been gelled and parted at the side when she'd first met him, but it was longer by several inches now and tucked behind his ears on both sides.

The stray thought found her that it must be someone's job to clip his fingernails. They were short and stubby where his hands rested at his sides.

Several feet ahead of Lilian, Maggie paused by the bed. "If you want to know the truth, Lil, I don't come here because I'm a bastion of Christian goodwill. I come here because he's the only living link I have to Diana and those missing years. To Cynthia. I hate what he did. But I can't get over the thought that he . . . that his father . . ."

Averting her gaze from the man in the bed, Lilian moved to Maggie's side and slipped her arm around Maggie's waist. She wished she could think of something to say. Some soothing, aloe-like words to cover the wounds Maggie had lived through in the years before she'd come into her life.

The wounds she still carried. Gracefully, and increasingly peacefully, it seemed. But they were still there.

"Sometimes I feel like I owe you all an apology."

Lilian startled. "What in the world for?"

Maggie nodded her head toward a pair of chairs along the wall. "All these years of looking for Cynthia. You all grew up under the shadow of Diana's death and Cynthia's disappearance." She lowered into a chair. "I've wondered more than once if it ever had any of you feeling as if a part of me was missing, unavailable to you."

Lilian dropped into the chair beside Maggie. "I'm pretty sure I can speak for all of us when I say that's not the case. You've been—you *are*—the best mom I could ever have asked for."

Maggie covered Lilian's hand on her armrest. "My gentle Lily Grace. You are the sweetest."

Sweet little Lily. She'd dreamed of the voice again last night. She'd gone months, even years in the past, without a visit from the recurring dream. This was twice in a week's time.

"I hope you know you're the only one I let call me Lily. And only once in a while."

Maggie grinned. "Yes. When we're having a moment."

"And I think it's hilarious that you call me gentle. I'm a lawyer. I argue for a living."

"Well, maybe there are things a mother can see in her

daughter that her daughter can't. Maybe while everyone else sees your strength and confidence, both admirable traits, I see something I admire even more—a softness that always finds just the right time to come out."

On the heels of Maggie's words, it didn't matter that Peyton Cornish lay in a bed only feet away, that machines droned around them, or that the air in the tiny room smelled of antiseptic. "I'm so glad it was you who found me. I'm so glad it was *your* doorstep." She leaned her head on Maggie's shoulder. "I used to pretend I was her, you know. Diana's daughter. When I was little, I used to pretend I was Cynthia."

"I had no idea."

She lifted her head. "Actually, it was more than pretending. I was half-convinced." Maybe wholly. "My age was almost right, even if my hair color wasn't. I came up with a reason for that. Came up with a whole justification for why you didn't recognize me as Cynthia when I showed up on your doorstep. Built a case for it when I was ten and wrote it all down in one of my old Mead Five Star notebooks."

A notebook she'd gone and thrown in the sea after Wilder's puncturing words at the houseboat.

"It's impossible, Lil . . ."

Yes, it was. But it'd been a happy dream for a while. A balm of her own, something to lose herself in when the questions got to her.

"I had a wild imagination, I guess."

"I love your imagination." There was a smile in Maggie's voice. "I remember long summer days chasing you around the farm because you'd convinced all of us the Legend of Muir Harbor was a true story and you'd figured out where Alec's treasure was hidden and you had all these plans for how we'd use the gold."

She laughed. "That old legend. I never got tired of it." The legend was local lore, telling the story of Maggie's ancestors, led by Alec Muir, who'd journeyed from Scotland and settled in Maine before it was even a state and founded Muir Harbor. According to the tale, when Alec died, he'd left behind a treasure of missing gold—a maybe fictitious, maybe not mystery that had been every bit as much a part of Lilian's childhood as the real-life mystery of Cynthia Muir.

"It never occurred to me, though, that you might think . . . but it makes sense. Like you said, you're close to Cynthia's age, and I'm sure hearing about her all the time planted ideas in your head. Goodness, it must've been so confusing."

"I think I just wanted it to be true so much. I wanted to be yours."

"Oh, Lilian, but you are—"

"I know. I do. I just . . . really believed it for a while. That the person you were so desperate to find was right in front of you. That the past I had so many questions about was right in front of me."

"This is one bond I wish we didn't share. The not-knowing." Maggie reached over and took hold of Lilian's hand. "So at what point did you stop thinking of yourself as Cynthia?"

"Oh, it didn't last long. Wilder did a pretty good job pummeling the truth into me. Told me my theory was impossible and that I'd probably never know where I came from and I just needed to accept it. I was ten. He was thirteen or maybe fourteen." A teenager, oblivious to how his words wrecked her. Of course, that was only part of the story. She'd left out the part about going to Harry's boat.

She'd left out what had spurred her to decide she was Maggie's long-lost granddaughter in the first place. That day in the school years earlier . . . standing up in front of a classroom. Feeling vulnerable and exposed and . . . lost. So, so lost in the wake of questions she couldn't answer.

Questions that swept her into a sea of confusion until her imagination had temporarily saved the day.

Maggie dropped Lilian's hand now and shifted to face her. "Oh." She said the word on an exhale. "Twenty years of annoyance and snide remarks finally make sense. That's why you don't like Wilder."

"It's not the only reason. Just the main one." Lilian managed a smile. "Do you still think I'm sweet and gentle? Now that you know I've held a grudge for this long?"

Maggie chuckled. "I do, in fact. Because you, my sweet and gentle Lily Grace, were trying to fill a hole in my heart when you imagined yourself as Cynthia. And in your own, no doubt. But I have a feeling there was as much love for me fueling that imagination of yours as there was curiosity about yourself."

It was true. She loved Maggie more than anyone.

"You know, if it helps ease your grudge at all, Wilder's had his fair share of heartbreak, too."

Lilian knew that. Had seen the evidence only days ago of how much he still missed his father. "He was pretty bad off for a while there after Harry died."

"He was more than bad off. I went to the houseboat the morning after the funeral." Maggie's eyes were fixed on the wall across the room, the memory playing in her expression. "He was a mess. Completely undone. I've never seen him like that. He was hungover and—"

"Wilder? Drunk?"

"He'd found a letter Harry wrote and I think he convinced himself . . ." She sighed and looked back to Lilian. "I shouldn't be saying this. It's his story to tell. But I don't know, Lil. As much as I sometimes wonder if I put too much focus on Cynthia when you were kids, I wonder if it's too much for Wilder now. At first I thought the case was good for him. Something for him to focus on after Harry, but now . . ."

Maggie suddenly straightened in her chair, her gaze sharpening into laser-focus. "Did you just see that?"

"See what?"

Maggie stood and moved toward the bed.

"Maggie, what is it?"

"His right hand. His fingers. I think they might've moved."

Lilian was on her feet in an instant. "Are you sure?"

"Well, no, but . . ." They both peered at the man for long, stretching seconds, until Maggie shook her head. "Maybe I was imagining things."

Lilian's focus moved from Peyton's immobile hand to his ashen face. Maybe it was because they'd just been talking about Wilder that his voice sought her out now, the memory of his words in the church.

"Peyton Cornish comes to Muir Harbor. Pretends to be friendly. But eventually, we learn the truth."

There was a piece he'd left out when he was recounting the man's entry into their lives. Intentionally? Had he been trying to spare Lilian the embarrassment by leaving out the fact that Peyton had befriended *her* before anyone else. He hadn't just befriended her. He'd taken her out to dinner, what she'd assumed was a date. Fooled her more than anyone with his preppy, nice-guy act.

All along he'd been trespassing, vandalizing, planning . . .

A chill started at Lilian's neck and slithered down her spine. "There was this moment, right before he went over the cliff. He looked right at me."

"Can I confess something, Lil? I come here and I bring snacks and I walk in this room and tell myself every time that I'm capable of forgiveness. But at the same time, there's a piece of me that doesn't want him to wake up. I can't stand the thought of him trying to hurt one of my children again. I want you all safe and sound and healthy forever."

Healthy.

Wilder's voice budged in again. *"She knows."*

Did she?

Lilian took a breath. This room, it seemed, with its eerie hush and unrelenting stillness, was a place for confession. "Maggie, there's something I have to tell you."

Γ

He shouldn't be in here.

Wilder knew it the moment he stepped over the threshold. Hanging around for mealtimes in the Muir family's kitchen, frequently crashing on the couch downstairs, keeping an extra toothbrush under the sink in the bathroom down the hall—a little unconventional, maybe, but reasonable.

Encroaching on Lilian's bedroom, though? *Unacceptable.*

He hadn't meant to trespass. He'd knocked, hadn't he? Wasn't his fault her door hadn't been latched closed. That his light rap had been enough to nudge it open an inch or two.

Maybe not, but he'd been the one to peek inside, let the door creak open a few more inches, squeaky hinges echoing into the deserted hallway, the subtle scent of her perfume greeting him. Dusk painted the walls of Lilian's domain in pastel brushstrokes, and the faint music of voices and laughter drifted through the register.

Maggie's fiancé had driven down from Augusta to join the family for dinner this evening, along with his grandson, Indi's boyfriend. Maybe Wilder should've felt out of place, crowded around the dining room table with this patchwork family stitched together by such an interesting crisscrossing of seams.

But the Muirs had a way of pulling him in, making him feel like another patch on the quilt.

He felt out of place now, though. Nonsensically inert mere feet inside a bedroom he had no business being in. *Just do what you came to do. Make the delivery and get out.*

If Lilian had joined the family for dinner, he'd have let her know then about the plastic tub filled with case files in the back seat of his Jeep. He'd decided to finally give in. Pass them on to her. But she hadn't been at dinner and it was getting late and he needed to make a painfully early start tomorrow if he was going to make it to D.C. by the time he'd agreed to meet Agent Franzen.

Agent Peter Franzen with the Federal Bureau of Investigation. He still couldn't quite believe someone from the FBI had reached out to him. Crazier still, the man had asked to meet with him.

Truthfully, it'd felt less like a request and more like a demand. Laughable, considering just the thought of sitting down to coffee with an agent was enough to make Wilder feel like a ten-year-old boy. Overly eager and dazzled by the sight of a badge, head filled with visions of a future that had never quite panned out.

Never mind that he had a badge of his own these days, along with a license he'd been obliged to flash a time or two over the years. But there'd been a time when he'd dreamed of a different badge. A whole different life.

A life that had been within a fingertip's reach when he'd made the decision to walk away. Leave it all behind. Follow his strongest gut instinct yet and return to Muir Harbor.

Thumping footsteps overhead drew him back to the present, reminded him where he was. That had to be Neil lumbering through the attic-turned-master-suite. Sydney's tread wouldn't be so heavy.

With a grunt, he hefted the plastic tub onto Lilian's bed, trying not to notice too many details of this room he absolutely shouldn't be in. But that was the problem with being a P.I. He couldn't help but take in the pale blues and greens of the pillows atop Lilian's cream-colored bedspread—earthy tones that felt fitting against the hardwood floors and walnut frame around her window.

"Light blues and greens—those are your colors."

Good grief, had he actually said that to her the other day? Ridiculous.

Leave. Now. You delivered the case files. So scram.

And he would've. He truly would've if his gaze hadn't picked right that moment to land on a scrap of paper sticking out behind a mirror over a squatty chest of drawers in the corner. Even from the other side of the room, he could make out its worn edges.

Even from the other side of the room, he knew what it was.

Don't do it, Monroe.

He was incorrigible. Or his curiosity was just that irresistible. He'd heard about the note, of course, but had never actually seen the original. Floorboards moaned underfoot as he moved and, crossing the last line between questionable and a full-on invasion of Lil's privacy, tipped the mirror to reveal the full index card.

The handwriting was sharp and angled. Faded from time, but readable.

Lilian. Birth date 9/12/88. Allergic to bananas.

"What in the—Wilder?"

His gaze jolted upward, instantly connecting with Lilian's wide eyes in the mirror. Heart thudding and conscience screeching, his guilt-laden apology was flying free before he even finished spinning around. "I'm sorry, Lil. I know I shouldn't have—"

Why did his blasted private-eye penchant for details have to pick just then to kick in again? It was a rapid-fire pinging of awareness as he took in first her wet hair hanging in tangles around her cheeks. Then her bare shoulders and arms, only a thin tank top above baggy pajama pants. She held a bundle of clothing and it must be her shampoo that smelled of apples, different from the perfume she always wore, and . . .

Bare feet. Again.

Lilian had been in the bathroom? He hadn't even realized she was home. He'd gone out to help Neil with evening chores awhile ago, before grabbing the tub from his Jeep, and apparently in that time, she'd—

A pillow hit him in the face. "What are you doing in my room?"

He blinked. "Lil—"

Smack. Another pillow. This one landed against his chest. It wasn't enough to send him reeling, but he took a step backward all the same, lifted his hands in surrender. "Really, I'm sorry. I was just leaving the case notes for you." But if she'd noticed them next to where she'd dropped her bundle of clothing on her bed, she didn't give any sign of it. She was too busy grabbing another pillow, taking aim.

He stepped out of the way and the thing whizzed past his head.

"This is my *bedroom*, Wilder."

"I know—"

"You might think you have free rein of this whole house, but not this room. Not my room."

Another pillow hit him in the shoulder and she'd moved closer. Close enough he could see the ire glinting in her blue eyes and feel the impact of her scowl. Except it wasn't anywhere near the impact she likely wanted. Oh no, all that blazing glower made him want to do was laugh. He'd felt guilty only a moment ago, but now . . . ?

Okay, he still felt a fair measure of guilt. But there was an unruly glee mixed in, and if Lilian sensed even a speck of his amusement, he'd earn another pillow to the face.

She was out of pillows, though.

And it was that realization that was simply too much

temptation. He felt the corners of his mouth lift.

"Don't you dare smile right now, Wilder Monroe."

"I'm not."

She bulleted him with a glare. "You're a liar and a trespasser."

"This might be a good time to remember that only a few nights ago, you snuck onto my boat."

"I didn't go into your bedroom."

"You might've if I hadn't caught you red-handed first." He shouldn't be arguing with her. He shouldn't still be standing here. Not when she had every right to be vexed.

Not with the light from her window falling over her just so, highlighting the faint dusting of freckles on her shoulders. He didn't know why, but he wished he hadn't noticed that.

"You and me—" her hand waggled between them "—we're not brother and sister. We're not siblings who get to go in and out of each other's rooms."

"I know that." Why did his voice come out so scratchy?

"Actually, not even my siblings barge in here. There's this little thing called privacy that we all choose to observe and respect. They *knock*."

He cleared his throat. "Lil, if this lecture's going to go on a lot longer, could you maybe . . ." He was too rattled to finish his sentence. Or even know what he'd meant to ask her. What was wrong with him?

He didn't have time to ponder it because in that same moment, Lilian became mindful of her own appearance. He watched it play out over her face. The quick glance down at her gauzy pajama top. The instant flush.

She whirled away from him and for a second, he thought she was going to march out of the room. Instead, she plucked a hooded sweatshirt from a hook on the back of her bedroom door and shoved her arms into it. She zipped it all the way to her chin as she twisted to face him again, releasing a huff that sent strands of damp hair billowing. "Explain yourself."

"The case files," he said weakly. "You kept asking to see them."

"You could've left them downstairs." She crossed her arms over her torso. "Or outside my door."

"I know. I should've."

She stared at him a moment more. "I wish I had more pillows."

He bent to pick up the closest one. Held it out in invitation.

She ignored it and pointed at the door.

All right, then. Suddenly, he wanted out of here as badly as she wanted him gone. And there wasn't an ounce of him that wanted to give an iota of thought as to why. He just wanted to escape.

He abandoned the pillow and gave her a wide berth as he passed. Was almost out the door when her sigh made him slow.

"Wilder. Wait."

He paused.

"I saw Peyton today."

Now he turned and saw that nearly all the bluster had leaked from her. The hoodie was still zipped as far as it could go, but she'd dropped her arms, if not her frown. "You saw . . ."

"I went to the care center with Maggie. She saw him move his hand. At first we thought it was a fluke, but then it happened again. The doctor said it's a positive sign he might wake up yet."

"Soon?"

She shrugged. "He said there's no telling. Could be tomorrow. Could be next month."

Tomorrow. Huh, now he didn't feel so great about taking off in the morning. But even if Peyton woke up from his coma tonight, it wasn't as if he'd be leaving his bed anytime soon. He wasn't a true danger to anyone.

Still. He didn't like the thought of Lilian in the same room as the man, unconscious or not.

No, he didn't like the thought of any of the Muirs in the room with him.

And yet, he'd known Maggie went to see Peyton now and then, and he'd never felt the need to issue a warning. But for some reason when it came to Lil . . .

He cleared his throat again. Why did he keep doing that? "Maybe we should talk to the police chief about stationing an officer outside his door. If not now, then starting when he wakes up. If he wakes up. I mean, he might not. There's still a chance of that."

She was looking at him as if she wanted to ask him something now. Fidgeting with the zipper of her sweatshirt, lips pressed together, an uncertainty he wasn't used to seeing in her expression.

She was going to ask him about the note, wasn't she? She'd caught him peering at it and—

"You were right."

So much for his dependable gut instinct. It might've been the very last thing he would've expected her to say. Against his better judgment, he let three long strides carry him back to her and lifted his palm to her forehead.

Which, of course, she promptly swatted away. "I don't have a fever, you—"

"Can you blame me for wondering?"

"Never mind. Just go away."

"No, this is a big moment for me. It's not that I've never been right before, I've just never heard you admit it."

Why wasn't she glaring at him right now? Shouldn't she be making some scathing comment? Reminding him of all the times he hadn't been right?

"Fine. Gloat. I don't care. But I told Maggie about the symptoms and the neurologist and the MRI and you were right, okay? She already sensed something was going on." She folded her arms across her chest again, but the stance seemed less a move of defiance or defense and more . . . a need for comfort or contact.

"How'd she take it?" he eventually asked.

"Okay. She hugged me. Asked what she could do. I told her there's not really anything to do. There's still the very real possibility that this whole thing is overblown and the MRI won't show anything and everything's going to be fine."

"Everything *will* be fine." Maybe it was the wrong thing to say. A faulty assurance he had no right to make.

But she didn't seem to mind. Not his words, not the hand he'd lifted to touch her elbow. A strange, senseless move. But they just stood there for a moment—she with her arms still crossed and him with his fingers skimming the cotton of her sweatshirt.

"Is that another gut instinct?"

He cleared his throat. How many times had he done that in the span of the past ten minutes? *A hundred, at least.*

He peered at her, thoughts too disorderly to form a response at first. Until, finally, he recognized the forced brightness in her voice for what it was. A need to lighten this moment. A need he could meet.

He eased a step back, dropped his arm. Gave her a diversion in the form of a smirk and joking tone that matched hers. "You're hoping it is, I'm sure. Because they're usually proven correct. As you've just admitted. Could you say it again just so I know I didn't imagine it the first time?"

Her frown was everything he'd hoped for. "Leave now or I start throwing pillows again."

WILDER

Meant to tell you last night. Heading down to D.C. today to meet with an FBI agent about Nicholas Cornish. Should be back tomorrow.

LILIAN

Umm . . . it's 5 a.m. You couldn't wait to text until a more reasonable hour?

WILDER

It's an eight-hour drive. Gotta hit the road. And since I try to avoid texting and driving . . .

LILIAN

You could've called me from the road.

WILDER

Maybe I will. True crime podcasts can only entertain me for so long. What are you up to today?

LILIAN

Since when do we swap agendas first thing in the morning?

WILDER

I'm getting the distinct impression you're not a morning person.

LILIAN

I'm working today. And going with Mariana to check out an apartment over lunch. Talking to Misty about Maggie's wedding cake. Satisfied?

WILDER

If Misty tells you she can't fit it in, mention my name and she'll change her tune.

LILIAN

. . .

WILDER

Have a good day, Miss Muir.

"You should be a realtor, Lilian. An apartment over a coffee shop? I couldn't have picked out a more perfect spot."

Lilian turned a slow circle in the modest-sized apartment above Trinna's Teatime. It wasn't exactly trendy, nor was it furnished. But it was within walking distance of the law office, Mariana's main requirement, and it was available. The woman had been living at The Lodge, Muir Harbor's only hotel, since her interview last week, and while it wasn't a terrible place to stay, it couldn't be all that homey and comfortable either.

"If you're going to live here, it's probably important someone warn you not to call it a coffee shop in front of Trinna. She's adamant it's a tea shop."

Mariana paused in the middle of the small living room

that opened into a narrow kitchenette. "Sure smells like a coffee joint."

It did, at that. The tantalizing aroma of coffee beans fairly seeped through the walls, and it was nearly enough to make Lilian groan. *Thirty-four days.* Over a month since her last cup of caffeinated bliss. Why hadn't she just given in and allowed herself to start drinking the stuff again? It wasn't as if Dr. Cho had told her to stick with tea.

He hadn't told her much of anything, really. A week later, and she still hadn't decided if that was a good thing or not.

To think, she still had eleven days to wait until the MRI and who knew how long after that until she had results. Possibly a diagnosis. Possibly not.

At least Maggie knows now.

Maggie had been so quiet and patient when Lilian had spilled everything to her, there beside Peyton Cornish's hospital bed of all places. She'd pulled Lilian into an embrace that spoke a world of comfort and peace and calm into being. *"I'm so glad you told me, Lil. I knew something was wrong, I just didn't know what. I'm here for you. I'm always here for you. And Neil and Indi—"*

"They don't know yet. I'll tell them eventually. But for now . . ."

She hadn't needed to say anything more. Maggie had hugged her again. *"Everything's going to be just fine."*

Wilder had come close to echoing those words last night. But there'd been something different in the way he'd said it. Coming from Maggie, it'd been a statement of quiet comfort. From Wilder . . . he'd meant to sound confident. Hopeful. But underneath there'd been a hint of something almost . . . needy.

As if he ached for his words to be true but wasn't quite sure . . .

Stop. She was being silly. It was her tiredness talking now. She'd stayed up too late last night culling through Wilder's and his father's old files. She'd been awoken too early by Wilder's text.

Because apparently they were keeping tabs on each other now and he was off to D.C. and why hadn't she asked him any questions about that? He was meeting with an FBI agent? How had that come about?

"Um, is there something concerning that I need to know about?" Mariana smoothed her hand over her sleek ponytail. The light of the window highlighted auburn threads Lilian hadn't noticed before. "You just went silent for a full two minutes."

"Sorry. Short night of sleep."

"I'm going to check out the rest of the place."

While Mariana disappeared into the bedroom at the back of the apartment, Flannel at her side, Lilian moved to the window and let the afternoon sun warm her face through the glass. With the pier only a short distance from Trinna's, on quiet nights Mariana might be able to open this window and enjoy the sound of the sea breathing in and out against the line of docks tucked into the curve of the harbor.

Lilian let her gaze drift over the sapphire ripples stretching into the distance, the pale sun-kissed wood of the docks, a few boats bobbing, Wilder's included. Faded white paint with a hunter-green stripe, curling letters. *The Marilyn*. Surely it'd been Harry Monroe who'd named the boat. Surely he'd laughed when he'd done so. *Monroe. The Marilyn. Marilyn Monroe.* She could picture the crinkles at the corners of the older man's eyes even now.

They were Wilder's eyes. The ones she'd seen looking back at her last night when she'd walked into her bedroom. She'd been so flabbergasted when she'd caught him leaning over her vanity, she'd legitimately thought she was imagining things at first.

Until she'd met his dusky gaze in the mirror. And for one

ephemeral moment, just before the rising of her ire, a picture had flashed in her mind. A picture of a different Wilder. The one Maggie had described earlier that day. Broken, anguished, nursing a hangover . . .

Completely undone. Those were the words Maggie had used. She wasn't sure why they'd lodged inside her so firmly but they had.

"Whoa, there's a walk-in closet in the bedroom." Mariana's muffled voice traveled from the other end of the apartment.

Lilian started to turn away from the window. Paused. Stepped back to the glass. *Who . . . ?*

There, just across the street, propped against a spindly lamppost, a man with his head tipped toward . . . her? She squinted, but the sun was too bright to make out his face or even really his form but—

He straightened. Spun on his heel. Walked off. He'd seen her.

Or . . . or she was completely imagining things. Why would someone be staring at this window? And with the sunlight so blinding, she didn't truly have a way of knowing he'd been watching her. *Silly.*

She turned away and moved into the hallway, peeked into the bathroom. Simple, but functional. Toilet, combo shower and bathtub. The pedestal sink was a con—no storage—but maybe the shelves behind the door made up for that.

"I think I'll take it."

At Mariana's pronouncement, she turned. Her coworker stood just outside the bathroom wall. "Really? It's the first place we've seen."

She winced. *Not the right word.* Mariana had told her not to get knotted up in semantics, but goodness, never had she realized how much of her life experience was tied up in sight. In colors and faces and shifting appearances. Mariana navigated the world without any of that. When Lilian had stepped into this apartment, she'd instantly appreciated the fresh coat of white paint but wondered why the landlord hadn't opted for at least one accent wall. She'd spotted the windows overlooking the harbor and knew exactly which wall would fit a couch best.

Mariana, she knew, had had an entirely different experience. She'd mouthed numbers as she'd counted the steps up to the second-floor entrance. Had run her hands along the countertops and kitchen appliances. She'd likely cataloged a whole host of characteristics about this space Lilian had missed thus far.

"The price is right. The location is perfect. And you said yourself Muir Harbor's rental housing options are limited."

"Not interested in buying?"

Mariana shook her head. "Not just yet. I need to save up for a down payment first. The divorce, uh, threw me for a bit of a financial loop. Going to take me a while to catch back up."

It wasn't the first time Mariana had mentioned her divorce in the days since they'd begun working together. She'd filled Lilian in on bits and pieces of her past. Apparently, she'd spent the bulk of her life in California, her father working on a fruit farm, no mother. She'd married at some point, but Lilian knew little more than that. Where exactly were the lines between friendly and prying when it came to a new coworker?

Mariana skimmed her fingers down the bathroom doorframe. "My dad will be so ridiculously glad when I tell him he can bring all my boxes of Braille books when he comes to visit in a couple weeks. He's been storing them for me for months now."

"How many boxes are we talking? Just so I know how many people to rope into helping."

"You don't have to help, Lilian. You're already doing so much. I have a job because of—"

"You have a job because you're insanely qualified and because my partner is smarter than me. He knew what I needed when I didn't want to admit it." Lilian leaned against the sink. "And of course we'll line up people to help with the move. No matter how many boxes of books you have."

Mariana let go of Flannel's leash and the dog took it as a cue to relax. He lowered to sit on the threshold between the bathroom and the hallway. "I've always loved reading. I don't think it was all that easy for Dad to find books in Braille when I was younger. Money was tight then. But he did his best to keep me well-stocked. Even found a few legal textbooks through the years. I started saying I wanted to be a lawyer when I was all of five or six."

"Five or six? It took me until at least ninth grade to set my sights on law school." That's when Lilian had participated in a mock trial for the first time and had taken home an award for her opening statement.

"Pretty sure I was influenced by a *Matlock* rerun on TV."

"Well, your dad sounds great. Supportive. Is he still in California?"

Mariana shook her head and smiled. "No, he lives in Iowa now. This little town called Maple Valley. He met his wife, Willa, on a dating website a couple years ago. She works at an orchard and they bonded over their shared experience with fruit." She let out a light laugh. "I'm happy for him. He's actually the one who found this job opening. I was a little tempted to hole up with him and Willa for the long haul, but I think he knew I needed the adventure."

Together, they moved from the bathroom back into the living room. "Do you mind if I ask—"

"Why me and my hoard of books never made it to law school?"

"You're a mind reader."

"No, I just know it's the question I'd be asking if our situations were reversed." Mariana leaned down to scratch Flannel's head. "Tale as old as time. Fell in love in college. Got married and let my dream go in favor of his. He had his heart set on medical school. Didn't work out, unfortunately. The marriage, I mean, not med school. Actually, last I heard, Emilio's part of a thriving family practice in a suburb near Ojai."

"That . . . seems terribly unfair." How in the world was Mariana still smiling at the end of that story?

"It's all right. You make your choices and you live with them. And now I'm going to make another one. A fun one." She nodded, as if affirming her decision. "Think I'll go downstairs and talk to Trinna. Tell her I'll take the place."

"Wonderful. Mind if I run a couple doors down to the bakery? I need to talk wedding cakes with the owner. Meet you out front in fifteen?"

"Sounds good."

They parted ways minutes later and Lilian started down the sidewalk toward the bakery. Misty Sprinkles had moved to Muir Harbor two years ago, bought the bakery from the former owners when they retired, and already she'd become legendary for her elaborate cakes. She'd been on some reality baking show a few years ago when she was only twenty-four, had stolen all of America's heart when she'd made a joke about how, with a name like hers, she'd been destined for the baker's life.

And, apparently, according to Wilder's text earlier, he'd managed to charm her along with everyone else in this town.

Or, huh, what if it was the other way around? Misty was sweet and, as far as Lilian knew, single. Hadn't Wilder said something last week about single-handedly keeping the bakery open? Did he *like* Misty? Did he come here daily and flirt with the woman?

Not that she cared if he did. Why would she care about Wilder's love life?

She halted in the middle of the sidewalk.

Why did she get the uncanny sense that someone was following her just now? Maybe Mariana . . . She whirled around.

Nothing.

Just a humming breeze and a striped awning flapping overhead. The low rumble of an engine. The jingle of bells at a storefront down the block.

She let out her breath and, with it, a tinny laugh. What had she thought she'd see when she turned? That same man from the lamppost? The man who probably hadn't been looking her way at all?

"Lilian?"

She spun again, this time to see Indi coming her way. Her sister's boho skirt fluttered around her legs.

"What're you doing just standing in the middle of the sidewalk?"

Thinking silly thoughts, that's what. Thoughts of being followed. Thoughts of Wilder Monroe's dating history. Both equally absurd things to dwell on.

Still. She glanced over her shoulder once more. Scanned the street, the empty sidewalk. Shook her head at her own ridiculousness and turned back to her sister. "Just heading to the bakery. Wanna come talk cakes with me?"

Once, maybe ten years ago, Neil had dragged Wilder to a massive farm implement warehouse in Augusta. The place had smelled of metal and diesel, with cement floors and fluorescent lights that glinted off machinery with wheels taller than he was.

Neil had all but drooled over a harvester while wearing the sort of woozy grin Wilder had never seen on his friend's face again until his wedding day.

The sort of grin Wilder was sure had to be plastered over his face just now as he tipped his head and squinted into the sun, taking in the sprawling cement building at 601 4th Street.

The Federal Bureau of Investigation's local field office in D.C., a different building from Bureau headquarters, which was where he'd originally thought he was heading. But a quick internet search at a rest stop somewhere in Massachusetts had set him straight.

He had to look positively provincial now, a small-town boy from Maine, surrounded by the bustle of the busy sidewalk, rumbling motors, and the occasional honk filling the air in the street behind him. Cigarette smoke mingled with the greasy smell of a pizza joint down the block.

I finally did it, Dad. Made it to the FBI.

Only seven or eight years late and not at all how he'd planned. But he was here. And Special Agent Franzen was waiting.

He smoothed his hand over the tie he'd roped around his neck before leaving his car in the parking garage. Felt appropriate, if unnecessary. An improvement, if nothing else, over the plain black tee he'd worn during his eight-hour drive. Closer to nine, counting the D.C. traffic.

He stepped up to the imposing door at the front of the building, attention careening through the glass to take in the speckled tile flooring of the lobby, the high ceiling, and lofty windows as scraps of memories he hadn't bothered sifting through in years dropped in one after another. His first appointment with a recruiter during his senior year of college. Being ushered into a community college classroom a year later for his Phase 1 exam, a proctor standing guard during the three-hour computerized test. A meet-and-greet at the field processing office in Baltimore.

"Wilder Monroe?"

At the sound of the voice behind him, he turned away from the door he hadn't even gotten around to opening.

A man stood next to a black sedan at the curb. Dark slacks, crisp white shirt, gray tie. A ball cap pulled low over his eyes didn't seem to match the ensemble, but the man tipped it up just enough for Wilder to catch sight of his gray eyes. "Monroe?" he repeated.

"Uh, yes. That's me."

The man closed his car door, his black loafers rapping on the sidewalk as he moved toward Wilder. "Special Agent Peter Franzen. Sorry, I meant to make it here ahead of you, but a meeting ran long. Have you eaten? There's a hot dog stand two blocks down. Okay with multitasking?"

"Sure."

"Good. Thanks for meeting me, by the way. Making the trip down." He held out his palm. "Don't know why I picked the field office for a meeting point. I'm only in town for a conference, don't have an office in this building. And I don't have clearance to commandeer a conference room."

When Wilder gripped his hand but didn't laugh, the man leaned a little closer. "That was a joke. Kind of. Unless the administrative assistants here are anywhere near as strict about reserving conference rooms via the electronic calendar as they are in our Atlanta office. In that case, I'm completely serious."

Wilder finally managed to muster something close to a grin. "The trip wasn't a problem."

"Good. Let's walk."

Wilder couldn't help casting a regretful glance over his shoulder as they started down the block. He'd been looking forward to an inside peek at the field office. Had wondered if he might be able to wrangle a tour out of this whole thing.

But he felt every bit as much at Special Agent Franzen's beck and call as he had when the man had first contacted him yesterday. "Gotta admit, I'm more than a little curious about what I'm doing here. I didn't realize making a few inquiries into Nicholas Cornish would catch the FBI's attention. It's true that I've been looking for him, but now that he's dead—"

"Take a beat, son."

Son? The man couldn't have more than ten or twelve years on Wilder, could he?

They crossed a street and rounded a corner, leaving the FBI building behind. Franzen pulled off his ball cap, revealing a mop of black hair. "I looked into you, Monroe. Turns out you're Harry Monroe's son. He's a bit of a legend around the Bureau. *You're* a bit of a legend."

"Uh . . . he is?" *I am?* "I mean, yes, of course. My father worked for the agency for a few years and—"

"Five years, and he closed more cases in that time than I have in my thirteen years at the Atlanta office. Then he up and leaves right when he's in his prime. Word on the street, according to a few senior staff who were here when he was, it's all because he fell in love."

Two versions of his father Wilder had never known. Harry Monroe the FBI agent. And Harry Monroe the besotted husband.

Or, well, he'd known the latter. In a way, at least. Dad hadn't talked about Wilder's mother often, but when he had, there'd been a weighty reverence in his tone. Along with the kind of heartache that revealed the depth of Dad's loss. When his mother had died only six months after Wilder's birth, Dad hadn't only lost his life partner, he'd lost a piece of his very soul.

Only to hear Dad tell it, the loss had begun long before

Ainsley Monroe passed. It'd sunk its claws into him in the weeks and months leading up to her death as he watched her waste away.

"It's the worst kind of pain, Wilder. Watching it happen. Seeing a disease run its course right in front of you and knowing there's nothing you can do."

Except there had been something they could've done. Something his mother could've done, anyway. Wilder hadn't known that part of the story until he was a little older, of course, but it'd gutted him. Thoroughly, completely . . .

"It was her choice, son."

He barred Dad's voice from his mind, forced the tight curl from his fingers at his sides. This wasn't what he'd come here for. "Actually, uh, my father passed away a few years ago. Leukemia."

If Agent Franzen had done his research, then he already knew that fact. Might also know it wasn't leukemia listed on the death certificate.

Sympathy filtered into the man's gray eyes. "I did hear that. I'm sorry."

Wilder looked away.

"You heard the part, though, where I said you're a legend around here, too?"

His gaze darted back to the agent. "I have to think you're exaggerating some."

Agent Franzen shrugged, twirling his cap around his finger. "You flew through SASS." *Special Agent Selection System.* "Off the charts on core competencies. High forties on your PFTs. There were higher-ups with their eyes on you. So why skip out eight weeks into Basic Field Training?"

Definitely not what he'd come here for. "It was, um . . . not a decision I ever planned to make. But it was the right one."

He waited for the agent to dig further. Ask if Dad had been

sick back then. Or if there'd been some other life-altering event that had, well, altered his life. His future.

But instead, Agent Franzen paused. Nodded. Then changed course. "Let's talk about Nicholas Cornish. I need to know why you've been on the hunt for him."

It was easy enough to spill his story. He started at the beginning, with Diana Muir running away from home. By the time he made it to the part where he'd taken over Dad's investigation, they'd reached the hot dog stand.

He was halfway through his ketchup-and-relish-covered hot dog when he neared the end of the tale. Well, not so much the end as the point of stalemate.

"Felt like such a big break, finally identifying Nicholas Cornish as the father of Cynthia Muir. But now he's dead and if there's any chance he *was* in Muir Harbor the weekend of Diana's death, if he was there or knows anything about what happened to Cynthia, I'm starting to think that knowledge died with him."

Franzen swallowed the last bite of lunch, then balled his wrapper and tossed it in a trash bin as they passed. "Huh. That's quite the story."

"Not what you were expecting when you asked why I've been trying to track down Cornish?"

The agent tipped his head with a thin grin. "I try not to be taken off guard by much, but that . . . yeah, not what I was expecting. I have a special interest in Cornish. I've been trailing him for a decade now."

"From the little I've learned about him, I'm not surprised. High-stakes gambling. Shady business practices." Wilder took another bite of his hot dog.

"Not just that. The man is—was—a fence. Buying and selling stolen goods. Art. Jewelry. Collectors' items. Which is why I'm interested in any of his associates you've talked to. We know it wasn't a one-man operation, and we know there are still pieces to be recovered. I'm ticked I never had the chance to bring him in but if recovering the goods and prosecuting whoever's left is as good as it's going to get, I'm willing to grasp at straws. Take a long shot."

So he'd called Wilder. If there was anything Wilder's stalled investigation could be called at this point, it was a long shot. "Well, guess I'm happy to help however I can. Not really sure what I can do, though."

"You can tell me who you've talked to. Exactly what they said. Names, details, anything you can remember."

"Okay."

The agent gave him a sidelong glance. "You're wondering why we couldn't just have this conversation over the phone."

"No, it's not that." He shrugged and crumpled his wrapper and napkin together. "I think I'm just having a sudden case of self-doubt. Your investigation into Cornish has legs. Mine? It's never sounded so far-fetched to me as it did just now saying the whole thing out loud. My whole search for Cornish . . . I haven't even been able to place the guy in Muir Harbor the weekend of Diana's death. For all I know, it's been a complete waste of time."

Unless he could come up with some tidbit of information to help Franzen. He'd brought along that photo of Cornish with some of his associates. He could at least tell the man who he'd spoken with.

They stopped at a crosswalk and he took the opportunity to level with the agent. "If you were in my shoes, would you keep going? Keep looking?"

"Look, Monroe, probably one of the most important lessons that comes with time at the Bureau is knowing when it's time to fold. For every cold case with a satisfying ending, there are hundreds more languishing. Sometimes the trail doesn't just go cold, it disappears altogether. And sometimes the most likely possibility isn't just a possibility, it's the truth, whether or not you can prove it."

The crosswalk light flashed, but they didn't move. "You're saying Cynthia probably died in the accident with her mother, body or no body."

"I'm saying, it's been close to thirty years. And from everything you've just told me, there's not a trail to follow anymore. I'm sure the thought of it stings, but it might be that the best thing you can do for this friend of yours, the one with the granddaughter—"

"Maggie."

"—is wave a white flag." Franzen replaced his hat and started across the street.

———

A hollering wind hurled itself against the house, almost enough to drown out a roar of thunder. Another spring storm. Howling and ferocious.

Her favorite.

Lilian felt around in the dark for her phone, bedsheets tangled around her legs, the remnants of a dream still fuzzy at the edges of her mind. But not the usual dream. Not the one with the man's voice.

Sweet little Lily . . .

No, it hadn't been him. Coffee—she'd literally been dreaming about coffee. *Okay. The caffeine drought ends tomorrow.*

Or maybe today? Her fingers closed around the phone and lifted it over her face, its bright light forcing a wince before she could make out the numbers. 1:16.

She kicked her bare feet free of her sheets and dropped her legs over the edge of her mattress. Might be the middle of the night, but the last time they'd had a good thunderstorm, she'd been too distracted to enjoy it. If trespassing on Wilder's boat and then going for an accidental swim in the Atlantic counted as distracted.

She pulled a knit blanket off the end of her bed and dragged it behind her as she padded to the window, pulling it around her shoulders just as a jagged gash of lightning slashed through the night sky. When they were younger, a storm like this would've sent Indi shuffling into her room and crawling into her bed. Lilian had always liked that. Had loved feeling like her little sister's safety net as she'd listened to the storm while Indi's breathing gradually slowed.

She huddled in front of the window, knees pressed into the floor, gaze drawn to the bend in the old oak tree in the front yard and then beyond it to the roiling sea, eerie wisps of moonlight fingering through the storm clouds.

Wait.

Her focus darted back, closer to the house. To a figure weaving through the darkness. *Who . . . ?*

Not Maggie, surely. She could sleep through a tornado. And in a house this old, with stairs that creaked and timeworn floors that made it impossible to creep through the quiet, she would've heard Neil or Sydney or Indi moving around. *Wilder's in D.C.*

Suddenly, she wished he wasn't. Because if someone was skulking around their farm with sinister intentions, there'd have been a certain comfort in knowing Wilder was down on the couch.

Don't be silly. Since when do you need Wilder Monroe playing security guard?

And just because someone was out there didn't mean something nefarious was afoot. Anyway, maybe she was seeing things. She pressed her nose to the cool glass again, a shudder twitching through her when she spotted the black shadow once more. Okay, she wasn't seeing things.

And it *could* be someone causing trouble. Wasn't all that long ago that Peyton Cornish had repeatedly trespassed, after all, even going so far as to break into their house during Neil's wedding.

Peyton's in a coma.

Well, someone was out there. Maybe the same person she'd seen earlier today. The one she'd thought might be following her.

Ridiculous. No one was following you. It was just the storm, making her think crazy thoughts.

But that *was* someone out there. She bolted to her feet, blanket dropping to the floor, and vaulted across the room. She snatched her phone from her nest of bedsheets as she passed—just in case—and hurried from the room. Down the hallway, down the stairs. In the entryway, she slowed just long enough to snag a jacket from the coat tree and throw it on over her flimsy pajama top, then reached for the front door.

Paused. Returned to the coat tree and plucked an umbrella from the basket underneath. A paltry weapon, perhaps, but it'd do.

Besides, she wouldn't need it. Maybe it really was just Neil, out there calling for Captain. All the same, she gripped the umbrella tightly, lifting it a few inches in the air as she pulled open the heavy door. Peered into the dark. Maybe Indi had taken up sleepwalking. Or . . .

Wilder.

She knew it as soon as her squinted gaze found his hulking form jogging through the rain, something that looked almost like a cape flailing in the gusty wind behind him. If she hadn't known it then, she would've a second later when another flare of lightning lit the sky.

She stepped onto the porch, rain pounding on the roof

above her. Or, no, not only rain. Sometime between the minutes when she'd left her bedroom and now, tiny pebbles of hail had joined the onslaught.

"Wilder?" Her call was swallowed up by rumbling thunder, so she moved forward, stray pricks of rain hitting her cheeks despite the shelter of the porch. "Wilder, what are you doing?"

But the answer was obvious a moment later when he threw a sheet of plastic tarp over Maggie's rosebushes. He disappeared for a moment, crouching, probably hooking the corner of the tarp over whatever he could find to hold it in place. And then he was up again, doing the same on the other side of the bush.

This time when he rose, he caught sight of Lilian. It was too dark to make out his expression, too late for her brain to comprehend how he could be here when he was supposed to be in D.C. So she just stood there, immobile while he lifted one hand over his head, as if it could ward off the hail bouncing to the ground beside him, and sprinted to the porch and up the steps.

And then he was standing in front of her, his drenched button-down plastered to his shoulders and chest, his hair soaked and matted, and was that a tie? It hung loose, fluttering in the wind.

"What are you doing here?"

"Saving Maggie's roses. Is that for me?" He nudged his head toward the umbrella.

"Yes. I mean, no. I mean, I thought you were . . ." Heart thumping, her nervous snort probably sounded as ridiculous as the sight of her holding the umbrella limply at her side. Wearing her pajamas. And someone else's coat.

Wilder's coat.

She hadn't realized it until now, but yes, it was definitely the warm weight of his leather jacket on her shoulders. Definitely a scent she wished she didn't recognize as uniquely his surrounding her. Musky and masculine and, good grief, she couldn't decide if she wanted to fling the thing off or stay wrapped up in it for the rest of the night.

It's storming. She should, they should both—

"Go inside, Lil. I gotta run back to my Jeep. Grab my bag."

She started to pull off the coat. "At least take this—" But he'd already turned and raced back into the storm.

Wilder shouldn't feel this good.

He'd driven almost eighteen hours in one day. He'd been told in no uncertain terms, by an FBI agent no less, that his investigation was dead in the water. He'd just been brow-beaten by a doozy of a spring storm.

So here in the closet-sized first-floor bathroom of the Muirs' farmhouse, he shouldn't feel like *this.* Awake and oddly energized. Almost . . . happy.

It made no sense. Unless the clean, dry clothes he'd just changed into—comfortable black track pants and a plain white T-shirt—had some kind of magical, mood-altering power.

More likely, if anything had tempered the frustration that had dogged his entire tedious return trip, it'd been the sight of Lilian Muir on the porch a few minutes ago. Pajama pants. Umbrella. His coat. He might actually enjoy that picture in his head even more than the memory of her panicking in his houseboat, hiding behind Dad's recliner.

Regardless, he should feel far more exhausted than he did just now. He should be itching to flop onto the couch and lose himself to sleep.

Instead, when he let himself out of the tiny bathroom, he bypassed the living room and followed the muted sound of movement in the kitchen. Soft light glowed from the doorway, at odds with the darkness that consumed the rest of the house and the storm still raging outside. Had the crashing thunder awoken anyone else?

And why did he hope the answer to that was no?

He paused under the arched opening, watching Lilian move at the counter, her back to him. She'd traded his leather jacket for a long blue sweater with a belt at the waist.

"Are you making coffee? At one thirty in the morning?"

Lilian spun so quickly, coffee grounds spilled from the spoon she held. "Geez, Wilder, make some kind of noise when you enter a room, will you?"

"Pretty sure creaky floors should've announced my arrival. You must've been distracted." He honestly would've been a little disappointed if she hadn't flashed one of her masterpieces of a scowl. *Classic.* "You didn't answer my question. Coffee? In the middle of the night?"

She bit her bottom lip. Then turned. "I had a dream about it. About coffee. I'm admitting defeat. The withdrawal is finally too much for me."

He plucked a chair from the kitchen table and dropped into it. "I noticed you switched to tea awhile back."

"You did?" She dumped one heaping scoop after another into the coffee maker. "I thought I'd been discreet."

"I'm a P.I., Lil. I notice things. Like your sweater. It's new."

"Indi talked me into taking a longer lunch than planned today. We stopped at the new boutique." She pressed the coffee maker's power button, then pushed it toward the back of the counter and faced him once more. "So yes, it's new. Indi thought I should get a pink one but—"

"Disagree."

Another timeless Lilian look—raised eyebrows. "Oh, right. Pink doesn't fit the color palette you've approved for me." The coffeepot gurgled behind her. "Thank you, Edith Head."

Brother, he never should've made that idiotic comment about blues and greens and whatever. But was he wrong? Even here in the dim light of the kitchen, that sweater did crazy things to her blue eyes. "Edith who?"

"Famous old Hollywood stylist. She picked out dresses for Grace Kelly and Audrey Hepburn and Elizabeth Taylor."

"Why do you know that?"

She shrugged. "I like black-and-white movies. Guess you don't notice everything, do you?"

Actually, he was pretty sure somewhere in the back of his brain, he was well aware of Lilian's love for classic films, but she looked so pleased with herself, he couldn't let her down. So he bit his tongue and watched her move around the kitchen. She pulled a loaf of bread from the breadbox in the corner of the counter, then a griddle from the cupboard under the island. Next, the fridge—cheese, butter.

"You know it's a little early for breakfast, right?"

She plopped a plastic plate onto the island counter and gave an annoyed huff. "I'm making you a grilled cheese sandwich, okay? If you made it home this fast, then you probably haven't had anything more to eat than Slim Jims and a bag of chips." She looked over to him. "And why are you home, anyway? I thought you were staying in D.C. overnight?"

Did she realize she'd just called the farm his home twice in one breath? "The meeting with Franzen was over pretty quick. It seemed dumb to pay for a hotel when I could be back in Muir Harbor and in my own bed in a matter of hours."

It was only half the truth. But he didn't know how to explain the other half. The muddled-up feeling that had overtaken him the second he'd collapsed into his Jeep under the cover of the parking garage. A need to move, to go. To be . . . not there.

To be here.

Same feeling he'd had all those years ago in Basic Field

Training. The one he'd never quite known how to describe to Dad. And yet, Dad had understood.

He waited now for Lilian to argue that the farmhouse couch was most definitely not his bed. Ask why he hadn't gone back to his houseboat. Point out that an almost-nine-hour drive didn't count as "a matter of hours."

Instead, she simply set to work assembling his sandwich. She cut thick slices of bread—he recognized Maggie's home-made sourdough. She slabbed on butter, added generous amounts of cheese.

Only when the sandwich was sizzling on the griddle did she finally turn back to him. "Well? Aren't you going to tell me what happened?"

"Did you know I almost joined the FBI?" Not an answer to her question. Not an answer at all.

She gaped at him for a moment. Then crossed to the island and pulled a spatula from a drawer. Eyed him again. "Today?"

He laughed. "After college. I . . . did all the stuff. Interviews, written tests, physical tests. Went off to Baltimore for Basic Field Training. But, uh, I came home after eight weeks."

She was tapping the spatula against her leg, clearly flab-bergasted. "I didn't know."

"You were in college. Racing toward law school." And they hadn't been exactly close back then.

And now? They'd made a pact last week. Had formed an unintentional habit of swapping secrets. What did that make them? Friends? Friend*ly*?

She turned away, reached into a cupboard for a mug. Filled it with coffee and set it in front of him. Then returned to the stove and flipped his sandwich. "Why'd you come home? Back then, I mean?"

He cupped his hands around the coffee mug, its steam wafting under his nose, pulling a gurgle from his stomach. "You know me, Lil. I get gut instincts. I got one then. Only it wasn't a wispy, cloudy sort of thing. It pretty much bowled me over. It was this . . . this knowing. That I had to go home. That I'd regret it if I stayed."

The kitchen was quiet for a moment, only the sputtering of the griddle filling the silence between them. But moments later, when Lilian returned to the table and set a plate with a golden sandwich in front of him, when he lifted his eyes to meet hers, he realized she'd heard everything he hadn't said.

"Your dad," she said softly.

He swallowed and looked back at the plate. "I would've missed those last five years with him."

He listened to the sound of her movements for the next few seconds. The opening of the cupboard, the sloshing of coffee. Padding footsteps and then the scraping of the chair across from his.

"I don't think I've ever put enough stock in your gut instincts."

He looked up and over. "They're mostly overhyped."

"Not that one, though." Lilian held her coffee cup up to her nose before taking a long, slow drink.

And the stray thought hit him that maybe *this* was the picture he liked best. Not Lilian diving behind a recliner or gulped up in his too-large leather jacket. But with her blond hair disheveled and her blue eyes contented, completely and entirely enthralled by something as simple as a cup of coffee.

You're staring. At Neil's sister.

Staring and thinking . . .

Well, he didn't know what he was thinking, but it felt . . . *impossible, preposterous, absurd.* They were Lilian's words from nights ago, but his mind was too blurry just now to remember why she'd said them or exactly when.

"Aren't you going to eat?"

He set his mug down and lifted his sandwich, took an enormous bite.

"When you're done chewing, will you finally tell me what happened today?"

He swallowed. "There's not that much to tell. Franzen wanted to know how much I knew about Nicholas Cornish. Which, obviously, isn't a whole ton. But I guess he'd been trying to pin the man for a whole array of white-collar crimes forever. Even though Cornish is dead, they're still trying to wrap up loose ends. Pin some of his associates with physical evidence. So I guess Franzen's ears perked when he found out a P.I. hundreds of miles away was looking for the guy. I'm not sure I helped him any."

He took another bite. "This is good." The sandwich, but also this. Sitting in Maggie Muir's kitchen in the middle of the night. With Lilian. Eating a sandwich she'd made him for no other reason than to be nice. Having another civil conversation. How many did that make now?

He just wished his conversation with Franzen had been half as heartening. Lilian was still watching him, waiting. Maybe already knowing what he was going to say next. "I asked him point-blank what he would do in my shoes. He said he'd give it up. The whole thing. Wave a white flag, that's what he said."

She lowered her coffee mug. "Oh."

He mimicked her movement, setting his sandwich down. "But I hate the thought of giving up. I hate the thought of letting Maggie down."

"She'd understand."

"But wouldn't she always wonder? Wouldn't the questions always be hanging over her head? What if Cynthia *is* out there? What if we'd just kept looking a little longer?" The questions had plagued him all the way home.

"Maggie is strong, and what's more, she's wise. If it's truly time to let it go, I think she'll know it, too. It's not all up to your gut instincts."

"That's a good thing, because this time around, I have no idea what my gut's telling me. No idea what to do."

"Look, Wilder, I read all those case files and notes. Your dad's, yours. I wish I could say some new piece of information jumped out at me, but nothing did. Except . . . well, you said you wanted a sounding board, someone to bounce ideas off of." Lilian traced the edge of her mug with one finger. "Here's an idea: What if you just take a day or two and try not to think about the case? Let it go just for a little while. See what it feels like."

He pulled at the crust of his sandwich. "I guess I could do that."

A few quiet minutes passed as he finished his sandwich and she drank her coffee. Would the caffeine keep her up the rest of the night? Would it keep him up? Would he mind if it did? Maybe they could just keep sitting here, keep talking.

"Hey, I think the storm settled down." Lilian's voice drew his gaze once more.

He hadn't noticed. The lack of thunder, the rain that had quieted to a patter—he totally hadn't noticed. "I've been meaning to tell you, I've got an idea for a wedding location."

"Really? I think Maggie's been coming around to the idea of the backyard—" At his shaking head, she cut off. "Okay, where?"

"I'd rather show you than tell you. Tuesday night."

She pushed her mug away. "Tuesday? Wilder, the wedding's five weeks from tomorrow. We should've had invitations in the mail forever ago. We can't put this off."

"Yeah, but we can't send out invites until Indi finishes the artwork anyway. No way we'll have them in hand earlier than the end of next week." And they'd already emailed out a Save the Date. They'd bought themselves some time. "I'll take you to check it out Tuesday night."

"At least tell me if this place is indoors or outdoors so I know what to wear."

That was Lilian Muir. Always with a need to be prepared. "I'm pretty partial to the combo of pajama pants and my leather jacket."

What possessed him to say the thought out loud, he didn't know. But when her gaze popped up from her coffee mug and collided with his, he was glad he had. In all his years of ruffling Lilian Muir's feathers, sometimes intentionally, sometimes not, he'd never quite realized how enjoyable it was to watch her blush.

But in the next moment, he regretted the impulsive comment.

"This is a bad idea." She bolted from her chair and moved to the sink in a flash, dumping her coffee down the drain. "I don't know what I was thinking, chugging coffee in the middle of the night."

He rose, carrying his empty plate. "Well, you were in withdrawal."

She turned faster than he would've expected, pulling the plate from his hands. She bent to place it in the dishwasher.

And he didn't move. He didn't know why he didn't move. But he didn't. Which meant when she came up, she was nose-to-nose with his chest. She froze for a moment that stretched, pulled taut.

Get out of her way.

His legs didn't listen.

Finally, she gave a shaky laugh. "Withdrawal cured. Good night." She took the long way around the island, hurrying toward the kitchen door, but slowed just as she was about to disappear. She looked over her shoulder. "Tuesday night?"

His voice was as stubborn as his limbs. All he did was nod. And then, finally, when she was out of the room, he let out an exhale and remembered to breathe.

8

The sun-kissed soil was warm underneath Lilian's fingers and soft under her knees. Every spring was another reminder of how much she loved this—the loamy smell of earth and seed, digging that always began with a wood-handled spade but eventually gave way to her hands in the dirt.

"Tell me I'm seeing things." Neil's shadow drifted over her at the same time as his voice, the faint lilt of his accent carrying on the breeze. "This can't be my little sister, home from the office before five on a Tuesday night."

She laughed and elbowed his ankle. "You're stepping on my carrots."

"I'm having a hallucination. Or maybe a stroke."

"Ha. Ha. Ha." She wiped her hands on her jeans and tipped her head, attempting to frown at her brother. But it was hard to do with the sky such a lovely shade of azure and Neil grinning down at her. Even the twinge in her back failed to bother her. Probably because she'd earned it from forty minutes bent over her little garden plot not far from the outbuildings where her brother spent the bulk of his days, rather than hunched and stiff at her computer.

Neil crouched down beside her. "Planting later than usual."

"Not too late." But yes, later into May than she usually did. Most seasons, she had rows tilled and seeds buried by Mother's Day. This spring, though, they'd had a late snow and just when the weather had finally begun to warm, she'd had that seven- or eight-day stretch of feeling worn down and unwell. The tremors and numbness . . .

One week until the MRI.

Captain trotted over, kicking up dirt under his paws, and burrowed his face against Neil's, his tail wagging and hitting the side of Lilian's head. Neil gave a chuckle and ruffled the dog's fur before nudging him out of the way. He reached for the spade she'd discarded and scooped a hole identical to the one she was currently dropping cucumber seeds into.

"Neil, you don't have to—"

"I know." He ripped open a new packet of seeds. "But we don't see each other as much these days. We should catch up or something."

She leaned back, knees still pressed into the ground. "Now I feel like I'm the one imagining things. The quiet Scottish blueberry farmer wants to talk? Sydney's done a number on you, big brother."

"Forget it. Let's just work in silence."

"Don't get me wrong. You've always mostly been a teddy bear of a person, but you don't try nearly as hard to hide it anymore."

He patted a mound of soil over the seeds he'd sprinkled into the hole. "So I guess I'm the only one working now."

She chuckled and bent over once more. "Nah. It's my garden. I'll do the work."

"Right now, maybe, but I'll be the one pulling weeds later this summer when you're buried in some important case."

"That's not—" She clamped her lips together and shrugged. "I want to say that's not true, but—"

"But we've got a whole string of summers behind us that say otherwise."

"Stretching all the way back to law school."

He harrumphed. "Try your undergrad years. You always had to pile on summer classes."

She watched him for a moment, her brother not by blood, but certainly by love and commitment and loyalty. He dug another hole, packed another miniature hill of soil over more seeds. "Hey, Neil?"

He grunted as he scooted down the row.

"Thank you."

He looked over, a question in his gray-blue eyes.

"For everything you do here. For keeping the farm going. For working so hard. I know part of you not going to college was because you knew I wanted to go to law school and money was tight—"

"Lil."

"No, just let me say it. I know I work too much, but I really love what I do. And I get to do what I love, in no small part because of sacrifices you've made. You help take care of this garden. Of Indi's beloved goats. Of a hundred different things around the house."

It was killing him not to interrupt her, she knew. Not to put a stop to her sudden show of gratitude. And honestly, she didn't fully know herself where it'd come from. Maybe there were simply moments when life reminded you of its best gifts. When you looked around and saw with fresh eyes and an open heart all the good. The glory of a normal moment in time, doing a normal thing.

"You take care of all of us in countless ways. I don't thank you for that enough."

Neil shook his head. "Who's the teddy bear of a person now?"

She chucked a clump of dirt at him, then they worked for a few minutes in quiet. Only when she reached the end of her row did she look over to Neil again. "You'd tell me if you and Sydney were feeling a little crowded, right?"

Realizing there were no more packets of seeds, he stood. "Huh?"

"You guys are newlyweds. I wouldn't blame you if you wanted your space."

"We've got the entire attic to ourselves."

"But I'm sure you'll have a bunch of kids eventually—"

"Define 'a bunch.'"

"—and between Maggie and Ray and me and Indi, I mean, that's a lot of people in one house. I know Indi will move out eventually, but—"

"What's all this talk of everyone moving?" Neil swiped the back of his palm over his forehead. "Ansel Barrett just came over earlier this afternoon to let me know he's pulling up stakes, moving down to Florida."

Lilian gathered up her empty seed packets, then rose. "I heard." Wilder had mentioned it at some point over the weekend, somewhere between an argument over real candles versus battery-operated for reception centerpieces—a reception they didn't even have a venue for yet—and Lilian's repeated, futile attempts to get him to tell her where he was taking her tonight.

"I went with Mariana, my new coworker, to look at an apartment last week. It got me thinking—I'm thirty years old. Maybe it's about time I get my own place."

"Lil, this farm is as much your home as it is mine. And as for feeling crowded—no, I don't. Or if I do, it's a good feeling, not a bad one. I spent the first half of my childhood without siblings, remember. Sydney grew up in foster homes. Living in a big old house with a bunch of our favorite people? We love it. It's perfect." He motioned his head toward the grove and they started walking. "Are *you* feeling crowded?"

"What? No." She wasn't. Was she?

"You talk about all that I do around here, but you do a ton, too. I know we pester you about working late, but your life is your life. Unlike me, you have a career that doesn't revolve around this farm. You're not tied down here. Unless you want to be. I think I'm mucking this up, but I'm just trying to say . . . well, I'm not sure what I'm trying to say."

"I think I know. And I appreciate you for it."

His look of relief was so palpable, she almost laughed. Instead, she knocked into his side with her arm. He bumped her back.

"So why are you off work so early? I have a hard time believing the garden was enough to draw you away."

"Don't be so sure. Mariana's basically amazing." She was fun, too. Today marked a full week of working together and already, they'd formed a habit of meeting in the kitchen for a snack halfway through the morning and again in the afternoon. "But no, I'm off early so I can go see a wedding venue with Wilder."

"Hmm, maybe Wilder will buy Ansel's farm."

Her gaze whipped to Neil. "What? Why would he do that?"

Captain raced past them, weaving through the trees. "It was our plan when we were teenagers. We used to sneak onto Ansel's property to fish at the creek and we'd talk about how someday, Wilder would buy Ansel's house so we could be neighbors. Funny that now he could actually do it if he wanted. Of course, every time we talked about it, I asked him how he planned to live in the middle of Nowhere, Maine, while working for the FBI."

"You know, I didn't even know about that until the other night? The FBI thing."

Neil turned to her with a look of surprise. "Really? I thought everyone knew."

She shook her head.

"I guess he doesn't really talk about it." Neil slowed as they neared the border of the grove, golden sunlight cascading through branches spotty with new leaves and landing in puddles on the ground. "It's funny, most people would probably say Wilder's an open book. He comes off so talkative and congenial you don't realize most of the time all the stuff he's leaving unsaid. For instance, he's been my best friend forever and I think I've heard him mention his mother all of three or four times."

His mother? "I don't think I've ever heard him mention her."

"Case in point." He scratched his fingers through his beard. "Or maybe not. You two aren't really known for your long heart-to-hearts."

Clearly Neil hadn't woken up on Friday night. The night of the storm when she and Wilder had lingered in the kitchen . . .

When there'd been that moment by the sink. When he'd come up behind her and she'd run into his chest and suddenly twenty years of irritation had dissolved into one muddled, momentous thought. The thought that maybe she didn't dislike Wilder Monroe so much anymore.

Maybe, incredulously, she'd found a thing or two to admire about him. His determination in chasing a dream. His decision to walk away when it was time. How well he seemed to know himself. How assured he was of his own mind most of the time.

How willing he was to admit it when he wasn't. *This time around, I have no idea what my gut's telling me. No idea what to do.*

"Can I ask you something, Neil? Do you . . . do you think

she's really out there? Cynthia? All these years, all the searching... do you believe...."

He let out a slow exhale and looked across the yard toward the farmhouse. "I don't know. I want to believe she is. For Maggie's sake. But... I don't know."

"I think maybe Wilder's harder on himself about the whole thing than anyone realizes. What if she's not out there and he's spending all this time beating himself up about it?"

The hem of Neil's plaid shirt lifted in the wind. "Don't tell me you, Lilian Muir, are worried about Wilder. Are you trying to make me go into shock twice in one evening?"

"I'm not worried about him." No, she was worried about herself. This wasn't normal. This inordinate interest in the man who'd driven her nuts for two-thirds of her life. "Do you think he'd really buy Ansel's place?"

Neil pointed across the lawn to where Wilder was just emerging from the back door. "Ask him yourself while you're off playing wedding planner." Neil took off again, crossing the yard in long strides and reaching his friend.

Lilian stood there watching them for a moment, trying to picture a younger Wilder wearing an FBI vest or working behind a desk. It was almost as hard to imagine as him taking up residence in Ansel Barrett's 1880s farmhouse.

"Hurry up, slowpoke. We've got places to be." Wilder waved her over. "Make that one place. We need to be there in —" He glanced to the sky. "About forty minutes."

With a sigh packed with more exasperation than she actually felt, she walked over, purposely unhurried. "Just give me a minute to change."

"No, what you're wearing is fine."

Dirt- and grass-stained jeans and a wrinkled gray V-neck? "Just fine? Oh, right, I'm not wearing your approved color palette."

Wilder's dark eyes sparked and yet, they didn't quite meet hers. "I never should've said anything about that."

"I could throw on your leather jacket if that'd make you happier." She had no clue what made her say it.

Or why in the world her stomach did a strange flip when he finally met her gaze, something daring in his expression. "Only if it's paired with pajama pants."

Neil coughed. "Uh—"

"Sandals," Wilder blurted. "You need to ditch the sandals."

"Okay." Her voice came out reedy and thin. And annoyingly obedient.

"Shoes. Or hiking boots would be even better."

Hiking boots? Where was he taking her?

***

"We can't have Maggie's wedding at the chapel, Wilder. It's too small. There's no electricity. And I doubt she's going to want to hike to the ceremony in her wedding dress."

Wilder clamped down on a grin and kept walking, following the sandy trail that cut through the clusters of evergreen and birch trees that adorned the rocky terrain. The evening air was piney and fresh, filling his lungs and fueling his steps. He didn't come up here often, to this craggy collection of hills several miles down the coast, but anytime he did, it was one more reminder of how lucky he was to have grown up somewhere so vast and rugged and wild.

"We're not going to the chapel, Lil." Even though it you asked him, the chapel at the top of the cliff, the one that overlooked the sea, would make a perfect spot for a wedding. There was an aura about the place . . .

"Then where—"

"You're not real big on patience, are you?"

She huffed and two-stepped to keep up with him. "Or surprises."

"Trust me, it'll be worth it." At least, he hoped so. Walter Wallace hadn't necessarily been exact when they'd talked timing, but he'd said twilight, and with the sun leaning into the west behind them and the sky a reflection of fiery color above, they should arrive at their destination just in time.

He supposed he could've just told Lilian about his idea. But that didn't seem nearly as thrilling.

Or nearly as rife with opportunity to disrupt those oh-so-easy to ruffle feathers of hers. Which was exactly what he should be doing. Because it's what he'd always done. Because it was comfortable and expected and routine.

Unlike late-night conversations in the kitchen or wayward thoughts about how cute she looked in pajamas. Or in his leather coat. Or barefoot. With wet hair. Holy blazes, he had a problem.

He *liked* Lilian Muir.

It'd become alarmingly clear to him Friday night, trying to sleep on the couch where he'd spent hundreds of nights before. But of course that night he'd noticed all its lumps and cursed the way his legs hung over the edge. He'd tossed and turned and tried to deny the truth that had hammered at him one hour into the next.

Not just that he liked her, he was *attracted* to her. Physically, intellectually, emotionally, all the ways. And he was sure there was something wrong about that.

She's Neil's sister.

So what? Lil was her own person.

She can't stand you.

Or maybe she could. At least a little. She'd made him a grilled cheese sandwich and hadn't poisoned it. Wasn't that some kind of hopeful sign?

"Wait, Wild, we aren't . . . we're not going *there*, are we?"

He realized she was no longer beside him and glanced over his shoulder, slowing to a stop when he saw that she had. *There. Right.* He was a dunce. He should've grasped that the tallest cliff overlooking the ocean wasn't a spot she'd be eager to return to. Not after what had happened there back in January with Peyton.

"I'm sorry. Yes, that's where we're going. But I obviously wasn't thinking." Not clearly, anyway. Not for weeks. Not with Maggie's case taunting him. And, more recently, thoughts he really shouldn't be thinking about the woman at his side, even if he couldn't articulate why he shouldn't be thinking them.

Lilian stuffed her hands in the pockets of her jeans. "We can't have the wedding on a cliffside any more than we can at the stone chapel."

"The cliff isn't the wedding venue I'm proposing. But it'll give you the perfect view of what I *am* proposing. But I should've realized . . ." His cheeks puffed with his sigh. "I'm sorry."

"Well, we've come all this way already." She dropped her shoulders and moved forward. "I guess if I fall to pieces from a flashback or faint or something, you'll just have to carry me back down the hill." She brushed past him.

"You aren't the fainting type, Lil."

Her light laugh echoed in the high-altitude air. "It's true."

He fell into step beside her. "And I've never seen you fall to pieces."

"I don't know, I screamed pretty loud the time you clobbered me with a dodgeball. I think I even cried. But you might've missed that part. I held it in until I was in the nurse's office."

He'd been what—ten or eleven the year of the infamous bloody nose incident? "I just realized something. I always think of my connection with your family starting when Neil moved to Muir Harbor. But I was already a teenager then. My history with you goes further back." They emerged into a clearing where weathered rock jutted over a plummeting landscape. The cliff was chiseled into the hills, overlooking a bottomless sea, its ripples brushed by the burnt-orange of sunset.

Lilian's steps slowed as she neared the cliff's edge, the burning sky tracing her profile. "It really is stunning." Her voice was infused with awe. "I'm glad we came. I don't want Peyton to ruin this place for me."

"And we're right on time, too." He moved to her side and pointed toward the endless horizon. "Look."

Out across the water, around a bend in the coast, lights and movement. A boat carving its way through the undulating blue, foamy waves parting with its slow progression. Just as he'd promised, Walter Wallace had made sure it glittered with light, dots of glowing yellow tracing both its upper and lower decks.

"Is that . . ."

"A yacht. A huge one. Room for at least a hundred and fifty guests. Maybe two hundred."

"What? I . . . I don't . . . are you serious? You want to have Maggie's wedding on a boat?"

He faced her. "You don't like the idea?"

"No, I . . . I love it. It's crazy and incredible and, oh my goodness, it'd be beautiful." Her every word was breathy with disbelief as she watched the yacht. "How did you even think of . . .? Can you even imagine? Maggie would love it. She loves the sea. I honestly can't think of anything more perfect."

"It's fitting, isn't it? Maggie Muir whose last name is the Gaelic word for 'sea,' having a wedding at sea. Just feels right."

"It does."

They watched the boat for a few hushed moments, only

the distant *caa* of a seagull, the rustle of the breeze, filling the quiet between them.

Until, abruptly, she spun. "But we can't do it."

He was so surprised by her sudden retreat, he didn't move at first. "What? Why not?"

She was already moving away from the cliff. "Wilder, we could never afford something like that. I mean, I've never reserved a yacht before, but it would be thousands of dollars, I'm sure." Twigs snapped as she marched into the trees.

"Slow down, Lil."

"In fact, I think I might be a little bit mad at you right now. Showing me something so enchanting, knowing it's impossible."

"It's not impossible."

"It is. Muir Farm isn't exactly flush with cash. You know this. You've seen the wedding budget. Obviously we all want Maggie to have the wedding of her dreams, but she's not going to want her kids paying for it. I mean, she'll let us contribute something, maybe pay for that cake Misty's making or the rehearsal dinner, but she's not going to accept—"

"Is there a reason you're walking so fast?" And where was she going?

That was clear a second later when the tannish-yellow walls of the chapel came into view. Perched at the edge of another bluff, its steeple piercing the sky. It was a study in contrasts. Small and ancient, to be sure, but somehow majestic with its foundation of rock and line of windows keeping watch on the sea below.

"I feel like I'm a rabbit and you just dangled the perfect carrot in front of me. Except, I guess technically Maggie's the rabbit and she doesn't know about the carrot." Lilian trooped toward the little church. "So it's probably best we just don't tell her about it. That way, she won't soar on wings of hope only to drop with a thud like me."

"I had no idea you could be this melodramatic, Lilian Muir."

She halted on the stoop outside the chapel's arched wooden door, her posture turning to liquid—shoulders drooping, arms hanging limp. "It was just a really, *really* beautiful idea, Wilder. But completely unfeasible. Even if we had the money, it's probably too late to book it by June."

"My turn to talk." Without thinking, he put his palms on her shoulders. "My dad was a boat guy. He knew everyone with a seaworthy vessel from here to Rhode Island. He and his friends used to go deep-sea fishing and sailing and once when they were sixteen, they boated all the way down to the Florida Panhandle. Scared their parents half to death. Dad loved talking about all his escapades with Ansel and Wallace. Wallace being the owner of the yacht we just saw. He rents it out for corporate events, parties, and yes, the occasional wedding."

A hint of hope feathered into her blue eyes. "You know a guy with a yacht."

"I do."

"So . . . it'd be free?"

He couldn't help a small smile. "Not free. But I'm sure Wally will give us a discount." Here was the part that'd really make her balk. "And I'm paying."

She stepped free of his hold. "Uh-uh. No way."

"Yes way. I want to do this. Maggie never has to know about the cost. You can tell her about the carrot, but leave off the price tag."

"Wilder, no—"

"Would you just listen to me for a second? I have money. Like, a lot of it. My mother had a life insurance policy that Dad never touched until I went to college. And even then, there was more than enough left. Then Dad . . ." His voice cracked. But he hurried on, hoping she hadn't noticed. "Dad had a policy, too. The houseboat's paid for. The dock fee is minimal. How do you think I can afford to only take a case or two at a time? I don't have a mortgage. And for reasons that really, *really* suck, I have more money than I know what to do with. I'd rather have Dad in a heartbeat, but I don't, so please, just let me do this. Let me spend a few thousand dollars on the closest thing to a family I have left."

He hadn't meant to say all that. Definitely hadn't meant for such raw emotion to find its way into his voice. To stand here and practically beg.

Stifling a groan, he grabbed the metal handle of the chapel door and towed it open. Musty air clouded around him as he stepped inside. Fled, more like. He was embarrassed. Dispirited. This wasn't how he'd envisioned the evening going.

The chapel's interior was dim and spare, only a few rough-hewn pews and a small altar up front. He dropped into a back pew and raked his fingers through his hair.

A moment later, Lilian sat down beside him. "I used to search for Alec Muir's treasure up here."

He felt his forehead wrinkle. "The Legend of Muir Harbor," he finally said.

She nodded.

He knew the legend well. It ended on a note of mystery. Supposedly, according to the story, Alec Muir's lost gold was still resting in its hiding place somewhere on Muir Farm.

When he'd been younger, he'd been as fascinated by the local lore as any other kid who'd grown up here. Whether there was any truth to the story, other than the indisputable fact that Alec Muir had been a real person, he didn't know. Yet it was all but a rite of passage for Muir Harbor teens to trespass at Maggie's farm at least once during junior high or high school and go looking for the treasure.

"Why would you come up here to search? The legend says the hiding place is at Muir Farm."

"This chapel, all the land around here, used to be Muir land. It was sold off in parcels through the decades when times got tough. But at one point, this spot right here was part of Muir Farm."

"Little Lilian Muir," he mused, "looking for lost treasure."

Dust particles danced in the waning light of sunset where it reached through the windows.

"I have fallen to pieces before," Lilian said softly. "A couple nights before the LSAT. I broke down in a study room at the library. I called Maggie and begged her to distract me, calm me down somehow. She recited the legend with a brogue that could give Neil a run for his money."

So that's why she'd brought up the legend. Because of his little outburst on the stoop outside. And now she was trying to make him feel better. "Lil—"

"And another time," she interrupted. "When I was a lot younger. Eight, almost nine." Her gaze was pinned to the chapel's lone stained-glass window at the front of the room. "We had to do this assignment in school, an oral presentation about our most prized possession. I brought the note. The one that was pinned to my overalls when Maggie found me."

The one she'd found him looking at that night in her bedroom. The one behind her mirror. Was that really only five days ago?

"Up until that point, I'd always thought I had the coolest story. I mean, I was curious about where I'd come from, but mostly I was . . . content in a way only a child can be before . . . before you start questioning things. I wasn't fully cognizant of the investigation into where I'd come from. I didn't really understand that the police and DHS and your dad and others had spent literal years trying to piece together who I really was. I was too young to comprehend what the meetings with a child psychologist were about. It was hard not being able to answer his questions but . . . I just . . . I just thought I had this neat story and I was excited to share it."

He didn't know why she was telling him this. Or what he was supposed to do with his growing urge to move a little closer. Reach for her hand. Because he might not know where exactly this story was going, but he could hear the small quiver in Lilian's voice.

"Anyway, I did my presentation and showed everyone the note. You know what it said. My name. My birth date. My dumb banana allergy. And then it was time for questions at the end and . . . it was like taking fire. Every raised hand a piece of shrapnel. *So you don't know who your real mom and dad are? What if they're bad people? What if they're criminals? You don't even know your real last name. What if you never know?*" She twisted her hands together in her lap. "They were just kids asking innocent questions. But their questions sabotaged my happy little story. And that night, when I was in bed, I fell to pieces. It was the first time words like *abandoned* and *unwanted* and *nameless* had ever plagued me and I just . . . lost it."

"Lil, I . . ." *Don't know what to say.* He knew what he wanted to do. He wanted to rewind time and burst into that classroom. Tell everyone to put their hands down or ask better questions.

Or if not that, then travel back to that same night and whisper in Maggie's ear that her little girl was upstairs crying. Because somehow he knew Lilian had never told Maggie about that day in school. Had very possibly never told anyone.

Until now. Until him.

"Just because you've never seen me fall to pieces doesn't mean I haven't." She stood, hugged her arms to her torso, shifted back on her heels. "You can pay for the yacht. That is, if Maggie wants a wedding at sea. You can pay and if anyone questions it, I'll convince them to let you."

His hands dropped to the pew on either side of his lap. *You just keep doing it, Lil. Keep throwing me for a loop.* "What changed your mind?"

She shrugged. "I'm a lawyer, Wilder. I appreciate a well-made argument."

⟶—•— —•—⟵

Lilian didn't feel embarrassed. She hadn't then and she still didn't now and she couldn't figure out why.

Any other time she remembered that day in school, any other day it played through her mind, she'd feel the same self-conscious flash of heat travel through her body. Feel the questions pressing up against her on all sides, exposing her. Exposing the truth that her story wasn't special; it was sad. Turning her inside out with disappointment.

But she'd felt none of that tonight sitting by Wilder in the chapel.

Nothing beyond a sense of something like . . . security. As if with Wilder, her vulnerability had a safe place to land.

Wilder tapped a rhythm on his steering wheel now, the hazy light of the streetlamps lining Main Avenue passing over his face one after another. Lilian's passenger-side window was cracked open, letting in just enough of the cool night air to flutter strands of hair that tickled her cheeks.

"You know, I think we've made it through this whole evening without one argument." He glanced across the console. "That has to be some kind of record."

He must be forgetting the part of the night where she'd stomped away from him, left him standing at the edge of a bluff while she marched through the trees, suddenly and stunningly disheartened at the thought that they'd never be able to

154

afford that yacht he'd shown her. Didn't that count as an argument?

That yacht. Oh, she could barely handle the thought of what Maggie would say when they presented the idea. A wedding at sea. What could be more perfect?

"You do still have to take me home, Wilder. We have plenty of time to break out into a knock-down, drag-out fight."

He shook his head. "Not really our style. We're more the war-of-words types. By which I mean, you repeatedly declare war on me and I usually sit back and take it."

At some point hours ago, between when they'd decided to grab dinner in town while going over the wedding to-do list she'd created and now, she'd given up trying not to smile when he said something funny.

Or in this case, something true. "Well, look at it this way. According to Maggie, you're Muir Harbor's golden boy and everyone adores you. Misty Sprinkles sure does. How boring would your life be if not one single person opposed you from time to time?"

He turned off Main Avenue and onto the road that curled past the harbor. "Opposed me from time to time? That's what you call the relentless disdain and snide remarks I've been subjected to over the years?"

She careened past smiling and fell right into laughing. "You make me sound terrible. A full-on shrew."

"I definitely did not say that. I did not use that word. Don't add that to your arsenal of justification for not liking me." He pulled up to the gravel lot in front of the harbor and braked. "And what was that barb about Misty supposed to mean?"

"Only that you were right, and the second I mentioned your name last week it was all, 'Of course I can fit another cake into the schedule. Do you want chocolate or champagne or red velvet? Here, let me give you a discount.'"

"Are you complaining because my friendliness with a local

businessowner got us a discount?" He narrowed his eyes, but it wasn't enough to hide the dancing reflection of the lamplight slanting in from the windshield.

"Your friendliness or your flirting? And why are you parking? You're supposed to be taking me home."

"I can't make sense of this conversation. Which, for the record, has definitely veered into argumentative territory, thereby ruining our longest-running streak of civility in history." He shifted into park and flopped against his seat. "I threw the 'thereby' in just for you, Miss Lawyer. I hope you appreciate it."

Honestly, she'd appreciated this whole night. Not just because they'd finally settled on a wedding venue or crossed several items off her to-do list. But because she'd had *fun*. Because she hadn't once thought about work or Dr. Cho or the MRI. And she was pretty sure Wilder hadn't given a thought to Maggie's case.

They'd just had a good time. Together.

The Jeep's engine idled, its soft rumble a backdrop for the awareness tingling through her. *Together.* That part was the surprise. That part was . . . something of a gift, really.

Last week in her office, talking with Mariana, she'd found herself longing for friendship. Hoping she might find it in her new coworker. And she'd begun to. But maybe there'd been another friend waiting in the wings, too. The last person she would've expected.

"Tell me the truth, Lilian." Wilder broke the silence now. "All these years . . . where'd the animosity come from? Something had to have happened to precipitate—" He motioned back and forth between them. "This."

Looking at him now, the man he'd become, it was almost difficult to picture the teenager he'd once been. Same dark hair and deep brown eyes, but with gangly limbs and a youthful swagger. She wasn't sure when he'd begun to fill out, shoulders broadening, the lines of his face becoming more defined until . . .

Until he'd become this version of himself. Only days ago, it would've galled her to admit how handsome he was, but now, she supposed . . . if she were pressed . . . if she took it all into account—the cleft in his chin and the strong jaw and, good grief, those eyes . . .

"Lil?"

She startled, looked away. Looked back. "You really don't remember, do you?"

"Remember what?"

When I was ten and you were a teenager. When I came to the boat. "Nothing."

"You've never liked me. There's got to be a reason."

"Look, I'm sitting in this Jeep right now with you, aren't I? I just spent, what? Five hours with you? I like you just fine."

"It's because now you know I'm loaded, isn't it?" He grinned and hopped out of the Jeep.

She pushed out of her side of the vehicle. "Seriously, what are we doing here? I need to get home."

He started toward the dock. "Past your bedtime?"

"Actually, yes. I'm old. Ten p.m. might as well be two a.m." She hurried after him, goosebumps rising on her arms, the air chillier this close to the water.

"I just want to grab a change of clothes. By the time I get you to the farm, I'm not going to want to drive back into town." He stopped at the edge of the dock and folded his arms as he faced her. "Aren't you going to say it? Come on, I gave you the perfect opening. You just heard me say I'm planning to spend another night on the farmhouse couch. That's your cue to call me a freeloader."

"Wilder, could you tell me about your mom?"

He dropped his arms. His jaw fell open. Why it felt so satisfying, surprising him like that, she didn't know.

"Where did that . . . why would you ask . . . ?" He lifted both palms to his bristly cheeks and rubbed them.

"I've never heard you talk about her." She shouldn't push him. He wasn't a witness on a stand. But the question had been heckling her ever since Neil had mentioned Wilder's mother earlier in the evening.

"I never knew her. She died when I was a newborn. That's why I don't talk about her. There's nothing to say."

"But how—"

"What don't I remember, Lil? What happened between us that I don't remember?"

He was redirecting her. Pushing the conversation away from a question she probably never should've asked. One he was making abundantly clear he didn't want to answer.

But she didn't particularly want to answer his question either. Hadn't they walked down memory lane enough for one night? That conversation at his father's houseboat had been every bit as painful as the day years earlier at school. The questions her classmates had hurled at her had opened doors of possibility in her mind. That afternoon at the houseboat had slammed them all shut. All but the one where the aching uncertainty lingered, the occasional yearning.

To know where she'd come from. To know why she'd been left behind. To know whose face belonged to the voice in her dreams . . .

She hadn't told Wilder that part of the story earlier. About the first time she'd ever dreamed of the voice, on the same night she'd cried herself to sleep after her worst school day.

She skimmed her palms over her bare arms.

Wilder accepted their stalemate for what it was. "Come on. I'll get you a sweatshirt while I grab myself some clothes." He nabbed her palm, then seemed to realize what he'd done. He glanced from their connected hands to her face and then his gaze just stayed there. He looked at her so deeply it was as if he was seeing right through her pupils into her tumbling thoughts.

"It wasn't just that one day in school, was it?" he finally said. "The not knowing, wondering who and why—it's been harder for you than anyone knows. For longer than anyone knows."

She wanted to shake her head, tell him he was wrong. She was strong, sensible Lilian Muir. She had a wonderful family and successful career. She was fine. She didn't need to know the rest. *It is what it is.* It was the mantra she played on repeat whenever the questions got to her.

So why couldn't she recite it now? Why, for pity's sake, did she suddenly want to cry? "I . . . I shouldn't care. It shouldn't matter. I already have so much."

"You're allowed to wonder, Lil. You're allowed to hurt."

Now she did shake her head. "I'm just not good at uncertainty, that's all. I hate unknowns. I want all the questions answered all the time."

He kept hold of her hand and gave her a small smile. "Probably what makes you a good lawyer."

"There have been times I've gone years without wondering . . . months without another dream." He wouldn't know what she meant by that. It didn't appear to bother him. He was doing it again. Being a safe harbor for her tossed-about heart. "But they always eventually chase me down—all the questions I don't have answers for, and then I'm that numb kid in front of a classroom again. I'm a lost little girl who doesn't even know her last name. And it makes me fall to pieces. It makes me do crazy things." Like convince herself, despite all logic, that she was Maggie's long-lost granddaughter. "Like break into your houseboat."

She blinked to trap the hot tears that threatened to fall, a shudder from tremoring through her body.

In the next moment, Wilder pulled her close. There was

nothing hurried in his movement. Nothing reckless. He still held her hand. But with his other arm, he circled her waist and nudged her toward him. "Technically, you didn't break in."

What could've been a sob was instead a choked laugh, muffled by his cotton shirt. "I stole your keys." His body was a shield of warmth against the cool seaside air, but she didn't know how to lean into it. This was too . . . new. Unexpected.

It was an unanswered question all its own.

She didn't know what to do with the hand that wasn't encased in his or how to let herself relax into the moment. But if she stayed here much longer, if his arm around her tightened and the last whispers of space between them dissolved . . . maybe she'd figure it out.

"If you ever do need to fall to pieces, Lil, I'm here."

She tipped her head to look at him. "Wilder, I . . ." His thumb was tracing a slow circle on the back of her palm and it was muddling her thoughts. Stalling her words. She pulled her gaze away.

And then pulled the rest of herself away, slipping her fingers free of his as she gasped. "Your boat."

"Lil—"

"I think someone's on your boat." She recaptured his hand and steered him around until he was facing the end of the dock with her.

To where a single light bobbed on the deck of his boat.

And then he was off, his long legs carrying him away from her too quickly. "Wilder!" *Be careful.*

She raced after him, but she was only halfway down the dock by the time he jumped onto the boat, bounded toward the upper deck above the living quarters. She knew when she heard the rumble of another boat's motor they were too late. Wilder was already barreling into his living quarters when she climbed aboard.

A second gasp choked her throat when she reached the doorway.

Tipped furniture. Open kitchenette drawers. Busted file cabinet. A glance into his bedroom revealed strewn clothing.

And Wilder, standing frozen in the middle of all of it. Eyes dark as midnight.

"I-I'll call the police."

9

*W*ilder couldn't believe what he was hearing.

He stalled, lifting a mug with the Muir Harbor Police Department emblem on its side and throwing back a long swallow of coffee, tepid and stale. How could it be stale already at only nine o'clock in the morning?

He eyed Chief Holloway from where he sat across from the man's desk in a chair too low to the ground. His knees could almost knock into his chest. "I'm telling you, Travis Sanford had nothing to do with the break-in on my boat."

Holloway palmed the back of his nearly bald head, scratching at what was left of his salt-and-pepper hair. "And I'm telling you, he's sitting in a room two doors down from here ready to confess to the whole thing. Strike that—he already did."

It made no sense whatsoever. When Holloway had called him an hour ago to let him know that first thing today, three mornings after the break-in, a local teenager had walked into the station to confess to the incident, alarm bells had gone off in his gut. They'd started clanging all over again a few minutes ago when he'd walked past the long glass window of the police department's lone conference room and seen the former star of the Harbor Hornets baseball team hunched over the table.

He'd known already Tuesday night that the chances of identifying whoever had been on the houseboat were slim. He hadn't gotten a look at the intruder, and though whoever it was had certainly done a number on his living quarters, he'd once again been smart enough to wear gloves.

For days now, he'd racked his brain, trying to conjure up any identifying feature of the boat the intruder had escaped in. Attempting to parse his memory or coax his usual premonition into action.

Nothing. Until now and the patent doubt burning through him. Except it was more than that. More than simple misgivings. He *knew* Travis Sanford had nothing to do with this.

It's about the case. It's about Maggie's granddaughter. It's about Peyton and Nicholas Cornish.

He couldn't say that out loud, though. Knew exactly how Chief Holloway would respond. Peyton was in a coma. Nicholas was dead. There were no straight lines between either man and his ransacked boat. After months of digging, there wasn't even any evidence Nicholas Cornish had a thing to do with Cynthia's disappearance.

He chugged the rest of the bitter, burnt coffee and willed it to massage his overwrought brain. *I'm sorry, Lil. I tried.*

Earlier in the week, he'd made a valiant effort at putting the case out of his mind, just like she'd suggested. And he'd kept trying even in the days since the houseboat incident. He'd focused on plans for Maggie's wedding. He'd put his boat back to rights. He'd helped the Muirs with preparations for Muir Harbor's spring market, opening tonight in the square.

But all along it'd been there, buzzing in the back of his head, the feeling that this—whatever it was—wasn't over. That there was something he'd missed. A breadcrumb he'd overlooked. Some mysterious something that was waiting for discovery.

And it sure as heck had nothing to do with the teenager sulking two rooms down. "Look, I know Sanford's gotten in trouble a few times lately." Last summer when the town's star pitcher was injured so severely it ruined his college prospects, there was no *not* being in-the-know. The kid hadn't handled the death of his dream well, and Wilder couldn't blame him. Something like that would be difficult for any teenager to handle.

Travis Sanford had fallen in with the wrong sort of friends, been involved in a string of petty misdemeanors. He'd been arrested a few months ago, hadn't he? Property damage or something. And then there'd been this spring's hazing of the younger players.

And Chief Holloway had already confirmed the kid had participated in the break-in at Lil's office last week. He had Morris Groves's old autographed baseball to show for it.

"I know Sanford's been building a rep for himself. But I'm just convinced this time it wasn't him."

Chief Holloway threw up his hands. "So what? He comes in to confess, why? Some misguided ploy for attention?"

"Maybe." The kid was used to seeing his name in headlines. If he couldn't make the sports page, maybe he could make the front page. "Or he's trying to impress his friends? Why don't you let me question him? I could—"

"You're not a cop."

"But I was there. I watched whoever it was leap from my boat to his. It'd probably take me all of three minutes to riddle Sanford's confession with holes."

Holloway's gritty stare drilled into him. "Because you can do our job so much better than we can, is that it?"

"That's not—"

"I like you, Wilder. What's more, I have loads of respect for your father, may he rest in peace. The number of times Harry consulted with us and served as a boon to this department, I couldn't venture to say. But Harry understood where to draw the line. He understood boundaries. He respected us enough to let us do our job."

Wilder perched his empty mug on the edge of the police chief's desk. "I'm sorry. I'm not trying to step on anyone's toes. I just—"

"I know. You have a strong feeling. A gut instinct. Everybody knows about Wilder Monroe's magic sixth sense."

The man wasn't trying to mock him, he knew it. Even so, each sentence felt like an indictment. His empty stomach roiled, but not with hunger, and his knuckles went white where he gripped the chair's leather armrests. "Do you think this is what I want?" His voice had gone murky and low. "This never-ending case is like a black hole. Do you think I want to be flailing around in the dark?"

He wished the words back the second they leaked out. He'd told himself to not even mention the investigation in here. He knew Chief Holloway likely felt exactly the same about the missing Muir granddaughter as did Agent Franzen. *A lost cause. Dead on the vine from the beginning.*

Understanding dawned in Holloway's expression and it mellowed his gaze. Even so, there was a firmness in his tone when he spoke next. "You always have a choice."

It was a nice thought.

But it was too simple. It didn't account for Maggie's hurts and hopes. It didn't account for the break-in on his boat that he knew—he *knew*—had something to do with his investigation. It didn't account for a missing body at the scene of an accident twenty-eight years ago.

It didn't account for the decades Dad had given to this search.

"I don't see any need to press charges."

"Wilder—"

He unfolded himself from his too-small chair, pulled from his reservoir of resolve, and forced any hint of exhaustion from his voice. "Even if he did it, he didn't take anything. Didn't cause any damage a few hours of cleanup couldn't fix."

Chief Holloway slowly stood. "If that's your decision . . ."

"It is." Maybe he was being stubborn. Maybe he was being stupid. But for all Dad's qualities Holloway had just recited, he'd left one off the list.

Dad had trusted him.

When Wilder had come home from Baltimore only eight weeks into what should've been a sixteen-week training, when he'd faltered his way through an explanation that had sounded half-baked and feeble even to his own ears, Dad had clapped him on the shoulder and looked him straight in the eyes. *"You're sure this is what you want?"*

Wilder hadn't been able to do more than nod. He might've made a mess of explaining himself. But he *was* certain.

"Then all I have to say is, welcome home and have a donut. I was planning to eat both, but for my son's homecoming, I think I can bring myself to share."

The memory followed him out of the police station, out into the brash morning light. Already the sun promised warmth and perfect weather for this weekend's Muir Harbor Spring Market.

But he couldn't seem to dredge up any eagerness for the event. All he wanted to do was go back to the houseboat and fall into a deep sleep.

Or find Lilian and interrupt her workday. Spill the frustration that already had a stranglehold on his day. What a shift. Neil was usually his first stop when he needed to vent. But now . . .

He paused at the curb, palms flat on the hood of his Jeep.

"Wilder, just the person I was hoping to run into!" Indi

Muir came jogging down the sidewalk, her brown ankle boots clacking on the sidewalk and colorful dress billowing around her legs. An oversized tote bag jostled at her hip. "Okay, in all honesty, it was actually Lil I was planning to track down. She left the house too early today." Indi came to a stop in front of him. "But this works, too."

He mustered an obligatory grin. "Happy to be Plan B. What's up?"

Indi pulled her bag around to her front and rummaged through it until she came up with a flat item wrapped in tissue paper. "The wedding invitation. Lil wanted to get it to the printer today." She handed it to him.

He unwrapped the tissue paper to find a thick piece of cardstock nestled inside. Indi's original artwork looked back at him—a watercolor print of the seaside. Somehow she'd captured all the wonder, all the splendor of the scene just outside the front door of Maggie's farmhouse. The rocky shore, the moody waves, bowing sunbeams. Above the photo, in feathery brushstrokes, she'd painted the bride and groom's first names and the wedding date. "Whoa, Indi, this is beautiful."

"Well, it won't be nearly as impressive as a digitized print, but it'll still be pretty. I'll need to get the original back, though. I'm planning to frame it as a wedding gift. Now, I think Lil already emailed all the info for the back of the invitation to the printer. So all the printer needs to do is scan this and they should have a proof ready to review by the end of the day. I meant to give this to Lil before she left for the office today, but I missed her and I'm supposed to be in the square helping set up market booths."

"I'll make sure she gets it." Or he'd save Lilian the work and take it to the printer himself.

"Thanks." She slung her bag over her shoulder. "Hey, you all right, Wilder? The way you were leaning over your car . . ."

"I'm fine. Could probably do with a little more sleep, that's all."

"I don't know why you're still crashing on the couch whenever you stay over. Both the guest room and Neil's old room are empty."

He'd stayed in the guest room plenty of times in the past. When there was a blizzard and the houseboat had lost electricity for days on end. When he was a kid and Dad had to leave town for a few days on a case. It'd never felt weird to camp out in that room at the end of the Muirs' second floor. He'd been an honorary Muir sibling for years.

But that title didn't feel quite right anymore.

In truth, nothing felt quite right today and he couldn't square it.

"Well, you have every right to be tired. Maggie's wedding is going to be the biggest event Muir Harbor's seen in years, and you and Lilian are making it happen. It's a lot of work on top of your jobs, not to mention a break-in on your boat and waiting for Peyton to wake up and, oh, then there's Lil's stalker—"

"What?" He almost dropped Indi's artwork.

She waved her hand and laughed. "I'm kidding. She doesn't have a stalker."

"Then why would you say—"

"There was this day last week where she thought someone was following her. Or imagined it. She told me about it at the bakery. She was laughing about it, said she needed to get more sleep. That's what made me think of it." Indi's bag slid from her shoulder. "Oh my goodness, Wilder, don't look at me like that. It was just a joke. There's no stalker."

Unless there was. Unless Lilian hadn't imagined whatever it was she'd seen. Whoever it was. Someone had broken into his boat. Twice. Someone might've been following Lilian. All the strange happenings were supposed to have ended with Peyton out of commission but . . .

His gut refused to stop hounding him. He was missing something. But how was he supposed to know what when he just felt so . . . off? He looked down to Indi's painted piece, intending to rewrap it in the tissue paper. But his attention landed on the words at the top. The date. *June 29.*

Four weeks from tomorrow. Tomorrow . . . June 1.

Which made today . . .

His lungs suddenly pinched, turning his breaths shallow. "I-I'm sorry, Indi. I need to go."

"The stalker comment really didn't mean anything. It was a bad joke. I'm sorry."

He fumbled to wrap the print, then shoved his hand into his pocket, came up with his keys.

"Are you okay?"

Okay? Hardly. "The date . . ." How could he have forgotten? How could he not have paid a speck of attention to the calendar? He should've known what day it was as soon as he'd awoken today. He should've known it was coming. Felt it in his gut. "I'll get this to the printer, Indi. Promise."

He rounded his Jeep and flung open his door, then wilted into his car seat and let the door thud to a close.

There were days when it was difficult to remember why Lilian had chosen to return to her quaint hometown instead of putting her law degree to work at some exhilarating high-rise in a big city.

And then there were nights like tonight. When late-spring loveliness wrapped Muir Harbor's downtown in a warm embrace and eventide glided in on a waterfall of color.

The sky was luminescent, liquid blues and lavender. Paper lanterns dangling from the trees added a misty glow to bustling activity all around.

The Muir Harbor Spring Market was off to a picture-perfect start. Booths and stands filled the entirety of the town square that wasn't a square at all, but an oval lawn framed by a cobblestone street currently dotted with food trucks and stands. The air smelled of funnel cakes and popcorn.

Lilian loved these nights. Muir Harbor's seasonal markets were a tradition that stretched back decades, coaxing visitors from surrounding counties and even all around the state. Vendors came in by the dozens, selling homemade wares, hand-crafted jewelry, all kinds of art and gift items.

Or in the case of Muir Farm, pies and jams and jellies, pastries and all manner of baked goods. In the summer and fall, their booth would also be cluttered with produce from Lilian's garden. They had one of the biggest booths at the market, and usually one of the busiest, too.

Which was certainly the case tonight.

Which was why she hadn't followed through on her promise to herself. Her promise to finally fill in her siblings about her upcoming MRI. She'd been putting it off ever since she told Maggie, but tonight felt like the right time. She could rattle off the update during a break between customers, quick and easy. Little time for questions.

But so far there hadn't been a break between customers. And anyway, Indi hadn't yet wandered over from her store's booth like she usually did a few times each market evening.

Lilian handed one of Maggie's packaged berry pies to Earl from the hardware store and accepted his twenty in return. "Just a sec and I'll grab your change." She waited until Neil's wife was done storing another customer's payment, then slid the metal money box over. She handed two wrinkled dollar bills to Earl.

"I should balk that your pie prices went up, but considering I know what's waiting for me, my taste buds and I won't complain." Earl gave her a friendly grin.

Actually, she'd made the executive decision to increase the price of Maggie's famed pies two seasons ago, back during the autumn market. Earl must not remember. She chuckled. "You know it'll be worth it. Plus, you're lucky to nab one at all. We've only got five or six blueberry pies left."

"Four," Sydney interjected beside her. "Just sold two to Tim Tompkins."

Hmm. On the one hand, the fact that their booth was doing crazy-good business was a huge pro. On the other, this was the first time community leaders had decided to expand the spring market to a two-day event—opening on Friday night and lasting all of Saturday—instead of their usual Saturday evening timeframe. Which meant a flimsy round of guesswork when it came to knowing just how many pies, their most popular item, to have on hand tonight and how many to hold back for tomorrow. "We're going to sell out and it's not even seven o'clock."

Neil squeezed in between Lilian and Sydney, added another twenty to the lockbox. "If we sell out, we sell out."

"I could run home and grab another load. Restock."

He shook his head. "Save 'em for tomorrow. We have plenty of other goods to sell."

"And if we run out altogether?"

He grinned and slid an arm around Sydney. "We close up shop and enjoy the rest of the night at our leisure." He leaned in close to his wife. "You remembered our pie, right?"

Lilian leaned her hip against their table. "What do you mean your pie? If there's an extra pie around here—"

"You mean this one?" Indi piped up from behind them and Lilian turned to see her holding a pie still nestled uncut in one of Maggie's antique dishes.

"Why isn't that one wrapped?"

"Because that one happens to be ours," Neil said as he crossed to Indi and plucked the pie plate from her. "Syd and I have a tradition. And aren't you supposed to be at your booth?"

"Philip and Holland insisted I take a break for a few minutes," Indi said, hopping onto one of the stools near the back of the booth. "They're manning my stand for a while. Figured I'd come see what's happening over here. And I'm glad I did because I need to hear about this tradition."

Neil tucked the dish away under a cloth. "No, you don't."

"But—"

"Oh, look, Patti Brighton-Smythe's on her way over. Who wants to take her business?" He waggled his dark brows at both sisters. "I thought so."

He turned back to the table just as Patti descended on their booth, her platinum hair piled as high as ever. Leaning as precariously to the side as ever.

Sydney sidled up to the sisters. "It was my first Muir Harbor market. And I'd made my very first homemade pie. And instead of selling it, we snuck away and ate it ourselves. It turned into a ritual. Never let him know you know he's so sentimental."

"I heard that," Neil called over his shoulder as he handed Patti two of their last desserts.

Indi laughed. "Sentimental Neil is adorable."

"Don't I know it." Sydney grinned and returned to Neil's side, chatting with Patti while he counted her change.

Indi slid from the stool. "I'd say they're so cute it's nauseating, but I'm pretty sure my stomach pains are from eating my weight in turnovers and muffins while helping Maggie bake. The house has smelled like heaven all week. It's the only scent my nose recognizes anymore—berries and sugar and butter." Indi paused. "Looking for Wilder?"

Lilian yanked her gaze to her sister, away from the crowd she'd been scanning. "Why would I be looking for him?"

"Because he usually helps run our booth, for one thing."

Yes, and though the market had been in full swing for two hours now, he hadn't made an appearance. Actually, she hadn't seen him all day. There'd been days in months and years past when she'd rejoice over that. But her old irritation was in tatters lately.

"And for another thing," Indi continued, "Wilder's usually wherever you are these days."

Not necessarily the case. Since Tuesday evening, since the houseboat break-in, Lilian had only seen the man sporadically. They'd texted about a few wedding details here and there. Crossed paths at the house now and then. But they'd both been busy.

Or maybe she'd been avoiding him. Because that thing Wilder had said a week ago—or was it two?—about how her perpetual annoyance with him was a comfort zone . . . he was exactly right. And now she was out of the comfort zone. Now he didn't annoy her. Now he . . .

Listened to her. Noticed things. How did he do that? How did he draw her out?

And then draw her in . . . *That hug.*

"Maybe he's under the weather. I saw him this morning, and he didn't look so hot."

She took her sister's abandoned seat. "You saw him this morning?"

"Yeah, he was just coming out of the police station," Indi went on.

Neil stepped up. "The police station? Did they figure out who ransacked the houseboat?"

Indi shrugged. "I don't know. I should've asked him."

Or he should've called Lil. At the very least, he could've

texted her. He had news about the boat and he hadn't told her?

Ignore that for a second. You just got your opening.

Oh, right. No customers. Her brother and sister both here.

"Uh, guys, I have to tell you something real quick."

Both siblings turned to her, and Sydney, too, moving to come up beside Neil. "You've talked to him?" Neil asked. "Since when does Wild start filling you in before me?"

She shook her head. "No, it's not about that." *Just say it. Get it over with.* "Back in April, I had a few days where I was kind of sick. Or, well, not really sick, I just had these weird symptoms . . . some tingling and numbness and something with my vision, and anyway, I went to the doctor and she sent me to a neurologist and now I'm getting an MRI on Tuesday. And it's probably nothing, but I just wanted to let you know what's going on because, you know, we're family."

Three sets of confused stares settled on her.

"Sorry, that was a ridiculous way to tell you."

"I don't think I understand." While Neil spoke, Sydney slid her arm around him. "A neurologist? That's . . . that's like your brain, right?" Neil's accent deepened. It was the one thing that ever gave him away. He could keep his expression masked, even his posture at forced ease. But that tilt into a Scottish burr had a way of betraying him.

He'd gone into instant big-brother worry.

Which was exactly what she didn't want. "Insurance made the whole thing a mess. I had to go to a specialist to get the MRI ordered. Hopefully my brain's completely fine." Except apparently it wasn't because she could see now that her logic had failed her. The night had been off to a perfect start and she'd ruined it for her siblings.

Indi hadn't even said anything. She just stood there, hugging her arms to herself, as if she were a reed the wind might bowl over any second.

"Guys, this is not a huge thing." Oh, she hoped it wasn't. "Maybe I shouldn't have said anything—"

"Why didn't you say anything sooner?" Neil cut in. "Like when you were having symptoms? We could've supported you."

"Neil." Sydney set her hand on his arm. "How long did it take you to tell your sisters about the farm's financial struggles last autumn? She told you when she was ready to. Let that be enough."

Lilian gave her sister-in-law a grateful smile. Or the closest thing she had to one in this moment. This wasn't how it was supposed to go. She was supposed to lightly fill them in and they'd experience a moment of surprise, but eventually realize it wasn't as serious as it might sound. A blithe, anticlimactic conversation.

Anticlimactic—yes. Hopefully that's how this whole thing would end. The MRI results would be in her favor. The symptoms would never return. They'd all look back and laugh at this moment of cloaking seriousness.

"I have questions," Indi said.

No, see, that's what she wanted to avoid. That's why she'd chosen this wrong moment in this wrong place. To avoid—

"Oh, that's Mariana." Lilian's feet dropped to the grass as she slipped from the stool. "I told her I'd be on the lookout for her."

"Lil—"

"I know you have questions and so do I." She gave her sister a brief, inadequate side hug. "But there just aren't really any answers right now. Honestly, I have a feeling I'm going to find out this was just stress-induced or something and I'm going to feel silly for even saying anything. But for now, can we just . . . I need to go say hi to Mariana. I'll . . . I'll be back in a minute." She turned and left through the back of the booth.

Coward. You're running away.

175

Or just giving herself space to breathe. She wished Wilder were here. He would've known what to say back there. He would've thrown out some funny remark and she would've rolled her eyes, but she would've been thankful for it.

Just as she'd been thankful he hadn't pelted her with questions when she'd told him the same thing she'd just told the others. He'd known for a week and a half now—no, longer, considering he'd found that appointment card over two weeks ago. And if ever she'd wanted proof of his high-functioning instincts, it was right there in the way he always seemed to know just what she needed. The comfort of a stretching quiet in some moments, a comment to make her laugh in others. Sometimes a distraction.

Sometimes a simple hug.

Where are you tonight, Wilder?

She wove through the crowd, hurrying to catch up with Mariana and Flannel. "Hey, Mari. You made it."

Mariana turned. Her eyes were hidden behind sunglasses, but her grin revealed her pleasure. "I was hoping I'd find you. I had no idea this thing would be so packed."

"Sorry, I should've done a better job preparing you. Most days of the year, Muir Harbor's just a speck on the map. But for four weekends out of every fifty-two weeks, our seasonal markets do us proud. Have you eaten yet?"

Mariana shook her head.

"Okay, a couple things you need to know. Food stands are around the perimeter and they're amazing. But don't try any of Lottie's moon punch. That is, unless you've got an iron stomach."

"Spiked, I take it?"

"The phrase 'packs a punch' was invented for that stuff. What kind of food are you in the mood for? I know all the best spots."

Flannel stepped closer to Mariana's side, moving out of

the way of an oncoming stroller. "You said something about pie earlier today."

Oh. Pie. She glanced over her shoulder, back to the farm booth where she'd abandoned her siblings. They were back to serving customers now, but she didn't miss Neil glancing her way in between handing Mrs. Jenkins a plate of muffins and accepting her cash. Indi was doing the same.

She swallowed her sigh. "Best pie to be had is Maggie's. Come on. You can meet my family." She threaded her arm through Mariana's and they walked toward the stand. "Guys, this is Mariana. She's my new coworker. Technically, her title is paralegal, but it should be lifesaver."

Mariana extended her hand and Neil was the first to take it, meeting Lilian's eyes for a strained second before speaking. "So you're why Lil's been home before dinnertime every night this week. Nice to meet you."

"My brother, Neil," Lilian offered. "And his wife, Sydney."

She introduced Indi next, then set about describing their booth for Mariana, explaining what they were selling and the fact that it was mainly Maggie's baking prowess on display at their stand. "Maggie's around here somewhere. This is her fiancé's first taste of a Muir Harbor market, so she's showing him around."

They chatted for a few more minutes, Mariana familiarizing the others with her dog, then lapsing into a conversation with Sydney about their shared experiences of being newcomers in Muir Harbor.

Indi moved to Lilian's side. "Because, you know, we're family?"

Lilian recognized her own clumsy words echoed back at her. "I know I fumbled in the way I told you."

"I'm just glad you did tell us. Everything's been so busy lately. So many things are changing." Indi's voice wobbled. "I wish I'd noticed something was wrong."

"I don't even know if something is wrong. I don't want anyone worrying—"

Indi threw her arms around Lilian and yanked her close. *Oh, Indi.* She'd always been the sweetly emotional one. And Lilian loved it about her.

"I just need my big sister to be okay. Perfectly healthy and perfectly okay."

"I feel perfectly healthy right now, I promise." She caught Neil watching them. He met Lilian's eyes over Indi's shoulder, gave her nod. "I feel perfectly okay, too."

"Good." Indi stepped back. "Then I guess I should probably get back to my booth." She paused. "Do you think we should be worrying about Wilder?"

Yes. No. "I don't know."

"It's just weird that he's not here. I would've thought he'd at least text Neil. Or you. For enemies you guys have been spending a lot of time together lately so—"

"We're not enemies." Lilian swiped wayward strands of hair out of her face, but the breeze pushed them right back.

"Definitely not the part of that sentence I thought you'd take issue with."

———•—   —•———

Wilder had spent all of five minutes at the market, but he'd known from the first that attending was a mistake.

He wasn't up to faking it. And why put off what he knew he needed to do?

He dropped a pile of shirts into the open duffel bag on his bed, shifting the contents he'd already stuffed in to make room. What else? A couple pairs of jeans should get him through. He'd already packed toiletries.

He had a dresser drawer halfway open when the knock billowed through the houseboat. He clenched the drawer's metal handles. He'd known it was coming. Four texts. Two unanswered calls. If ever he deserved Lilian Muir's ire, it was now.

He closed the drawer and forced his legs to move, the heaviness of the day weighing each step. The blinds on the houseboat's living room windows were drawn, and it felt like too much to work to find the light switch, so he let muscle memory guide him through the dark.

But it was a poor guide. He'd moved the trunk earlier today, the one he usually positioned in front of the couch like a coffee table. He'd left it out of place and he tripped over it now, stubbing his toe, knocking into an end table, tipping a lamp.

"Wilder?" Another rap. "You in there?"

"Hold your horses."

"Don't bark at—" Lilian's words swooped to a stop when he flung open the door.

"What?" Oh Lord, why had he all but growled the word? None of this was Lilian's fault. Today's date. The fact that he'd forgotten. The case that just wouldn't go away. That horrible, impending sense of failure. Dad, Maggie . . .

Lilian. Her stare raked over him from top to bottom and he knew whatever she was seeing wasn't good. He'd seen it himself in the bathroom mirror as he'd thrown his toothbrush and soap and razor in his duffel bag. The dark stubble shadowing his face, the gloom in his eyes. Wrinkled navy henley and gray sweatpants.

He'd change before he left. But it wouldn't do much to improve the picture.

"You look terrible," she said.

"You flatter me."

"What's going on? Is your phone dead or something?" She

took a step closer. Sniffed the air and grilled him with an accusing gaze. "Have you been drinking?"

"No, Lil, I haven't been drinking. But I'm kind of busy, so—"

She budged past him, barging into his space, laser-focused. And all he could do was watch her scour the place and find what she was looking for. The tipped-over plastic cup he hadn't bothered to throw away.

She spun to him. "You *were* at the market. What'd you do? Make a beeline straight for Lottie's and then hole up here? You know that stuff's lethal."

"I didn't drink it." He let out a ragged breath. "Not most of it, anyway. Three sips on my way back and I poured the rest in the Atlantic."

"Great, so you've killed every fish in a half-mile radius."

"Is there a reason you're here?"

She crinkled the cup and tossed it in his trash. "Is there a reason you're being a jerk?"

"I'm sorry." He let it out on a puff of air, smoothing one palm over his chest. Tried again. "I'm sorry, Lil. It's been a bad day."

"That's not a good enough explanation."

But it was all he had right now. Because he couldn't do this with her. He couldn't tell her what today meant because that would require talking about Dad, and if he started talking about Dad, he might not stop. He might tell her everything.

He might tell her the one thing he'd never told anyone. The suspicion that had tangled his thoughts or maybe his very soul three years ago and had him knotted-up still. All because of a letter and the resounding refrain it'd left him with.

What if? What if? What if?

He hadn't read it again, not even once, since that first time. But once had been enough to burn it into his brain.

"Lilian—" He broke off when he realized she wasn't

looking at him anymore. No, her gaze had slithered past him and through his open bedroom door to the open duffel on his bed.

"Where are you going?"

"Atlanta."

She jerked her focus back to him. "Why?"

She was in lawyer mode and he was a witness on the stand. If she hadn't given up after those texts and calls, she wouldn't now that she had him in her sights.

And for a moment, he almost let himself find some sense of comfort in that. She might be glaring at him right now, but this wasn't the old glare. This one had an undertow of worry. And if she was worried, it meant she cared.

He turned away from her, retreated into his bedroom, then returned and held out the photocopied newspaper clipping. As soon as she took it, he explained. "You probably already know that's Nicholas Cornish in the middle. The five men around him are all business associates. I'd already identified three of them. Franzen was able to name the fourth. Fifth is still a mystery."

"I don't understand."

"There's also an old housekeeper I haven't spoken with yet. And a childhood friend of Peyton's I found on Facebook."

"The case . . . you're going to Atlanta to . . . for the case." She looked completely bewildered. "Why?"

It was the second time she'd asked it. "Because I have to."

"You don't."

She didn't understand and he knew he couldn't make her. Did he even understand it himself? He moved past her, into his bedroom once more. Was he being stupid? Reckless?

Was that even a question? His gaze landed on the photo on his dresser. Him and Dad. *I'm sorry, Dad. I should've taken the boat out. I should've remembered.*

Just like he should've come home earlier that night three

years ago. He should've been there when it happened. No, before it happened. He might've been able to—

"It's too much, Wilder." Lilian followed him into the bathroom. "The chances that any of these people you're going to talk to actually know anything . . . I don't see why you have to go. Can't you just make phone calls? Send emails?"

"Emails go into spam folders." He moved to his dresser. "People don't like answering calls from numbers they don't recognize."

"Or if they do recognize the number, sometimes they just ignore it."

"I said I'm sorry—"

"You know what? You want to know why I didn't like you for all those years?" She budged in front of him, blocking his path to the dresser. "It's because you told me the truth when I didn't want to hear it. You might not remember it, but I do. I remember every detail. I was ten years old and I came to this boat and I had a long talk with your dad. I spent forever telling him all the reasons I thought *I* was Maggie's granddaughter. I had it all written up in a notebook, presented my case right in that living room out there. And when it was all over, when Harry had let me down as kindly as he could, you took over. You overheard the whole thing and the minute I walked out onto the deck, you made sure every last tether connecting me to that silly, illogical dream had snapped. *It's impossible, Lil. You'll probably never know. You need to accept it.* That's what you said."

At some point while she'd pitched one sentence after another at him, he'd backed up, lowered onto the bed. He combed through memories, scouring his brain, looking for that day.

"That killed me, Wilder, and I held it against you for years and, yeah, I know how immature that was, but my point is, you did me a favor. You told me the brutal truth and got me back to reality. You were right. I'll probably never know where I came from. Just like no one will ever find Alec Muir's treasure. And you . . ."

She didn't say it.

But he heard it loud and clear and as earsplitting as a clanging gong. *And you won't ever find Cynthia Muir.*

"You don't believe she's alive."

"Wilder, that's not . . ." Her sigh was nearly a groan. She raked her fingers through her hair, her frustration palpable.

"I hate that I hurt you like that." He slouched over his knees, braced his head in his hands. It thudded, ached. Maybe he *should* have finished off that punch from Lottie. But no, then he'd just be putting off the headache until tomorrow.

He'd drunk himself into a stupor on this boat once before. Once had been enough.

"I hate that I hurt you," he said again. "I'm sorry." He kept saying that. It didn't feel like enough. "It's too late but . . . I'm sorry."

"And I'm sorry for holding a grudge for twenty years." The mattress shifted as she sat beside him. "But I didn't tell you that to try to get an apology out of you. I just don't think you should go to Atlanta. I don't think you should keep pursuing this. It's making you miserable."

She was wrong. She was trying to help, but she was wrong. This case might exasperate him to no end. It might have him grasping at straws more than he liked. But it wasn't the thing threatening to eat him alive.

It wasn't what had trapped him in this boat for most of the day with the blinds drawn or what was buzzing in the back of his head now, prodding him to hurry up and leave.

"I'm sorry, Lil." Another worthless apology. "But you should probably go."

"What? Why?"

He lumbered to his feet. "I already booked a red-eye out of Portland. I should've hit the road fifteen minutes ago."

"But—"

"I know what you were trying to do in telling me that story, Lil, and maybe if it were another day, maybe if it wasn't May 31, it would've worked. But I'm just not ready to let it go. If the brutal truth is that this case is unsolvable, I'll have to believe it someday. But I can't believe it today, okay? So I have to go. And so do you."

She rose slowly. "What does the date have to do with anything?"

"Please, Lil. Just go."

*L*ilian took a sip of the champagne one of the bridal store attendants had handed her as Maggie disappeared into a changing room. The bubbles tickled her nose and scratched her throat, and for the hundredth time this morning, she begged her errant thoughts to stop running away from her.

To Friday night and Wilder.

To the way he'd looked when his houseboat door had thrust open and his six-foot-something frame had sagged in the doorway, some invisible weight hanging over him. No, swathing him, dragging, pushing him down.

To the voicemail he'd left her the next morning when she'd still been asleep.

Hey Lil. I made it to Atlanta. Wanted to . . . wanted to say I'm sorry again. And also that before I left, I looked through Dad's filing cabinet for any of his old notes from back when Maggie found you. I couldn't find anything. He took meticulous notes about every case, so there should've been something in there and I don't know why there's not. I'm really sorry . . . Anyway. I'll be back in a couple days. Um, if you ever want to talk . . . well, I'll see you soon, okay? Oh, Indi said something about someone following you and that it was nothing. It is nothing, right? If it's not, tell me, and I'll hop on the next plane back. I can't believe your voicemail hasn't cut me off ye—

How many times had she listened to it on Saturday? And then again on Sunday?

Sydney's gasp and Indi's squeal, simultaneous and startling, yanked her attention back to where it was supposed to be. Firmly ensconced in this cute little boutique in the heart of Bar Harbor. Fixed on the woman emerging from a back room with a shy grin lighting up her whole face.

"Oh, Maggie." Lilian let out a soft breath and rose from the velvet-covered chair where she'd waited with the others. "I know it's only the first dress you've tried but . . ." She couldn't even finish her sentence. Stunning. Maggie was stunning.

It was a simple dress, understated yet elegant, with lace sleeves that reached to Maggie's elbows and soft folds of white that traced her figure and glimmered their way to the floor.

Indi was the first to reach her, arms outstretched as if she was itching to touch the dress, but her hands stopping short of brushing the pristine fabric. "Don't take this the wrong way, Maggie, but oh my word—you have *curves.*"

Maggie burst out laughing even as she turned in front of the three-way mirror, craning her neck to catch every angle of the dress. "I'm not one to preen, but I must say, sixty-five looks okay on me."

"Are you kidding me? Just okay?" Lilian came up on Maggie's other side. "Ray is going to lose his composure the second he sees you coming down the aisle."

"He already loses his composure anytime Maggie enters a room," Indi countered. "It's a thing with the men in that family."

If Lilian had to guess, she'd bet money it wasn't Maggie's beau Indi was picturing right now, but the man's grandson.

Philip West still stumbled over his words every now and then when he was around Lilian's sister. Indi would probably be disappointed if he didn't.

Sydney's reflection joined the rest of them in the mirror, her adoration of Maggie glistening in her eyes. "It's gorgeous, Maggie. You're gorgeous."

The store owner approached, her sleek blond hair pulled into a tight bun. "Dare I say this is the one?" She broke the mood with her question.

Or maybe not entirely. Because Maggie's gaze was still shimmering and she reached both arms out to her sides, drawing her daughters and her daughter-in-law close. "I prayed for this, you know."

Indi sighed. "For a wedding of your dreams to the man of your dreams?"

Maggie's grin widened. "No. I prayed this wouldn't take long. You know I'm not a big shopper."

They broke into fits of giggles, a tangle of arms and happiness.

The store owner eyed them in the mirror. "There's a ten percent discount when you buy off the rack."

For some reason that only made Maggie laugh harder, and then the rest of them, too.

Lilian's hair fell over her face as she giggled, and for a moment, there was no voicemail on her phone itching to be listened to for the dozenth time. No MRI waiting for her tomorrow. There was only this—a beautiful present. And all the joy in the world at the thought of Maggie's future.

"We did pull several other gowns for you to try—" the storeowner offered.

But Maggie pulled herself together enough to shake her head. "Oh no, this one will do."

"You're not just choosing it because of your aversion to shopping?" Indi slid her arm from around Maggie.

"Or not trying any of the others because of their price tag?" Lilian added. "Because you can't let that hold you back. We made a killing at the spring market, so you should spend to your heart's content." After all, the most expensive piece of Maggie's wedding was already covered thanks to Wilder.

Whether or not Maggie knew the full extent of that situation, Lilian didn't know. She'd told Wilder he should be the one to present the possibility of holding the wedding on his friend's yacht. It was his idea, after all.

And a brilliant one. It was going to be incredible—a night to remember. Unique, romantic, all for Maggie. All because of Wilder.

Who was somewhere down in Georgia. Doing who-knew-what. She couldn't decide whether she wanted to throttle him or chase him down with the sole purpose of making sure he was okay. That the unkempt state she'd found him in on Friday night had been a fluke.

He's fine. Of course he is.

"This is my heart's content." Maggie's voice drifted in. "I love this dress. I love my girls. I love that our mission is accomplished and we'll get back to Muir Harbor and Ray sooner than planned."

Maggie's fiancé lived up in Augusta, but when he'd learned about the women's late-afternoon shopping trip, he'd offered to drive down to Muir Harbor and have dinner waiting for them when they arrived home. He'd probably bring Philip and Holland along, too. They'd have a full house tonight.

With one obvious missing person.

The storeowner looked dubious at Maggie's fast decision-making. Or maybe disappointed that Maggie hadn't chosen one of the more expensive gowns. "Would you like to look at bridesmaid dresses? We also have a wonderful selection for flower girls."

Maggie knew they'd already mostly settled on a selection of bridesmaid dresses from an online store. But she waved her hand toward the rack near the front of the store. "Might as well take a look. Just in case." She wove her arm through Lilian's, though, before she could move toward the rack. "Come with me?"

"Sure."

She left Indi and Sydney to finger through the selection of dresses and followed Maggie through the doorway behind the tall mirrors, toward the cluster of curtain-covered dressing rooms.

Maggie paused outside the middle curtain. "Help me with the buttons?"

"Of course." She stepped up behind Maggie and set to work on the string of pearls that drew a line down Maggie's back. "Wow, Ray's going to have fun with this on your wedding night."

Maggie *tsk*ed but Lilian knew she wore a smile. "Don't be indecent, Lil."

She chuckled. "I'm just saying, I hope he's got deft fingers because these buttons are no joke."

"I'm worried about him, too, you know."

She's not talking about Ray. Obviously. "I'm not worried."

"I'm your mother, Lilian Grace. Don't lie to me."

Lilian Grace. She'd gone five years without a middle name, from the day Maggie had found her on the front porch until the day they'd stood in a judge's chambers and her adoption had been finalized. "I'll never forget you asking me how I felt about Grace as a middle name. You gave Indi the middle name Joy and you said Grace felt just right for me." She reached the last button.

Maggie turned. "You're trying to change the subject, my dear. Don't think that escapes me." She winked and ducked behind the curtain. "You should know that when Wilder comes back, I'm going to ask him to drop the case once and for all."

"Maggie—"

"It's not the worst thing in the world to admit you care about him. He has a way of wriggling under a person's skin. It's his Wilder way." The rustle of the dress sounded from behind the curtain. "Of course, leaving town stubborn and half-cocked is his way, too. But then, we're all a bit of a mixed bag, aren't we? He's only a human."

"Not you, Maggie. You're pure goodness."

"Trying to flatter me to get me off-topic won't work either."

"Okay, fine, yes, I am a little worried about him." She flounced into a chair identical to the ones out front. "But I also want to wring his neck." And against all reason, to then circle her arms around the very same neck and whisper that it was all going to be okay.

Get a grip. This is Wilder you're talking about.

And she didn't even know what was wrong with him. It wasn't just the case that'd had him coiled so tight and ready to spring the other night. She'd realized that before she'd even reached the end of the dock after leaving the houseboat. He'd said something just before asking her to leave. Something about the date. *May 31.*

Clearly it was significant. But how? It wasn't his birthday. Nor the anniversary of his dad's death.

"Hey, Maggie," she called through the curtain. "Do you remember when Harry Monroe's birthday was?"

"Actually, yes. But only because it was on Halloween. It's an easy one to remember."

Oh, right. Maybe she'd known that.

"Why do you ask?"

"I'm trying to figure out why May 31 is significant to Wilder."

"You should ask Neil."

She'd considered that more than once over the weekend. Every time she'd talked herself out of prying. But with every day that passed, she was losing a little more of her resolve.

A little more of her common sense, more like. Wilder Monroe wasn't her BFF. He wasn't some kindred spirit whose every thought and move and emotion she should understand. He wasn't her brother.

An image slipped in of the way he'd looked several evenings ago, standing out on the dock, holding her hand, moonlight tracing his profile. Tall and steady and caring. *Definitely not a brother.*

Oh, what was happening to her? What had she eaten for breakfast this morning? The champagne was messing with her head, surely, causing her to forget how mad she was at him for the way he'd ignored her calls and texts on Friday and skipped the market and barked at her when she'd shown up at his door.

And what had possessed her to remind him about the day she'd gone to the houseboat when she was a kid? It was clearer than ever that he still didn't remember it. One of the most momentous experiences of her childhood and he didn't even remember it.

Well, she did. More than she wanted to. She could still feel the flutter of little-girl nerves that had plagued her as she'd walked down that dock. Could still smell the muddy coffee Wilder's father had offered her. Remember how grown-up she'd felt saying yes and how terrible it'd tasted.

Then had come Harry Monroe's mild-mannered patience as she'd presented her case. The tender way he'd let her down.

She'd spent so much time brooding over Wilder's part in that day through the years that sometimes she forgot about Harry's part. About how gently he'd pointed out the holes in her case as if he knew how much it meant to her to be taken seriously.

You had a good father, Wilder. A kind father.

Maggie slid open the dressing room curtain, dressed back in her tan slacks and frilly white shirt, her favorite yellow cardigan around her shoulders.

"No second thoughts on the dress?"

"Not a one. I'm not as into to-do lists as you are, but if I was, this would be an awfully big one to check off the list."

Lilian stood. "Speaking of which, we're down to pretty small details now." Thankfully, the printer had rushed the invitation print job and they'd been ready by Saturday morning. "Invitations should start hitting mailboxes by tomorrow. No thanks to Wilder." Except that wasn't entirely fair. He'd helped her stamp and address envelopes last week. He just hadn't been there for the impromptu envelope-stuffing party with the family around the kitchen table after Sunday dinner yesterday.

"He'll be back soon, Lil."

"I'm not . . . that's not . . ." She huffed and started back the way they'd come. "Do you know anything about his mother?"

Maggie's forehead wrinkled, probably from the abruptness of the question as much as the question itself. "She died when he was a baby. I believe it was a very aggressive breast cancer."

Oh. It'd been cancer for both parents. Although, she was pretty sure it wasn't the leukemia that had caused Harry's death in the end. Hadn't there been something about a bad reaction to a medication?

"Actually . . ." Instead of reentering the store's main area, Maggie paused. "Now that I'm thinking back, I remember some talk around town. I think maybe Ainsley refused treatments. Yes, I'm pretty sure that was the case. She was pregnant when she got the diagnosis. So for the baby's sake . . ."

For Wilder's sake. "Oh, that's . . ." Terrible. And somehow also beautiful. Tragically beautiful. "Does Wilder know that? Did he grow up knowing his mother made that kind of sacrifice?"

"Honestly, I don't know. But if he did, that's an awful lot for a young boy to understand."

Maybe an awful lot for a grown man to deal with. "I don't think I've ever been all that fair to him, Maggie."

"Or maybe you simply never saw him. And now you do. Or you're beginning to. So the question you have to ask yourself is, what are you going to do with that?"

This was a long shot. A wild goose chase so ridiculous, it was probably about time he admit he'd gone off course.

Admit defeat.

Wilder stepped into the funeral home located in a section of Atlanta he'd just as soon never visit again. Seedy motels and derelict apartment buildings, enough potholes riddling the pavement he had serious worries about the condition of his rental car's tires.

This is it. Last stop. That's it.

Because he was tired. And—maybe he could finally admit it—he was done. Since his plane had landed at ATL Saturday morning, he'd managed to track down two of Nicholas Cornish's old business acquaintances from that old newspaper clipping and had come up empty-handed. Not a one remembered any talk of a child other than Peyton. Not a one recalled any mention of Muir Harbor.

He'd found two of Cornish's old residences, including his latest home, a grand modern affair located far from this run-down funeral home, long since emptied and placed on the market. He'd even scoped out the old housekeeper who used to work for the man.

He'd gotten absolutely nowhere. If Cynthia Muir had survived that car accident three decades ago, if Nicholas Cornish had been anywhere around Muir Harbor when it happened and had somehow whisked her away, no one here knew it.

Which meant this final stop was most likely in vain. But he had five hours before his flight home. Why not give himself one last shot of discouragement?

The interior of Brazelli's Funeral Parlor wasn't quite as neglected as its peeling exterior, but it was close. Faded burgundy carpet and a low ceiling made the lobby feel small and congested. A wooden rack was secured to one wall, crowded with pamphlets advertising coffins and crematorium services.

"Good afternoon, can I help you?"

A stooped man with bare wisps of silver hair approached from a darkened hallway. His wire-rimmed glasses magnified his eyes and his suit jacket appeared to be a size too big.

"Hi, I'm sorry to show up without an appointment." It was his standard opening these past days as he'd intruded on the lives of Nicholas Cornish's old acquaintances. "My name's Wilder Monroe. I'm a private investigator. I'm here because I think this funeral home conducted services for an individual I'm looking into. She died in April 1991."

The man—Mr. Brazelli?—looked entirely taken aback. And rightfully so. Wilder hadn't exactly cushioned his introduction.

"Her name was Sophia Cornish." Nicholas Cornish's ex-wife. Peyton Cornish's late mother. A strand of this investigation so far removed from its center, it was entirely illogical to even be wasting time on it.

But then, this whole trip to Atlanta had been illogical. Impulsive and irrational and . . .

And he wanted to go home. He didn't want to be here, didn't want to do this anymore. He wanted to go home to Muir Harbor and see a dozen familiar sights and a hundred familiar faces.

He wanted to see Lilian. There was the blunt truth. He owed her an apology, yes, but more than that, he just wanted to *see* her. To be in the same place she was. To laugh when she made some snide remark or feel that unforeseen sense of wonder when she pulled back the curtain just long enough to divulge something personal.

She'd done it all over again Friday night on his houseboat and he couldn't stop thinking about it. He'd scoured his memories during his entire middle-of-the-night flight to Atlanta and finally crumbs of a stale recollection had begun to scatter in. A humid summer afternoon. A long bike ride back from fishing at Ansel Barrett's creek with his new best friend. Climbing onto his boat only to hear someone else's voice intermingling with Dad's, coming from the living room.

And eventually, skinny, tow-headed Lilian Muir emerging from the living quarters. It was as much as he could remember.

Or maybe as much as he wanted to remember. Because he didn't want to remember hurting her. Didn't want to remember the oblivious, careless words he'd evidently tossed at her like the oblivious, careless teen he'd been.

"Perhaps we should sit down?" The man in the glasses motioned toward a small chapel, visible through the glass windows that edged one half of the lobby. Wilder followed him through a set of double doors, then sat in the cushioned pew the man indicated. "I'm Gomer Brazelli, by the way. This is my establishment. Mine and the missus's."

"It's . . . a very fine place." He might not have meant the statement thirty seconds ago. But a quick glance around the chapel revealed a certain degree of care. Yes, the carpet was washed-out and worn in here, too, a match for the discoloring of the pale gray tufts on each pew seat. But the wooden backs of every pew shined with polish. A lemon scent hovered in the air. Every bow on every curtain was knotted just so, and the windows gleamed. "It's nice to meet you. And again, I'm sorry to drop in like this."

Mr. Brazelli's knees creaked as he lowered onto a pew in front of Wilder. He twisted in his seat to face Wilder. He nudged his glasses up with his knuckle. "Tell me the name of this woman again. And what you'd like to know about her."

He didn't even know what questions to ask. What did any of this amount to? Nicholas Cornish had abandoned his first wife before Diana had ever returned to Muir Harbor, before Cynthia had ever disappeared. *Or died.* As for Sophia, from what he'd learned, she'd died of liver failure after years of intense alcoholism, leaving behind Peyton and Elizabeth, the daughter Cornish had sent away.

What did any of that have to do with the search for Maggie's granddaughter?

Off course. You're so far off course.

"I'm sorry, Mr. Brazelli. I think maybe I've wasted your time."

"Her name," Mr. Brazelli repeated.

"Sophia Cornish."

The man lifted two fingers to rub his creased brow. "That's what I thought you said."

Wait. "You recognized the name. You remember—"

Mr. Brazelli rose. "Please wait here."

"But—"

The man was already shuffling away, disappearing out the doors they'd just entered. What had just happened? Did Mr.

Brazelli actually know something that might get him somewhere? Or was this another practice in futility?

He wanted to hope, but considering the wasted stretch of days behind him and the way he'd run away from Muir Harbor . . .

Yes, that's exactly what he'd done. He'd run away. Not because of the case or even so much because of what Friday's date had meant to him. But because of what he'd done. That day when he'd realized the date, he hadn't just shut himself up in the boat like a recluse and sulked. No, when he'd felt his heart fragmenting, he'd decided to go ahead and smash it to smithereens.

He'd pulled Dad's letter from its buried resting place in the living room trunk and, God help him, he'd taken it into his bedroom and unfolded it for the first time since the day after Dad died.

Son, I'm writing this note by the light of the alarm clock . . .

He hadn't gotten any farther than that. Just one line and it'd been enough to completely wreck him. Just the sight of Dad's handwriting . . .

"Do you know where he is?"

The voice flooding into the chapel from behind him wasn't Mr. Brazelli's. He turned to see a woman rushing toward him. Strands of gray hair frizzed around her face, her purple headband not enough to contain them. A pair of red reading glasses bounced over her chest, dangling from a string around her neck.

"Do you know where my brother is?"

Mr. Brazelli came up behind her as she stopped beside Wilder's pew and gently laid his hands on her shoulders. "He doesn't know yet, *mia cara*. I haven't explained."

Wilder rose slowly. "I-I'm sorry. I don't . . . I'm here about Sophia—"

"Yes, I know," the woman interrupted. "My brother

worked for her husband. Or, no, I suppose he wasn't her husband anymore when she died. But he was at her funeral. I tried to ask him then, but he put me off, just like all the other times."

Mr. Brazelli offered Wilder a consoling nod. "I'm sorry. You said the name Cornish. You said you were a private investigator. My first instinct was to tell my wife. Her younger brother disappeared decades ago. He'd only been working for Mr. Cornish for a few years, but—"

"We knew something wasn't right," his wife interrupted. "Nicholas Cornish had a reputation even then. Leo would go on these trips for him. He was so young. The last one . . . he never came back."

"I'm sorry," Mr. Brazelli said again. "I know you've come here about Sophia, but when I heard that last name . . ."

Regret. It slithered in, coiling him in a squeezing guilt. This sweet couple looked at him just the way Maggie had so many times. Every time he thought he had a new lead. Every time he thought he was so close.

"We asked for help from the police back then. We asked Nicholas Cornish." Mrs. Brazelli gripped her husband's hand at her shoulder. "We would've hired someone like you if we could've afforded it."

Why had he come here? Why did he have to keep making things worse? "I'm afraid . . . I don't know if I can help. I'm looking for a different missing person. I've been looking into any old connections of Nicholas Cornish on a long shot." And coming here for information about his ex-wife's death had probably been Wilder's most ridiculous reach yet. Look what he'd done in the process. Raised someone else's hopes, only to let them down. Unless . . .

It was another pipe dream. Another ridiculous shot in the dark. Even so. He reached into his back pocket and took out the creased copy of the newspaper photo. There was still that fifth man he hadn't identified. He unfolded the paper and handed it to Mrs. Brazelli.

She gasped in the next moment. "That's him! That's Leo." She pointed.

The fifth man.

He told himself not to let his thoughts spin. Not to mistake that gallop in his pulse for a gut instinct that might not mean anything. But he had to ask. "When did Leo work for Cornish?"

"He started in 1987," Mr. Brazelli answered.

"And when did he go missing?"

"1990." It was Mrs. Brazelli who supplied the information this time, her gaze still glued to the photo in her hands. "September 1990."

He gripped the edge of a pew, his knuckles tight. His lungs tight. Everything tight. *It doesn't necessarily mean . . . it's probably . . . coincidence.* "Do you know the exact date? When did you see him last?"

Mrs. Brazelli finally looked up from the paper. "Yes. We recited it over and over back when the authorities were still willing to look. Before they gave up. The last time I saw my brother was on September 27, 1990. He told me he was going out of town. I called him two days later. It was his birthday, you see. We didn't talk long. He was distracted. He wouldn't tell me where he'd gone. That was the last time I talked to him. September 29."

September 29, 1990. The last day Maggie had seen Cynthia Muir alive.

———————

A clammy but cool breeze swirled in from the open window over the kitchen sink. It caught in the leaves of

Maggie's plants on the sill and ruffled the curtains.

"What are you doing all alone in here?"

Lilian turned at the sound of her brother's voice. He stood in the kitchen doorway, looking as he always did. Staid. Calm. But instead of his usual faded Levi's and dirt-stained shirt, he wore darker jeans and a thin beige sweater. Probably on account of the company filling their farmhouse. In addition to Maggie's fiancé and his family members, Sydney's father and grandfather, Tatum and Tate Carter, were joining them for dinner, too.

To think, just a year ago, half of the people talking and laughing out there in the living room right now hadn't been a part of any of their lives.

"I was just checking on the lasagna," she answered Neil.

"Ray and Philip said they're in charge of kitchen duties tonight. They wouldn't even let Maggie set the table." He ambled into the room. "You should leave the lasagna to them, otherwise they'll worry you don't trust them."

"Actually, I have to show you something." She motioned him over and opened the cupboard door under the sink, reached in for the flattened cardboard box she'd found in the garbage can, and held it up. "Do you think Maggie knows?"

"That someone threw cardboard in the trash instead of the recycling bin?"

"No." She tapped the front of the box. "It's freezer lasagna, Neil. Ray Camden is serving a premade lasagna to his future wife who's probably never so much as tasted one of those frozen individual pot pies."

Neil's chuckles filled the kitchen. "The audacity."

She slipped the box back into its hiding place. "Not that I'm personally a snob about freezer meals. I lived on Bagel Bites and frozen pizza in law school." When she turned back around, it was to see Neil leaning over the island counter, looking at her with that way he had. "What?"

"Tomorrow. I really wish you'd let one of us drive you down to Portland for the MRI."

"We've been over this. I want to drive myself."

"But—"

She held up her palm. "I'm not being put to sleep. It won't even be that long of a thing. And besides, I just feel like it would be good to have that time in the car . . . alone."

He splayed his palms on the countertop. "Hmm."

"What's that supposed to mean?"

"What do you mean what's that supposed to mean? It was just a *hmm.*"

"Your *hmms* are never just *hmms.*"

Neil straightened. "You know, sometimes I think you like arguing for arguing's sake."

"Neil, I'm a—"

"Lawyer, I know. And as for my *hmm,* all I was thinking was that I hadn't realized it before, but you probably don't get a lot of alone time. We've got a houseful most of the time."

"Same goes for you. And you've got a spouse in the mix."

"Yeah, but sometimes I can go an entire workday with only Melba and the goats and chickens to talk to. You've got a partner and a paralegal and clients." He scratched his chin. "We've all been hovering over you a little too much, haven't we?"

"To be blunt, yes. Indi keeps showing up at my bedroom door in the morning with a cup of coffee when I'm barely awake. You've asked me to let you drive me to Portland at least five times now. I love you both, but it's a little much. I hate to imagine what it's going to be like if I find out I actually have some terrible disease—" She cut off the instant she saw Neil's eyes go stormy. "Which I won't."

"You can't joke about stuff like that, Lil."

Wilder would let me. The thought caught her off guard.

"But we'll stop hovering. Or at least, I will. Can't speak for

Indi. As for alone time, if that's what you were in the kitchen for, then I won't try to coax you back into the crowd."

No, that's not what she'd come in here for. But if she admitted why she had . . .

The voicemail she'd listened to again. The call she'd almost made.

"Maybe you simply never saw him. And now you do. Or you're beginning to. So the question you have to ask yourself is, what are you going to do with that?"

Maggie's words had woven in and out of her thoughts on the whole drive home from Bar Harbor. She'd wanted to kick herself for the way she'd spoken to Wilder on Friday night. She'd gone to his houseboat intent on checking on him, yes, but at some point, it'd turned into an effort to change his mind. To make some kind of point and get through to him.

Instead, she should've said to him what he'd said to her earlier in the week. *"I'm here."*

Just two simple words that could mean the whole world when the right person said them.

Neil had turned and he padded toward the doorway now.

"Don't go yet. I have to ask you . . ." She waited until he faced her again. "May 31. Do you know what that date means to Wilder?"

He'd had one hand on his chest when he turned, but at her question, he slid it down and closed his eyes. "Oh, crap."

"What?"

Neil dropped into a chair at the kitchen table. "I'm an idiot. How did I not remember? Syd and the pie, our tradition. That's all I was thinking about that night."

She pulled out the chair beside him and sat. "Tell me."

He stretched his neck back, looking to the ceiling. "Wilder and his dad. They had this tradition. May 31 is the anniversary of the date Harry bought the boat when Wilder was like four or five. Every year they would celebrate it like it was a holiday. Harry would even pull him out of class if it fell on a school day. It's the one time a year they took the boat out on the open water. To hear Wilder talk about it, it was better than Christmas. Fishing, gorging themselves on junk food, I don't know what all. I just know that every May 31st that's rolled around since Harry died has wrecked him about as much as the funeral did."

She was the one to close her eyes now. She propped her elbows on the table, let her hair fall over her face. "I knew something was wrong Friday night. And I lectured him. I cross-examined him and then I lectured him and—"

"You didn't know. I'm the one who should've been there for him."

They sat in silence for a moment.

"Maybe I should go to Atlanta. Drag him home."

She looked over to her brother. Saw the care written in every angle of his face. "He'll come home on his own."

"I know. I just . . . I don't know if I've been there for him as much lately. I'm new at being married. I don't always know how to balance . . . I pull back from one person too far and hover over another too much—"

"Don't beat yourself up, big brother. You've been there for everyone in this family a thousand times. Wilder, too. Give yourself some grace." Could she do the same for herself, too? *You didn't know what that date meant to him.* "And like you said, you've only been married a few months. You went from thirty-four-year-old bachelor to brand-new husband so quickly. Of course it's going to take a while to find your new balance."

Just as it might take her a while to understand how to be Wilder's friend instead of . . . whatever they'd been before. Not enemies, but well, maybe antagonists.

"A new balance." Neil let out a breath. "If I tell you something, can you keep it to yourself for a few days? Why am I asking that? You didn't tell us about your health stuff for a month." He offered her a half-smile as he met her eyes. "Not an accusation. Just the truth."

"Fair enough."

"Anyway, I'm going to have to do even more balancing come this fall. And the house is going to get a little more crowded, too."

She popped out of her chair so fast, it toppled to the floor behind her. "Are you saying what I think—"

"Don't freak out. We want to wait and tell Maggie after her wedding shower. But yes. Due in October." He stood, opening his arms for the hug he obviously knew was coming.

She embraced her brother, blinked back tears that surprised her. A baby. A little niece or nephew. "Congratulations. If I'm this over the moon, I can't imagine how you and Syd are feeling."

"Guess that's probably another reason I didn't remember Wilder's boat day. I've kind of been wrapped up in this. That's what they always called it—him and Harry. Their boat day." He released Lilian and stepped back. "What are we going to do about him, Lil?"

She picked up her chair and righted it at the table. "I think . . . we just be here. Waiting for him when he gets home. And we remind him he has a place here with us."

11

She was small and swaddled, wrapped in a downy blanket and held close.

She'd been anxious only minutes ago. Upset over something she couldn't quite remember now. It'd gone fuzzy, whatever had upended her, and instead, her favorite voice whispered in her ear. "Shall I tell you a story?"

"Mm-hmm." A contented little murmur and a wispy thrill.

"It starts, as so many Gaelic stories do, with two clans and an ageless feud . . . and eventually, a family set adrift at sea. As the legend goes, the famed and ferocious Alec Muir said it was only fitting that the sea gift his family their freedom and their future."

Lilian's eyes fluttered open, but only darkness returned her gaze. Slowly, awareness trickled in. Cold metal underneath her. Circular walls hemming her in. MRI-safe headphones covering her ears and a voice droning.

Oh brother. What had made her think listening to a murder mystery podcast during her MRI was a good decision? Apparently it hadn't even been an interesting episode because she'd just dozed off, hadn't she? Dreamed about the Legend of Muir Harbor.

How long had she been in this torture device, anyway? So

far, she'd managed to ward off any claustrophobia, but much longer and she just might suffocate.

Think of happy things. Like the hazelnut coffee she'd guzzled a few hours ago. Neil's doing and he didn't like flavored coffees. Love without words. Then there'd been Maggie's hug on Lilian's way out the door. The note from Indi she'd found taped to her steering wheel before she'd left for Portland.

She'd wondered if she'd hear from Wilder this morning. He'd been the first to know about today's test, after all. He had a mind like a steel trap. He wouldn't have forgotten the date.

Yet, after the way he'd pushed her away Friday night . . .

Happy things. You're supposed to be thinking of happy things.

It was all going to be okay. She'd just keep believing that.

Forty minutes later, she was shrugging back into her thin hoodie. She'd specifically picked it out for today, assuming she'd want to be comfortable while lying immobile inside an oversized tube. But she'd forgotten she couldn't wear metal inside the thing, which ruled out a sweatshirt with a zipper.

While she slipped on her shoes, a technician explained that the images taken by the machine would be reviewed in the next week or two and she'd receive a call from Dr. Cho's office when he was ready to discuss the results.

And then it was all over. She was shown into the lobby and she was free. *Now the waiting begins. Again.*

"Lil."

Her gaze zoomed to the far end of the space, to the figure unfolding himself from a waiting room chair, his clothing a wrinkled mess and his hair as much in need of a cut as ever. But his eyes—they were different than on Friday night. They were bright and alert, trained on her.

She rushed to him. "Wilder? What are you doing here? When did you get back? Have you slept?" His gaze might be clear, but it couldn't hide the tiredness tugging at him.

"Just now or last night or, like, in general?"

Her mind fumbled to process his reply. Her last question—the one about if he'd slept—that's what he was jokingly answering. Or, well, not exactly answering. "I'm still recovering from claustrophobia. And I'm very confused right now."

"Right. No clowning around, then. No, I didn't sleep last night. My first flight got delayed, which made me miss the connecting flight, so it turned into an overnight travel mess. Then I drove straight here from PWM. But yes, I think maybe I did fall asleep for a few minutes just now."

"That only answers one question. And the least important one."

"I consider sleep very important. Especially when I don't get enough of it."

"Wilder—"

"Okay, okay. What am I doing here? Waiting for you. Check. When did I get home? I haven't yet. Refer to previous answer about coming straight here after I landed. Check. Any other questions?"

"Why?" She didn't like how tinny her voice sounded. Or how impatient she was for his answer.

Or how forcefully the truth slammed into her—that when she'd been trying to think of happy things earlier while trapped in that machine—Wilder Monroe's face had lingered in the background the whole time.

"Because I had a feeling you'd be here alone." He reached out one hand, then froze for no more than a moment. Just long enough so she could glimpse his doubt and then his resolve. He awkwardly patted her arm, at first, then slid his palm up and down. Once, and again.

The movement left a trail of warmth with each brush. "Neil offered to drive me," she said. "Everyone did. But I wanted to be alone. I wanted to be able to think. Pray a little."

His hand stilled. "So I shouldn't have come."

"No," she blurted. "I'm glad you did." And then, maybe because she was worried he'd drop his hand, maybe because she feared just how bereft she might feel when he did, she leaned toward him. At first, the hug was every bit as hesitant as the one from last week. When they'd stood out on the dock, the tips of their shoes touching and her heart trembling in confusion.

But all it took was a moment's awakening of her senses—the feel of his scratchy chin against her forehead, the solidness of his chest, the faint spice of his aftershave that had somehow survived a flight and a drive and . . . Her arms went from hanging limp at her sides to circling around him, and in that one spontaneous movement, all her reluctance was gone.

He joined in, twining his arms around her back, lifting one had to tuck her face into the crook of his neck. Had he just sighed? Or had that been her?

Everything else had gone silent and still. No front-desk receptionist talking on her phone. No revolving door whirring. All she could hear was a clock ticking or maybe her heart . . .

"I have a lot to tell you."

At the sound of his voice, her reluctance whooshed back in. Only this time, it was an unwillingness to step away.

But she had to. She had to because this was *Wilder*. Because so much bewilderment was swirling to life inside her that if she didn't move away from him, she might combust. Because she couldn't just stand here forever in this waiting room wrapped in a man's arms who, up until a few weeks ago, had been the bane of her existence.

Wilder Monroe, what are you doing to me?

She gulped and stepped back.

He dropped his arms.

"Y-you have a lot to tell me?" Good grief, she sounded like she'd just swallowed a cloud, her voice a cottony rasp.

"I do. I might have a new lead on the case. Or I don't know, it might be a different case altogether. Another missing person. Could all be a coincidence, but my gut says it's not and . . . but no, that's not the main thing. I need to apologize for Friday—"

She was already shaking her head. "You already did. And it's okay. Neil told me—"

"It's not okay. You were being sweet and nice, coming to the boat to check on me like that, and I bit your head off and sent you away. I'm really sorry about that."

Despite her quivering nerves, she managed a partial smile. "I'd accept your apology but I'm stuck on that spot where you called me sweet and nice."

He lifted his shoulders. "If the shoe fits." He gazed down at her. "How are you? How was the MRI?"

"It was fine. I fell asleep for part of it. Dreamed about Maggie telling me The Legend of Muir Harbor, if you can believe it."

Or, well, no, she wasn't so sure that'd been Maggie's voice in her dream. But it hadn't been *him* either. The man without a face. It'd been a woman's voice, one she didn't know now. But she'd known it in the dream.

It was just a dream.

Wilder chuckled. "I can believe it. We are talking about the girl who used to go treasure hunting at a hilltop chapel." He reached his hand out to tuck a strand of her hair behind her ear and didn't give her any time at all to catch her breath before he spoke again. "Got plans for the rest of the day?"

"I'm really struggling to reconcile this Lilian Muir—the one who'd take an entire Tuesday off work for a medical test that only took an hour—with the workaholic Lilian Muir I've known all these years."

Lilian didn't give him any indication she'd heard him.

So Wilder contented himself with watching her as she watched the shoreline slowly fade from view. They stood close enough to the edge of the yacht's lower deck that a haze of sea spray misted their cheeks, and the afternoon breeze wreaked havoc with Lilian's hair. It fluttered around her face, but she didn't bother pushing it away, clearly entirely enthralled with the eddies of blue and turquoise rippling into the distance.

Breathtaking.

Not the horizon, but her. Lilian. Just a week ago, he would've berated himself for the thought. Come up with a whole list of reasons why he had no business drinking in the sight of her with anything other than complete objectivity.

Objectively, obviously, she was a beautiful woman.

But subjectively, palpably, undeniably . . . she was a whole different kind of beautiful to him. It wasn't just the sapphire eyes and heart-melting smile and figure he'd lately learned fit absolutely perfectly against him. It was her spark of intelligence and wit and humor that ignited his awareness. Her depth of thought but also emotion. She tried to keep a tight lid on the latter, he knew, but every once in a while, she let the lid slide.

Like when she'd pressed against him in the waiting room of the medical center and suddenly he could hear everything she didn't say. *I'm surprised at how much I missed you. I'm a little scared at how happy I am to see you.*

He'd felt the echoes of his own thoughts in those heady seconds when his arms were around her.

"It's all because of Mariana."

He blinked and a small cough escaped. "Oh, uh, what?"

Lilian leaned with her hip against the railing, a little smile on her lips that convinced him she'd caught him staring and inexplicably didn't mind. "Normally I would've rushed back to the office, but Mariana's already so totally at home and on top of things. I even took off a little early yesterday to go wedding dress shopping with Maggie and I didn't feel a smidge of guilt. You'd think with all the reading and paperwork the job entails, it might be difficult for her, but she makes it work. She's got all these devices and this Braille printer and . . . well, I guess you were there when she was unpacking her stuff. I have a small fear that she's so good at the job, she'll eventually replace me."

He had the notion to tell Lilian she was irreplaceable. But that would be going too far, wouldn't it? He could try to say it with a tease in his voice like usual, but what if it came out dripping with intensity instead? The last thing he wanted to do was scare her off. Sure, she'd been the one to initiate that embrace back at the medical center in Portland, but she'd also been the first one to pull away.

They were in completely foreign territory here, and though he'd finally stopped denying his own frisson of shifting feelings for her, he had no idea if she was in the same place.

So he held his tongue and turned, leaning his back against the edge and hooking his arms through the railing. "So what do you think? Will this do? I mean, I hope it does, because the invitations have been printed."

"Will it *do*? Wilder, this thing is incredible."

They'd already taken a tour of the whole ship, including the sprawling interior room they'd fill with chairs for the wedding ceremony, then transform into a ballroom for the reception. They'd set up stations serving hors d'oeuvres on the upper and lower decks, where guests could mingle in between.

The yacht had been docked at the marina throughout their

tour, and Wilder hadn't expected his father's friend to actually offer to take them out on the ocean this afternoon. But he'd been thrilled when Lilian agreed. It was a chance to spend a little more time with her.

But also an opportunity to shake off the seriousness of the conversation that had filled their drive to the marina. They'd initially had to drive separately since they both had cars in Portland. So they'd gone back to Muir Harbor first, where Lilian had left her car at the farm and then hopped into his. Then on the half-hour trip down the coast to the marina where Walter Wallace docked his yacht, he'd filled her in on his time in Atlanta, ending with his stupefying visit to Brazelli's Funeral Parlor.

"Honestly, I'm not even sure what possessed me to go there. It's like this search is a tree and Cynthia's disappearance is the trunk, and the more the investigation drags on, the farther and farther out on the branches I go until . . . I'm standing on the ground holding a twig, not even knowing if it's from the right tree."

Lilian had chuckled at that. *"I didn't know you were so good at metaphors. So the funeral home's the twig?"*

"Yeah. And I have no idea if this Leo's disappearance is at all tied to Diana and Cynthia or not. But he worked for Cornish. He disappeared the same weekend Diana left Atlanta and came to Muir Harbor. So I have to at least look into it."

He could find out what kind of car the man used to drive and see if the tire tracks matched any of those at the scene of Diana's accident, for one thing. Call around to local hotels and lodgings to see if he could place the man in Muir Harbor that weekend. Of course there was confidentiality, but he could usually find his way around that. He'd already asked the Brazellis if they knew the name Diana Muir. They didn't. But that didn't mean Mrs. Brazelli's brother hadn't had some connection to her. There was every chance they could've met through Nicholas.

"My biggest question is whether to tell Maggie. I'm so tired of telling her I have leads and then the leads not panning out. Maybe this time I just follow the trail and fill her in later if it actually goes anywhere."

"She's not breakable, Wilder. You don't have to protect her."

Maybe not. But he didn't have to keep disappointing her either.

"You're still thinking about Atlanta."

He looked over to Lilian now.

"We're on this amazing boat in the ocean, there's not a cloud in the sky, I didn't pass out during my MRI, and you're somehow still standing after sleeping for all of ten minutes in the past twenty-four hours—"

"Nah, I'm sure I squeezed a good twenty in."

"I just think all of that put together is total justification for letting yourself relax. Even if only for an hour or two."

How could she think he wasn't enjoying himself? "For the record, I am having a splendid time right now."

"Those three lines in your forehead a second ago would say otherwise."

"Fine. No more thoughts about Atlanta." Twenty-eight, almost twenty-nine years this case had stretched. It could wait another day. He would think about what he'd learned in Atlanta later. Decide whether to tell Maggie later. "What do you want to talk about, Miss Muir?"

She studied him for a moment. "How'd your dad become a boat guy?"

Her hair was still whipping in the wind. She'd left her hoodie in the car. Were those goosebumps on her arms?

"We should move inside. You're getting chilly."

"You're getting evasive."

He lifted her elbow from the railing and tugged her toward the door that led into a sheltered seating area. "My dad's dad worked on a lobster boat. Spent his whole life on the water, casting nets. Dad used to joke he came out of the womb with his sea legs already intact."

He led her toward a bench along an observation window and they sat.

"Dad also joked that he probably would've followed in my grandfather's footsteps if he didn't absolutely hate the smell of lobster." He could almost hear Dad's laugh now. "Anyway, he went a different route, but never lost his love for the water."

Dad had always said it was falling in love with Wilder's mother that had pulled him away from the Bureau. But maybe it'd been the seaside, too.

"You really miss him."

Lilian's soft words didn't require an answer, so he looked down. When had he knotted his hands together in his lap?

"I was at the funeral, but I don't think I ever said how sorry I was for your loss. How sorry I am. I-I wish . . . I wish I'd been kinder to you when you were going through such grief."

He needed to say something. Let her off the hook. Tell her there'd been days in the last three years when her caustic comments had been the only thing to make him smile. But his voice didn't want to work.

"Your dad was so nice to me that day I came to your boat," she went on. "When I tried to prove to him that I was the missing Cynthia Muir, he sat there so patiently and attentively. It's like he knew how fragile my naïve emotions were and took so much care to handle them tenderly."

"And then I came along swinging a figurative bat. I'm sorry, Lil."

Suddenly, her fingers were closing around one of his hands. "That's not why I brought it up."

"It's why you loathed me for decades, though."

"*Loathed* is a little strong." She held his palm between both of hers, one of her thumbs tracing his knuckles.

Surely it was the surprise of it that loosened something inside him, letting words he never meant to say tumble free. "It's not just the grief." He could feel her questioning gaze without even looking at her. "That's not all of it. You know how my dad died?" One of her hands slid away, but he gripped the one that remained.

"A reaction to one of his leukemia medications, wasn't it?"

"Not one. He was on multiple medications and they all had different dosages. The wrong mix of the wrong dosages . . ." He finally looked over at her, holding her gaze. "He left me a letter, Lil."

She didn't say anything but her fingers laced through his.

"I didn't find it until after the funeral." He closed his eyes. Oh Lord, he'd already been such a wreck that day. He'd felt like a corpse himself, his broken soul entirely disconnected from his body as he watched Dad's coffin lower into the gravesite.

After finally escaping from a luncheon where he couldn't taste a thing, he'd made his first and, to this day, only visit to a liquor store, then hightailed it to the boat.

And that's when he'd found it. He hadn't slept on the boat since discovering Dad's body, so until then he hadn't seen the edge of the envelope peeking out from under Dad's mattress.

Suddenly, he was on his feet, needing space, needing this story over with, out of him. "He was a smart guy, Lil. Yes, it was a lot of medications to keep track of, but his mind was in perfect working order. There was no reason for him to mess up those dosages."

"Wilder, what are you saying?"

"I'm saying he left me a letter. Nicest thing I've ever read in my life, but there's a reason he wrote it."

"Because he loved you." She stood and moved toward him. "Because his prognosis was terminal and—"

"He always said how hard it was watching my mother

waste away. How much he wanted to remember her before the cancer, not the way she was in the end. He said watching her die was almost worse than missing her after she was gone. He wouldn't have wanted me to experience the same thing." His breathing had gone tight and rapid, his lungs heaving with each painful sentence. "So it's not just the grief. It's the worst gut instinct I've ever had. It's wondering if he took matters into his own hands and . . ."

Why was he shaking now? He wasn't cold.

"It's not just the grief," he said again. "It's knowing I'm never really going to know—" His voice didn't just crack then, it broke.

All of him broke. Hot tears and pain as deep as the sea, rising up to drown him even as Lilian wove her arms around him.

"It's okay, Wilder. I'm here. I'm here."

<hr>

Son,

I'm writing this note by the light of the alarm clock you make fun of me for still using. Yes, I know I could use my phone instead, but admit it, you'd miss making fun of my alarm clock that looks straight out of the 70s. (True story: It IS out of the 70s.)

I think if you asked a lot of men my age how they'd feel about sharing a tiny bedroom with their grown son, one with only two small bunks and barely any room to maneuver, they'd recoil. But not me. You've turned out to be a darn good roommate, Wilder. I could do without the snoring, but since I'm fairly certain you have to put up with the same thing, I won't heckle you for it.

I've tried to be the kind of father who shows his love in lots of different ways. I've always felt like it was important to say how much I love you rather than solely depending on what comes a little more naturally to me—expressing what I feel through actions instead of words. I hope I've said it enough. But just in case I haven't, or in case you might appreciate having it in writing (we both know the value of written evidence!), let me say it here:

I love you, son.

I'm proud of you. I'm proud of the man you've become.

Being your father has been the greatest honor of my life.

I love you, Wilder John, and I need you to hold on to that in the days to come. We do not grieve as those who have no hope. I forgot that from time to time after your mother died. But God would always find some way to remind me—and more often than not, He'd use you. My brilliant, bold, wild son.

You are loved beyond comprehension—by your

earthly father and another. Hold on to that.
Love, Dad

Lilian was weeping by the time she finished the letter, the words blurring in front of her as she let the frayed single page fall into her lap.

Oh, Wilder.

He'd left her alone with the note in his living room, the sound of his shower running reaching through the wall behind her.

Never could she have pictured Wilder Monroe so shattered as how she'd seen him back on the yacht. He'd cried like a child in her arms, but silently, his body shaking as she held on and begged God to tell her what to do or what to say. There had to be some way to comfort him.

But maybe this is it, she'd finally thought. Just being there. Just holding on.

To a man she'd never thought would need her. To one she never could've imagined being needed by.

She brushed her hands over her cheeks, used the edge of her hoodie to wipe her tears, then picked up the letter Harry Monroe had written and read it once more.

She knew now what Wilder thought this letter was. Or, at least, what he suspected. Not just a father expressing his love, but a man saying a purposeful goodbye. One who hadn't accidentally messed up his medications but . . .

She shook her head. *No, it can't be that.* It wasn't as if this letter spelled anything out. That is, nothing more than Harry Monroe's deep, abiding affection for his son. *Your gut is wrong this time, Wilder.*

Oh, how she hoped it was. But that was the part that was killing Wilder, wasn't it? Hope wasn't an answer to the *what-if* that had rooted itself in his mind and refused to let go. Wilder was a detective. A man committed to evidence, to facts.

But there was no trail to follow this time.

She heard the squeak of the faucet's turn in the bathroom and, a second later, the sound of the water stilled. Poor Wilder had been so embarrassed earlier. It was written there right alongside the exhaustion evident in every inch of his face. He'd tried to make a joke, said something about how he owed her dinner after a display like that.

But she'd convinced him to come here instead. *"You need to sleep, Wilder. In fact, I'll drive. The only question is whether you want to sleep at the boat or at our house."*

Any other day and she knew he would've laughed. Said something about how Lilian Muir had just issued an invitation to sleep at the farm after years of calling him a squatter and asked if an alien had taken over her body.

But instead, all he did was hand her his keys. *"The boat."*

She'd only walked with him down the dock to make sure he didn't fall asleep on his feet. He'd told her to come inside, though, and after she followed, he'd disappeared into his bedroom, reappearing a moment later with the letter.

Then he'd turned without a word and eventually she'd heard the shower running.

Should she leave now? Or stick around a little longer? Make him something to eat? *He needs sleep more than food.* Right, then there was no reason for her to be here.

She stood, folding his letter, intending only to slip it under his bedroom door, maybe give a soft knock and let him know she was leaving. Except, wait, she didn't have her car.

Okay, then. She pulled out her phone, opened her contacts, and tapped on her sister's name.

"Lil! Where are you?" Guess they were skipping the greeting. She opened her mouth, but Indi raced on first. "You should be here. We're just putting supper on the table. You owe us all an MRI report."

She moved away from Wilder's bedroom door, just in case he'd already flopped into his bed. She hoped he had. "I texted you all. Didn't you see it?"

"Yeah, but you didn't give details."

"I was cloistered in a metal tube. It was cold. There's not much more to report."

"How about where you've been all day?"

"Uh, I'm with Wilder. I was wondering if you could—" Her words cut off as her attention hooked on the window across from the little kitchenette and its view of the harbor front, the lot where they'd left Wilder's Jeep.

"If I could what?"

Another vehicle was parked right next to the Jeep. Headlights on. Pointed right at the houseboat.

Nothing weird about that. There were other boats moored at the harbor, after all. Which meant there was no reason at all to leave Wilder's letter on the table, move to the door and step up to the deck, train her gaze. But she did it anyway.

"Lil—?"

The headlights blinked off.

It's nothing. It's just a car . . .

"Hey, never mind, Indi. I'll talk to you later, okay?"

"But—"

She tapped out of the call and moved toward the dock.

Instantly, the vehicle's engine rumbled to life, and seconds later, it was speeding away from the harbor.

Heart thudding, she reversed course, crossed the deck, and let herself back inside. This was ridiculous. It was just another car. It could be anything, anyone.

But someone had broken into Wilder's boat last week. And after everything he'd told her about what he'd learned in Atlanta, well, caution was a good thing, wasn't it?

She walked to Wilder's bedroom door and knocked. "Hey, Wild?"

No reply.

She nudged the door an inch. "I hope you're not in there wearing only a towel or anything," she said softly. "I'm coming in."

Oh, she was glad she'd whispered. The man was sprawled on top of his bed, his long limbs jutting in every direction, his face smashed into a pillow. Humid warmth seeped from the bathroom, and for a moment, she just stood there, her heart a puddle of confusion. She could smile at the sight of him passed out or start crying all over again at the memory of his sorrow.

One thing she knew—no way was she waking him up just to tell him about a set of headlights that probably meant nothing. Instead, she padded to the side of his bed and lifted a comforter that was hanging off. She spread it over him.

Then did something she knew she'd have no explanation for if he happened to wake up and find her here. She perched on the edge of the mattress beside him, reached one hand to touch his damp hair.

And whispered, "You really need a haircut, Wilder Monroe."

12

*O*nly one coherent thought slipped past the fuzziness of sleep, nearly lost to a haze of cozy warmth and pure contentment.

Someone must've bought a different brand of laundry detergent.

Lilian curled into the sheet tucked around her, her pillow a perfect cushion, and tried to carve a mental trail through her drowsy comfort. When had she last done her laundry? She didn't remember paying any attention to the detergent. Had she even washed her bedsheets last week? Why did they smell so . . .

She forced her eyes open. Or, well, one eye. It was too bright to keep them both open with sunlight pouring through the window and heating over her. Had she forgotten to close her curtains last night?

She rolled onto her back, confusion cresting over her in one small wave after another. Navy blue sheets. Hers were white. The light was coming from the right, beside the bed instead of across the room and . . .

She lurched upward with a gasp.

Not my bed. Not my room.

Her bedroom didn't have that slight sway, and oh, why,

why was she in Wilder Monroe's houseboat? In his bed? Her heart slammed against her chest as she flung a sheet and comforter away and looked down. Yesterday's leggings and loose tee, minus the hoodie.

She squeezed her eyes closed once more. *Think. Last night.* She'd wanted to tell Wilder about that vehicle she'd seen but then she'd found him passed out and she'd sat down on the mattress beside him and . . .

"There's an arm movement that's supposed to go with that."

She gasped again, only this time it came out as a squeal and was accompanied by a jerk that caused the back of her skull to bump against the headboard. Her gaze reeled to the open bathroom door, where Wilder leaned against its frame, a toothbrush hanging from the side of his mouth.

And no shirt.

Well, it'd been a nice life for the most part. But all good things came to an end. And this was the end of the road for her. She was going to expire from mortification right here in this bed that definitely wasn't her own.

Wilder lifted his arms and lined them up in front of his chest genie-style. "Like this."

"W-what?" she croaked.

"A second ago. You closed your eyes so forcefully you looked like the blond-haired lady from *I Dream of Jeannie.* Trying to make breakfast appear or something?"

"You watch *I Dream of Jeannie?*" That was the question she chose to ask right now? Not, for instance, what she was doing here, or what time it was, or why, for goodness' sake, he wasn't fully dressed.

"Dad liked Nick at Nite reruns. I'm more of a *Bewitched* man myself, but what can you do?" He went back to brushing his teeth and turned away.

She clambered from the bed, or tried to. But she was more

tangled in Wilder's bedsheets than she'd realized and in her hurry to flee the scene, she only toppled to the floor.

The thump brought Wilder back to the bathroom door and with a laugh, he rushed over to her. "Guess you don't have your sea legs yet." Before she knew what was happening, his palms were on her arms and he was lifting her to her feet.

And oh no—*oh no*—that was bare skin way too close to her face.

She wrenched away from the man, but only ended up tumbling backward, into the bed she'd just been trying to escape.

"Uh, is everything okay?"

Good grief, he looked genuinely confused. "Why aren't you wearing a shirt?!"

He glanced down. And instead of bumbling or blushing or even having the decency to look just the tiniest bit chagrined, when he lifted his head back up, a grin not even the Cheshire cat could pull off was spreading over his face. "Why, Lil? Is this making you uncomfortable?" He took a step toward the bed and she scrambled backward. "Well, maybe try imagining for a moment how uncomfortable I might've felt when I woke up to discover I wasn't alone in my bed. Put yourself in my shoes for a moment—"

"They'd never fit. You have Sasquatch feet." Finally. She'd gotten a witty rejoinder in.

Which he didn't even bother to acknowledge. "Consider, if you will, how disorienting it might be for a man to find a woman in his bed with no memory of how she got there. It has a certain effect."

"It doesn't explain your lack of shirt!"

"I have as much memory of taking it off as I do you climbing in bed with me!"

"Gross. Don't say it like that. I did not—"

"I sleep warm, okay? And there was an extra body in the bed. I must've taken it off in the middle of the night."

"Well, find it," she hissed through gritted teeth, "and put it back on."

"You are sitting on it." He matched her rhythm and tone perfectly.

With a sound somewhere in between a snarl and a shriek, she pulled it out from underneath her and sent it flying at him.

He caught it with one hand. "You are definitely not a morning person."

Why wasn't she moving just now? She should be attempting to make it off this stupid bed, preferably without crashing this time, and hurrying out of here.

"I've got coffee perc-ing, by the way." Wilder stuck his arms inside his shirt to turn it the right side out. "It's probably about done so—"

The sound of the houseboat's front door flying open jutted in and then, "Wilder, I'm so sorry to barge in but apparently you didn't hear me knock and we can't find . . ."

Oh, please God, no.

Indi appeared just outside the bedroom door. Just in time to see Wilder's arms lifted over his head, his shirt only halfway pulled on.

"Lilian," Indi finished weakly, looking from Lilian on the bed to Wilder and back to Lilian again. "Um? Okay?" Her voice had gone high-pitched. "I mean . . . okay. That answers that question."

"Indi, this is not what it looks like." Lilian climbed from the bed again. No falling to the floor this time. Small mercies.

"Well, it looks like you spent the night here." Indi's tone went up another notch. "But who am I to make assumptions?"

Okay, so maybe it was exactly what it looked like. But in an incredibly innocent, inadvertent, oh-so-accidental way.

Wilder cleared his throat. "If it helps, I was in the process of putting my shirt *on* not taking it off when you walked in."

Lilian threw a glare to Wilder. "How does that help?"

"Listen, we can talk about this later," Indi said. "Or never talk about it. I'll just pretend I never saw anything—"

"Because you didn't," Lilian and Wilder said at precisely the same time. Which made Lilian feel the need to frown at Wilder all over again.

To which he responded, of course, with another catlike grin.

"We've been trying to get ahold of you, Lil. The care center called. Peyton's awake."

Lilian's gaze whipped to her sister. "He is?"

"Technically, I'm not even sure they were supposed to call us. We're not family. But one of the nurses knows Maggie goes there regularly so . . ."

Wilder had burst into movement while Indi was still talking. He pulled open a dresser drawer and plucked out a pair of jeans, then closed himself into the bathroom.

Indi immediately turned on Lilian. "So, yeah, forget what I said about never talking about what I saw, and don't say I didn't see anything because I definitely did. And it included abs."

"Not now, Indi." Preferably not ever. She looked around the room. Hoodie, where was her hoodie? "Peyton's awake as in *awake*? Is he talking?"

"I don't know exactly, but I was thinking you might want to—"

The bathroom door flung back open and Wilder hiked out, grabbing his wallet off the dresser and stuffing it in his back pocket. "I'll go check out what's happening. There's no reason for anyone else to go."

He slipped past Indi and out of the bedroom.

Oh no, you don't. She shot through the doorway after him. "I don't think so, Monroe. I'm coming with you."

He spun too quickly for her to react, taking her by the shoulders before she knew what'd happened. "I'd really feel better if you didn't. Let's not forget what happened the last time the guy was around a Muir sister."

"He's just coming out of a coma, for Pete's sake. No one's going to be in any danger."

"I probably won't even be able to see him. There's no need for everyone to rush there."

"Then why are you rushing there?"

"Lilian."

"Don't *Lilian* me." She shook free of his hold.

So instead, his hands lifted to her cheeks, cupping her face as her eyes went wide. "You just woke up. You're still wearing yesterday's clothes. It's a weekday, and you need to get to the office. Drink some of my coffee. Get a ride home from Indi. Take a shower and brush your teeth. I'll call you later." He rotated and the next moment, he was on his way out the door.

"You're so condescending sometimes, Wilder Monroe," she shouted after him.

He let the door fall closed behind him, leaving her to stand there, fighting the ridiculous urge to stomp her foot.

Why fight it, though? She stamped one foot and then the other, and then remembered her sister. She whirled around to see Indi with her eyebrows raised and her hands on her hips.

"And I thought that nurse's phone call was going to be my biggest shock of the day."

There were some things a man just couldn't shake off.

And waking up at the crack of dawn to Lilian Muir's arm

slung over his chest and her face pressed into his bicep ranked pretty high up on his list of unshakable experiences.

He really shouldn't have laughed at the adorable mix of shock and bewilderment on her face when she'd jolted up from underneath his sheets. Hadn't he felt the same double-edged thunderbolt when he'd realized that not only was someone in bed with him but just who that someone was?

Hadn't he lain there with his eyes bugging and his lungs no match at all for the sudden uptick in his breathing? He should win some kind of medal for eventually accepting the situation, remaining so still for what felt like hours while his pounding heart battered his rib cage.

Accepting, my eye. You were downright basking in it.

The only reason he'd finally carefully removed her arm and slid from the bed was the very real fear that she'd have a heart attack if she woke up to find herself curled against him. Pure reluctant compassion.

The elevator dinged and he wrenched his mind free of the memory. Or as free as he could manage considering he was convinced he could still smell the faint citrus of Lilian's perfume. He emerged onto the second floor of the care center and followed the corridor to the long-term wing, rounding a corner in time to see Chief Holloway speaking with a doctor.

"I can assure you, Chief, we have a very good security system in place. Considering that and the patient's current condition—"

"The patient," the police chief cut in, "has been accused of attempted murder. Now that he's awake, I'd feel better about having a guard outside his door 24-7."

"So would I." Wilder inserted himself into the conversation, earning himself only the slightest of greetings from Chief Holloway, thinly veiled exasperation in the man's expression.

For his part, the doctor appeared ready to be done with this discussion. "If that's what you think is best."

Wilder only barely managed to keep himself from echoing Chief Holloway's "I do." Instead, he turned to the doctor. "Any chance I could speak with Cornish?"

The doctor gave an adamant head shake. "He's only just woken up. He's disoriented and likely incredibly anxious, and even if he was capable of fully taking in anything you said, he wouldn't be able to answer. He's got a tube running down his throat and he hasn't used his voice in five months."

"But—"

"I know, you both have questions. But you're just going to have to wait."

Wilder tried to look past the man, get a glimpse into the room where Peyton was located, but the doctor stepped in front of the door and held his hand out. "You'll wait and you won't cause a scene." With that, he slipped into the room.

Wilder let out a sigh and rubbed his hand over his scruffy chin. "Guess he told us."

"What are you doing here, Monroe?"

He dragged himself into position to face Chief Holloway. "Same thing as you, I expect."

"Peyton Cornish stopped being your concern as soon as a police report was filed. Don't worry, we're not going to let him off the hook."

"I know that, but considering he's the one person we know for a fact has a connection to the old Muir case, I'm hopeful you'll let me talk to him, too. Plus, there's more at play. There's an ongoing FBI investigation." He needed to call Agent Franzen. The man had said to get in touch if Peyton woke up. "They're going to want to see Peyton. His father—"

"What the heck are you talking about, son?"

Son. It was a jolt. Like sand thrown in his face.

Of course, at some point while he'd been lying in bed this

morning, he'd remembered what'd happened the night before. His complete loss of composure, breaking down on the yacht. Like, seriously breaking down in a way he hadn't since the day he'd found the letter in the first place.

At least this time he hadn't gone and added alcohol on top of his emotional distress.

But then, Lilian's presence while he'd lost all semblance of dignity had been an intoxication all its own. She'd been . . . amazing, really. Water for a parched soul. Both soothing and strong in a way he couldn't quite come to grips with.

It'd be a lie to say there wasn't a piece of him embarrassed at the thought of her seeing him like that. But there was another piece that was strangely glad. He'd felt a similar gratitude when Maggie had found him the morning after Dad's funeral, heartbroken and hungover. She'd saved him that day.

But apparently he still needed saving. Three years he'd kept his fears about the truth of Dad's death locked inside and he wasn't sure he'd ever been fully aware of the slow erosion it'd caused. Or maybe he was perfectly aware and he'd simply never wanted to face it. It was easier to bury himself in a different mystery.

Until Lilian. Until she'd burrowed past his defenses and tugged on his secrets.

The truth of it was, this gratitude wasn't anything like what he'd felt toward Maggie, after all. Because there were myriad other accompanying emotions, not to mention a heady, heartfelt longing attached this time. And he was so far past trying to pretend away its existence, he couldn't think of one good reason why he had in the first place.

So why was he standing here right now? What was he even doing?

Peyton Cornish wasn't going anywhere. He could call Franzen later. The doctor wasn't about to let him in the room and he wasn't in the mood for Chief Holloway's exasperation and—

Ding.

From around the corner and down the hall, he heard the elevator, and the familiar flicker he knew so well, the perfect gut instinct at the perfect time, took hold.

He was already moving down the corridor, walking backward at first, then with a grin he couldn't hope to contain, twisting to face away from the police chief, rounding the corner and knowing exactly who he'd see . . .

God bless his infernal gut instinct.

Lilian had only made it a few feet from the elevator when Wilder appeared around the corner.

"Don't you dare try to reprimand me for showing up here, Wilder. I followed every single one of your stupid instructions even though you had no right to boss me around." She held up a metal travel mug. "I drank your coffee. I went home and took a shower and brushed my teeth, and yes, I'll go into the office eventually, but for now I have as much right to be here as you."

He reached for her hand and towed her back the way she'd come. She was still trying to catch her breath when he hit the elevator button.

"What the—"

"You drive me crazy, Lilian Muir."

The elevator door opened. "That's my line."

He pulled her into the elevator and instead of waiting for the door to close on its own, he slapped the button behind her to force it closed.

"Sheesh, why are you in such a hurry? And why are you

leaving already? What'd the doctor say? Did you see Peyton or—"

The moment he closed the distance between them, she lost her train of thought. She'd been in the middle of an interrogation, hadn't she? A whole list of questions. But he disarmed her in one fluent move. "Wilder, what are you . . . ?"

She took a step back, but there was nowhere to go, not with the elevator wall bumping into her from behind.

"Why'd you stay last night, Lil?"

"Why are you standing so close?" He was using up all the air in this tiny space. And she . . . needed someone to remind her how to breathe.

"Why'd you stay?" he asked again, moving another step closer. Close enough he could splay one palm over her waist while the other slid up the wall beside her.

"I didn't mean to fall asleep." Why was he touching her? Why was *she* touching him? Certainly her right hand, the one not holding a travel mug and dangling uselessly at her side, had entirely disconnected from her brain, traded common sense for compulsion as it wandered to his chest. *What am I doing?* "I just wanted to make sure you were okay. I didn't intend to . . ."

Her eyes fluttered to a close as she felt the whisper of his lips against her cheek.

And she simply had nothing left. No words to finish her sentence. No arguments left to make. Not a single coherent thought.

Save the one turning her into a shuddering mess of anticipation: Wilder Monroe was going to kiss her. And she was absolutely going to let him.

He dipped his head just a little lower, drew her just a little closer.

Ding.

Her breath caught in her throat at the sudden loss of his warmth, his face pulling away, the hand at her waist dropping.

Open your eyes.

A throat cleared. Not Wilder's. Not hers.

She opened her eyes.

And for the second time this morning, wanted to sink into the nearest hole and disappear. Neil stood just outside the now-open elevator door, his eyes every bit as narrow as Maggie's were wide beside him.

13

*H*e was teetering on a tightrope, holding his breath while the world went quiet around him, knowing any moment his balance would give and he'd find himself falling.

The only question was which direction.

Ignore their audience and do exactly what he'd pulled Lilian into this elevator to do? Or face the fact that he'd just put both of them in an incredibly awkward position?

And that Neil was looking at him right now as if he might want to deck him for the first time in their twenty-year friendship.

He could feel his Adam's apple virtually leap out of his throat as his gaze drifted back to Lilian. He'd been so focused a minute ago on her soft skin and her ready lips, the feeling of her leaning into him, that he hadn't noticed the tips of her hair were damp. Or that apparently she hadn't done whatever she normally did to style it, because instead of reaching to her shoulders in one silky, straight sheet, it fell in unruly twirls.

Time stretched but somehow he was aware that only a second had passed. Maybe two.

When no one stepped on or off the elevator, its doors

began to close, and he let out a relieved breath. Option A, then. Kiss Lilian Muir senseless.

But she was too fast, scurrying from her spot between him and the wall, throwing out one palm to keep the door from closing. "Morning." Her voice was too bright.

And delectably breathy. At least he knew he wasn't the only one who'd been affected by what had almost happened. He stepped out of the elevator behind her, caught between delight and regret and . . .

Neil cleared his throat again.

And just a little trepidation.

But not enough to keep him from grinning at the sight of Lilian's flushed cheeks.

"I have to get to the office." Her tone was still hilariously perky. "Uh, if anything happens with Peyton, someone call me, okay?" And then she was all but running for the exit.

Wilder made to go after her, but Neil intercepted him. "For the sake of my blood pressure, I'm gonna need you to get that look off your face."

"Oh, for pity's sake, Neil." Maggie rolled her eyes from behind her son.

Wilder clamped his palm on Neil's shoulder. "I've never before seen you lose your temper, old friend. Usually I'm all for new experiences, but I need to catch your sister."

And say or do what exactly, he didn't know. But it didn't stop him from angling around Neil and striding toward the door Lilian had just disappeared through. He pushed his way outside, the vivid morning sun momentarily blinding him before he caught sight of her already in the driver's seat of her car, backing out of a parking spot.

Sheesh, the woman really had gone into an all-out sprint. "Lil," he called, knowing there was no way she'd hear him. And that even if she did, she probably wouldn't stop. A rushing wind blew through the parking lot, bending the spindly trees planted in a tidy row along its edge.

Shoot. Had he just made some terrible tactical misstep? Had whisking her into that elevator and putting every scrap of his desire on unmistakable display been a blunder?

She wanted to kiss you every bit as much as you were desperate to kiss her. Her grip on his shirt had signaled as much.

And, well, the fact that she hadn't slapped his face or pushed him away or even so much as taken a breath in the moment right before that cursed elevator door ruined everything.

Still. He probably could've picked a better time. Maybe a different location.

"She's my sister, you idiot."

Reluctantly, he turned to face his best friend's glower. "She's a thirty-year-old woman who knows her own mind and doesn't need her big brother protecting her." *Especially from me.*

Neil skulked a few steps closer. "So what exactly is happening here? Are you two dating now? Or did you just skip right to manhandling her?"

"I was not manhandling—"

"Wait, was she with *you* last night? Is that why we couldn't find her?"

"Neil, I need you to calm down and process your thoughts like a rational human being. And when you do, I think you'll realize neither I nor your sister owe you any kind of explanation of our relationship."

"So there is a *relationship.*"

"Define relationship."

Neil crossed his arms. "I'd rather not. I don't want to picture the various connotations."

"Fine, then. Conversation over." He started toward the door once more. He needed to find out if Peyton was *awake-*

awake before he called Franzen. But he didn't make it two steps before turning back to face his friend. "What's so wrong about it, though? The idea of Lilian and me? Do you think I'm a horrible person or something?"

Neil dropped his arms. "Of course not."

"Because in two decades of friendship, I kinda thought maybe you respected me at least a little."

"Obviously I do."

"So what's your problem, then?"

Neil tipped his head to the sky in exasperation. "It's just not what I expected to see when that elevator door opened. You should've seen her all weekend, Wilder. After you took off to Atlanta . . . she was worried about you."

"I know. The way I left was stupid—"

"It was." There was finally something close to his usual calm settling into Neil's expression. "But also . . . understandable. I'm sorry I didn't remember the date."

"It's okay. I didn't at first, either." He felt the breeze comb through his hair. "You know I'd never intentionally hurt her, right?"

Neil eyed him for a moment. "She comes off confident and unflagging, but she's got the softest heart of anyone in this family."

And that was saying a lot. "I know that." After last night, he really knew it. What he'd told her on the yacht, the way he'd broken down . . . how she'd kept saying, *"I'm here. I'm here."*

"She doesn't let people in easily."

"Trust me, I know that, too."

Neil sighed. "And I really, *really* thought she disliked you."

"Dislikes how much she likes me, absolutely." At his friend's groan, he wiped his smile off his face. "Sorry. Too soon. Would it make you feel better to take a swing at me?"

"No. I've got too much to do today to spend time icing my hand." Neil turned back to the building. "Speaking of which,

I'm not even sure why Maggie and I came here. There's nothing for us to do. But hearing Peyton's awake . . . it felt significant."

Because it was. "If you need to get back to the farm, I can give Maggie a ride home."

"Yeah?"

He nodded and was relieved to see the gratitude in Neil's eyes. Back to normal, then. He hoped.

Except nothing was normal because he'd almost kissed Lilian Muir only minutes ago. And that felt about a thousand times more significant than Peyton Cornish waking up from a coma.

Neil called to him just as he was about to reenter the care center. He turned.

"It was just the surprise of it." Standing at the spot where the pathway met the parking lot, Neil lifted his hand to shield his eyes from the sun. "I actually think you and Lil could be ... I don't know. It was just surprising. Seeing my sister, my best friend . . . like that."

"Well." Wilder shrugged. "You've never liked surprises." He grinned.

And then didn't stop grinning as he walked back inside. As he stepped into the same elevator where his world might've just tilted a little. As he reemerged into the care center's third floor.

He found Maggie standing in the same spot where he'd left Chief Holloway earlier. The police chief wasn't around. Had he left?

Maggie raised her eyebrows when she saw him approach. "Well, you don't have a black eye. That's something."

He laughed. "I think your son and I have made our peace."

"And my daughter?"

"Indi and I tend to get along just fine so—"

She elbowed him. "You think you're so funny. Fine, I won't

ask any questions. Other than what made you come back here instead of . . ."

Chasing Lil down? An annoying surge of common sense, that's what. If Lilian had left, it meant she wanted her space. He was smart enough to know to give it to her. "Call it a strategic retreat. Also, Neil left and I'm giving you a ride home." He hurried on before she could say anything else. "Have you gone in?"

Maggie shook her head. "The doctor doesn't want anyone in there. I'm not really sure why I even came." An echo of Neil's words. "But he's a link. I told Lilian as much a couple weeks ago. He's the only link we know of and so . . ."

"He might not be the only link." Wilder said it without thinking. He still hadn't decided whether to tell Maggie about what he'd learned in Atlanta. But his thoughtless words had opened the door. "I found out someone who worked for Nicholas Cornish in Atlanta disappeared the same weekend Diana came here. He's been missing ever since. It's flimsy. It's conjecture. It might be a coincidence. But I'm going to look into it."

Maggie didn't say anything at first. But then, when she reached for both of his hands and held them between hers, he knew what her next words would be. "It doesn't have to be you."

"Maggie—"

"I need you to hear this because I don't think I've ever said it. Or if I've tried, I wasn't clear. It doesn't have to be you, Wilder."

His hands grew clammy inside hers. "Are you giving up on her being alive? Are you starting to believe she died in the accident? Is that what this is about?"

"No, it's about you. It's about me wanting you to be free. I want you to be free, Wilder. You've spent three years on this—"

"My father spent twenty-five."

"Yes, but it was a side thing for him. Something he looked into when he had time. For you . . . it's become so much bigger. And I don't think I'm okay with that anymore." She squeezed his hands once more before letting go.

How could he make her understand? How could he make her see that it did have to be him? He *needed* this. Maybe it was selfish and stubborn and a whole host of other things, but he needed the lifeline solving this mystery would provide.

Because maybe, just maybe, it'd save him from drowning in the one he couldn't.

"He wouldn't want to see you like this, Wilder—trapped inside questions that were never yours to answer."

Dad. It always came back to Dad.

Somehow Maggie knew it. Because she'd been there, of course. Found him when the drowning first began.

But what if he wasn't drowning anymore? Showing Lilian Dad's letter last night, losing himself in an onslaught of emotions . . . *Another life preserver.* Lilian had thrown him another life preserver.

And if he held on to that, perhaps it truly would be possible to let go of the rest. The what-if that had plagued him for so long.

And the investigation?

"Oh, you're still here." The doctor emerged from Peyton's room. "Fine. You can have two minutes. But I'm telling you, he won't be able to talk."

Permission to see Peyton? He looked to Maggie and read the resignation in her eyes. "I'll think about what you said, Maggie. I will."

She only nodded. "I'll wait out here."

Was he disappointing her by stepping into the room? He didn't know what to think—about anything she'd just said, about the thoughts churning around in his head. There was so much. Dad and Maggie and the case. That missing man from Atlanta . . .

Lilian.

He approached Peyton's bed. The man's eyes were closed. Had he already slipped back into the coma? Or was he simply asleep? Peyton's face was almost the same color as the bedsheets. Wilder hadn't come here since the man had been transferred from the hospital five months ago. There'd been no reason to. And he'd only encountered Peyton a few times before the incident that had landed him here.

And yet, his face, even gaunt and pale, looked familiar. Probably because Wilder had spent so much time staring at photos of his father.

His attention snagged on the bedside table. A potted plant rested underneath a metal lamp, a small gift shop card propped in a plastic holder. Who would've sent that?

He glanced over his shoulder. Maggie came here once a month. But no, why would she give a plant to the man who'd tried to . . .

He plucked the card free and turned it over. Only a few scribbled, generic words. *Get well soon.*

Who . . . ?

"There's a man who's stopped in a couple times." The voice behind him was a surprise. He turned to see a nurse.

"A man?"

"He's been quick. Just in and out. He brought the plant the first time."

Franzen?

Would the agent from the Bureau have been so impatient to interrogate Peyton about his father's activities he'd have come all the way to Maine already? That didn't seem to make sense.

Nor did the handwriting on the note. Wilder could swear he'd seen it somewhere before. He knew it.

He knew this handwriting. But how? Where?

⸻

She was only imagining things.

That was it. Lilian had woken up this morning in a bed that wasn't hers. She'd had four cups of coffee. She'd almost been kissed in an elevator. That's why her nerves were jangled and she was standing in the middle of her office with the strangest feeling . . .

That someone else had been in here.

Sunlight squeezed through the bamboo blinds at the window, landing in lines on the opposite wall. Everything on her desk was in its place—computer, two framed photos, brushed nickel lamp. The chairs in front of her desk were in their usual spot, with their usual symmetrical tilt. Not a crease to be seen in the tasseled rug under foot.

Of course, the tassels were in tangles, but that was nothing new, was it? She didn't know. She never paid attention. She knelt down to fan out the beige strings and in the process realized her hand was trembling.

With a start, she straightened and held her palm up in front of her. Then let out a puff of relief. *Not the same.*

No, the jitters she had now weren't the same as the tremors she'd experienced more than a month ago now. *Just a caffeine buzz.*

Or a result of the impossible sensation that had slammed into her when she first stepped into her office. Or . . .

Or she might as well admit it. She was a frazzled mess. A frazzled, frenetic, practically feverish mess, and the ridiculous alliteration was only further proof. She was a mess because she just couldn't get it through her head, what had happened this morning. Or what had nearly happened. What she wished had happened?

Wilder Monroe had almost kissed her. And she had almost let him. Absolutely would have let him if that elevator door hadn't opened.

"Are you okay?"

Not even close. She spun on her heel to see Mariana standing in her doorway. No Flannel. Now that Mariana had grown comfortable in the small cottage, she often left him in her office when stopping in to see Lilian or walking to the kitchen.

Comfortable. There was something Lilian hadn't experienced for a single minute yet this day. Unless she counted those drowsy moments when she'd first awakened, right before she'd realized where she was. She'd been comfortable then. Incredibly so.

But every second since? Especially the ones she'd spent backed up to an elevator wall, while every nerve inside of her simmered and sang? Not comfortable. Not comfortable at all.

Since when was discomfort so exhilarating? And confusing?

"I don't think I am okay. I think I've had too much coffee." More like too much proximity to a man she'd only just gotten used to liking, let alone . . .

"No such thing as too much coffee." Mariana moved into the room and sat in one of the chairs in front of Lilian's desk. "So what's on the agenda for the day? I've got all this month's billables invoiced and notes from the Danberry deposition are waiting for you in your inbox. I've been reading up on real estate law, and I don't think getting Mr. Barrett's parcels separated will be much trouble. So what's next?"

Do your job. Good night, for weeks she'd been worried about mystery symptoms and appointments with a neurologist and yet, she'd managed to carry on with her duties. One kiss that hadn't even come to fruition shouldn't be enough to upend her.

But it wasn't just the almost-kiss. It was weeks' worth of conversations and revelations and a growing closeness. It was the infuriating discovery that she was attracted to him. And the alarming truth that he fascinated her.

It was Wilder.

"Okay, your silence tells me we're somewhere beyond an overwhelming to-do list. Do you need a listening ear?"

Yes. Maybe. Or no, definitely not. Because right now she wasn't even sure she could utter Wilder's name without feeling like fireworks were going off in her chest. "I think I might be at a crossroads. I don't know whether to take a step forward or take a step back or no steps at all. But no steps might not be possible. Because, I mean, I'm going to have to see him again eventually. But going backward might not be an option either because after this morning . . ." She wasn't making a lick of sense. She dropped into the chair beside Mariana. "I'm sorry. I'm being weird. Let's talk about Ansel Barrett's property. I'm still hoping he doesn't end up divvying it up because it just seems a shame to separate that house from the farmland but—"

"Can I tell you what my dad told me when I was at the biggest crossroads of my life?" Mariana leaned forward in her chair.

"Um . . . what?"

"I have the strong feeling you need a friend right now instead of a paralegal. We've only worked together a few weeks, but a new friendship is still a friendship, right?"

Lilian nodded, then caught herself. "R-right."

"When I was at my biggest crossroads, when I'd packed my suitcase but hadn't yet walked out of the bedroom, with Emilio just downstairs and a thousand doubts pulling me a thousand ways, I called my dad. And I'll never forget what he told me. He said, 'Mari, don't let fear make your decisions.' I've repeated it to myself about a thousand times since, including when I flew out to Maine to interview for this job."

"Don't let fear make your decisions."

Until this moment, Lilian wasn't sure she would've thought of herself as a fearful person. But maybe it'd been her companion for years without her knowing it. Fear of all the questions she couldn't answer. Fear of the unknown. She'd made a skill of running away from it.

Whereas Wilder had a way of running right into it. It was his job. It was his way. To trust his gut and move forward no matter the uncertainty in front of him.

"I don't know how you did it—leaving everything behind, moving across the country." Lilian ran her fingers through her tangled hair. It was finally dry. "You're talking to someone who went to college and law school less than two hours away and then promptly returned not just to her hometown, but to her literal childhood bedroom." She paused. "Do you mind if I ask what happened? With your marriage?"

Mariana leaned back in her seat. "I think the bottom line is that Emilio didn't want a blind wife."

Oh. Mariana's goldish-reddish hair shimmered in the sunlight. What she'd just said . . . how had she said it so evenly? "He doesn't sound great."

Mariana actually laughed. "He was, in the beginning. And, I mean, obviously he knew what he was getting, but also . . . he didn't. Blindness has been a part of my life since before I can remember. Sometimes in weird ways on random days, I even find myself grateful for it. And when Emilio and I first started dating, he said it didn't matter. But later, I realized it did. I think it frustrated him more than he let on that I didn't have opinions on the paint colors in our townhouse. That I didn't notice when he'd gotten a new haircut or wore a new tie."

"That seems incredibly superficial and unfair."

Mariana shrugged. "And I'm sure he could've gotten over a lot of it. But he couldn't seem to get over the idea of having a baby with someone who . . . He was scared. That's what it came down to. He was just scared. And I couldn't convince him that he didn't have to be. We argued about it for years but there came a point when we were just done. We both knew it."

Mariana was quiet for a moment. Lilian wished she knew what to say. But Mariana spoke again before she could find the right words. "I have a disability. I'm not frightened of that word. I'm not frightened of the reality. But if I'm ever going to fall in love again, it's going to have to be with a man who can accept it. More than that, a man who doesn't just wave it off and pretend it doesn't matter, but who can recognize both the challenges *and* the gifts of it." Her expression turned wistful. "Someone who's up for the adventure."

Up for the adventure. It sounded like something Wilder would say.

Wilder. Who'd tugged her into an elevator this morning with enough determination and desire in his magnetic brown-black eyes to make her knees go weak. No, she hadn't felt comfortable in that moment. But she hadn't felt fearful either. She'd felt . . . the adventure of it.

"Thank you for this, Mariana. For talking."

"It's a great skill of mine." She smiled. "Dad used to say it would aid me in my future career as a lawyer."

"I think I'd like to meet your dad."

"You will. He's coming out next week, remember?"

"You know it's not too late, right? You could still do law school. Although, what am I saying? I don't want to lose you. But maybe you could take online classes. Maybe we could even find a way to help with the expense. A lot of workplaces do that for their employees' further education."

"I definitely wouldn't be opposed to talking about it sometime. For now, I'm just happy to be here. But listen, I should probably go let Flannel outside." Mariana stood. "The poor thing's been weird all morning." She moved to the office door. "He keeps sniffing around the office. Morris or Danine or someone must've been in there after we left yesterday. Do we have someone who comes in to clean the offices?"

Lilian stilled. "What?"

"I'm pretty meticulous about knowing where and how I leave things. I always leave my chair pulled out a few inches, but it was pushed all the way in this morning, so I'm pretty sure someone was in there. Which I realize sounds ridiculous, but . . . well."

Ridiculous? No, it didn't sound ridiculous. It sounded familiar.

14

"What's all this?"

Lilian had walked into the house expecting to find her family already sitting down to dinner. Instead, an empty dining room and the sound of voices floating from the kitchen had sent her moving toward the back of the house.

Where she found all her family members and then some. Maggie and her fiancé stood at the kitchen table, packing plastic plates and disposable silverware into an oversized picnic basket. Everyone else—Neil and Sydney, Indi and Philip—were crowded around the counters. Making sandwiches, packing carrot sticks and grapes in tiny bags, and from the looks of things, just generally getting in each other's way.

"It's the first seventy-five-degree day of the spring," Maggie called over the hubbub. "It seemed like as good a reason as any to go on a picnic."

They knew it was evening now, right? That the sun was on its way to bed and the temperature had dropped at least into the high sixties? And if they were planning to trek to their usual picnic locale, a perfect little stretch of sand about a half-mile down the coast, it'd be even chillier by the water.

Clearly none of that mattered to the chatter-bug collection of people in front of her.

"I've got blankets." Wilder burst through the kitchen's back door, his arms piled with blankets and—

Oh my word.

The man had gotten a haircut. Nothing drastic, but his hair no longer skimmed over his ears, and wait, had he shaved? What's more, he wore an olive green button-down she'd never seen before and it *did* something to his dark eyes, added just a hint of light, miniscule flecks of bronze, and . . .

She was staring.

As was almost everyone else in the room. Except they weren't only staring at Wilder, but zigzagging their gazes from him to her and back again. Neil and Indi had clearly blabbed to their significant others about what they'd seen today. *Bunch of busybodies.* Only poor Ray looked befuddled at the crackling tension that'd just entered the room.

"I guess if we're picnicking I should go change out of my work clothes." Yes, it was a cowardly escape, but it was all she could think to do under the circumstances.

She half expected someone to follow her. One of her nosy siblings, if not Wilder himself. But she made it all the way to her bedroom without a tail, then made quick work of peeling off her gray pants and scoop-necked blouse, replacing them with a pair of loose jeans and a simple black V-neck.

Which she traded out at the last minute for a light blue top she found at the back of her closet. Not that she was willing to spare a thought for why she'd made the swap. Definitely not. Because there was no reason.

Certainly not a reason who'd lately developed the uncanny ability to make her palms sweat.

He was also not the reason she dabbed on some light pink lip gloss and ran her fingers through her hair. Why hadn't she dried it this morning? It was a windblown wreck. But if she stayed up here any longer, everyone downstairs would think she was up here primping and hadn't she suffered enough indignity today?

She stared at herself in her vanity mirror. "You are Lilian Muir. You are sensible and practical and you scored a 178 on your LSAT." *You're also talking to your reflection.*

And, oh yeah, you fell asleep in Wilder Monroe's bed last night and almost kissed him in an elevator this morning. Real sensible. Real practical.

Didn't change her LSAT score, though.

She grabbed a pair of sandals and marched from her room, willing herself down the stairs. Dignity and decorum, that's what she'd strive for when she walked back into the kitchen. If she acted like nothing had changed, nobody had seen anything, ahem, interesting today, then everybody else would act normal, too, right?

She marched into the kitchen.

No one even looked up. They were back to assembling sandwiches and packing the picnic basket, as if Wilder had never shown up and she'd never left and, wait, where was Wilder?

"I sent him ahead with the blankets, dear." Maggie sidled up beside her, her voice low. "To our regular spot."

"You did? I mean, I don't know who—" Her hands found her waist. "Did you just snort?"

"I would never do something so unladylike." Maggie stepped closer and lifted her hands to Lilian's cheeks. "I'm not going to ask you any questions or say one single word. Other than don't talk yourself out of anything before you've given it a chance."

She could pretend she didn't know what, or rather whom,

Maggie was referring to, but what was the point? "That was more than a single word, Maggie."

"I'm your mother. Deal with it." She patted Lilian's cheeks once more and nudged her head toward the back door. "Go on ahead with Wilder."

Everyone else was still chattering, preparing their picnic supper. But surely they all had one ear trained on this exchange. If she followed Wilder out the door—

"Or you can stay here." Maggie interrupted her thoughts. "And field a cross-examination from any one of the people in this room who I'm guessing aren't going to be quite as willing to let you off the hook as I am. I don't think Indi's told Neil exactly where she found you this morning yet but it's possible it could come out if the questions start flying."

Well, when she put it that way . . .

Wilder had known exactly what Maggie was doing when she'd ushered him out the door. Her whispered, "Don't say I never did you any favors," on his way out only confirmed his suspicion.

Which was why he'd dawdled in the grove for the last—he held up his wrist and glanced at his watch—eight minutes. How long was it going to take for Lilian to change her clothes and catch up with him? He could only walk at a turtle's pace for so long.

At the snap of a twig behind him, he stopped and grinned. "Took you long enough."

Lilian was at his side in seconds, but instead of pausing to greet him, she barreled on ahead. "Come on. We're supposed to be getting our spot ready."

He hurried to keep up with her. "It's a big job, I know.

Three whole blankets to spread out on the sand. Do you think we're up to it?"

"Wilder—"

"I like your shirt. It's a pretty color on you."

She sputtered to a halt. "I didn't wear this for you."

"Of course you didn't."

She snatched the whole pile of blankets from his hands and kept walking. And it took every ounce of his self-control not to laugh. Instead, he caught up to her in a mere two or three strides and compelled his big mouth to refrain from anything that hinted at teasing. "So how was work today?"

"Fine."

"Just fine?" They turned the opposite direction from the edge of the grove that would've spilled them into the main farm grounds. Instead, up ahead they'd soon reach a clearing where the coast curved. Much of the seaside around these parts consisted of rugged, uneven rock, but they were nearing a hidden patch of sand and grass where the Muir family had been picnicking for as long as he'd known them.

"Well," Lilian finally added, "maybe not exactly fine . . ." She stopped walking. "I have to ask you something, Wilder. Those gut feelings you get. What do they feel like?"

"Uh, where did that question come from?"

"I walked into my office today and got the distinct impression that someone had been in there. But nothing was out of place. Nothing's missing. And I probably wouldn't have given it another thought except Mari had the same feeling. And she's pretty sure her chair had been moved."

He was struggling to keep up. Mari . . . oh, yes. Her paralegal. "Did you call the police?"

"No. There weren't any broken windows, no busted locks. Like I said, nothing's missing. And who knows, Flannel could've bumped into Mariana's chair. It's just strange that we both had the same feeling, right?"

Strange, yes. Like the card by Peyton's bedside with hand-writing he recognized but couldn't place. Like the knowledge that another man had visited the care center and signed in as John Smith. He'd checked at the front desk before leaving.

Strange like his boat being ransacked. Like Lilian feeling as if she was being followed.

"I shouldn't have said anything. You're starting to look less like Captain and more like Flannel."

He took the bundle of blankets from her arms. "I have no idea what that means."

"Neil's dog is playful. Mariana's is all business, all the time." She started walking again.

He hurried to her side again. "You seem rather businesslike at the moment yourself."

"Everything's been weird today, Wilder. I'm . . . off-kilter."

They left the cover of the trees and emerged onto the beach, the evening sky ablaze with color. Reds and pinks and oranges, spilling over the coast in a show of light and skipping over the ocean. Tall grass danced in the breeze, the air tinged with the saline scent of the sea.

Lilian pulled a blanket free from his arms and began spreading it over the sand.

"I like it when you're off-kilter, Lil."

She grimaced and grabbed another blanket.

"I like it when you frown, too." There were whole worlds contained in her scowls. "Well, as long as the frown isn't about something serious. Like someone trespassing in your office."

"We don't know for sure if anyone did. And aren't you going to help?"

"I think you've got it handled." She so didn't. The wind had already flapped three corners of the first blanket up and she wasn't faring any better with the second.

He dropped the third in a heap and crossed to her.

"Wilder—"

He grabbed her hand just like he'd done this morning, towing her closer to the water, then dropping to his backside in the sand and pulling her down with him.

"What are you doing?"

"Everyone else is going to be here in a few minutes. Let's just enjoy this until they get here."

"Enjoy what?"

"The view, silly." And the feel of her arm pressed up against his. Strands of her hair brushing his cheek. The fact that she grumbled and yet didn't make a move to put any space between them. "Let's not think about intruders or anything else for a few minutes." Legs bent in front of him, he wrapped his arms in front of his knees and looked to the sea. *So much blue.* Vast and bottomless. "It never gets old, does it?"

When she didn't answer, he leaned just the slightest bit closer. "I was eight, by the way."

She turned to him with a wrinkled brow.

"First time I ever had a gut instinct that I remember clearly. I was eight. I was in Sunday school. Pastor Hastings was teaching. He was talking about sacrifice and trying to explain to us what it meant. He told a story of someone he knew, someone in Muir Harbor, who'd made a great sacrifice for someone she loved. He kept it vague but . . ." He paused. "I felt this weird flash of heat in my gut, a jolt, and suddenly I knew exactly who he was talking about. Or thought I knew. I, uh . . . confirmed it later."

"You were a detective even then."

"Guess so." He cleared his throat. Not a memory he wanted to dwell on. And yet, more and more he was discovering the unexpected feeling of, well, rightness that came with sharing pieces of himself with Lilian. "Anyway, you asked what my gut instincts feel like and I think that sums it up."

"A flash of heat. A jolt." She was quiet for a moment before turning her gaze to the ocean. "This really has been the strangest day."

While she watched the undulating sea, he watched her, could practically hear her thoughts returning to this morning. To the houseboat, then the elevator. There was no stopping his slow smile from forming.

"Wilder, what are we doing?" Her fingers were knotted together in her lap.

"Well, I'd say you're gearing up to depose me. Regarding certain events that took place earlier today, I would guess. Meanwhile, I'm trying to work up the nerve to ask you on a date."

"*What?*"

"I know it's a little backwards. We woke up in bed together. *Then* almost kissed. *Then* got to the part where I ask you out. But I'm okay with being unconventional."

She jumped to her feet. "Unconventional? Wilder, this whole thing is—"

"Impossible, preposterous, absurd?" He craned his neck to look up at her, her hair a glowing halo in the setting sun.

She crossed her arms with a huff. "Exactly."

Slowly, he rose. "See, that's the thing, Lil. I don't think it's any of those words. And I don't think you're nearly as irritated with me right now as you're pretending to be."

"I'm not pretending. I am irritated."

"Why?"

"Because you got a haircut!"

That did it. He was plumb out of restraint. Nabbing both her palms this time, he hauled her to him, and only when she freed one hand in order to catch herself against his chest, did he give himself the luxury of sliding his newly unoccupied fingers over her cheek and into her hair.

"I think you like my haircut, Lil."

"Don't be cocky."

He took no small amount of satisfaction in her frayed voice. "What's more, I think you like me."

"So?"

He dipped his head toward her ear, only just stopping himself from letting his lips graze her skin. "So, I think you should let me take you on a date. And before you argue, consider the fact that we have unfinished business."

He could feel her catch her breath, the rest of her body so close and so still it was all he could do not to finish what they'd started earlier right here and right now.

But somewhere past the haziness of his yearning, he was pretty sure he could hear voices in the trees. So instead of giving in to impulse, he allowed himself only the briefest contact. A feather of a kiss beside her ear.

Not enough.

And maybe not for her either. Because when he pulled away, it wasn't just her rosy cheeks or glazed blue irises looking back at him. But a pair of upturned, glossy lips.

Which immediately drooped into a frown when the moment was broken and confusion set in. Or, dare he believe it, disappointment? He just couldn't help it. He lifted one eyebrow and like an idiot, gave in to the urge to smirk.

She glared at him.

"So . . . Saturday?"

She marched past him and went back to work spreading out the blankets. But not before flinging over her shoulder the only word he needed to hear. "Fine."

$\mathcal{L}$ilian held the phone to her ear, wishing she hadn't recognized the number when it'd lit up her phone's screen. Wishing she'd simply ignored it.

Instead, standing alone at the bottom of the farmhouse stairs, the choir of voices from the living room a dull buzz in the background, she tried not to let the nurse or receptionist or whoever it was she was speaking with ruin what was supposed to have been a special day.

"On Monday morning? Monday as in two days from now?"

"Yes. Does ten o'clock work?" The woman on the other end had already explained that Lilian's MRI results had come in yesterday afternoon. That Dr. Cho wanted to schedule an appointment, and that since they'd had a cancellation for Monday morning, they wanted to offer the slot to Lilian.

Ten o'clock. She tried to picture her work schedule. Came up blank. "I think so. Actually, I'm not entirely sure. It's Saturday, so I'm not at the office and don't have my calendar in front of me—"

"Yes, and I apologize, we don't usually do scheduling on weekends, but we're open once a month on Saturday mornings. I was hoping to get you called yesterday, but the day got away from me. Anyhow, how about I pencil you in and you can call first thing Monday morning if it's not going to work out? Otherwise, we'll plan on seeing you at ten."

The woman spoke quickly and, moments later, the call ended before Lilian could process it. *MRI results. Monday morning. In two days.*

They'd found something. They had to have found something. Why else would they want her to come in? If the MRI had come back clear, someone could've simply called and told her that.

You don't know that. Don't assume. Don't think about it at all.

Because Maggie's wedding shower was going on in the next room over. Because Wilder was taking her on a date tonight.

Because she wasn't going to spend the rest of this weekend fearing the unknown. Besides there was a positive to this. On Monday, she'd have answers. There *wouldn't* be an unknown anymore. This was exactly what she needed and wanted. *This is a good thing.*

She moved back to the living room, where so much tissue paper littered the floor, it was almost impossible to catch a glimpse of the hardwood underneath. Scattered bows and scraps of wrapping paper added to the mess.

The shower had been a complete success. Thanks, in no small part, to Lilian's sister-in-law. Sydney's arms were currently loaded with emptied dishes, not a single mini-quiche or slice of fruit left in sight.

Instead of going back to the rocking chair that had been her perch throughout the morning's festivities, Lilian trailed after Sydney. "Let me help you. If you stack one more plate on that pile, we'll have a whole new mess to clean up."

Sydney laughed and went right ahead propping another

plate on her load. "You forget, I've got more than a decade's worth of waitressing experience behind me."

"Still. Let me grab the silverware, at least." It was hard to remember sometimes that Sydney had lived a whole different life halfway across the country before coming to Muir Harbor last fall. Why, she hadn't even been at Muir Farm a whole year, and yet, she'd become such a part of the fabric of this household that it seemed impossible she'd once been a stranger.

In her place of honor on the couch, Maggie was fingering through the cards she'd received in between sneaking peeks at Patti Brighton-Smythe's wig as the woman prattled on. It leaned to the side, in definite danger of toppling into the pile of gifts Maggie had received.

Prior to the shower, Maggie had tried insisting on no gifts, saying that after decades in this house, there wasn't a single household item she needed. But Sydney had talked her into a compromise—none of the usual sort of wedding shower gifts. Instead, guests who wanted to bring presents had been instructed to buy all manner of scrapbooking supplies. Maggie had been saying for years she wanted to do something with the shoeboxes full of photos in the hallway closet upstairs.

Most of their guests—Maggie's friends from church, women from the community—had departed in the last half hour or so, but a few stragglers remained.

"We owe you big-time, Sydney. Maggie loved every second of this shower." Holding as many pieces of silverware as she could handle at once, Lilian followed Sydney into the kitchen and they deposited their dirty dishes in the sink. "If I'd tried to plan this thing on my own, my personal disdain for traditional shower games would've gotten in the way of planning good entertainment."

"I thought I kept the games pretty brief and painless." Sydney started back the way they'd come.

"Oh, you did. And skipping the part where we pass around every single gift and ooh and ahh for two hours? Chef's kiss. My hat's off to you."

"I'm getting the definite idea you have definite opinions on wedding showers. I'll keep this info in my back pocket for future reference." Sydney snuck her a teasing grin as they entered the living room once more.

Which Lilian chose to ignore. So she was going on a date with Wilder Monroe tonight. So that hadn't been on anyone's list of predictions for the year. Didn't mean she owed anyone a statement, written or oral, on the matter.

Besides, it's not like she would've been able to clearly communicate where she stood on the man anyway. She was a jumbled wreck of foreign feelings and flustered anticipation, and every instance of being around Wilder in recent days had only made it worse. He'd winked at her last night after they'd finalized details with the caterer and she'd had to chug an entire glass of ice water to keep herself from dissolving.

If he'd winked at her a few weeks ago, she'd have probably tossed the water in his face.

"It's Indi whose shower preferences you should learn. I bet Philip proposes by the end of the year."

"Maybe." Sydney pursed her lips as if to keep herself from saying more. But then Sydney turned to Lilian, a different sort of smile, rimmed with a hint of shyness, tugging at her mouth. "Actually, the shower's not quite over. There's one more gift . . . I was going to wait until it was mostly just family left . . . and I told Neil he needed to be here for this part . . . but for some reason, I'm suddenly nervous."

"This gift—is it of the happy news variety?"

Sydney gasped. "Neil told you?"

"I'm sorry. But also overjoyed." See, another reason not to

obsess over that call from Dr. Cho's office, her appointment on Monday. There were so many reasons to be glad today. "I didn't know if you knew I knew—"

"And he thought I'd be the one who wouldn't be able to keep the secret." Sydney tucked her red hair behind both ears with a pretend pout. "At first we thought we'd wait to say anything until after the wedding, but after trying on bridesmaid dresses a couple days ago, uh, I'm thinking it's going to be fairly obvious fairly soon. I wish Neil would hurry up and get here—"

"He's here," Lilian's brother's voice interrupted from behind them and a look of relief splashed over Sydney's face.

Lilian glanced over her shoulder to see not only Neil, but also Philip and Wilder, the latter of whom dipped his head in greeting, then winked. Again.

Where was a glass of water when a woman needed it? And what was she supposed to do when he did stuff like that? Wink back? Probably not go mute and frown. Or was she smiling? She couldn't tell lately.

He was smiling.

"Are you sure we should be doing this today?" Sydney tucked herself into her husband's side. "It's Maggie's day. I don't want to steal her thunder."

"Are you kidding? She's going to be ecstatic. It'll only make her day all the better." Neil put his arm around Sydney and steered her toward Maggie. Philip had already moved through the room to find Indi.

Leaving Wilder to step up beside Lilian. She could feel him watching her as she watched Neil and Sydney approach Maggie. He smelled like fresh air and sawdust, which probably meant he'd spent the morning helping Neil on the second treehouse he'd begun to build.

"They're due in October." His low voice grazed over her like a trail of tiny sparks.

"Did you use your brilliant P.I. skills to deduce that?"

"Did you just call me brilliant?" He bumped her with his elbow. "And no. I wheedled it out of Neil this morning."

"You look proud of yourself. What would you say if I told you I've known since Monday?"

He smirked down at her. "I've known for like a month. Just didn't know the due date 'til today."

"Impossible."

He only gave her a playful shrug and an expression that said, *What can I say?* Of course, Wilder and his gut instincts.

"Hmm, October." Neil had told her the month the baby was due earlier in the week, but she hadn't done the math at that point. Her brain ticked off the months now. "Holy honeymoon baby, Batman."

When she dared a glance at the man beside her, she could tell he was remembering the same thing she was. That first night out on the porch after Maggie had asked them to plan her wedding. He'd called her Batman then and she hadn't had a clue what he'd meant and oh, if anyone had told her then she'd be standing next to him now fighting the urge to run the pad of her thumb over that ridiculous dimple in his chin . . .

A happy shriek rescued her gaze from his face. Indi, clearly having overheard Neil and Sydney's news as they'd shared it with Maggie. For her part, Maggie was tearing up even as her face beamed with joy.

Oh yeah, Neil was right. This wasn't stealing Maggie's thunder. It was the sun shining even brighter on her day.

And Lilian wouldn't dim it by telling her about the appointment. That could wait until tomorrow. But as for the man beside her . . . She turned to face Wilder. "I got a call from Dr. Cho's office a few minutes ago. They want me to come in on Monday morning."

He didn't say anything. He simply lifted his hand to brush one of hers. And now she was thinking of another night. Out on the dock, yards from his houseboat. When he'd taken her hand and she'd realized she might want something she'd never wanted before. To be close to Wilder Monroe instead of far, far away.

"I feel like it might not be a great sign that they want me to come in. But . . . but at least I'll have answers, right?"

His pinky locked around hers. "Do you want a discussion or a distraction?"

She leaned closer. "Definitely the latter."

"Then how do you feel about starting our date a little earlier than planned?"

"How early?"

"Now?"

"It's barely lunchtime." She motioned her head toward the ruckus across the room. "And I have people to hug, baby news to celebrate."

"I'm a people you could hug."

"Also, I should probably change."

"So that was no to the hug, I guess."

"Except I don't know whether to dress up or dress down." She glanced down at her mint-green sundress. "You still haven't told me what we're doing for this date."

His fingers brushed her elbow. "We're going to have to work on this whole having two separate conversations thing." He leaned in close even as he turned her toward the crowd in the living room. "Go hug your people and celebrate Neil's news. And then let's get out of here."

"But—"

"You don't need to change. You look perfect."

———

"What are we doing at Ansel Barrett's house?"

At Wilder's side, Lilian leaned forward in the passenger seat. He was getting used to having her next to him in the Jeep. To the subtle fragrance of her perfume reaching across the small space. "Patience, Lil."

When she reached for her door handle, he stilled her with one hand on her knee. "And let me get the door. This is a date and I'm a gentleman." He waited a beat. "You're not going to counter that?" Ah, there was the scowl he'd been waiting for. But it disappeared so quickly, he couldn't help a chuckle. "You totally don't know what to do anymore now that you know how much I like your frowns, do you?"

He used to think goading Lilian Muir was an entertaining pastime. Turned out, flirting with her was even better.

And if it helped her get her mind off Monday—if it helped *him* get his mind off Monday—all the better. If he had his way, neither one of them would give it another thought today.

Nor would he think about the case. About how Agent Franzen had never called him back, even after he'd tried calling the Bureau's field office in Atlanta. About how Peyton had eventually fallen back into his coma. Or about a man named Leo who may or may not have anything to do with anything.

He certainly didn't have anything to do with today. Today was about right here and right now. It was about exploring something new.

Or perhaps not so new. Lately he'd begun to wonder if maybe there'd been a piece of his heart just a little bit lost to Lilian Muir for a whole lot longer than he'd realized.

He bounded outside and rounded the vehicle, his shoes crunching over the gravel of Ansel Barrett's driveway. Hopefully the man had remembered to leave his spare key where he'd indicated.

Wilder reached Lilian's door and pulled it open. But when she didn't move from her seat, he leaned in. "Coming?"

"This is so weird."

"I know, but I'll explain everything when we get inside."

"No, I mean *this*. Us. Everyone watched us leave the house together, you know. They've been watching us all week."

"Lil—"

She turned her head to him. "You said you were going to come to church with us tomorrow. Well, are you going to sit by me in church? The second you do, every person in that congregation will take note. Then we'll have an entire town of busybodies eyeing us. It just all feels awkward, and I feel uncertain and I don't like feeling uncertain."

He leaned closer and tapped the edge of her knee until she got the hint and shifted to face him, letting her legs dangle over the side of the seat and tucking her hands in the pockets of her dress. He planted his fists on either side of her, pressing into the leather.

"Lil, I know everything's been wonky this week. But we don't have an audience right now. It's just you and me."

"And my uncertainty."

"And your uncertainty, which I find pretty charming, if you want to know the truth."

She rolled her eyes. "Right. About as charming as my prickliness and my bossiness and my list-making and my constant need to be organized and have a plan, all of which you've had a front row seat to as we've tried to plan Maggie's wedding."

"Yes. And all of which I find charming."

"You can't possibly. People like you are supposed to tell people like me to loosen up. Go with the flow. Ditch the list."

He shook his head. "I like your lists. And I like you. Exactly as you are. You don't need to loosen up."

"I don't?" She'd never sounded so unsure.

He reached up to tuck a strand of hair behind her ear. "No.

You just need to get out of the Jeep so we can have ourselves a date."

"Is Ansel here?"

"We've got the place to ourselves."

"Why?"

Questions—she asked so many questions. And darn it, if he didn't like that, too. But suddenly it was driving him just a little bit crazy, hovering this close, gazing into her pretty eyes and reading such an endearing mix of rare insecurity and shy eagerness there. "You'll see," he said thinly, then coaxed one of her hands free and closed his palm around hers.

She didn't pull away, letting him tug her from the Jeep and lead her toward the old farmhouse. Neither the homestead nor the house were quite as large as Maggie's. Several towering evergreens surrounded the house and the hedges edging the porch looked in need of a good trimming. The house could use a coat of paint. Actually, no, first it could use a good scraping considering the state of the peeling siding.

But he liked the shutters framing large windows and he could see the promise in the exterior. Wouldn't take much of a makeover to make the place a little more presentable.

That was the outside, though. He had no idea what they'd find on the inside. But it'd sounded fun—taking a tour of a house nearly as old as Maggie's, observing Lilian's reactions as they wandered through another man's space.

A space that would go on the market soon. The *For Sale* sign still sat on the porch, but it would be out in the yard before long.

He let go of Lilian's hand long enough to crouch by the porch stairs and feel around for a key in the dirt underneath. When he rose, Lilian pursed her lips. "I don't know whether to be relieved we're not breaking in or concerned you know where Ansel keeps his spare key. Do you know where we keep our spare key?"

He climbed the porch stairs. "Don't need to. Maggie gave me a copy forever ago." He unlocked the door and pushed it open, then moved aside so she could enter first. "Have you ever been in Ansel's house?"

"Once or twice when we were kids. He and Cherise babysat us a couple times. I don't really remember much, though."

He stepped inside and immediately a muggy warmth enveloped him. "Ansel said we might need to mess with the thermostat. He's down in Florida visiting his daughters and the house has been closed up for a few days." And it'd been unseasonably warm lately.

He glanced around the living room—shaggy brown carpet, faded light blue couch and two matching chairs. No thermostat that he could see. He moved toward an opening that led into the dining room. *Bingo.*

"Ansel's out of town?"

The thermostat read seventy-seven. That explained the mugginess. He fiddled with it until he heard the air conditioning kick on, then turned to survey the dining room. It was small and the same shag carpet trailed in here, but the ceilings were a nice height and he sure couldn't fault the amount of natural light spilling in through the bay windows.

"Wilder, what are we doing here?"

Lilian stood behind one of the chairs circling a dining room table that felt far too large for just one man. She gripped the chair's scalloped edge.

"Well, I don't know if you've heard, but Ansel's planning to move down to Florida later this summer. In fact, I think that's why he's there now—he's looking at condos."

"I know. He came into the office awhile back. He had questions about dividing parcels and . . ." She raised her eyebrows. "Wait, I thought Neil was joking but . . . are you thinking about buying this place?"

He lifted one shoulder. "Maybe. I mean, I've only seen two rooms so far."

"Are you wanting my opinion or something? I haven't done a ton with real estate law, Wilder. If you need info on land value and buying the house alone versus the house and land together, you need to talk to a realtor. Or assessor."

He mimicked her stance, leaning over a chair at the opposite end of the table. "I don't want info at the moment. I just wanted to see the place. See if I could picture myself here."

"But what about your boat?"

"I don't know."

"Would you sell it?"

"I don't know."

"Why am I here?"

That one, he could answer. He pushed away from the chair and ambled to her side of the table, stopping in front of her. "Partially because I value your opinions. Mostly because I just like being around you."

She tilted toward him, one hand still on the back of the chair. He propped his own right next to hers, brushing her thumb with his. She was looking past him, to the window where sunlight poured in, doing magnificent things to her already magnificent eyes. "As it turns out, I like being around you, too."

"Good to know."

"It's hard to picture you not living on the houseboat, though."

"It shouldn't be. I squat part-time at your house, a fact you seem to love reminding me of."

Except that she hadn't lately. Nor had he stayed at the farm lately, either. Because somehow camping out on the couch just a floor below this woman no longer made for a good night's sleep. Made him feel both too close and too far away from her.

"You are so far gone, I can't even make fun of you for it. It'd go right over your dopey head." Neil's words from earlier in the morning as they'd worked on his next treehouse—accurate.

"Would it be hard, though?" Lilian met his gaze. "You and your dad shared that boat for so many years. Would it feel a little like . . . losing another piece of him?"

He heard the hesitance in her tone, and his first instinct was to rush past the question. Give a pat answer and move on. But there was such a sincere concoction of curiosity and caring in her expression. He'd let her so much further into his pain than he'd ever meant to earlier this week. "I'm sure it would." He swallowed. "But I think . . . I mean I know . . . there's a reason I've crashed at the farm so often in the past three years. There's a lot of memories at the boat."

"Good ones, yes?"

"And a couple really, really bad ones." Finding Dad hunched over in his recliner—eyes closed, but not sleeping. And then, only days later, finding the letter.

He still couldn't believe he'd let Lilian read it. They hadn't talked about it. But the topic had been a specter in recent days, hovering in and around stolen glances and bouts of flirting.

"You know when I told you about coming home from Basic Field Training? Leaving the FBI dream behind? It wasn't just wanting to be home in the immediate future. It was knowing I wanted to have a family, be a dad, and I wanted to do that here. Not in D.C. or Baltimore or Philly or whatever." He gave her a small smile. "And yeah, Neil and I used to joke about me buying this house, but to me it wasn't really a joke. I actually loved the idea then. And I think I might love it now. I'm ready for something different. I'm ready . . . for life to feel a little easier. More settled. Plus, I don't know if . . ."

That's where his words stalled. Where he wasn't sure he wanted to keep going. Until Lilian covered his hand over the back of the chair with hers. "I don't know if I can move on if I keep living on the boat. But I know that I want to."

"I want you to be free, Wilder."

He'd heard Maggie's voice in his head so many times since the other day outside Peyton's room. She'd been talking about the case. But maybe, certainly, also this.

"I want to stop replaying Dad's last couple of weeks over and over in my mind looking for clues. Thinking that if I'd just paid more attention, noticed something, maybe I could've changed things. I want to stop wondering if he composed that letter all while planning . . ."

Lilian moved closer to him, fingers curling around his hand, her other arm going around his waist. "I read your letter, Wilder. It's beautiful. Obviously you know your father better than I did, but from an outside observer, it sure didn't sound like that kind of goodbye. Have you reread it lately?"

He shook his head. Sure, he'd tried last Friday, before he'd gone running off to Atlanta, but he hadn't been able to make it through.

"Then I just really think you should read it again."

He didn't need to. He remembered every word from the first time he'd read it. And yes, it was beautiful. But Lilian didn't know the rest of the story. "Do you know how my mother died, Lil?" Absently, he lifted his hand to her back. "Why she died? Because she refused treatments for her cancer. Because of me. She was sparing *me*. Did you know that?"

She nodded against his shirt. "Maggie told me."

"Pastor Hastings unknowingly told me." He hadn't meant to go here. This wasn't what today was supposed to be about. But he just couldn't seem to stop baring his heart to this woman.

Slow understanding dawned on Lilian's face. "That day in Sunday school. Your first gut instinct."

"Yeah, Hastings is talking about sacrifice and using my mother as an example, though obviously he didn't name her, and I'm the kid in the corner suddenly having an epiphany. I'd heard Dad talk before about how hard it was to watch my mother die. But I never knew . . ."

"Oh my goodness."

"I interrogated Dad about it after church, asked him a hundred questions, got him to admit it was, in fact, my mother the pastor was talking about and that, yes, she delayed treatments because she was pregnant, because she didn't want to endanger me." He felt his shoulders drop. "Dad got pretty emotional. Tried to make me feel better by saying her prognosis had been so bad, treatments likely would've done little more than put off the inevitable. I think he was worried I'd feel guilty and maybe I did. But mostly I was just so confused. I couldn't grasp a love that big from someone I didn't even know. But . . ." He let out a long, ragged breath. "But I do know Dad. And I just can't shake the thought that he was trying to do the same thing. He was trying to spare me, too . . . but I didn't need sparing. I would've been there for him. I would've done whatever I could've to make however long he had left as easy and comfortable as possible."

"I know you would've."

"It would've been a privilege to . . ." He wrapped both arms around her now, pulling her closer, relishing the feel of her leaning into him, even as the angst carved through his chest. "I didn't need sparing," he said again.

She tipped her head to look at him. "You needed your dad."

And that was all it took. A look. A glimpse at the tears in her eyes. And for a moment he wished would go on forever, the sharp twist of his pain stilled. "Right now, I think I need you."

She moved her hands to his cheeks, the touch of her fingertips so soft, he might be imagining it. But no, that was her thumb skimming lightly over his chin, then his bottom lip. And then she was lifting onto her tiptoes, brushing her lips over his.

It took him less than a heartbeat to catalog a hundred sensations. The soft pressure of her lips. Her fingers drifting into his hair. The warmth of her skin through the fabric of her dress. Her feathery sigh that became his cue to take over.

He tightened his arms and kissed her exactly like he'd been dreaming of for days. Only this was so much better than a dream.

It was a healing. It was hope tucking itself in and around all the broken pieces. It was weighty and light, all at once. Sheer perfection.

It was everything.

"If you buy that house, you have to keep the pink tile in the bathroom."

Wilder smiled as he walked Lilian from the driveway in front of the Muir family farmhouse toward the porch. He wasn't sure he'd stopped smiling once in the past hours. He'd probably go to sleep tonight still wearing his grin and wake up in the morning with sore cheeks.

"And that lovely green kitchen linoleum. You've got to keep that, too."

"Whatever you say, Lil." He'd keep the whole darn house the way it was now if it'd make her happy. The Pepto-Bismol bathroom. The old linoleum in the kitchen. The shag carpet almost everywhere else. Fine by him, if it stayed.

As long as she stayed right where she was now. At his side.

They climbed the porch stairs, moonlight sloping under the roofline, a light wind winnowing through the wind chimes and rocking the swing in the corner. He had no clue what time it was. The hours had drifted by all through the afternoon and into the evening, and he would've been happy to stay at Ansel's for as many more. They'd toured the whole house. Played a game of hide-and-seek like kids, finding all the nooks and crannies of the old farmhouse.

They'd lounged in the faded but surprisingly comfortable sofa in the living room, talking about everything and nothing. At some point he'd gone back out to his Jeep and returned with two bags full of groceries for everything they'd needed to make a Margherita pizza.

"Are you sure this is what Ansel meant when he said to make ourselves at home?"

Lilian had been wearing an apron when she'd asked that, one she'd found hanging on a hook behind the pantry door, bearing the words *Grandmas make the best cookies* embroidered in bright blue letters. She'd had a streak of flour on her cheek and a limp circle of pizza dough over one fist.

And he'd had no choice in that moment but to abandon the tomatoes he'd been slicing and kiss her again.

He didn't know how it'd happened. He didn't know how he'd gone from pouring out the broken pieces of his heart to then up and laying the whole beating thing at her feet. So this was what it was like to fall and fall hard. Never again would he make fun of Neil.

"Eighties décor aside, Ansel's house is pretty great," Lilian said. "There's so much space. So much you could do with it. I like it a lot. Do you?"

He was thinking less about Ansel's house right now and more about how much he liked seeing Lilian wearing his hoodie over her dress. "I think I do. I think I really love it." He paused. "I'm just now realizing, though—I made that whole date about myself. The house. My . . . stuff." Dad and his death and, whoa, had he really talked about his mother? He never did and he didn't even know why. It just felt so distant some-times, like some other person's past. Some unknowable love he could never fully comprehend.

"You're forgetting. You made my favorite pizza. And if it makes you feel better, you can make the next date all about me."

The next date. She said it like it was a given, and he liked that. Really liked it. "We'll go treasure hunting at the old chapel."

Their steps slowed as they reached the front door.

"Wilder?"

"Hmm?"

"Your mother . . ."

Had she heard his thoughts a moment ago? He came to a stop on the porch. Clearly, Lilian sensed his hesitation, because quiet seconds stretched before she finished her question. "Do you know much about her? Other than . . . how she died?"

He nodded slowly. "I didn't really like talking about her as a kid. I had a lot of complicated feelings after I found out . . . still do, I suppose. But at some point when I was a little older, I realized how much Dad wanted to talk about her. I forced myself to get past the discomfort and ask some questions. Always made him light up."

The breeze fluttered the hem of Lilian's dress. "You were a good son."

He looked away for a moment. Then back. "She was an elementary school teacher. An only child. Grew up on Army bases, moved around a lot. She fell in love with Muir Harbor the second Dad brought her here. And apparently she was a terrible cook." Oh, he could almost hear Dad's laughter when he recounted her failed attempts in the kitchen.

"I wish I could've met her. I wish *you* could've met her."

"In a small way, maybe I did. Through Dad's stories, his

memories." They'd always been clouded, though, by what Wilder knew about her death. Somewhere along the way, he'd settled into an emotional detachment of sorts.

But maybe that could change. Maybe . . . he was ready. "Actually, um, Dad had some of her old scrapbooks." They were stored in the same trunk where he kept Dad's letter. "I haven't looked at them in a long time. If you ever want to . . ."

"I do." Lilian touched his arm. "Date three?"

"Only if you bring whichever shoebox in the hallway closet has all your old elementary school pictures."

"You really do know all this house's old secrets, down to what's in every closet, don't you?" She glanced to the door. "Are you staying here tonight?"

"Ah . . . I don't think so."

"If you buy the house next door, you'll probably never stay here anymore, will you?"

Before she could reach for the door, he closed the space between them and pulled her close. "Would that disappoint you?"

She released the smallest gasp as she landed against his chest, her voice breathy when she spoke. "It'd mean more hot water for the rest of us."

With a pretend rumble of dismay, he bent his head to kiss her cheek. "Pick you up in the morning?"

"We could just meet at the church."

"I'd rather pick you up. And yes, I do plan to sit by you, by the way. If people want to talk, they can talk."

"Well, okay, then."

She'd barely finished the sentence before he covered her lips with his and sank into satisfaction at the feel of her molding herself to him as she twined her arms around his back. He kissed her until his lungs begged for air, and then kissed her again.

And how he ever found the willpower to pull himself

away, he didn't know. But somehow, eventually, he said good night and opened the door and watched her slip inside. He walked back to his Jeep and made the drive to the harbor. He might sleep like a baby tonight or sleep not a wink. He didn't know. He didn't care.

"I want you to be free, Wilder."

He parked in his usual spot in the sandy lot and watched the inhale and exhale of the sea, the harbor lights waltzing over the water. *I think maybe I am, Maggie.*

Free and very possibly head over heels in—

He straightened behind the wheel, his gaze sharpening. Movement and light. At the end of the dock. By his boat.

Déjà vu. It smacked him free of his contented trance and he bolted from the vehicle. His long legs made quick work of the distance. He attempted to keep his steps light. This time he'd face off with his repeat intruder. This time there'd be no jumping to another boat and disappearing into the night. This time . . .

The intruder didn't flee at all.

No, but he did whirl when Wilder came up behind him and reached for his arm.

Not a he. It was the only thought he could finish before *she* shook free of his hold, slammed one palm into his chest, and lifted something that glinted in the moonlight with her other. A badge?

"Wilder Monroe?"

"Yes, who—"

"Agent Hannah Green. FBI."

The saline smell of the sea crowded the air around him as he took a step backward. "Another agent. Here? I've been trying to get ahold of—"

"Peter Franzen, I know. You called the Atlanta field office yesterday."

"I left a message with . . . I'm not sure who. A secretary? She wouldn't give me Agent Franzen's voicemail."

The woman—Agent Green—lowered her badge. "How do you know Franzen?"

What was happening here? "I met him last weekend. No, two weekends ago." Or was it three now? He was too confused in this moment to know. "He was in D.C. for a conference."

"And he presented himself as an agent?"

Presented himself? "Yes, of course. We spoke about—"

"Mr. Monroe, Peter Franzen is not an agent with the Atlanta office or any office with the Bureau. Not anymore."

"I don't . . . I don't understand. I met him at the D.C. office." *Outside the office. You never made it in the front door.*

"I think we better go inside and sit down," Agent Green said, her voice hard. "And then you're going to tell me everything."

16

WILDER

Make it to Portland?

LILIAN

Yes, and guess what. The carpet in this waiting room is the exact same mustard yellow as the carpet in Ansel's bedroom.

WILDER

Am I the only one who feels weird about how familiar we are now with your neighbor's bedroom?

LILIAN

You half live at our house. I think he counts as your neighbor, too.

Except you never stay the night anymore.

Finally realized how lumpy our couch really is, didn't you? You do remember we have two empty bedrooms upstairs, right?

278

WILDER

Is that your subtle way of saying you miss seeing me in the mornings? Neil's with me right now. Maybe I should see how he feels about me claiming his old bedroom. Right next door to yours. I bet he'd love that. I'll tell him it was your idea.

LILIAN

It was nice knowing you, Wilder. It really was.

WILDER

I wish I was there with you.

"*W*ilder?"

At the sound of Maggie's voice, Lilian looked up from her phone. The waiting room smelled of vanilla and spice. An aroma meant to be calming, no doubt, but it was messing with Lilian. Her churning stomach, her churning nerves . . . "Yes. He really wanted to come today."

And she'd wanted him here. So much it scared her a little. Their date on Saturday had been so very perfect. But then Sunday morning had rolled around, and with it, the memory of something Wilder had said the day before.

"I'm ready for life to feel a little easier."

Just one sentence squished between so many others. He'd gifted her with such heartfelt vulnerability that at first, she'd missed that one sentence. But yesterday it'd whispered in her ear, again and again. And this morning . . .

This morning she was meeting with a neurologist who might tell her life was about to get the opposite of easy. *It could be MS. It could be a brain tumor. It could be . . .*

Nothing. It could still be nothing.

One of Maggie's knees bumped into Lilian's as she shifted

in the padded waiting room chair. "He could've come with us. Or I could've stayed home if—"

"No, I'm glad you're here. I'm just sorry this is happening so close to your wedding. You should be enjoying your last days as a single woman, not carting me around to an appointment." Especially one that should've started half an hour ago. The receptionist had already come over to apologize to them twice. Dr. Cho's previous appointment was running late.

Lilian had been illogically relieved every time.

"You drove today so technically you did the carting." Maggie nudged her arm. "And you have no reason whatsoever to apologize. This is exactly where I belong."

"Well, Wilder couldn't come, no matter how much he wanted to. That FBI agent is meeting with him this morning." The one who'd upended everything all over again.

Poor Wilder. When he'd picked her up for church on Sunday morning, he'd looked as if he hadn't slept at all the night before. And maybe he hadn't. He'd spilled the whole thing, or as much as he knew of it, on their short drive into town.

"This agent, Agent Green—she was Franzen's partner. He was a dirty agent. By the time they knew, he'd disappeared and now she's tracking him. They know he's in Maine. They think he's right here in Muir Harbor, waiting for Peyton to wake up." Wilder had taken one hand off the steering wheel to undo the top button of his dress shirt, his long sigh rife with exasperation and exhaustion. *"Nicholas Cornish. Peyton. Peter Franzen. Agent Green. Mrs. Brazelli's missing brother. This thing has grown so many tentacles and I don't know anymore if a single one even connects to Cynthia."*

She'd almost insisted he stop the car. Or turn it around, head back to the farm or his houseboat instead. The man had needed sleep. Needed a break from trying to fit a bunch of puzzle pieces together. Pieces that might not even belong to the same picture. He needed . . .

He'd told her what he needed. He needed things to get a little easier.

Lilian leaned her head against the wall behind her.

"If we aren't called back to Dr. Cho's office pretty soon, I'm going to have to resort to an old-school tactic." Maggie cast Lilian a soft grin. "I'm going to have to put on my story-teller hat and don an accent and tell you The Legend of Muir Harbor."

Lilian rolled her head to look at Maggie. "Remember the time I called you before the LSAT?"

"How could I forget? I thought I was going to have to drive to your apartment and give you some of my blood pressure medication. But no, a little story time did the trick." Her hazel eyes scanned the waiting room, her gaze distant. "You and Diana. You both had such a fascination with that old legend."

"I really believed I was going to find that treasure once upon a time." Just like once upon a time she'd truly believed she was Maggie's missing granddaughter. That Diana was her mother.

Of course, it had never made sense. But she'd tricked her young mind for a while there. Convinced herself. Wanted to believe it so badly. Wanted to know . . .

"You've always been the imaginative one, Lily. People look at you and they see the accomplished lawyer and confident, capable woman. But you're more than one thing—we all are. You have a wild imagination and it's a lovely facet of who you are."

"I don't know why, but that feels like one of the nicest compliments I've ever received." So nice she had to look away for a moment. Swallow her rising emotion. "But you also forgot the part where people see me as straitlaced and bossy."

Maggie gave a hearty laugh. "I don't know, would a strait-laced woman sneak onto her enemy's houseboat?"

"How in the world do you know about that?"

"Or wake up in said houseboat by accident a few weeks later?"

She groaned. "No one's ever going to let me forget that, are they?"

"It's just such a hilarious picture in my mind."

She narrowed her eyes at Maggie. "I can't believe you. You should be concerned about propriety and inappropriate behavior and—"

"Wait, the way I heard it, there was no inappropriate behavior. Did I get the story wrong? If so, I would be more than willing to give you the requisite scolding if you really want it. But you're a thirty-year-old woman, so it feels like those days should be behind me."

"You're doing a very good job distracting me, by the way."

"I'm glad."

She studied Maggie for a moment, this woman who had taken her in and made Lilian her own. The mother of her heart. "Maggie?"

"What, dear?"

"Does it ever bother you that none of us call you Mom?"

Instead of answering quickly, Maggie considered the question. "No. No, I don't think so. I happen to like my name, for one thing. But for another, I guess I never needed to hear the title to know who I was to each of you. You weren't mine biologically, but I always felt . . . that I was yours. That God had written each of your names on my heart before He brought you into my life. What I was called wasn't nearly as important as the calling I was living out."

Why did tears seem to come so easily these days? "Did you have to give such a beautiful answer?"

"You asked."

"I know, but I'm overly emotional today. It's vexing."

"It's understandable. You're sitting outside a neurologist's office waiting for test results. Meanwhile, you're wrapped up in the most unexpected romance ever—"

Romance. "That word makes me uncomfortable."

"That word makes you blush."

"Okay, I think I'm ready to hear The Legend of Muir Harbor now."

Maggie laughed again. Then folded her hands in her lap. "Diana called me Mom, you know."

That was twice in the span of one conversation she'd brought up Diana. "You don't talk about her as much anymore."

Maggie was still for a moment. "I know. With the wedding coming up . . ." Maggie sighed. "I tormented myself for a lot of years, wishing I'd done so many things differently when Diana was young, wondering where we'd gone wrong, why she ran away, how there could be any purpose in her finally coming home if God was only going to take her away that same weekend, and my granddaughter . . ."

Another long sigh. Another moment of stillness. Then Maggie went on. "We tell ourselves stories, don't we? We tell ourselves the stories we think we need to hear to make it through. To find meaning. For the longest time, I told myself the story of my own failure as if that could explain everything. I told myself the story of Cynthia's disappearance because it felt like the one fixable thing in the middle of an unfixable tragedy. I still tell myself the story of her reappearance. Sometimes out of hope, sometimes, though less often recently, out of desperation."

Maggie looked to Lilian once more. "It's taken me a long time, but I've begun to tell myself a different story. The story of how I loved Diana the best I could as a young adoptive mother and how, despite the ups and downs, she loved me, too. I've been telling myself a story that's filled with what I do know instead of what I don't. I know that I told her about

Jesus, and that He was holding her close, even when I couldn't. I know that if I never know with certainty what happened to Cynthia, I can listen to a still, small voice promising me He knows. And He cares." Maggie laid her hand over Lilian's. "They matter—the stories we tell ourselves, which ones we choose to believe."

"But what happens when it turns out that's all they are— just stories? Just things we try to talk ourselves into?"

Like talking herself into believing she was Maggie's granddaughter.

Like talking herself into believing the tremors meant nothing. The numbness meant nothing. The MRI would show . . . nothing.

It would show something. Somehow she knew it. Somehow she knew she was going to walk into Dr. Cho's office with one story of her life and walk out with another.

"I think there's a little truth in every story. After all, sometimes truth isn't a fact, it's a light shining on an unexplored place in our heart that's hungry for healing. Stories can show us those places." Maggie squeezed her hand. "And then there's an invitation, a question. Not just what story will I listen to, but what story do I want my life to tell?"

They sat in silence for a few moments, Maggie's words wrapping around her. And somewhere in the background, Wilder's voice, too. *I'm ready for life to feel a little easier.*

And then, "Ms. Muir? Dr. Cho is ready for you."

"How could I have been such an idiot?"

Wilder slapped his paintbrush against the outer wall of the houseboat's living quarters. Eggshell white, Dad's preferred shade. He'd given the boat a fresh coat of paint every three years like clockwork.

She may not be the newest boat in the harbor, but she can still shine.

Three years. His first time painting without Dad.

"You're not an idiot, Wilder. You had no way of knowing." Neil dipped his brush into the nearly empty paint can at his feet.

Rollers would've made this so much easier, but with the boat's wood siding, grooved and uneven, it was impossible. "I never asked to see his badge. I didn't ask to see any proof." Peter Franzen had said he was with the FBI and Wilder had believed him without a second thought. "I'm supposed to be the guy with the infallible gut instinct, and the man didn't even have to try to fool me. Why didn't I think to question it when we didn't go inside the D.C. office?"

And why was he here on his boat right now instead of with Lilian in Portland? Agent Green would be here any minute, but he could've stood her up. Lilian was more important, and he wanted to be at her side when that neurologist told her the results of her MRI.

But she'd said Maggie was going with her, and he was trying not to read anything into that.

One date. You've only been on one date. Unless he counted the entirety of yesterday—church and lunch at the farm and an afternoon of card games with her family, an evening walk out to her vegetable garden after dinner. They'd pulled a few early weeds and then simply sat in the dirt and watched the sun set.

Perfect as the day had been, it'd been difficult not to let his unexpected visit from the Bureau agent the previous night intrude on his thoughts. The stern expression hadn't lifted from Agent Green's face once as he'd let her into the houseboat, tapped on the lights. He'd opened his fridge hoping to find something to offer her, but he ate so few meals there, he'd come up empty.

He'd finally settled for filling a glass of water. She'd never even taken a sip. It'd just sat there untouched on his small table, all through his recounting of how Franzen had first contacted him, how they'd met in D.C., how the agent—ex-agent—had told Wilder to call him if Peyton Cornish ever woke from his coma.

"But you haven't spoken to him since you met in D.C.?"

Wilder had shaken his head. *"I'm struggling to come to grips with what's going on here."*

"What's going on here is you've gotten yourself into the middle of a hushed-up manhunt. Franzen wasn't lying when he said he's been after Nicholas Cornish for over a decade. But about seven months ago, we got an anonymous tip that there might be a reason we've never been able to make anything stick where Cornish is concerned."

"Franzen was in on it. He was a dirty agent."

Agent Green nodded. *"Not sure how long it stretches back, but we know at least several years. We think the tip came from someone inside Cornish's circle. Something went wrong between them. There has to be a reason he'd risk contacting you."*

"Wilder." Neil nudged him, pointed to the drips of paint Wilder's brush had dropped on the deck.

"None of it makes sense. All I've ever been trying to do is find Maggie's granddaughter and somehow I end up in the middle of a turf war." The pungent odor of the paint fused with the briny scent of seawater, and the afternoon sun felt overly warm for this early in June. "I should be in Portland right now."

He abandoned his paintbrush, then crossed the deck, sandals slapping against the wood, to retrieve an unopened can of paint. He found a screwdriver and pried the lid from the can, legs protesting at his prolonged crouch.

"Are you really going to do it, Wild? Sell the boat? That's why we're painting it, right?"

"I don't know. Maybe." He rose, accepting Neil's questions for what they were—a distraction. "To tell you the truth, I'm thinking about changing more than my living situation. I'm thinking about . . . well, turning in my badge, as it were. Saying adios to the private eye life."

Neil had reached for his paintbrush, but now he let it drop onto his paint tray once more. "No way, seriously? What would you do?"

Wilder poured a lake of syrupy paint into the tray. "Not sure. I'm not really strapped for cash, so there'd be no rush to decide. Maybe I buy up all Ansel's land." He glanced to his friend. "Maybe I keep the house but turn around and sell the fields at a steal of a price to this farmer I know."

"Wilder—"

"Or fine, I rent them out at mutually-agreed-upon terms that are beneficial to all parties until one of said parties is in a good place to buy the land at a reasonable but slightly-under-market-value price." He went on before Neil could argue. "And then maybe I take my time fixing up the house, seeing what it feels like not to be at the beck and call of a case."

Neil studied him. "You wouldn't miss it?"

"The P.I. work? I doubt it." When he'd left Basic Field Training, walked away from his old FBI dream, it hadn't been because of some deep desire to be a private eye. He'd just liked the idea of working alongside Dad. Coming home. Being around the people he loved.

Maybe the FBI hadn't ever been his real dream in the first place. Maybe some people didn't dream of a thing to do but a place to be. And people to be with.

Somewhere to belong. Someone to belong to.

He'd lost his someone when Dad died. But now . . .

"Morning, Monroe."

Wilder rose, head turning to the sound of Agent Green's voice, drifting from where she stood at the edge of the dock. Same slick ponytail as Saturday night. Dark slacks, gray shirt —a shadow juxtaposed with the bright day.

Why had he agreed to meet with her again this morning? He'd already told the agent everything he had to tell the other night. *I shouldn't be here. I should be in Portland.* "Good morning," he finally uttered.

She stepped onto the boat, sliding a glance to Neil. "Should we go inside?"

Wilder lifted a hand to shield his eyes. "That's Neil. He's connected to my case. There's no need—"

"It's fine," Neil cut in. "Go on. I'm ready for a break anyway. I'll run downtown and grab lunch."

Wilder swallowed his sigh and nodded, then led Agent Green inside. It was the same song and dance as Saturday. He motioned to the table, opened the fridge. This time, at least, he'd had the chance to think ahead. "Soda?"

She looked like she might refuse, but then she shrugged. "Sure."

He handed her a can of Coca-Cola, then took the seat across from her. "Sorry it's so warm in here." He'd opened the windows last night, had fallen asleep to the whoosh of the wind and the gulping tide. The clammy breeze pushed its way through the houseboat now. He liked the airflow, but the humidity made his soda can sweat. "I could turn on the A/C."

The agent waved her hand. "I need to be back at the hotel in forty."

Which apparently meant there was no time to waste. "Staying at The Lodge?"

She nodded. "We've set up a mini-headquarters. Took some work convincing my superior it was worth me sticking around for a few days. But we've got Peter on a gas station security cam fifteen miles from here. There's only one town in Maine he'd have a reason to come to. *Two* reasons—you, Peyton Cornish."

He downed half his soda in one gulp just to avoid the directness in her stare. "Doubt I'm a reason. Already told you —he hasn't contacted me since D.C. I called and texted him, never heard back."

"Still. He contacted you in the first place. There had to have been a reason."

It was the same thing she'd said Saturday night. And all he had to offer was the same response. "He wanted to know what I knew about Cornish. He said he was still trying to track down stolen goods, track down others in the fencing ring."

Agent Green nodded. "I think what he's really trying to track down is a storehouse. Cornish didn't just fence artwork and jewelry and any number of things. He provided storage, which can be as valuable to a thief looking to offload his loot as finding a buyer. Twice, we almost nailed his location. And twice, we found ourselves staring into emptiness. A warehouse, a shipyard building—both times, someone tipped him off before we made our move."

And they believed that someone was Franzen.

"If Franzen's in Muir Harbor, it must be because he thinks Peyton can tell him something," she added. She'd said that Saturday night, too. "Or . . . there's one other possibility."

He lowered his can and spread his hands. "He has to know by now I've got nothing for him to go on."

"Not what I meant but—"

"We can go over all of this again if you really want, but I've got my own investigation going."

Two investigations, if he counted Leo James. Since returning from Atlanta, he'd made some inquiries. He'd called The Lodge and other hotels in surrounding towns, charmed his way into finding out if a man by that name had stayed in Muir Harbor in late-September 1990. He'd gotten the make and model of the man's vehicle from the Brazellis and looked for it on security cameras, just as the Bureau had done in their search for Franzen.

He'd come up empty over and over again. Calls to area hospitals had been just as fruitless. Without a court order, no way was he getting ahold of patient information.

He was chasing another pointless lead, wasn't he? A lead that wasn't a lead at all. And he didn't know what to do anymore. Doggedly keep going or throw in the towel? He'd just told Neil a few minutes ago he might be ready to leave the P.I. life behind. But there was such a difference between choosing to walk away from something and realizing maybe there was nothing left to walk away from.

Other than a distinct sense of failure.

"It's not his handwriting, by the way."

He looked across the table. "Sorry, I was lost in thought for a second there."

"The plant at Peyton's bedside, the card." Agent Green finally popped the tab on her soda can. "It's not Peter's handwriting."

"Oh." He'd mentioned the card to the agent on Saturday night, along with the break-in at his houseboat, the possibility that someone had been at Lilian's law office. *Maybe some of it's related, maybe some of it's not. But I do know someone has been visiting Peyton. Could be Franzen, I suppose. And I know I know that handwriting.* But then, he'd never seen Peter Franzen's handwriting.

So the plant and card weren't from him. At least not directly.

He downed the last of his cola, frustration chugging through him. "Look, I apologize that I'm not more help here. I wish I could be." He might as well be honest. "No, what I really wish is that you could be of some help to me. But we're after separate things here so I—"

"I can be."

"—can't help feeling like I'm wasting . . ." His voice lagged as her words sank in. "What?"

"Leo James. We ran his VIN. His car was pulled over on September 30, 1990, here in Maine. Sanford, to be exact. Middle of the night. Broken headlight."

"How . . . I . . ." He had a cop buddy looking for any trace of the vehicle's VIN showing up in police records, but apparently the FBI worked faster. He'd told the agent all about his search for Cynthia Muir and the possibly related, possibly not disappearance of Leo James on Saturday. "He was here. He was in Maine." September 30. The day after Diana's death.

"Well, the car was," the agent said. "If James was the one driving it, he was using an alias, complete with an ID and registration. But if it wasn't him . . . then what? He just happened to offload his car to someone who just happened to be in Maine at the same time as your other mystery is unfolding? That's a bigger stretch to me than the alternative."

The alternative being that Mrs. Brazelli's brother, who'd worked for Nicholas Cornish, had known Diana. That when they'd both left Atlanta, they'd been together. That he'd come to Muir Harbor with her.

Agent Green pulled out her phone and started tapping. "I'm texting you the info we have, including the name the person driving the car used. You'll have to take it from there."

Middle of the night. Broken headlight. Leo James could've been at the site of the accident. He could've been speeding away. He could've—really, he could've—had a child in that car with him. He could've had Cynthia.

Which meant, if Wilder could find this man . . . "Thank you. Seriously, I'm more grateful than I can say. I've been so close to giving up."

Agent Green pocketed her phone, her eyes never straying from Wilder's face. "You can't. You won't."

"How do you know that?"

"Because somewhere along the way, it got personal. It's written all over you. And once it gets personal, you don't have a choice." She flicked the tab on her soda can with a look that said, *Ask me how I know.*

She knew because her partner had betrayed her. And he recognized that look of bleak resignation on her face. The one tinged with desolation.

That night when he'd found Lilian Muir on his houseboat, when he'd trudged into his bathroom and looked in his mirror . . . that's what he'd seen staring back at him.

Agent Green hunched her shoulders as she leaned forward now, elbows digging into the tabletop. "I've looked into you, Monroe. You've got a rep. You're not just a P.I., you're a good one. That means you notice details. You see things other people don't. Keep thinking and call me if something else comes to mind about Franzen, your meeting with him, anything."

He nodded and she rose.

And right then, as if on cue, his phone blared into the silence. He pulled it from his pocket and let out a shallow breath at the name on the screen. *Lilian.*

17

*G*ilded early evening light teased the edges of Lilian's bedroom window like a frame. How long had she been sitting here like this on her bed, legs bent and knees pressed against her chest, waiting for telltale thumps on the creaking old stairs?

Waiting for Wilder. Wondering how to tell him what she hadn't told him before.

Maybe she and Maggie should've come home sooner. Should've skipped a late lunch at that sidewalk café in Portland, an afternoon of shopping for candles and wedding favors and simple jewelry to go with Maggie's wedding dress.

Maggie's attempt at soothing Lilian the best way she knew how—by helping her cross items off a list. And all the while, Lilian had known . . . he knew.

Because he was Wilder Monroe. Because she was positive she hadn't been at all convincing in the half-answers she'd given him over the phone earlier.

"It was basically a non-diagnosis. I don't have much in the way of answers. I don't really know any more now than I did before. I'm fine, just . . . well, I think it's great to have this one-on-one time with

Maggie before her wedding, so we're going to do some shopping. Tell you more when I'm home, okay?"

He knew. Of course he did.

"Lil?"

She startled, letting her legs drop and her feet hit the floor. She hadn't heard his steps. She should've heard him coming up the stairs. Or sensed him standing in her doorway. Something told her he'd been there for more than a few seconds.

He was wearing that olive green shirt again. The one that turned his eyes to agates and stretched just right over his chest.

Which was suddenly the only place she wanted to be. She covered the distance to him in a few long strides and pressed herself against him, kissed the jaw he hadn't shaven today and breathed him in. "I missed you."

He combed his fingers through her hair, then rested his palm against the back of her head, her face tucked into the curve of his neck. And for a moment, she was back in Portland, back to that day when she'd found him waiting for her after her MRI. Back to an embrace just like this one.

Only then, amid a swirl of other feelings, had been a shockwave of surprise revelation. The surprise that she was so very happy to see him. The surprise of how much she'd missed him. How much, how incredibly, impossibly much, she needed him.

But there was no surprise this time. This thing between them had gone from unlikely to undeniable.

Which only made the push and pull going on in her heart all the more unbearable.

"I need you to tell me the rest of it, Lil. That phone call . . . you didn't say much. And I didn't want to push, but you have to know it kind of killed me. I know there's more."

"There is." She took a step back, and then, at the sound of the front door opening, Indi's voice drifting up the stairs, she reached behind him to close her bedroom door. She'd already talked to the rest of them. But something told her this conversation would be harder than the rest.

Not so much because of what she had to tell him. But because Wilder would see what the others might not. His dark eyes would look right past her calm words and her stoic acceptance and he'd see . . . everything.

She retook her place on her bed and half expected him to sit beside her. Instead, he dipped into the chair at her desk. She could feel his probing gaze. *Just start talking.*

"So, the MRI showed a lesion on my brain. It's consistent with the kind of lesions people with MS have."

He scooted his chair closer to the bed. Took a breath. "Okay. So then it's—"

"No. Or, well, not yet. And maybe never . . . but possibly eventually . . ." She shook her head. She needed the logical side of her brain to start working so she could get this out.

Her brain might turn on her someday. Or not. And that was the thing—she didn't know. She didn't know. She still had questions, but the questions didn't have answers. At least not right now.

"Dr. Cho said to receive a diagnosis of MS, you need to see two areas of damage from two separate neurological episodes. When I told my regular doctor about that time in law school when I had some of the same symptoms as I did this spring, that clued her in apparently. Both she and Dr. Cho thought the two things might be related. One plus one equals . . ." She slid her palms over her jeans. "But the MRI only showed one lesion. So maybe that first time it really was just stress. Or something else. I don't know."

I don't know, I don't know, I don't know.

She couldn't stand those words. Ever since that day in front of her class, all those raised hands, all those questions. And the same answer every time. *I don't know.*

"Anyway, Dr. Cho is calling it clinically isolated syndrome. It's a term that describes the first instance of a clinical episode that could suggest multiple sclerosis. Not everyone who has CIS goes on to develop MS, but Dr. Cho said because of the one lesion and how long my first episode lasted, he considers me a high-risk of developing it. He wants me to consider starting treatments. He called it disease-modifying therapy." She hurried through the facts, like a train racing over its tracks, trying not to feel too much. "He also wants to do a spinal tap. Sometimes they find a-a band or something in the fluid. I can't remember what it's called."

He moved from the chair to the bed, sliding his arm around her waist. "I'm just so happy it's not as bad as it could've been."

She pulled back. "I don't think you're hearing me. High-risk, that's what Dr. Cho said. People considered high-risk have a sixty- to eighty-percent chance of going on to have MS. And for half of those people, it ends up being debilitating. Not usually right away, but eventually."

"Yes, but what I'm hearing is there's a chance you never have another episode."

She needed space. Room to breathe. She needed someone to tell her why she couldn't embrace the hope and relief she saw written all over Wilder's handsome face. She'd seen the very same on Maggie's when they'd left Dr. Cho's office.

"Clinically isolated syndrome. I say we focus on that second word. We pray this was absolutely just an isolated incident."

Why couldn't she be happy about this? Why couldn't she build a case like she always did? A case for why this *was* good news.

Because you've been here before.

Because she'd talked herself into the best-case scenario once before only to have the hope knocked right out of her.

"It's impossible, Lil. You'll probably never know. You need to accept it."

Wilder's old words from so long ago didn't apply now, though. She'd been a child then. She'd built up a fantasy in her head and watched it topple, but that didn't mean this would, too.

But what about his words from just two days ago? *"I'm ready for life to feel a little easier."*

"I guess it's good news and bad news and no news. All I can do now is wait and see if it happens again and try to decide whether or not to start that therapy. Dr. Cho said there are a variety of factors to consider, but . . ." Her voice finally cracked. "I'm just . . ."

She didn't know what she was. All she knew was that all day she hadn't been able to stop thinking about how Wilder Monroe had already been through so much. He'd lived through the trauma of a life-changing diagnosis already. He'd never known his mother because of one disease. Lost his father because of another.

She slipped away from him and stood. "Have you had dinner yet? Maggie and I had a huge lunch, so I'm not really hungry but if you are, we could . . ."

His marble eyes told her the truth. She'd been right. He was seeing everything. Hearing everything she wasn't saying.

"This doesn't change things for me, Lil."

"But what if it does for me?" It slipped out so quickly, it took her aback every bit as much as it clearly did Wilder.

She hadn't meant it. Or maybe she had. *God, I don't know. Please . . .* The prayer hung there, unmoving, unfinished.

Wilder rubbed one palm over his face, the tic in his jaw pronounced, and when he finally spoke again, his words came slowly and deliberately. "You heard me say I would've given anything to be there for Dad. To walk with him through whatever was waiting for him. I didn't need sparing then. And I don't need sparing now."

She couldn't tell if her pulse had slowed or pounded into a sprint. Whether her heart was begging her to fall into his arms or warning her away. "You just told me the other night that you're ready for life to get easier."

"I didn't mean—"

"This whole thing, you and me, it's happened so fast. And it's happened in the middle of so much craziness—your case, my health. All these unknowns." She sagged against her dresser. "I'm so tired of unanswered questions."

"Then start asking different questions." He stood abruptly, agitation fueling his tone and each of the steps he took toward her. Even so, his hands were gentle as they took hold of hers. "I don't think this is about me, Lil. I think it's about you."

"You think I don't know that? I've already got a past that's a blank slate. Now I'm looking at a future where nothing feels clear anymore."

"But I'm here. That should be clear. I'm right here." He waited to go on until she looked up at him. "But you can't see that because you're afraid."

"Don't tell me what I am, Wilder."

"You're pulling away because you're afraid. Because none of this, not me, not a disease you may or may not have, fits into a neat and tidy plan like a wedding to-do list. But no plan, however perfect, was ever going to give you what you really want."

She slipped her hands free, stepped back and bumped into her dresser, hard enough it'd probably leave a bruise. "And what is that? If you know me so well, what is it I really want?"

"Certainty, Lil. You want absolute certainty that no one's ever going to abandon you again. So if you need to jump ship first, you will."

Her breaths were coming hard and fast now. She was

overly warm and overly worked up. She turned away from Wilder, but she couldn't escape his gaze. Because there it was, looking back at her in the mirror over her dresser.

And then, there it wasn't. His gaze drifted away, off to the side.

To where that old, insufficient note peeked out from behind the mirror. All she knew of her *before*. Her name. Her birth date. Her allergy.

Wilder inched backward, staring at the corner of the note.

"Wilder, I-I'm sorry. I didn't mean . . . It wasn't supposed to be like this." What *it* did she even mean? This conversation? This relationship they'd stumbled into? "It was just a difficult day and I'm . . . all muddled up. I have some hard choices to consider."

Wilder didn't answer.

"I haven't even asked . . . your conversation with the Bureau agent. How did it go?"

It was as if he didn't hear her. He turned away, raked his fingers through his hair. Then turned back. "She was wrong. Agent Green was wrong. We do get a choice."

"I don't understand."

"I don't want to be the reason you make a hard choice, Lil. I want to *be* your choice. You're mine. If I haven't made that clear yet, I choose you. MS or no MS. I won't ever abandon you. I guess you just have to decide if you believe that or not."

He glanced again at the note. Why?

But there was no asking him. He was gone in the next moment.

⚬──────⚬

The steering wheel of his Jeep was no lifeline, but Wilder's fingers gripped it in desperation all the same, knuckles white, the tightness stretching all the way into the muscles in his arms.

Ahead of him, the taillights of another car bled red into the night.

He was such a fool. He'd handled every second of that conversation with Lilian so very wrong. He *knew* her. He knew how hard it was for her to feel exposed, uncertain. And what had he done?

He'd made her feel like a child again, standing up in front of a classroom and getting pummeled. Only instead of lobbing questions at her, he'd hurled accusations. *I'm a fool.* Why couldn't he have just listened? And if he had to open his big mouth, why couldn't he have found better words?

And then the way he'd left . . .

But he'd had to. Because of that note. Because of what he'd realized.

Wan sunlight poured over the landscape, though clouds hovered in the distance. Any other night, he'd take the long way, enjoy the scenery, the curve of the coast, the rollicking sea on one side of his Jeep, trees and rolling hills on the other.

But he couldn't tonight. He had to know for sure. He pressed harder on the gas pedal.

And yet, with every mile between him and Lilian, his gut twisted all the more. He'd meant every word he'd said to her before he'd left. Maybe it was too fast. Maybe it was too soon. One date—they'd only been on one date. And yet, he'd meant those words more than he'd ever meant anything—*I choose you.*

Truthfully, his heart had chosen her long before now. Forget his old FBI dream. Forget buying Ansel Barrett's house. Lilian Muir had become his dream. It'd happened like a bolt of lightning hitting the water. It'd happened like a slow ripple drifting out to sea.

It'd just *happened.*

And now he feared he was losing her. Already. Too soon. Why was it always too soon?

She's not Dad. She's not dying.

No. But she might be pulling away. And he might've only made things worse with everything he'd said tonight. Why couldn't he have just given her some space? He lifted his phone. Should he call her?

Listen to yourself. One second regretting that he hadn't given her space. The next . . .

He abandoned his phone in the console, rubbed his palm over his forehead. Tried to focus. The note . . . He should've realized earlier.

How many minutes passed while his murky thoughts pulled him deeper and deeper into an abyss? Enough to get him to his destination. Enough to temporarily numb him.

He parked his Jeep and climbed out, crossed the parking lot in a near trance. He'd have to talk his way into the room. Visiting hours would've ended long ago, and Agent Green would have the room under close watch.

Because she was convinced Peter Franzen would show up here, intent on talking to Peyton Cornish.

Well, Franzen wasn't the only one.

Fatigue hounded his every step—through the lobby, up the elevator. Of course, the memory found him. This same building. This same elevator. *Lilian.* An almost-kiss that had paved the way for more. More closeness. More togetherness. More kisses.

God, I can't let her go.

The elevator spilled him into the hushed third floor, the evening lights dim, the hallway empty and still. His stomach growled into the silence. He should've grabbed food on the way. His clipped steps echoed in the vacant corridor.

And then, a hasty explanation to the young FBI agent

posted at Peyton's door. The agent's text to Hannah Green. Thankfully, a quick reply.

And just like that, he was in. Details crowded altogether. IV bag. Monitor. Odors—latex, then bleach. From the shining floor or maybe the crisp sheet tucked around Peyton's motionless form.

He stopped short halfway into the room. The plant. Where was the plant he'd seen on the bedside table?

"What are you doing here?" The voice was little more than a scratch, coming from pasty lips. Peyton's head was turned toward Wilder, a near-tangible lethargy hanging heavy in his drooped gaze, along with a dark, unmistakable recognition.

"So you know me." He'd wondered how much Peyton would remember of the days and weeks leading up to his fall from the cliff. Five months in a coma could've wiped whole swathes of the man's memory.

Wilder had only ever talked to Peyton a few times, long before he'd known who the man really was. Even then, he hadn't liked him. Hadn't liked the way Peyton had latched on to Lilian.

The thought was a jolt. *Even then . . .*

Even then, maybe his heart had known something his head hadn't yet. Harbored feelings for Lilian that had yet to surface. A gut instinct he'd failed to interpret. Which seemed to be happening more and more. Maybe that's what happened when a man fell in . . . *love?* Was he really there already?

Was it even a question?

No, it wasn't. And yes, he was. He knew it now, standing in the dim lighting of this eerie room. He was completely and absolutely in love with Lilian Muir.

And if he lost her . . . if she left him like Dad did—

"I have nothing to say to you. You should leave."

Did the agent outside know Peyton was awake? Last

Wilder had known, Peyton had been drifting in and out of consciousness for days.

"Where's your plant?"

Peyton struggled to sit up in his bed, ignoring the question.

"More importantly, who brought it to you? Do you know?" And the note. Where was the note?

The note with the handwriting. Handwriting that might be . . . couldn't be . . .

"I want to see Lilian."

His eyes flashed once more to Peyton. "Why?"

"You think I don't know there's an agent on the other side of that door? I'm going to need a lawyer."

"There's no chance in—"

"I talk to Lilian or I talk to no one."

Wilder was breathing too heavily. Feeling far too much temptation to stalk the remaining distance to the bed and . . . do what? Lose his last hold on his temper and injure a man who'd already suffered broken bones and internal injuries and months in a coma? "Why her?"

The answer was right there, circling around at the edges of his brain. Something he'd missed. A detail.

"You notice details. You see things other people don't." Agent Green's voice.

But he hadn't seen this. In all the mess, in all the chaos, he'd missed it. But it was staring at him now, a glaring truth, hammering in his head. Twisting in his stomach. "The plant—"

"It probably died."

"The note. Who . . . ? I need to see the note."

Peyton's quick glance at the lamp wasn't quick enough. *Finally.* Wilder strode to the bedside table, lifted the lamp with one hand, and swiped the other underneath. And when he came up with the note, when he held it up in front of him, he could all but hear it mocking him.

It was right here. Right here in front of him.

The truth.

Yes, he knew this handwriting. It was the same writing that was on the note behind Lilian's mirror. The note someone had pinned to her overalls before leaving her on Maggie's porch.

"You've figured it out, then."

Heart pounding, he turned, slowly, to Peyton. The man had given up on his attempt to sit up. He was lying prone again, his gaze lifted to the ceiling, growing hazy.

"I need to know who wrote this, Peyton. I need you to tell me—"

The man's eyes were drifting to a close.

"Don't you dare go to sleep. Who wrote this?" Was he shouting? Was that why he was hearing footsteps rushing into the room behind him? The agent, maybe a nurse. Didn't matter. All that mattered were answers.

"Peyton—"

"I came for her." He closed his eyes, his last words barely a murmur, but clear enough to send a chill through Wilder. "Now he has, too."

*T*he hallway was too quiet.

Lilian sat at the top of the staircase, the spot where she'd landed she didn't even know how long ago. After Wilder had left her bedroom, eventually she had too. But she'd gotten no farther than here.

This hallway that was slowly emptying. Neil's bedroom—empty. The guest room—unoccupied. Indi would move out eventually. She'd marry Philip and . . .

There'd be just Lilian in her middle room.

"Hey, you."

She'd missed the padding of Indi's steps behind her. She'd been sitting here like a zombie. Frozen and forlorn.

And missing Wilder. Missing him with every inch of her heart and kicking herself for doing exactly, *exactly* what he'd said. *"You're pulling away because you're afraid."*

Indi lowered onto the step beside her. "You okay?"

"Yeah." No. "Just thinking."

"About?"

"About how hollow this second floor is going to feel when you marry Philip and leave."

"Certainty, Lil. You want absolute certainty that no one's ever

going to abandon you again. So if you need to jump ship first, you will."

Good grief, it was like her skin and bones were nothing but a glass window for Wilder to look straight through. Straight into her heart. Why did he have to see everything?

"Uh, is there something you know that I don't? Because Philip and I aren't in a rush. He's got a book deadline and Holland still has another year of high school. I've only just connected with Olivia."

Olivia, yes. The daughter Indi had given birth to as a teenager. "I'm so happy she's in your life now, Indi. I've been so self-focused lately. There're so many good things . . ." All the healing in Indi's life. Neil and Sydney and a baby on the way. Maggie about to marry a wonderful man.

"Wilder. He's a good thing, yeah?"

A good thing? Try myriad good things—so incredibly good —wrapped up in one person. There'd been days last week when she'd counted his touches—a brush of his hand while they finalized the wedding reception menu, his arm around her shoulder while they sat on the porch swing—the way he'd once tracked their growing collection of civil conversations. Until, just like him, she'd lost count. Until his touch, just like his company, had become completely normal.

And yet, the opposite of normal. Because how could you call something normal when everything about it, everything about him, felt vivid and interesting and exhilarating?

"I think I messed things up with him. I pushed him away."

"Lil, you've spent two decades pushing him away and he hasn't gone anywhere."

"It's different now. We're different."

"I know, and it's been fabulously entertaining to watch."

She couldn't even muster up a glare for her sister, playful or otherwise. All she could manage was a groan. "I don't know why I'm like this. The news I got today wasn't nearly as bad as it could've been. I should be grateful. And this man comes along who I honestly think might know my heart better than I do and what do I do? I get scared and retreat. It's like . . . there's something broken inside of me. Wilder's completely right. I'm still afraid of being left behind. I'm still that little kid who doesn't know who she is."

"Oh, Lilian." Indi scooted closer on the stair and draped her arm around Lilian. "You went through something traumatic as a child. You're going through something difficult now. There's not a manual for navigating any of it."

"I've accepted that I'm probably never going to know where I came from. Or, at least, I've tried. I've really, really tried. But now this. Now I'm supposed to accept a future where I may have a neurological disorder. And if I do, I don't get to know ahead of time how bad it's going to be. There's no planning for this." She lowered her forehead to her knees. "I hate how whiny I sound."

"Stop berating yourself, please. You are allowed to be upset in this moment, Lil. You're allowed to be sad and angry and confused and a thousand other emotions if you want. You're allowed to be a human and you're allowed to be weak. You don't always have to be the capable one who has it all together. Take it from the younger sister who has looked up to you for your entire life, who's never quite felt as put-together as you—you'd be doing that sister a favor to just throw a good, old-fashioned fit right now."

At some point while Indi was talking, tears had pooled in Lilian's eyes. They spilled down her cheeks now, even as a mangled laugh tried to push free. "I've never had it all together."

"Well, you could've fooled me." Indi stroked the back of Lilian's head as the tears kept coming. "You did fool me."

"I don't want to have MS." Her voice shook around a sob. "I don't want to wonder every day if . . . if it's coming."

"I know. I know."

"I don't want to still be living in my childhood bedroom while everyone else is moving on. I don't want to be stuck."

"Lil—"

"I'm scared and I don't want to lose Wilder—"

"You haven't. I'm sure you haven't. The man adores you. You've usurped Neil's place in his life."

Another frayed laugh tried to push through her clogged throat, but she was crying too hard now. There was nothing more to do but give up, to let it all out, every crumpled emotion. Just spilling and spilling, until she was out of breath and out of tears. Until her head hurt and eyes were swollen.

Until she could find her voice once more. "W-well. You got your wish."

Indi still had her arm around Lilian, but somewhere in the past few minutes, she'd lifted her other arm, too, circling around Lilian's front, huddling around her big sister on the perch at the top of the staircase. "I did. I really did."

"I hope my breakdown was everything you dreamed." She finally found something close to a laugh, a hiccup cutting through it.

Indi pulled away just slightly, dropping one hand to Lilian's knee. "I've never truly wished for you to break down. I hope you know that. I also hope you know that it doesn't matter if I do marry Philip and move out of this house or if Neil and Syd have a dozen kids. The three of us are bonded for life. And you have a built-in support system for whatever comes your way. One that's probably going to include Wilder, whether you like it or not."

She hiccupped again, nearly managed to smile. "He's so annoying. He's so right all the time."

"I can't believe I just heard you say that. If ever I needed proof you've completely reversed course on the guy, that was it."

"He's been through more than you know, Indi. If I have another episode, if I get sick . . ." She pushed out a sigh, strands of hair billowing around her face. "I wish I knew what the future held."

"What do you want it to hold?"

Such a simple question, and yet it made her catch her breath. It slowed the rushing river of her emotions.

"I'm so tired of unanswered questions."

"Then start asking different questions."

Oh, Wilder. He'd been so exasperated but so . . . wise.

What did she want her future to hold? *There* was a different question. There was a question she could answer. She didn't have to build a case in order to answer it. She didn't need a plan and there was no list.

There was just the plain, indisputable truth.

"Don't let fear make your decisions." Mariana's voice.

And then Maggie's. *"What story do I want my life to tell?"*

"I have to go." She stood and started down the stairs.

"What?" Indi jumped up behind her.

"Thank you, Indi," she called over her shoulder. "Thank you so much." She was out the front door in seconds, halfway to her car before she realized she didn't have her keys. She raced back into the house, fumbled for her jacket on the coat tree, waved at Indi, and let a laugh free once she was outside. She'd left her sister clueless and bewildered.

Or maybe not so clueless. Because by the time she reached her car, Indi was on the porch. "Tell Wilder he owes me."

Clouds rumbled in the sky, casting shadows over the landscape. She made it to the harbor in under ten minutes. Jogged from her parking spot down the dock, to the houseboat, her heart lifting at the sight of a light on inside. She stepped onto the deck, the smell of fresh paint and coming rain blowing around her as the breeze picked up. She didn't bother knocking, pushed open the door.

"Wilder, I'm sorry. I'm so sorry. I did what you said. I asked a different question. Well, Indi asked it but I'm going to answer it right—"

Her words evaporated into the air at the sight of the man rising from Wilder's green couch. *Not Wilder.*

"Um, I'm . . . who . . ."

The man was tall and thin and not at all familiar. Mossy black hair, hawkish features. Eyes pinned on her. "I was waiting for Monroe, but this will do just as well. Better, really. Lilian Muir, nice to meet you."

"I-I don't know—"

"Peter Franzen, at your service."

The agent. The *ex*-agent. "Oh."

"Recognize the name, do you? Good. In that case, I trust you'll be cooperative?" His shadow loomed over her as he approached.

"Cooperative?" Dread pooled in her stomach. She needed to call Wilder. Her phone—had she even grabbed it before leaving the house? She turned to the door, but the man—Franzen—was too quick.

He blocked her path with ease. "You've saved me a trip, you see. I was going to ask Monroe a few questions and then fetch you, but Monroe isn't here and you are. So . . . change of plans."

Something told her the man had wanted more than to ask Wilder a few questions. Something told her he knew Wilder knew the truth about him. Maybe even that Wilder had been in contact with the Bureau. He wasn't here to talk to Wilder. He was here to hurt him.

"I don't know what you want but—"

"I want you to come with me. No arguments. No difficulty."

She steeled herself. "Not happening."

Instead of replying, he nudged his jacket aside. And she

saw exactly what he wanted her to. Her inhale was sharp, but it didn't do a thing to slice through her instant alarm. Even so, as she dragged her gaze from the gun at his waist to meet his eyes, she refused to shrink back.

If going with him meant sparing Wilder whatever he'd intended, then okay. She'd go. But she wouldn't cower.

He met her scowl with a sneer of his own. "Let's go, Miss Muir. We have somewhere to be."

19

"What do you mean she isn't here?"

Everyone in the farmhouse kitchen was staring at him. Maggie and Indi standing at the counter, dishing out bowls of ice cream. Neil and Sydney at the table. All staring.

And he didn't blame them. Certainly they'd heard him thundering his way up the staircase minutes ago, then barreling back down. And then, considering how he'd burst into the kitchen, he probably looked half-crazed.

He felt half-crazed. He didn't even know how many times he'd tried calling Lilian on his way home from the care center. His heartbeat was stuck in some kind of staccato that made it impossible to take a deep breath.

But worse was the flash of heat in his gut. The feeling that it was happening again. That he was too late again. Like with Dad . . .

Too late, too late.

"I need to find her."

Indi rounded the island counter. "She went looking for you an hour ago. She's probably at your boat right now, impatiently waiting for you to show up."

"Okay." He spun and started down the hallway, toward the front door.

"Wilder, wait." Neil hurried after him. "What's going on? You look freaked out."

"I found something out. About Lil. And Peyton. And . . ." And it didn't make sense. And he still wasn't sure he believed it. And . . . he didn't have time for this conversation.

Because he couldn't shake it. He just couldn't shake the feeling that had grown stronger and stronger with every mile that had carried him closer to Muir Harbor. Something was wrong. Something was very wrong. "I need to find her. If she shows up, call me, but I'm going—"

"I'll go with you. Just let me run upstairs and grab my phone, get some shoes."

"Can't wait. Follow in your truck if you want."

And then he was out the door, breaking into a jog, bolting into his Jeep. He sped down the lane and gunned the engine as soon as he hit blacktop, passing every car he could on the way into town.

Relief flooded him the moment he spotted Lilian's car in the harbor's parking lot.

And then left him less than a minute later when he stood in the middle of his empty boat. "Lil, where are you?" His voice was a whisper, almost a moan.

He'd tried calling her two more times on his way, and he tried again now.

Nothing. *Nothing.*

She was here.

He knew that much.

And not alone.

He froze. Yes, someone else had been here. The cushions on the couch, the trunk-turned-coffee-table, Dad's boots . . . everything was just slightly askew. And there was a can of soda sweating on an end table, probably leaving a ring. Lilian would never . . .

Neil charged in. "Is she here?"

Wilder shook his head, the dread crawling up his throat stealing any words. Maybe any rational thought at all. *Something's wrong.*

"Wilder, you've got to tell me what's going on here. Everyone back at the house is—"

"In a minute." He lifted his phone and tried to pray, tried to think. Then froze all over again when he actually got an answer.

"Monroe, what is this I'm hearing about you yelling at Peyton Cornish?" Agent Green didn't bother with a greeting. "I got a call that he was awake, that you were—"

"I need to know about the other possibility." The harbor's waters pitched underfoot, jostling the boat.

Silence crowded the line. And then, "What are you talking about?"

"When we met this morning." Was that really only this morning? "We were talking about Franzen. About how he was going after a storehouse. How he probably came to Muir Harbor to talk to Peyton. But you said there was one other possibility. Something else he's after. Did you mean *someone* else?"

"Wilder, what's going on?" Neil spoke at the same time as Agent Green attempted to.

"Monroe—"

His voice was hard as granite. "Who's he really looking for?"

a looming storm held the sky in its grip, leaden gray clouds rimmed in an eerie yellow, as if the setting sun, though desperate to break through, had gone weak and frail.

"I don't understand what you want with me." Why hadn't Lilian grabbed a raincoat before leaving the house? The air had been so clammy today. She should've sensed the coming storm. Should've been prepared.

But how could she have prepared for this? Forced at gunpoint into a black sedan. Then minutes later, coerced back into the sticky night air. Why had they come here of all places? The cemetery at the edge of town?

Dusk painted the graveyard in shadows, tombstones poking from the earth, an unnerving stillness draping over the hilly field.

Peter Franzen marched forward, his fingers curled around his pistol. Her warning to keep walking, to keep up.

"Please, this is crazy. Whatever's going on here, it has nothing to do with me."

"It has everything to do with you." The man was impenetrable. Thin lips pressed into a line, grim and nearly white. He hadn't hurt her. Hadn't even touched her. But there was a forbidding severity in the slant of his brow.

"How—" A squall heaved over the hill and through the trees, and she wobbled, one foot rolling, coming free of her sandal. Franzen's hand was at her elbow in a second. *Maybe not so impenetrable.* He'd kept her from falling. He waited as she righted her sandal and slipped her foot back inside.

It gave her the nerve to try once more. "If you could just explain. I've cooperated with you. I'm here, walking through a graveyard for no possible reason I can discern. The least you could do—"

"We stop here."

They'd halted in front of a slate-gray tombstone and . . . Oh. Oh, she knew this stone. They'd come here as kids—she and Neil and Indi. Curious. Wondering. Just enough brittle light remained to make out the etched words.

Diana Christine Muir
1971–1990
Beloved Daughter. Treasured Forever.

A distant rumble ricocheted in the sky. Why was she here? What use did an ex-FBI agent have for her?

"I know you see us, Cornish. You might as well come out."

Her gaze flew to Franzen's face. "Cornish? Peyton's in a care center. He's barely out of a coma. There's no way—"

"You went too far this time, Peter."

It came from behind them. A voice, gravelly, on the cusp of hoarse. When Franzen turned, she did too. It wasn't fast, the eventual recognition. It took long, muddled seconds, the wind whipping around her.

Another man, and she'd seen his face before. Not in person, but in pictures. High cheekbones, sharp angles. She knew him.

Or, no, she didn't. She only knew his name.

His name and the fact that he couldn't be standing here now. Because he was supposed to be dead. Nicholas Cornish couldn't be standing only feet away from her, watching her as if any second he might spring into action.

"You're him. You're Peyton's father. But you died. A-a plane crash. Isn't that what it was? You're not supposed to be—"

"Hello, Elizabeth."

What? *What?*

"My name's Lilian."

"Elizabeth Lilian. It was a compromise. Or, no, I suppose it wasn't. We were past compromising by that point. I called you Elizabeth. She called you Lilian. Neither one of us was willing to give in. And Diana . . ."

Her heart thrashed inside her chest, the gummy air coiling around her. A raindrop landed on her cheek. No, no, something was wrong here. This man who was supposed to be dead was saying words she couldn't make sense of. "I'm not Elizabeth. I don't know who that is. That's not me."

The man took a step closer, his white hair flattened by the wind. "'Lilian. Birth date 9/12/88. Allergic to bananas.'"

The note. Her note. Why was he reciting it to her?

"I ruined Sophia's life. I figured the least I could do was leave you with the name she wanted."

No. *No.* It was starting to come together—a picture, the truth, blurred but slowly taking form. And she wanted to look away. Didn't want to see this or know this. *I'm . . . he's . . .*

The face she could never see in her dream. The dream where she was safe and swaddled and warm and wanted. Was this his face?

It's not his voice. That's not his voice.

The voice in the dream was deeper, gentler. Soft like cashmere.

And yet, as another fat raindrop slid down her cheek, too many facts lined up in a neat and tidy row. Peyton—the way he'd befriended her before anyone else. The way he'd looked at her just before falling from the cliff. *"Hello, Lilian."*

She squeezed her eyes shut, listened to her memory replaying everything Wilder had told her about the Cornishes. *"There was a sister. Elizabeth. But after Sophia died, Nicholas sent her to live with relatives."*

Elizabeth. Elizabeth Lilian . . .

And the note. Nicholas could recite the note from memory.

She opened her eyes to find him still staring at her. And, oh Lord, the falling darkness, the falling rain, neither were enough to sweep away the final fact as obvious as anything else. He had her eyes. Or she had his. *God, this can't be true. It can't.*

"We tell ourselves stories, don't we?" She'd told herself a hundred different stories a thousand different times about where she'd come from, who had left her. But never a story like this. With an ending like this.

He's not the ending, he's the beginning. He left you. He pinned a note to your overalls and left you on his dead lover's old porch.

"How could you?" She could barely hear her own shaky voice above her pulse pounding in her ears. Above the brutal certainty of it all clanging with every beat of her shell-shocked heart.

Could he hear her over the growling clouds?

Yes. Yes, he could. She saw it in the deepening creases in his face. The set of his jaw. "I loved her. Diana—I loved her."

"She was a teenager." Her voice was strangled, goosebumps crawling up her arms.

"She was mine. And when she died, when she took our child with her, I was lost. You kept crying for her. Crying and crying and crying. You didn't want me. You didn't even want

Sophia. You wanted *her*. Just like I did. Then Sophia died, too. And you just kept crying."

She was crying now. Or maybe it was the rain, those rivulets tracking down her cheeks. A shudder wracked through her. "If that was your defense of everything, of anything at all, it's weak. You're a criminal. And you're not my father. I won't believe it."

Except she did. She did and it was a truth as jagged as lightning.

"I did the only thing I could. I gave you the closest thing to Diana I could. I delivered you to her family and walked away and it was for your own—"

A click interrupted Nicholas's words. And she felt it—cold metal, pressed up against the side of her head. Peter Franzen. She'd almost forgotten . . .

"The family drama has been a nice little show, but I'm running low on patience."

"Peter—"

Nicholas swallowed whatever he'd meant to say next as Franzen butted the gun closer to Lilian's temple.

Oh, God . . . please . . .

"You made a lot of promises, Cornish, and you didn't keep any of them. I was supposed to be on that plane, not you. You reneged and ran away like a coward. But I know a faked death when I see one. And you're a fool if you think the FBI's not well aware you're still alive and kicking."

"You're the fool. We'd have both been in the clear if you'd let it go. If you hadn't gone looking—"

"They were going to track me whether or not I went after you." Franzen nudged the gun into her head again. "I want the plane you promised me. I want a wire transfer. And then I never want to see you again."

Bait—that's what she was. It was so clear now. Somehow

Franzen had known who she was. He'd used her to draw out Cornish. And now . . .

For once, she didn't want to know. The question of how this was going to end—she didn't want to know the answer.

———◆·————··———◆———

"You should've told me." It was killing Wilder not to be the one behind the wheel. Not to have the option of shoving the pedal to the floor. "If you had any inkling Cornish was still alive—"

"Just count yourself lucky you're in this car right now. I didn't have to pick you up." Agent Hannah Green turned a sharp corner, crackling static issuing from the walkie-talkie at her waist.

Lucky? He was supposed to consider himself lucky in this moment? When one criminal or another—maybe both—had Lilian. He *knew* it. And the worst part was, Agent Green hadn't tried to talk him out of it. When she'd finally told him over the phone that Nicholas Cornish was still alive, that he was here in Muir Harbor, when he'd sputtered his fear that Cornish or Franzen had taken Lilian . . .

"I'll pick you up."

It was all she'd said. No attempt to calm him or brush him off or convince him Lilian was safe.

And if he was this frantic, how must Neil feel? They'd left him at the harbor, helpless and grappling to understand the truth.

Lilian was Peyton's sister. Nicholas Cornish's daughter.

She was the detail Wilder had missed. Hours upon hours, days upon days spent with her . . . and he hadn't realized. Hadn't noticed.

"Where are we going?"

"We found Cornish this afternoon, not long after you and I met. We've had agents tailing him ever since. But we've been waiting. We knew he'd draw out Peter, or vice versa." She finally slipped him something of an apologetic expression. "I'm sorry we didn't realize your friend would be involved."

Friend. Had a word ever sounded so feeble? Lilian was so, so much more than that and if they didn't get to her soon —*wait.* "You're telling me you know where Cornish is right now?"

"He's been waiting at a cemetery for forty minutes. Who else would he be waiting for but Franzen?"

"He's there alone?"

She nodded.

Then that meant Franzen was the one who'd been on his boat. Franzen had Lilian.

It made too much terrible sense, all of it. When Lilian had thought she was being followed—he'd been in D.C. meeting with Franzen. So it was Cornish then, wasn't it? After faking his death, he'd come to Muir Harbor, had visited Peyton in the hospital, left that plant. He'd sought out the daughter he'd abandoned twenty-eight years ago.

Wilder's ransacked boat—had that been Cornish, too? Or had that been Franzen, looking for some kind of proof as to Lilian's identity? *Dad's files.* He'd never found any files from Dad's long-ago investigation into Lilian's parentage or birthplace.

All this time he'd been caught up in one mystery, clueless, while another had been spinning like an eddy. Faster and faster, a riptide, and now Lilian was caught in it and he'd . . .

He'd failed. He'd missed the one detail that mattered most. And they might be too late.

Agent Green's walkie-talkie crackled again, but this time a voice cut through the static. "He's here. Franzen. And you're right, there's a woman with him."

Lil!

Agent Green plucked her walkie-talkie from her waist. "And?"

"They're talking. Franzen's got his gun out."

"Don't go rushing in." The words clamored from Wilder. "If Lil's there, if someone has a gun, you have to be—"

"I'm a minute away," Agent Green interrupted. "Wait for me."

They parked near a cluster of trees, then jogged to where three other agents huddled, drizzle slinking from the clouds. And then he saw it. He saw *her.* Lilian, with her arms hugged to her torso, but her back ramrod straight. And a glint of metal, he saw that too. Right up against her temple.

Oh God, oh God . . .

"Do not move, Wilder. We've got this." Agent Green's voice was low and stern. "Do not move."

"Surely you know they're here right now."

If Nicholas Cornish's voice had been like gravel before, it was an all-out growl now.

Trembles vibrated through Lilian. *No cowering.* Isn't that what she'd told herself earlier? But that'd been before. Back when she still knew who she was. Or no, hadn't known.

"Over in the trees." Nicholas took a step closer.

Oh, please let him mean the FBI. Or the police. Someone who could help. Should she risk stepping away from Franzen? Or simply keep standing here? Waiting.

"They've been on me for hours."

In an instant, the gun was no longer at her head. Franzen whipped it away, jutting his arm toward Nicholas instead.

Her father.

No. *No.* This wasn't the man from her dream. His wasn't the voice. All those years of wishing she knew . . . she didn't want to know *this.* Him.

"You'd risk yourself to—what? Lead them to me?" Franzen stalked toward Cornish.

Run. The single word fell over her like the steady rain. Why couldn't she listen? Why wasn't she moving?

Your father.

No. No! She didn't care about him. He'd stolen Maggie's daughter away. He'd betrayed his wife. He'd abandoned Lilian. He was steeped in a world of criminal activity. She would not let herself care about what happened to this man. This man who'd called her Elizabeth. Not Lily.

Sweet little Lily.

"Yes, maybe I would." Cornish's voice filtered through the rain. "Yes, maybe I would risk myself. If it's what I had to do to protect my children, yes."

"Well, you did a shoddy job of it. One's hooked to a machine and as for the other—"

Voices. Steps sloshing through puddles. A crack of lightning.

Run.

This time she listened. But it was too late. Because she knew, even as she twisted and moved, that boom wasn't thunder. It wasn't her heart thudding. And then, a second one . . .

"Lil!"

She was on her knees. Why was she on her knees? The wet ground soaked through her jeans and her hands landed in the mud. Somewhere outside her own confusion, chaos swirled. She could hear it. Shouts and grappling. Had Franzen shot Cornish?

"Lilian." The same voice from a second ago. Wilder? I-it couldn't be. He wasn't supposed to be here. It's why she'd gone with Franzen willingly, to get him away from the houseboat . . .

She felt like she was on the houseboat now. Everything rocking, swaying.

And then someone was holding her. Pressing in close even while yelling for help. "Lil, I'm here. You're going to be okay." *Wilder.* She wanted to see his face, but everything had gone blurry. Dark.

"It wasn't his voice. The one from the dream. It wasn't him, Wilder."

And then . . . nothing.

21

*S*he's swaddled again. Warm again. Held close and coddled.

Only there are two voices this time. His—the low, soft baritone. He calls her *sweet little Lily* just like always. But there's her voice, too. A singsong, laughing voice. The voice of a storyteller.

The legend. She's telling Lily the legend.

"It starts, as so many Gaelic stories do, with two clans and an ageless feud . . . and eventually, a family set adrift at sea. As the legend goes, the famed and ferocious Alec Muir said it was only fitting that the sea gift his family their freedom and future."

The man laughs and Lily can feel the rumble in his chest. *"It's always the same story. Don't you know any others?"*

"Ah, but this is a true story."

"So you really believe there's a lost treasure somewhere?"

She reaches for Lily. *"There's a treasure right here."*

Something changes then. They aren't laughing anymore. Their voices drift into whispers. *"She's not ours."* He's the one to say it.

She's the one to sigh. *"I know."*

She says something else then, but Lily can't hear it. She's pulled away. She's cold. She's . . . hurt.

It's a snake slithering through her body, poisoning her with a pain she doesn't understand. She tries to open her eyes but colors blur. She's moving, the sound of wheels squeaking and whirring squeezing through the chaos of her confusion. And the voices she hears now, she doesn't know.

Except for one. *Maggie.* "Hold on, Lil, just hold on."

He wasn't supposed to be here.

Wilder was supposed to be in his Jeep, on his way to the houseboat or maybe the farm. Not here in this dimly lit hospital chapel, wearied body wilting into a hard-backed chair.

Maggie had pleaded with him to go home. Get some rest. Take a shower. It was Tuesday, probably afternoon by now, and he hadn't left the hospital. Sixteen, maybe seventeen hours . . .

Since Lilian closed her eyes. Since his heart stopped.

So much blood. So much yelling. He hadn't realized until later, when it'd all replayed in his exhausted brain, just how much of the yelling had been him. One minute everything had been in slow motion—Peter Franzen turning, moving his gun again, pointing it at Lilian—and then in the next, a flurry of madness.

One gunshot.

Lilian dropping.

Then another.

There'd been no listening to Agent Green. No staying put. He buried his head in his hands now, trying not to remember the metallic smell of blood mixing with the residue of gunpowder. The glue-like air, the grumbling clouds, the shock of looking down later and realizing his shirt was damp from more than rainwater.

Someone had brought him a T-shirt later. He'd pulled off his soiled shirt right there in the hospital hallway, unwilling to leave his post just outside the OR door, the closest he was allowed to be to Lilian at that point. Entirely inappropriate. Neil had told him after the fact that he'd made a nurse blush.

Couldn't bring himself to care.

"Had a feeling you didn't make it far."

Wilder didn't turn. He hadn't heard the chapel door open, but he could've guessed that Neil would find him. "Couldn't leave. Not when she hasn't woken up yet." Lilian had made it through surgery long hours ago, but she was still unconscious, so no, he wasn't leaving.

Though why he'd picked this spot to land, maybe to hide, he didn't know. A chapel. What use was a chapel when a man had forgotten how to pray?

He tipped his head, his bleary eyes lifting to the stained-glass cross at the front of the small room. It must be backlit. It was the only thing that offered any light in this windowless room. How many chapels had he been in lately? There was that chapel in the funeral home in Atlanta. The chapel on the cliff. He'd gone to church with Lil on Sunday.

And this place. Silent and still and useless.

It doesn't have to be useless. And you haven't forgotten how to pray.

Perhaps not. He'd uttered a hundred panicked prayers last night. First when he hadn't been able to find Lilian. Then when he had. When he'd seen that gun at her temple. When he'd watched her hit the ground. Held her while she bled.

He'd prayed then, and all through her surgery, too.

But now he was here. And all he could feel in this room where family members and friends and loved ones were supposed to pour out their fears and fill up on hope . . . was empty.

"She's going to be okay, Wilder. The doctor just checked on her again. He said things are looking good. She'll wake up soon." Neil paused. "It's not your fault. If that's what you've been sitting in here thinking—"

"It was right there in front of me, Neil. I had dozens of pictures of Cornish. I had a few of his ex-wife, too." Lilian's birth mother. "And Peyton. All of that and I couldn't see any sort of family resemblance?"

"All of us met Peyton. None of us saw anything familiar."

"I saw that card by Peyton's bed. I recognized the handwriting. If I'd figured it out sooner . . ." Or if he hadn't left Lilian last night. If he'd stayed with her in her bedroom, stuck around even when the conversation got hard, none of them might be here right now.

But that's what he too often did, wasn't it? That last day in May when the memories got too painful, he ran off to Atlanta. The day after Dad's funeral, when the letter ripped his heart in half, he escaped in another way—drank enough to lose himself, at least for a little while.

And when the running didn't work, he did the opposite. Picked a distraction and held on for dear life. The truth was, everything he'd said to Lilian last night before all hell broke loose, he could've said to himself. He'd accused her of grasping for certainty. Well, what was he doing? What had he been grasping? Since Dad died, he'd held on so tight to Maggie's case, to a need to solve this mystery. Before, he'd held on to Dad, to the life they'd shared and the boat they'd shared and the career they'd shared.

There was more. For years, he'd been holding on to Neil's friendship. To the Muirs and his place as a surrogate family member. Even to his reputation as the P.I. with the uncanny instincts.

And for weeks . . . for weeks it'd been Lilian.

Holding on—he was always holding on so tightly. White knuckles, clenched fists. Scared of being left behind, just like Lilian. Scared of being left alone.

"One of these days, Wilder, you're going to have to learn how to let yourself off the hook." Neil dropped into the chair two seats down from him. "You're a human. You're not in control."

"I know that."

"I don't think you do." Neil palmed his cheeks and rubbed his eyes. He probably hadn't slept any more than Wilder since last night. "I think you're convinced you could've stopped all of this, could've stopped Lilian from ending up a target. I think you're convinced . . . you could've saved your dad."

He whipped his head to Neil. "Don't bring Dad into this."

"Your dad is in everything. You think I can't see how terrible the past three years have been for you? You're my best friend. I know Lil has pretty much lapped me when it comes to my place in your life—"

"Neil—"

"But I know you. I still know you. And I know you spend most days carrying around more weight than one person should have to. If you don't want to talk to me about it, talk to Lil when she wakes up."

He had been talking to Lilian. He'd told her more than anyone. He'd cried in front of her, for heaven's sake.

"Or Maggie or a counselor or all of the above," Neil went on. "Talk to God."

"I can't." The words slipped from him without his permission. But once they were free, they opened a floodgate. "I can't pray. I haven't been able to since Dad . . . not really. You think I blame myself for everything? Maybe I do. But I also blame Him. I'm angry, okay?"

He was angry at the God who'd let this happen. He was

angry at the God who kept taking and taking and taking. His mother and his father and then any peace he might've found over the latter. Because of that letter and the thoughts it'd planted in his mind.

He was angry that Lilian was lying in a hospital bed right now. And that when she woke up, she'd have to face the truth of where she'd come from. And what the future might hold. The unknown, the thing she hated the most, in the form of a disease that may or may not come to fruition.

"How am I supposed to pray if I don't know if I can trust Him? How am I supposed to believe He cares when there's so much hurt? What am I supposed to do with all of this? Just pretend it all away?"

"No."

"Then what?"

Neil sighed. "Maybe exactly what you're doing. Keep asking questions. It's what Harry always told you to do, right?"

Keep asking questions, son.

"God's not going anywhere. He can handle your anger. He can handle every single question. You might think you're in a stalemate or that you can't pray. But maybe the questions are prayers. Maybe the emotions we wrestle with—they're groaning, soul-deep sorts of prayers, whether we acknowledge it or not."

Wilder leaned over his knees. "I can tell you've spent twenty years living with Maggie."

"She rubs off on a person, I guess." Neil stood. "I'm going back to the room. I don't know how much longer the nurses are going to let us get away with breaking the only-two-visitors-at-a-time rule."

He didn't leave, though. Not right away. He stepped closer to Wilder and touched his shoulder. "He sees and hears it all anyway, Wild. You might as well have an honest conversation."

He moved away then, the chapel's door closing softly behind him.

───────•─────── ───────•───────

The light trickled in through the creases at the edge of her consciousness.

And the trickle turned into a stream. A stream that carried with it voices, like driftwood, floating along and waiting for her to reach out. Open her eyes.

Lilian saw Maggie's face first. Hazy and distant and dear. So very dear. It was the one thing she knew amid a ripple of confusion. She was the driftwood now, caught and carried, turned about. And bruised—yes. Oh, she hurt.

Maggie. Just focus on Maggie.

"She's waking up." Another vague voice.

She blinked and tried to concentrate. "W-where am I?" The words were sandpaper, scratching her throat.

Maggie, again, her face closer now. She peered down at Lilian with tears in her eyes. "Oh, Lily Grace, how good it is to hear your voice."

She felt a hand curl around her own, and then more faces crowded in. She blinked again, and then once more. Neil, Indi . . .

"You're in the hospital," Maggie said softly. "You've been here since last night. You were . . ." Her words caught.

Neil bent over the bed then, taking over. "You were shot, Lil. You had to have surgery. We've been waiting for you to wake up."

Shot. *Shot.* And oh . . . oh, it all came roaring back in. The graveyard. Two men. One gun. Her knees hitting the ground and a rush of darkness enveloping her. *Wilder.*

"Wilder?" She rasped his name.

"We finally convinced him to go home for a little bit." Maggie's fingers tightened around hers. "He hasn't left the hospital once until now. I thought he was going to end up in one of these beds if he didn't get some rest. Or at least take a shower and change his clothes. He's been a wreck. We all have."

"He didn't go, though." Neil. "I was just with him. He's in the chapel."

She tried to sit up, but it was as if she was shackled to the bed. Her limbs were too heavy, her head throbbing. And her side, her stomach . . . She glanced down.

"The bullet went straight through your side. Just missed your abdomen." Neil answered her unasked question, helping her get situated, propping pillows behind her. "But you're all fixed up now. Still got all your organs and everything." Even in her haze, she could tell he was trying to smile. Trying and failing so terribly, his accent going to that deep place it always did when he was emotional.

"Oh my gosh, this is torturing me. Do you even know how bad I want to give you a hug right now?" Indi threw up both hands, then buried her fingers in her hair. "I know we're all trying to stay calm, but—"

Neil did grin then, sliding one arm around Indi's shoulder. "You might as well just cry again."

"No. Lil's awake now. I'm done with the tears."

If Lilian had the strength, she might've laughed at the way Indi's welling eyes fully betrayed her.

"Well, I'm not." Maggie lifted a tissue to her eyes. "I'm a watering pot. No, a fountain. But I have every right." She leaned in closer, reaching her hand to smooth the hair away from Lilian's cheek and tuck it behind her ear. "You almost left us. Neil gave you the short version. It was touch-and-go. You lost so much blood. If the bullet had been only a centimeter over . . . I don't know why I'm saying this."

"I'm glad you're saying it. I need to know what happened. I'm so confused."

And sore. And tired. And almost desperate to see Wilder.

Neil perched on the side of the mattress. "Peter Franzen shot you. Apparently he went berserk, knew the gig was up. He shot you and then Cornish."

Nicholas Cornish who was supposed to have been dead already. Nicholas Cornish . . . who was her father. Did they know?

She looked at their faces, one to another. She could read it all in their expressions. The whole story—yes, they knew it. And it had an ending now. Because she could read that, too. "He's gone."

Maggie nodded. "He died at the scene." She glanced away for a moment. "His last words were about Diana. That's what an agent told me. Something about how he loved her, how he was sorry."

"He told me the same thing—that he loved Diana." Was it love or an obsession, though? And what did it matter anymore? He was gone. Dead. For real, this time. Why did knowing that feel like a knife slicing through the place where a bullet had already done damage? She didn't know him. She didn't love him.

"He said I wouldn't stop crying. That's why he left me. I wouldn't stop crying after Diana died. And then Sophia . . ." Oh Lord, Sophia. Her mother. She'd had a mother once.

No, she had a mother now. She had Maggie. Maggie, whose hazel eyes were filled with such tender care that it almost hurt. Probably, certainly, because it was so clear how much Maggie was hurting for her.

"It wasn't supposed to be like this, Maggie. I've always

wondered . . . I've always wanted to know. But not . . . this. He abandoned her, too. My . . . the woman who gave birth to me." More pieces of the puzzle began to fit together, a jigsaw image she never could've pictured herself a part of. "I've always known I was born close to the same time as Cynthia. But it wasn't just the same time. It was to the same man. Do you realize that? He had me with Sophia right around the same time Diana had Cynthia. Oh my word."

And then he'd lost . . . every one of them. Diana, Cynthia, Sophia . . .

But he didn't lose me. He left me.

Hot tears slipped down her cheeks. "I don't want to cry over this. I definitely don't want to cry over him."

"He was a broken man, Lil. It's okay to cry about the marks his sharp edges left on you." Maggie handed her a tissue.

"How could he do that to . . . everyone? He took your daughter away." And oh, maybe more. There was something he'd said, something she'd been too terrified to latch on to before, but now . . . *"When she died, when she took our child with her, I was lost."*

Nicholas believed Cynthia had perished in the accident with Diana, didn't he? Wilder had another theory, yes. There was another man. Someone who'd gone missing from Atlanta. Leo . . . someone.

But Nicholas believed his daughter was dead. Was that an answer all its own? Wouldn't he have sensed if she was still alive? His own flesh and blood?

His own flesh and blood. That included Lilian, too. He'd had no problem walking away from her. It'd been so clear in his retelling. The way his jaw had set, his chest puffed as he defended himself. He didn't have any regrets. Other than losing Diana.

The tears—why wouldn't they stop? Why couldn't she slow and soften her shuddering breaths? "I'm n-not crying for him. I'm crying for everything he took . . . H-he ruined lives. My father . . . h-he was . . ."

Maggie bent over her, placing her palms on both of Lilian's wet cheeks. "He took one daughter, yes." She touched her forehead to Lilian's. "But he didn't take you. You, my daughter, the daughter of my heart long before a judge's signature ever made it official . . . he didn't take you."

※——◆——————◆——※

She's awake.

Wilder lifted his thudding head. How long had he been sitting here?

Lilian.

He felt it in his gut—the flash of heat as familiar as ever. But never had he been so desperate for it to prove true. *She's awake.* Which meant she might be sitting up and talking and wondering why he wasn't there.

He bolted to his feet, the movement enough to pull a groan and keep him from immediately racing out the door. He stretched. Every muscle in his body had gone stiff and sore, and his fatigue was a heavy cloak. And yet . . .

Something inside of him had loosened. He didn't know exactly how. Unless Neil was right. Unless the emotion that had overtaken him in this silent, still room—all of it, the anger, the fear, the heartbreak—had been a prayer. A surrender of sorts.

A giving-up. Years of worrying that's exactly what Dad had done, given up, when possibly all this time, his soul had been aching for him to do the same.

He didn't know. He really didn't know.

He just knew he was tired. He just knew he couldn't keep clenching his fists and grasping, grasping, grasping for the wrong things. Or even the good things. Because they could go away. In an instant, everything could change, and he'd find himself with a white-knuckled grip on nothing at all.

He stood in the middle of the aisle and looked to the cross. *God, I feel like all I know is everything I don't know. And I don't know if I trust you enough to hold on to you.*

But he was reaching. He was trying. He'd sat here in this chapel for he didn't know how long and let his hollowed-out soul have its way. And maybe, for right now, that could be enough.

Let it be enough.

Another glance to the cross. Another nudge in his gut. *Lilian.*

He turned and hurried from the room. Too quickly, because as soon as he was out the door, he collided with a woman.

Her *oomph* was accompanied by a laugh and the sound of her purse's contents spilling to the floor. And, oh, he knew her. Her eyes didn't quite meet his as he, along with the man at her side, helped steady her. "Oh gosh, Mariana, sorry. I wasn't looking."

Lilian's coworker smiled. "Wilder, right? That means we must be in the right place. Is Lilian awake? I wanted to come earlier but wasn't sure if I should, but eventually Morris told me to go, so Dad gave me a ride and . . . I'm rambling. I do that when I'm worried. No, I do that all the time. Is Lilian—"

"Her surgery was successful. There was a lot of internal bleeding, but I think she's going to be okay." *And she's awake. And I should be there.*

Relief flooded Mariana's expression. "Thank goodness. This is my dad, by the way. He's in town visiting for the week."

Wilder shifted his gaze to the man at Mariana's side. He'd

bent over to pick up the purse Mariana had dropped, was scooping items inside.

"Nice to meet—" The rest of Wilder's sentence fled from him when the man looked up. The impact slammed into him. Instant recognition. Not a gut instinct, but a revelation.

He looked from the man to Mariana.

It's not possible.

Back to the man. "Leo James." The name released on an exhale, rife with disbelief and bewilderment and absolute certainty.

Mrs. Brazelli's brother, the man from the photo, slowly stood, mouth parted halfway. Sun-bronzed skin and dark hair that nearly reached his shoulders.

Mariana tipped her head to the side. "Uh, no, this is my dad. This is—"

"Leo James," Wilder said again.

"No. I mean, you're half right. James is his first name. Last name is Sherwood. Same as mine. I took it back after the divorce."

Wilder couldn't stop shaking his head. Couldn't stop looking back and forth between them. Was it resignation passing over the man's face? Or relief? If this man was Leo, then . . .

Heat claimed every inch of him. Heat and knowing.

"I . . . I wondered if . . ." The man closed his mouth. Then opened it and tried again. "I haven't heard that name in a long time."

"*F*ranzen's in custody now." Neil stood near the window in her hospital room. He'd been texting Sydney ever since he returned to the room, asking her to bring Lilian's favorite sweatshirt, a couple of books since it sounded like Lilian was going to be here for at least another day or two. He pocketed his phone. "The FBI's already mostly cleared out, if you can believe it. Though they're going to want a statement from you when you're ready."

Lilian took a sip from a straw, the water in the glass a nurse had handed her lukewarm.

"Wilder was at the scene."

Neil nodded. "He knew you were in danger before anyone else. I guess he'd gone to see Peyton earlier. He figured everything out, came racing back to Muir Harbor. Scared all of us half to death when he burst into the house, looking for you."

"Him and his darn gut instincts." Shouldn't he have had an instinct that she was awake by now? *I wish you were here.*

They'd tried texting him to let him know Lilian was awake, only to find his phone stuck in the vinyl cushion of the chair by Lilian's bed that Maggie occupied now. Indi had offered to fetch him, but Neil had said they should wait a few minutes. *"I think . . . he needs a little time."*

Neil ambled over now. "He'll be here any minute."

"I'm here right now."

At the sound of his voice, Lilian dropped her cup, water sloshing over the bed, soaking through the sheet that covered her bottom half. She might've squealed if her throat wasn't so scratchy. As it was, a gasp slipped free and then, something like a laugh as everyone else moved into action. Indi shifting Lilian's bedsheet, saying something about keeping the spilled water away from her incision. Maggie using her sweater to try to sop up what she could. Neil picking up the cup rolling its way across the floor.

All the while, Lilian didn't move. Partially because she couldn't. She had a tube taped to her hand, a wound making its presence known with every tiny shift of her body.

Mostly because she didn't want to. After everything that had happened, here was a moment she wanted to stay in. Locking eyes with Wilder. Drinking in his soft smile. Goodness, how had she ever disliked that grin?

"Hey, sleepyhead."

"Hey."

Neil straightened, cup in hand. "I feel like maybe this is our cue to leave."

"No," Wilder blurted.

No? Frankly, she would've been fine with a little privacy just now.

But Wilder wasn't looking at her anymore. His eyes were on Maggie. And his expression had morphed into something that hovered between apprehension and anticipation. "Wilder?" Her voice still wasn't working as it should. His name came out a mere scratch.

"Um, I think you all might want to be here. There's something . . . someone . . ." He moved farther into the room, covering his mouth and chin with his palm, rubbing his hand downward. He looked so very tired. But also . . . jittery. Had he been ODing on caffeine?

"I had to sweet talk everyone at the nurses' station to let all of us be in here at once. There's someone waiting . . ." He shook his head, motioned with one hand behind him.

Mariana walked in, one hand gripping her walking stick, the other resting on the arm of a man next to her. Lilian looked to Wilder. Why was he being weird about this? Why did Mariana look so uncertain?

"Mari, I'm so glad you're—"

She was interrupted by a gasp from Maggie and then the sound of Maggie's chair hitting the floor as she jolted to her feet. Then wilted in the next moment.

Wilder reached Maggie before anyone else could, chastising himself for the foolishness of this even as he slipped his arm around her, steadying her on her feet. "I'm sorry, Maggie. I shouldn't have done it like this. I'm an idiot—"

"Don't you dare call yourself an idiot when you've just . . ." Maggie couldn't finish her sentence, her gaze glued to Mariana, shock stealing all the color from her face.

"What in the world is going on?" Neil moved to Maggie's other side. He righted her chair and tapped her shoulder, clearly wanting her to sit.

But Maggie was having none of it. She pulled away from Wilder and stepped toward Mariana. "It's you. All this time and . . . it's really you." She lifted her hands as if to reach for Mariana. To do what she did so often with the rest of them. Cup the woman's cheeks or maybe pull her into a hug. But she paused. "I, uh . . . I'm afraid I'm about to completely over-whelm you and I'm so sorry but . . ."

She started weeping then. Or maybe laughing. He honestly wasn't sure. But it was beautiful—watching Maggie Muir embrace her granddaughter. Watching Mariana's own eyes fill with tears as she smiled over Maggie's shoulder. The poor woman had to be overcome, incredibly confused, the hasty conversation they'd had outside the chapel nowhere near enough to answer all her questions.

But in this moment, Mariana—Cynthia—was a picture of graceful acceptance. She returned Maggie's embrace, the light from the room's narrow window just enough to glint in her hair, highlighting strands of red mixed in with the gold.

"Wilder?"

Lilian.

He scooted past Neil and bent at her side, the sight of her —awake, alert, adorably disoriented—every bit as wonderful as the reunion taking place just feet away. "You can never get shot again, Lil. I forbid it."

"What—"

"And I'd very much like to see one of your classic glares and listen to you tell me I don't get to forbid you from doing anything, but first . . ." He brushed a strand of hair away from her cheek and pressed a kiss to her pale skin. "Never again. I mean it."

"Is it really her, Wilder? You found her? It's Mari . . . she's . . .?"

Even hoarse, her voice was the best thing he'd heard all day. "I didn't find her. I had no idea. Not until I saw him." He motioned to the man standing behind Mariana, then reached for Lilian's hand, desperate to keep touching her, suddenly wishing everyone else out of the room.

But he'd had more time to come to terms with what was happening. More time as in only a few minutes, but still.

341

While he might want Lilian all to himself just now, she was every bit as dazed by what she was seeing as he'd been when he'd first recognized Mariana's father as Leo James. When he'd had the staggering realization of who Mariana really was.

Except for Maggie. She wasn't dazed. She was dazzling, radiant with joy as she finally released Mariana and took a step back. "You're alive. You're here. First Lily wakes up and now this."

Was Wilder the only one who noticed it? Was he the only one who saw the look on Mariana's father's face just then? The man's gaze flew to Lilian and though he didn't move, every shade of emotion colored his eyes at once. A pulsing shock. A disbelieving hope.

And a tremulous but clear recognition. Oh. *Oh* . . .

Lilian hadn't seen it. She was still staring at Maggie and Mariana. Just like Neil. Just like Indi.

"I have a thousand questions. How are you here? Where have you been?" Maggie held both of Mariana's hands now. "Wait, Lil called you Mari. So you're her . . . you've been here in Muir Harbor . . . oh my goodness, my brain is going a mile a minute."

Mariana was grinning. "Mine too. I'm insanely confused. All I know is Wilder told me I'm your granddaughter. And my dad said it's true."

The man, Mariana's father, finally tore his eyes away from Lilian long enough to glance around the room, then step up to his daughter's side. "I, um . . . I guess I have some explaining to do."

Lilian's fingers went limp in his.

That low, velvety voice. *His* voice. She knew his voice. She *knew*.

"Wilder?" If her throat was parched before, it was shriveled now. Too dry for anything more than a whisper. She felt his hand tightening around hers, but she couldn't make herself return the gesture or look anywhere but at the man standing next to Mariana.

A man with kind brown eyes. A man who'd only said a few words, but whose tone was so impossibly familiar. *Sweet little Lily.*

"You know me." She forced the words through her dry lips. "You know who I am."

His Adam's apple bobbed as he nodded and she could swear he mouthed her name. *Lily.* "I think so. You were only two the last time . . . I don't understand how you're here."

"I don't understand any of this."

Lilian barely registered Indi's comment. She couldn't stop staring at the man. Mariana's father? Mariana's father was the man from her dream?

Mariana . . . who's Cynthia . . . Maggie's granddaughter.

She closed her eyes for a moment, struggling to take it all in. She felt Wilder's warmth as he leaned closer, perching on the mattress. "You just woke up, Lil. Maybe we should all—"

"No." Her eyes flew open. "No, he said he was going to explain." She looked to the man. "Please explain."

Maggie nodded. "Yes. Please do."

He reached his palm to the back of his neck, his mouth opening and closing as if he hadn't a clue where to start. He kept looking from Mariana to Lilian and back again. "I'm so sorry," he finally said.

And it hit Lilian all over again. His voice. The face in her dream she'd never seen. This wasn't some morphine-infused hallucination. This was . . . *him.*

He lowered his hand and exhaled. "I'm Leo James. I

worked for Nicholas Cornish. I met Diana for the first time when Cornish had a few of us over to his apartment for a meeting."

Maggie blanched.

"I didn't realize at first . . . the arrangement. I knew he was married to someone else. Had a son and a newborn. I thought maybe Diana was a sister, but then I saw them together . . . and she had a baby, too." He shook his head.

"You knew Diana?" Maggie asked softly.

He swallowed and nodded. "Cornish was, uh, kind of possessive of her. Sometimes when he went back to Savannah to be with his family, he had me be a sort of bodyguard, I guess. I got to know her. She wasn't happy with him, but she didn't think she could leave. She was so young."

Maggie drew in a shaky breath. "I think maybe I should sit down."

Neil got her a chair, Indi came to stand at her side. How was this happening? It was . . . so much. Lilian felt herself sinking farther into her pillows. But she had to stay awake for this. Couldn't give in to the pain in her side or the sudden need to close her eyes.

"Lil?" Wilder squeezed her hand again, his voice a murmur.

"It's his voice. He's the man from the dream. He knew me. He knows me."

She could feel Wilder's tense worry even without looking at him. Was she making any sense at all? *He doesn't know about the dreams. You never told him.* Which meant he couldn't know about the ache in her heart right now.

When she'd realized who Nicholas Cornish was to her, it'd been an unmaking. It'd been like wallpaper, ripping and peeling away until it revealed cracked plaster. And all she'd wanted to do was slap the paper back in place, to wish she'd never peeked behind it.

But trying to comprehend who this man was to her, who she was to him . . . it felt so much more real somehow. So much more significant. And she just . . . didn't understand.

"I should get a nurse," Wilder whispered and started to pull away.

But she shook her head, letting go of his hand and clinging to his arm instead, even as the thudding in her head grew louder.

The man went on. "I watched Diana get more desperate to leave, especially after Cornish left his wife and moved in with her permanently. And . . . I cared for her. I wanted to help. The plan was to head west and disappear, but she wanted to stop in Maine first. We decided to drive separately. If Cornish was going to follow anyone, I wanted it to be me."

They all knew the rest of it. Or, most of it.

"The accident?" Maggie asked. "There was another car."

Anguish filled the man's face. "It wasn't me. It was one of Cornish's men. He'd figured it out, sent someone after her. Couldn't even be bothered to . . ." He shook his head. "We'd made plans to meet. I was on my way." He cleared his throat. "I heard it happen. I was almost there. I saw a car go flying past me with a broken bumper and, I don't know, I just went into a blind panic. Got out of my car and started running toward the smoke. I found Cynthia . . ."

Was there anyone in this room who wasn't riveted to this man's words? And, oh, poor Maggie. Was she reliving it all? She'd heard the crash, too. She'd gone running, too.

Was she sitting in that chair right now thinking that if she'd only gotten there a few minutes, maybe even seconds, earlier, she might've been the one to find her granddaughter?

"I'm so sorry." Leo James's voice sounded farther away now, and Lilian was struggling to keep her eyes focused. "All I could think was that I had to get her away. That Cornish would keep looking. If he knew she was alive . . ."

"You protected her," Maggie said, her voice clogged with emotion.

Or, at least, Lilian thought it was Maggie. But everything was going a little too blurry.

"Lil." Wilder peered down at her. "This is too much . . ."

She tried to shake her throbbing head. "I know him. He knows me. I need to understand."

"You will. Later." Wilder's lips were soft against her forehead. "But for now, go ahead and go to sleep."

"Stop telling me what to do." Her voice faded at the end, her eyes closing. *Later.*

*E*verything had changed since Cynthia Muir had come home.

Everything, and yet, nothing.

The farmhouse still smelled of butter and sugar and the seaside air whispering through open windows. Neil was off somewhere, and Indi's voice drifted from the kitchen. On the phone with Philip, if her frequent bursts of bubbly laughter were any indication.

Home was still home, and as for Maggie . . .

From her nest on the living room couch, Lilian watched as Maggie pulled an afghan from the crowded quilt rack across the room and held it toward her granddaughter. "I started crocheting this the day I met you. If you think I've been emotional these past few days, you should've seen me then. I hadn't seen my daughter in two years and until that day, I hadn't known you existed. I went from weepy to laughing with joy to weepy all over again. I'm sure I freaked you out then, and I can't believe I haven't scared you away now."

Mariana draped the afghan over one arm, skimming her fingers over the yarn. Flannel stood at her side, stern and serious as ever. "You haven't scared me at all. I have a grand-mother. I just keep saying it to myself. I never knew . . ."

How many times had Lilian heard her say the same thing since Tuesday? It'd been four days and the shock hadn't worn off for anyone, had it? Somehow they'd all moved through the days but every minute had been tinged with discovery and myriad accompanying emotions.

". . . only if Lil's comfortable. I don't want to leave her stuck here."

Maggie's voice flitted in, pulling her back to the present. Today was Saturday. Lilian's first full day at home. *Home.* She'd probably never loved it more than she did now, after nights of sleeping on a hard mattress, being interrupted by the beeping of monitors, by nurses checking on her. She'd come home late yesterday afternoon and slept in her own bed last night and it'd been glorious.

Or, almost. It would've been better if Wilder hadn't left so early in the evening.

He'd been here along with everyone else to welcome her home, but he'd seemed a little distant. Just as he'd been at the hospital over the past few days. She'd assumed it was because every time he was in her room, someone else was too.

But he could've found a moment. At the hospital, here at home . . . he could've captured a few minutes alone with her. Didn't he realize how much she wanted him next to her? Other than one measly kiss on her cheek yesterday when she'd come home, he'd barely touched her.

It wasn't a measly kiss on the cheek, though.

No. No, it might've been too little and too brief, but it hadn't been nothing. His bristled cheek had lingered near hers for more than a moment. He'd smelled like heaven, and his fingers had skimmed her waist. *"Welcome home, Lil."*

No. It hadn't been measly. It just hadn't been enough.

She blinked, then realized both Maggie and Mariana faced

her. Even Flannel. "Oh . . . I'm sorry. Were you saying something to me?"

"I was going to give Mari a little tour of the farm before dinner. But only if you're all right here. Do you need anything?"

She laughed. "I'm absolutely fine. And I'm actually supposed to be walking a little bit here and there, so if I need anything, I'm totally capable of getting it."

Maggie grinned. "You sound more and more like yourself every day." She leaned down, kissed the side of Lilian's hair. "Lily Grace, I'm so glad you're home."

"Me too. If I never have to eat Jell-O again, it'll be too soon."

"Yell for Indi or Syd if you need something. You shouldn't overdo it. Mari, let me grab some shoes and I'll meet you on the porch." Maggie moved from the room.

Mariana, though, lingered for a moment, Flannel's leash wrapped around one hand. "I'm still in shock. Half sisters. It still feels unbelievable, doesn't it?"

"I don't understand how you're taking all this in stride, Mari."

"I'm not the one who was shot."

"No, but . . . you and your father. He kept so much from you." Lilian hadn't seen the man since Tuesday, and it was starting to get to her. She had so many questions.

Oh, she'd pieced together enough to know Leo—no, he went by James now—must've spent time around her when she was a baby, a toddler. When Nicholas Cornish had left his wife, he must've had Peyton and Lilian in Atlanta at times. Which meant they likely spent time at the apartment Nicholas shared with Diana.

Which meant they'd spent time with Diana . . . *and* the man who'd grown to care for her. Enough time that Leo's—James's—voice had worked its way into Lilian's subconscious and into her dreams. *Sweet little Lily.*

It'd never been her father's voice in her dreams. It'd been *his.* The man who'd raised Mariana as his own.

After Lilian had awakened again later Tuesday night, Neil and Indi had filled her in on the rest of his story. Leo had whisked Cynthia away from Maine, convinced it was the only way to keep her safe. He'd taken her to California, changed their names. She became Mariana. He became James. It'd been easier to disappear back then. No social media. No cell phones to track.

Not until weeks later had he begun to notice something different about the toddler's eyes . . . how it seemed she struggled to focus. She'd had a head injury, an impact from the accident. Something hidden away, unnoticeable until it started slowly eroding her eyesight.

Mariana skimmed her fingers along the edge of the coffee table, then lowered to sit on its corner. "It hasn't been easy, Lil. There've been moments in the past few days where I was convinced I didn't know him at all. I think I've felt every emotion in the universe."

"I don't blame you. Did you even know he wasn't your biological father before?"

She nodded. "Yeah, he was always honest about that. Actually, he sprinkled truth into a lot of things. I've always known I was blind because of a car accident, a head injury. He told me the other night he wept for weeks back then, thinking if he'd gotten me to a doctor earlier, maybe my eyesight could've been saved. Finally, I guess one of the doctors set him straight. It was irreparable damage. His actions didn't cause it."

"No. But they caused Maggie nearly three decades of hurt."

"I know. But maybe they also saved my life. Maybe they also kept Nicholas Cornish away from the rest of you." Mariana lifted her palm to Flannel's head. "I'm not making excuses for any of it. The whole thing is weird and twisted and complicated. But at the bottom of it all, underneath all the confusion, behind all the secrets, there's the simple fact that I love him. And I know he loves me. Despite everything, that's worth holding on to."

Lilian heard the front door open, footsteps in the entryway. The man himself appeared in the arched opening on the other side of the living room. Leo. James.

"Hey, Dad."

Mariana must have instincts that rivaled Wilder's. Or she was simply that attuned to her father's footsteps.

Technically, Nicholas Cornish was her father. Your father.

Half sisters. Mariana was absolutely right. It still felt so incredibly unbelievable.

It's not only that. You have a brother, too.

Yes, Peyton. Who knew when that would sink in. Who knew when any of it would. Tangled mysteries, FBI agents— good ones, bad ones.

With Franzen now in custody, it'd been confirmed that he was the culprit who'd ransacked Wilder's boat weeks ago. He'd been looking for the same thing Lilian had last month— old case files regarding not Cynthia, but *her*. Apparently Nicholas Cornish had let it slip to the ex-agent years ago that he had unfinished business in Muir Harbor. Franzen had begun to put the pieces together, had come to Maine looking for proof that Cornish had not only a son, but a daughter in Muir Harbor—and planning to use one or both to lure the man out of hiding.

Cornish, of course, had already been in town. After faking his death to escape arrest, he'd visited Peyton. And the working theory was that he'd been the one to break into Wilder's boat that first time, on the same night when Lilian had gone looking for Harry's old files, probably because he'd been curious about the ongoing investigation into Cynthia's whereabouts. Authorities also believed it was Cornish who had broken into the law office and followed Lilian around town.

It was all enough to make her head spin. How was she supposed to make sense of it while at the same time dealing with that unhelpful diagnosis she'd gotten on Monday? The same day she'd been *shot*.

The same day she'd pushed Wilder away. Was that why he'd seemed so disconnected these past few days?

Or was she the disconnected one? Everything was discombobulated.

"You're early," Mariana said, standing now, moving toward James. Maggie had invited him to come to dinner tonight. Another thing that felt unbelievable. Maggie's willingness to forgive and accept the man who'd taken her granddaughter away.

But then, maybe Mariana was right. Maybe he'd saved her, too.

Maybe there was no black or white or fully good or fully bad in this situation. Maybe it was all shades of gray and the best thing to do was what both Maggie and Mariana were trying to do. Face all of it. Feel all of it. The parts that were hard and painful. The parts where hope shined through the cracks.

And the love underneath it all. The love in Maggie's heart that had held on for all these years.

The love in Mariana's that allowed her to hug her dad even now. "I'm glad you came. Maggie's going to give me a tour of the farm. Want to come?"

James looked over his daughter's head, his uncertain gaze connecting with Lilian. "Actually, I was wondering . . . hoping maybe I could talk with . . ."

Lily. That's what he wanted to say. Somehow she knew it. He cleared his throat, but she could hear her name as clearly as she'd heard it in her dreams. Moments later, Mariana was leaving with Maggie and he was padding across the room. He sat in the rocker in the corner. Then must've decided it was too far away. He moved to the end of the couch instead, only a few feet away from her, shifting so he could face her.

"The thing I want you to know . . ." His eyes were the color of caramel, tiny wrinkles at their corners. His hair was nearly black, a few strands of silver threaded in, and pulled into a haphazard ponytail. He started again. "I want you to know, we wanted to take you, too."

She didn't know what to say. Couldn't digest his words. "I don't understand."

"When Diana and I left, we wanted . . ." He shook his head and cleared his throat. "I need to back up. Cornish had you in Atlanta every other week. Peyton didn't come as often. He was older, in school. But you were there all the time and he left you with Diana when he was at work. Which I thought was horrible at first because she already had a newborn at home. But she adored you. Loved you. She would talk about how fun it was going to be for you and Mariana . . ." He shook his head a second time. "Cynthia, to her. She would talk about how fun it was going to be for the two of you to grow up together. She pretended you were twins. She would tell you stories."

Lilian gripped the edge of a blanket Maggie had covered her with earlier. "She told me the Legend of Muir Harbor, didn't she?"

"She loved that story." He glanced away. "She was so young. And she felt trapped. But the two of you were her great joys. Cornish's ex-wife had a drinking problem and the worse it got, the more he kept you in Atlanta. And the more Diana and I . . . I was young, too. And I'd fallen for her. But I knew Cornish would kill me if he knew. I knew he was dangerous." He cleared his throat again and looked to Lilian once more. "She wanted to take you with us, and I did too. I was just as attached as she was, but I told her we couldn't. Mariana was her child, but you weren't. It would've been kidnapping."

She pulled the blanket up, over her arms, almost to her chin. Each small movement tugged at the stitches in her side, sent tiny shoots of pain through her.

Sweet little Lily.

He'd held her, this man. He'd loved her.

He'd left her.

"I . . . I never thought . . ." He took a breath. "I never thought I'd see you again. I kept tabs on Cornish through the years. I thought he sent you away to live with relatives. I was relieved. And now . . . I just can't believe you're really here. I had hoped when I sent Mari here she'd find her biological family. But I had no idea she'd find *you*."

"You sent her here?"

He nodded and rubbed one palm over his mouth. "I always wrestled with how I'd kept Mari from knowing her grandmother. How I'd never told her the truth. But more than anything, I wanted her safe, away from anyone or anyplace that might draw Cornish's attention. Then last month, when it appeared he'd died, I thought it might finally be safe to come clean. But I wrestled with that, too, because what if I told her everything and she rejected me? Or what if her Muir Harbor family rejected her? She'd already been through so much, with the divorce and all. Then I found that job opening. Here in Muir Harbor. With you. Though, I didn't know you were . . . you."

"Yes. She said you were the one who told her about the job opening."

Another nod. "Maybe it was wrong, sending her here without telling her but . . . I don't know. There was all this uncertainty and I didn't know how any of it was going to work out, but I prayed and took a risk and waited to see what would happen next. And now . . ." Tears glistened in his eyes. "I just want you to know how much you were wanted. Diana loved you. I loved you. And I'm so sorry for leaving you behind, Lily. I've never forgotten you. I've prayed for you. I've thought of you. Every single day. I know the things I've caused. I don't expect anything from you. I certainly don't expect anyone to forgive me. The fact that Mari's even still speaking to me . . ."

Lilian let her blanket drop to her lap. "She's Maggie's granddaughter."

His reddened eyes met hers.

"I think it must be a Muir thing. Finding the strength to forgive. Choosing love above everything else." Choosing a new story to tell. Not an easy one. But a healing one. "I'm a Muir, too, you know."

All those dreams. All those times she hadn't been able to see his face. What a sight it was now. A stranger, but not, managing a smile through his tears. Who'd prayed for her and thought of her and wanted her.

A beautiful unknown, out there all this time. One who'd made mistakes, who'd battled with uncertainty.

Who tentatively reached for her head now. "Sweet little Lily. Who could've known it would be you? That you were what would happen next."

———◆——— ———◆———

It was a little like medicine—or it should be—the western sunlight bathing his skin, the sound of the sea lapping at the houseboat in lazy ripples as it moved through the open water.

It's not May thirty-first, Dad. Sorry about that.

Wilder watched as a seagull glided toward the ocean, its

belly skimming the surface. Stray drops of saltwater spritzed his face, despite the slow pace of the boat, and he leaned back in his canvas chair, closing his eyes against the brightness, trying to let these minutes be the salve he knew he needed.

But it was hard to entirely relax. He'd only slept in fitful snatches all week long. Even after Lilian had come home from the hospital Friday, yesterday, he'd still struggled to rest last night.

He should be glad. Maggie's long-lost granddaughter had been found. The mystery that had held him in its grip for three years . . . done. Just like that.

More importantly, Lilian was recovering. Each day, a little more color returned to her cheeks. It'd been all he could do not to hover at her side every hour she spent in that hospital room. Eventually, the medical staff had begun enforcing the rule that only two visitors be in the room at a time. They'd had to start taking shifts—and he'd had to share his every visit with her.

He'd told himself that was a good thing. It kept him from being overbearing. He didn't know where they stood. There'd been chaos and a slew of shocking revelations since that conversation in her bedroom Monday night, the one where he'd made a mess of things . . .

And all he wanted to do was fix it. All of it. But if Lilian had needed space before everything had happened, how much more might she need or want it now?

Or he was wrong. Or he shouldn't be here at all right now but back at the farm, making sure Lilian knew exactly how he felt about her. Exactly how terrified he'd been when he'd thought he lost her. Exactly how much he'd meant it when he'd said he'd never abandon her.

The problem was, his gut had gone silent. He didn't know what was the right move or wrong move when it came to Lil. Maybe when it came to anything.

"I'm a wreck."

"Clearly." Neil, his accent thick and a little too packed with amusement, even in just one word.

Wilder peeled his eyes open and glanced at his friend. Neil had his feet propped up on the boat's railing. Almost the exact spot where Lilian had gone over the edge weeks ago.

Feels like a year ago.

"Don't be smug." It was exactly the kind of thing Lilian would've said. *Had* said to him, plenty of times, usually with one of her glorious scowls. Good grief, he missed her scowls. That's how he'd know when she was really feeling better— when she finally glared at him again.

Neil dropped his feet to the deck. "So what are we doing here? Is this really one last hurrah before you sell the boat?"

"I don't know."

"Are you going to buy Ansel's house?"

"I don't know."

"Have you talked to Lil about it? Or about anything?"

Wilder's chair creaked as he rose. "What's with the twenty questions?" He moved to the edge of the boat and leaned over the railing.

"I'm sorry—"

"Don't be sorry." He whirled around to face Neil. "Just tell me what I'm supposed to do. I'm done with gut instincts. They're a thing of the past and I'm . . ." The boat bobbed and his elbow hit the railing behind him. He winced. "All I've wanted for years is to be done with this case, but now that it's over, I'm unmoored. I'm . . ." *A mess.*

Neil looked up at him. Steady as ever. Like the rocks of the shore. Solid and sound. "It's been your harbor. The case, ever since your dad died."

"I know that. And now I'm adrift. I don't need to know what's wrong with me, Neil. I need to know what to do."

"Well, you could start by not leaving my sister in the dark.

You've been keeping your distance, and I'm pretty sure it's driving her crazy." Neil grinned then. Actually had the nerve to grin when Wilder felt like he was coming apart at the seams. "Although this is you we're talking about. Driving her crazy is sort of par for the course."

He turned his back on his friend and faced the sea once more. "Lil's had a million things thrown at her this week."

He heard Neil stand behind him. "All the more reason she might really need you right now. She'd probably even admit it."

The wind scraped his cheeks and combed through his hair. He tried to breathe it in, let the sea salt air do what it was supposed to. Cleanse and calm. But nothing felt right.

How could it? He was out on the open water without Dad. He was on this boat without Dad. He was trying to navigate his life . . . without Dad.

"What if I can't ever get over it?" He wasn't sure Neil could hear him. Wasn't sure it mattered. Because the question wasn't for him.

It was for the God he'd been trying to make his way back to. Dad had told him to keep asking questions. Neil had told him to keep asking questions. So, okay. Here was a question. *The* question.

What if it just never stopped? The pain of losing Dad. The grief. The need to hold on to something, anything—a case, a family that wasn't his, Lilian—to keep the loss and loneliness from eating him alive?

The ache of reading that letter and wondering . . .

"I just really think you should read it again." Lilian's voice floated in on the breeze, the memory hovering at the edges of his mind. They'd been in Ansel's house. He'd had his arms around her.

She'd been so uncertain at the start of that date. He'd had to coax her from his Jeep. Then, mere minutes later, she'd

358

been the one coaxing the anguish from his heart. Letting him ramble on as they stood in Ansel's dining room.

He pushed away from the deck's railing, strode past Neil.

"Where are you—"

"Inside. I need a minute."

It only took seconds—hurrying inside, crossing the room to the trunk, dropping to his knees. Instead of buried at the bottom of the trunk, the letter waited for him on top of piles of his mother's, where he'd left it after Lilian had read it.

Folded and faded. Waiting to torture him like always.

But maybe not this time. Maybe this time . . .

"I just really think you should read it again."

For Lilian, he'd read it again. For the piece of him that was desperate to let go, he'd read it again. Slowly, he let himself lower to the floor, leaning his back against the couch, and unfolded the letter.

Son, I'm writing this note by the light of the alarm clock . . .

That ridiculous alarm clock. That ridiculous, beloved alarm clock. Wilder might've switched out the old mattresses in the bedroom, but he'd kept Dad's clock.

He could feel his throat clog as he read his father's words. Could feel his muscles loosen, his body somehow, bit by bit, begin to relax. *I love you, son. I'm proud of you.*

It didn't gut him this time, his father's expression of love. It didn't empty him out.

Being your father has been the greatest honor of my life.

There was no clanging in his head or flash of heat in his gut. For once, he didn't wonder, he just . . .

He just believed his dad.

I love you, Wilder John, and I need you to hold on to that in the days to come.

That's when the tears found him. *Hold on.* Those two words. How could Dad have known? Days ago in that hospital chapel, just minutes ago out on the deck . . . he'd kept thinking about all he was holding on to. White knuckles, clenched fists. Holding and grasping and trying and failing to let go.

And here it was in his father's crooked handwriting. Not a prying open of his hands, but a gentle touch. A redirection. A mooring.

Something to hold on to. Someone.

You are loved beyond comprehension—by your earthly father and another. Hold on to that.

The letter fluttered to his lap and he was undone. Finally and fully.

*H*e was weightless yet grounded. Emptied out
and filled back up.

He was . . . okay.

A tranquil breeze washed over Wilder as he leaned over
the houseboat railing, the sun dipping lower into the western
sky, sending streaks of pale color through gossamer clouds.

Maybe he should've felt embarrassed at the way Neil had
found him long minutes ago. Sitting on the floor, his shirt
stained from using it to wipe his eyes, which were likely red
and swollen.

But there hadn't been room for embarrassment. Not with
so much else crowding his heart, making it feel alert and alive,
even as his body felt wrung out.

After reading Dad's letter—and then reading it again—he'd
pulled out one of his mother's old scrapbooks, thumbed
through its pages, found a picture of her and Dad together,
more tears falling. There was grief, yes. How could there not
be? But there was gratitude, too. And an intense relief he
wasn't even sure he understood.

He just knew it was there, stronger than any gut instinct
he'd ever had.

"Let's go back."

It was all he'd said to Neil when his friend sought him out, and apparently, it was all Neil had needed to hear. They'd turned the houseboat around, and now, the lights of the harbor were in sight.

"I have a feeling we're going to be late for dinner." Next to Wilder, Neil propped his arms over the railing, his gaze on the dusky sky.

Dinner at the farm. Suddenly it was the only place he wanted to be. At the farm. Not, for once, because he needed to get away from this boat and all its memories. But because along with all the other emotions humming in his heart, was a pulsing need to be wherever Lilian was.

He missed her. He wanted to see her. He wanted to tell her what had just happened even if he struggled to find the words. *You were right, Lil. I needed to read it again. It was different this time. Somehow . . . it was different.*

"Maggie invited Mariana and her dad." Neil shook his head. "I still can't get over it. All these years, Cynthia's been alive. I doubted it for a long time."

"I know. You were mad at me when I dragged Sydney here last year, thinking she was Cynthia."

"I was worried about Maggie. I thought you were getting her hopes up again."

"Yeah, well, the way I see it, you still owe me the world's hugest thank-you. You're a happily married man and soon-to-be father all because one of my gut instincts proved wrong."

Neil grinned. "I thank you and your faulty gut instinct."

It was almost incomprehensible—all that'd happened since Wilder had first brought Sydney to Maine. All that'd changed. What he wouldn't give to be able to tell his father all about it. To have one of their long conversations, to see Dad gasp when he got to the part in the hospital corridor where he realized who Mariana was.

Would that have been the part that surprised Dad most? Or would it have been the part where his son fell hard for his best friend's sister?

Or perhaps that wouldn't have surprised Dad at all. *You would've known she was everything I wanted long before I did, wouldn't you?*

Because Dad had been . . . Dad. He'd known Wilder better than anyone.

Well, maybe until Lilian.

You would've liked us together, Dad. And he would've scolded Wilder for keeping his distance this week. He absolutely would've.

Within minutes, they were steering the boat toward its usual spot in the harbor. Wilder tossed a thick rope onto the dock, then climbed out of the boat and went to work securing the rope to a mooring cleat.

"Your turn to thank me, Wild."

"What's that?"

"I'm dying to see how this turns out. And when I get back to the house, there's going to be a whole passel of curious women, too. And they'll all be mad at me for what I'm about to do."

"I have no idea what you're talking about. What are you about to do?" He straightened to see Neil looking past him.

"I'm about to walk away, my friend." Neil hopped onto the dock. "You can thank me later."

He turned just as Neil brushed past him.

Lil. She stood at the end of the dock, her hair fluttering in the wind, the prettiest silhouette he'd ever seen.

Oh yes. He was going to be very late for dinner.

It was déjà vu, walking down the dock, feeling it sway underneath her feet, wondering what might happen when she reached the end.

But she hadn't swiped Wilder's keys this time. And it wasn't dark. She wasn't wearing a raincoat and there was no storm hovering in the clammy air.

Unless the storm that was her thundering heartbeat counted.

She'd seen Wilder's houseboat in the distance when she'd first parked at the harbor. She'd watched it near and recognized her brother standing with Wilder. He'd strode past her a few seconds ago, the kind of smirk he rarely wore tugging at his lips.

"I'll tell Maggie not to set you a place."

"She already knows. She's the one who drove me here."

Because Lilian hadn't been cleared to drive yet. But also because she'd needed those quiet minutes alone in the car with the woman who'd given her the gift of a family. She'd told Maggie all about her conversation with James. She'd told her about Diana. About how she'd dreamed about both of them through the years.

"Can you believe it, Maggie? I was connected to you before you ever found me."

Tears had glistened in Maggie's eyes as she'd steered her car toward the harbor. *"Somehow I can believe it. We've been surrounded by miracles for so long. We didn't know it, but they were there all along."*

And there was something else, someone else, that'd been there all along, waiting for her at the edge of the dock. When she'd started walking his way, she'd half expected Wilder to come barreling toward her, but no, he was still just standing there. Waiting.

As if he knew this walk was something, well, momentous really.

She'd come to the houseboat when she was ten, hoping to convince Harry Monroe she was Cynthia Muir. She'd come here again at thirty, hoping to convince herself there were still answers to be found.

But who could've known the best answers would find her all on their own? Answers made up of words such as *wanted* and *known* and *loved*. By the family of her heart. By a familiar stranger who'd known her name and never stopped thinking of her. By the God who, she was coming to understand, had seen her all along.

And, she was pretty sure, oh she hoped, by the man whose grin was widening by the second.

Her side pinched by the time she reached Wilder. Was this the farthest she'd walked since waking up in a hospital bed with a hole in her side? And for the love of all that was good and holy, did he have to look so handsome just then? All dark-eyed and rugged, his hair windblown and just a touch of sunburn on his cheeks. How long had he and Neil been out on his boat?

And why hadn't she at least put her mussed hair in a pony-tail? Dashed on some makeup? "You could've met me halfway. I was shot a few days ago, you know."

It was like watching a light switch off, then turn back on. His smile vanished, then reappeared in an instant. "I have really missed your scowls, Lilian Muir. But also, I can't talk about you being shot. It's too terrible."

"Tell me about it. I'm going to have a scar, and I can't walk twenty feet without feeling like someone's punching me in the stomach."

There went his grin again. "You're hurting? Why didn't you say something? Should you even be up and about like this?"

"I'm fine. Certainly fine enough to be here."

"Why *are* you here?"

"Because . . ."

Because she's been reminded today that sometimes the unknown wasn't a ghost waiting to pounce, but a gift waiting to be unwrapped. Because she was ready—so very ready—to spend less time fearing what she couldn't see in her future and more time wondering about all the good, all the surprises, it might hold.

Because she couldn't get James's words out of her head. *"I prayed and took a risk and waited to see what would happen next."*

Wilder simply watched her, patient as ever.

"Because I'm curious," she finally said. "I want to see what happens next."

Wilder's gaze didn't leave her, and for once it didn't bother her—knowing he could see her so completely, could likely hear her every cluttered thought, sense her every hopeful emotion.

"Well, I'd very prefer that what happens next not include you pushing yourself too much."

"I said I'm fine—" Her retort dissolved into a squeal when he swept her off her feet, somehow managing to lift her into his arms while being careful of her side. "Wilder!"

He stepped onto the boat, his every movement sure and soft. "No more walking for you tonight."

"If you drop me—"

"I'm not going to drop you."

"If my stitches open up—"

"I'm being excessively careful, Miss Muir." He crossed the deck, his arms secure around her. "Also, I'm really good with a needle and thread."

She was trying so hard to glare. She was trying so hard not to notice how he smelled of soap and sunshine and the sea. But why? Why was she trying to do anything at all other than melt into the warmth of him and attempt to remember what she'd come here to say?

"Wilder—"

"I'm sorry for being so distant the past few days." He ducked under the doorway and into the houseboat's living room. "I wanted to give you the space I didn't on Monday night. I feel awful about how that conversation went." He skirted around the trunk. "I accused you of being scared—"

"I was." Was that his father's letter lying on the floor? His mother's scrapbook?

"I'm the one who was scared of being left behind, Lil. I've clung to you and clung to your family and clung to Maggie's case." He stopped in front of the couch and she thought he'd lower her onto it. Instead, gently, he lowered himself, sinking into its green cushions and bringing her with him, carefully arranging her in his lap.

"Wilder, your dad's letter . . ."

"You told me I should read it again. You were right."

She couldn't feel the pinch in her side anymore. Nor could she look away from his face. There was something new in his eyes, something light. She touched the collar of his shirt, and felt the heat of his gaze traveling through her.

"So why'd you come here tonight, Lily Grace?"

"You already asked me that. And where'd you hear that nickname?"

His head dipped lower, his chin touching her cheek. "Maggie said it in the hospital. I like it."

"Usually she's the only one I let call me Lily." But now there was James, too. Not the father she'd always imagined, but he was real. The man from her dream, who called her Lily . . . he was really real.

And so was this right here. Only this was a dream she couldn't have imagined. Gloriously real and gloriously relentless, and if Wilder wanted to call her Lily, he absolutely could. He could call her anything as long as he made a habit of holding her like this.

"Your answer before about why you're here . . . it wasn't very specific." His thumb traced her arm. "I could do my P.I. thing and hunt for clues as to your real purpose, but I have to tell you, I might be taking a little sabbatical from the P.I. life. There's this old house I'm thinking of fixing up—"

"You can't sell this boat, Wilder."

"I know—"

She gripped his collar. "Yes, you should totally buy Ansel's place, but you can't sell the *Marilyn*. It's too special. It means too much to you."

"I know, I know, Lil. What I don't know is why you're here." He kissed her cheek.

"Because Maggie's wedding is in two weeks and we still have a dozen things to do." She slid her arms around his neck. "We've lost a whole week. We haven't figured out where to have the rehearsal dinner or how many people are coming or—"

Finally, he cut her off, smiling even as he captured her mouth and pulled her closer, kissing her until she couldn't possibly have remembered what came next on her to-do list. Until she was pretty sure she couldn't breathe.

But then, who needed air? She was just fine drowning in the feel of him. He had one hand on her cheek and the other on her waist. He was still grinning against her lips. Or maybe that was her. She broke away just long enough to gasp. "Fine, fine, I came here for this, too."

"I thought so."

Then he had his fingers in her hair and she was the one to kiss him. Long and languid and another answer, another assurance that of all the things she might not know, she knew this: She loved Wilder Monroe. Wildly and impossibly.

"I'm probably going to drive you crazy, Wilder."

"Done." He kissed her cheek, then her chin.

"No, I'm serious. This whole CIS diagnosis—I don't want

to constantly fear what it might mean but even so, there's going to be days where it gets to me. I'm going to worry that my hands are shaking or wonder if my headache's more than just a headache. There's still tests I have to do and I have to make a decision about therapy and I might get MS, Wilder, I really might, and I don't know what it'll be like or how I'll handle it—"

He stilled her with a look, his fingers brushing her neck, his thumb tracing her jaw. "We'll handle it together. Whatever happens. We'll be in it together."

"I could get the bad kind of MS. I could lose my eyesight. Or my ability to walk."

"Then it will give me great pleasure to carry you around. Haven't I just proven my talents in that area?"

She curled into him and reached up to touch his cheek. "You read your dad's letter."

"I think . . . it wasn't his goodbye. It was his heart on the page." He turned his head and pressed a kiss into her palm. "And I've spent too long thinking about how he died. I want to start thinking about how he lived."

There was such a peace in his eyes and she wasn't sure she'd ever seen anything better. Not even a brilliant sunset spilling over the ocean could compete. She buried her face against his neck. This right here. This is the new story she wanted to tell. This is what she wanted to happen next. Today and tomorrow and for every *next* to come. "Just for the record, you can cling to me anytime, Wild. I don't find you nearly as off-putting as I used to."

Laughter rumbled in his chest and he pulled her even closer than before. "I love you, too, Lilian Muir."

25

*H*e had absolutely no clue how they'd pulled this off.

Wilder's gaze traveled the sprawling room at the center of Walter Wallace's packed yacht. It was his P.I. gaze, cataloging details, one after another. Glowing centerpieces of floating candles and white flowers. Live music and laughter. People, so many of them, scattered around tables and crowded onto the dance floor. Fairy lights and Indi's whimsical décor, made all the better by a radiant sunset spilling in from every direction.

Okay, he knew exactly how they'd pulled this off. Miss Lilian Muir had had them running around since the crack of dawn this morning. Never mind she was only a few weeks out from a gunshot wound and subsequent surgery.

Never mind it felt like a hundred things had happened in the month and a half since Maggie had first asked them to take on the planning of her wedding. Oh no, nothing had slowed Lilian down.

She'd gone full-on drill sergeant.

And he'd loved it.

Loved every minute of being bossed around. Being told where to hang what and how to arrange the slipcovers over

370

the chairs and for goodness' sake, not to trip over the cords by the sound system.

He just wished he knew where she was now. He'd barely taken his eyes off her through the ceremony itself. Hadn't been able to. She'd stood just behind Maggie—she and Indi serving as Maggie's maids of honor—wearing maybe the most stunning dress he'd ever seen. Or probably it wasn't so much the dress as her.

And probably he was supposed to have been paying more attention to Maggie. He'd done his best. He'd watched with enough welling emotion, certainly, to rival anyone else's as the woman who'd saved him from himself three years ago, who'd pulled him close and given him a place to belong, pledged her love to the man standing across from her.

Maggie's eyes had sparkled and if she'd stopped smiling even once during the ceremony, or the meal afterward, or her first dance with Ray, he hadn't noticed.

But then, there'd been Lil in the aforementioned dress that slanted off one shoulder and hugged her figure, and really, how was he supposed to notice anything else anyway?

But also, how had he lost her?

"Well, I'm glad I waited on my move to Florida long enough for this." The voice came from behind him, rising above the music and the crowd, but just barely.

Wilder turned to see Ansel Barrett ambling his way, a clear plate in hand, a piece of tiered cake half-eaten on it. "Wouldn't have been right without you here, Ansel. Even if you had moved, we'd have sent a private plane for you."

"I'd guffaw at that, except we're having this shindig on a private yacht, so . . ." The older man grinned and shrugged. "Come outside for a minute? I'm tired of yelling."

He followed Ansel toward the back of the room and out a set of double doors that led onto the yacht's lower deck. Lilting music followed them into the cool night air. A few people lingered here and there on the deck in small clusters. Was this where Lilian had disappeared to?

Strings of light traced the deck's railing and eventide was even more spectacular out here, the sky flaring with color—purples and yellows and a peach-hued orange stretching into the distance. Breathtaking.

"Phew." Ansel took a bite of his cake. "I love a crowd, but I also love talking at a normal decibel. I need to talk to you about the land."

Right now? "Happy to up my offer, Ansel. Which I realize is a stupid thing to say to a seller, but I guess you already know I'm pretty intent on going through with the purchase, so you've got the upper hand."

"Don't be silly, son."

Son.

There'd been a day not very long ago when that word from anyone else's mouth could make him flinch. When all it could do was bring his pain to the surface. But now . . .

It still hurt a little. But it healed a little, too. He could hear it in Dad's voice and savor the memory. He could choose, as many times as he needed to, not to dwell on the old *what-if.* To release it and hold on to something else instead.

Love. He could keep holding on to love just like Dad had asked him to. Holding on to a Father who'd been holding on to him all along.

He could remember Dad's life. He could find ways to get to know his mother, even now. He could share it all, every emotion, even the difficult ones, with the woman he loved.

"I just want to know if you've talked to Neil yet about farming the land," Ansel said. "I had someone ask about buying my harvester, but if it's all the same, I'd rather throw it in with the rest of the equipment that's already included in the sale. But only if I know it's going to someone like Neil. Well, not someone like him. Preferably him."

"You are a very good person, Mr. Barrett. And yes, I've talked to him. He's still being stubborn about leasing the land at way too high of a price, but don't worry. I can talk him down. I'm very persuasive."

"He really is."

Lilian.

There was no stopping his smile as he angled to see her, and why in the world would he have wanted to stop anyway? Lilian Muir was worth smiling about every day, all day.

She came up next to him, the evening wind or maybe just the busyness of the day having long ago messed with the intricate hairdo she'd worn earlier. Strands of tousled hair had escaped from beaded pins and they fluttered around her face now.

"Although what he calls being persuasive, some might consider coercive. It's how we ended up planning a wedding together."

He chuckled and towed her to his side. "We ended up planning a wedding together because Maggie asked us to."

"She asked us and I said no and you coerced me into it."

"I think you mean charmed you into it."

"I know what I meant."

"So do I, and where've you been?" He tucked a piece of hair behind her ear.

"Ansel just walked away."

"A good man, indeed." He tugged her closer. "Where've you been?"

"You're repeating yourself."

"Because you haven't answered. And you haven't danced with me either."

"Well." She propped her free hand, the one not wrapped around his side, on her waist. "You haven't taken me on that date to the chapel. I thought we were going to go treasure hunting."

"We are. We will. After you've fully recovered—"

"If I've recovered enough to dance, then I've recovered enough to hike."

"I've always liked arguing with you, Lil. But it's even better now." He kissed her lips once, twice. "Where've you been?"

"On the upper deck. Everyone's up there waiting for you." She moved her hand away from her waist and around his neck instead, her voice going breathy. "Family photos."

"Family photos?"

"Yes, the lighting's perfect, but we couldn't take them without you." She pressed her lips to his cheek.

Family photos. And they were waiting on him.

***

She might never recover from this. She might never want to.

Pure joy, that's what it was, tickling over her skin, pooling in her heart, filling her lungs until she might burst. It was just too lovely, seeing them all together, huddled near the railing of the upper deck, talking over one another and just generally ignoring the poor photographer waiting for them to come to some semblance of order.

Lilian slowed her steps as she and Wilder wound their way toward her family.

Maggie and Ray were at the center of the group, hands clasped together. Had they broken apart even once since the ceremony? Lilian didn't think so. Maggie was resplendent in her dress, but even more so in her contentedness. Twilight streaked her white hair with color and lightened her already beaming face.

It might've been Neil and Sydney's wedding day, too, for all they'd had eyes for only each other all evening. Sydney had been convinced her pregnancy was on full display in her bridesmaid's dress, but who would notice a tiny bump with the way she kept beaming at Neil?

He's happy. And her big brother deserved it. So very much.

Indi fairly bounced with energy from her spot near the yacht's railing. And Lilian couldn't blame her. She had her dear Philip on one side. She had Holland, Philip's half sister, her shadow and confidante, on the other. And in front of her, the daughter she'd given birth to almost twelve years ago. It was the first time Olivia had joined their whole family for an event, thanks to Indi's budding friendship with the family who'd adopted her, and how the girl wasn't completely overwhelmed by the lot of them, Lilian didn't know.

But wait, this wasn't everyone. She came to a full halt in front of her gathered family and shook her head. "Seriously, guys, can no one follow orders?" Somehow, above the clatter of voices and the music of the sea, they clearly all heard her, turning at once as she folded her arms. "No one fetched Mariana?"

Blank gazes stared back at her, Indi speaking up. "I thought that's where you went."

"No, I went to find Wilder. One of you was supposed to go after Mari."

The photographer leaned in. "We really need to get a move on. The lighting—"

"Of course. I'm sorry." Lilian spared the man an apologetic glance before turning back to her family. "I'll go find her. No one else move."

Neil smirked. "Someone is extra bossy today."

Lilian tried to glare, but doubted it had any effect at all. She turned to Wilder, took in his extra wide grin and lowered her arms. "I *am* extra bossy today."

"I know. I love it."

"Your job is to make sure no one leaves before I get back. We are getting this family picture."

"Aye, aye, captain." He gave her a mock salute that would have made her roll her eyes a month ago.

But now . . . well, she still rolled her eyes. But only because she knew he'd enjoy it. Because she knew it'd make his handsome smile grow all the more and that was something *she* loved.

She spent the next minutes retracing her steps until she was back in the crowded reception hall, scouring the place for Mariana. It didn't take long to spot her. She stood near the dessert table, holding a plate with a piece of cake and flanked by her father and stepmother.

Yesterday Mariana had introduced Lilian to Willa, the woman from Iowa her father had married. Maggie had insisted on inviting the pair to the wedding, though James had been uncomfortable with the idea at first. But in a way only Maggie could, she'd managed to convince the man he was welcome.

They'd had several private conversations—Maggie and James—in the days after the revelation about Mariana's identity, her past and James's role in it. Lilian didn't know what all they'd said to each other, but she knew it couldn't have been easy for either one of them. But then, maybe forgiveness and healing went all the deeper the more hard-fought they came.

She was beginning to think that's how hope worked, too. Hope was stronger when it was chosen and chased and held close despite the odds. Despite a diagnosis or an unknown. Despite questions that didn't have answers or answers that were hard to understand. It took effort, it took curiosity—but there was hope to be found and cherished in all of it.

James spotted Lilian's approach first, the subtle shift in his expression telling her he still hadn't quite gotten over the surprise of her. He really had cared about her all those years ago. Cared still. "Lilian."

"Hey, I'm sorry to interrupt, but we're doing family photos up on the deck. Your presence is required, Mari."

Mariana's delight at being counted as family was nearly as heart-tugging as Wilder's. "Of course. Lead the way." She handed her plate to James. "Don't eat my cake, Dad."

"Can't make any promises." He chuckled, then glanced to Lilian, gave her a soft smile and a nod. They'd have more time to talk in coming days, if not in person, then by email or phone. He'd already invited Lilian to come with Mariana next time she visited Iowa. *"You'd be surprised at how much our little Maple Valley is like your Muir Harbor."*

She'd take him up on the invitation. She'd relish the opportunity to get to know him every bit as much as she'd loved coming to know Mariana, her half sister.

Maybe, eventually, she'd even find a way to get to know the brother she now knew she had. *Peyton.* She hadn't been ready to see him right away, but earlier this week, amid all the final wedding prep, she'd mustered up the courage. Wilder had accompanied her to the care center, only to have Peyton refuse to see her. Apparently, since he'd learned about his father's death, he'd gone to a dark place.

He was still facing serious charges and likely, prison time. But . . . he was her brother, even if that reality felt strange and difficult to digest. He wasn't beyond redemption. *Hope.* Yes, there could be hope for him, too. So when the time was right, she'd reach out. She wasn't sure how or when or what might happen, but she'd try.

Lilian returned James's nod and wound her arm through Mariana's. "We better get up on deck before our poor photographer has apoplexy."

Minutes later, they squeezed into place among the family members the photographer had arranged during Lilian's absence. Lilian tucked herself in at Wilder's side, and Mariana took her spot next to Maggie, looking almost as if she'd been a part of them all along.

And maybe in a way she had. Maybe time and distance, tragedy and mystery had kept her away for a time. A loose thread, snipped and separated.

But never lost.

None of them had ever been lost, not really. They'd been pieces of a tapestry, stitched together by a divine hand. In different times, in different ways, and it hadn't always been easy or pain-free.

But they were connected now. They were together now. A tightly woven family, found and forever.

"Whoa, look, Lil."

Wilder's whisper in her ear sent a shiver down her back. While the photographer made last-minute adjustments to his camera, Lilian followed Wilder's pointing finger toward the glowing skyline. The chapel on the cliff, backlit by the setting sun, its steeple reaching for the clouds.

"I'm absolutely going to cash in on that date, Wilder. How does tomorrow sound? After church. We could really find it, you know. We could find Alec Muir's treasure. With your instincts and my intelligence—"

He grinned down at her. "Your wild imagination, I think you mean."

"You promised to take me treasure hunting and I'm going to hold you to it. You know I will. You, me, the chapel, a long-awaited second date."

"Two things." With his hand on her elbow, he turned her to face him. "First, and this is going to make you groan, but I'm going to say it anyway: I've already found my treasure."

Her breath caught in her throat and she didn't even care that her entire family surrounded them. She didn't care that they'd tease her endlessly or that, for years, decades to come, they'd still be talking about how Wilder Monroe, once the very bane of her existence, the closest thing she'd ever had to an enemy, had worn her down and won her over.

She just didn't care. "Why in the world would that make me groan?" She slid her arms around his waist, underneath his suit jacket. Any minute now and the photographer would scold them. "What's the second thing?"

"You're thinking too small, Lilian Muir." Wilder dipped his head to her ear, another delicious shiver gliding over her skin. "You, me, the chapel . . . we can do a lot better than a second date."

Epilogue

a summer breeze rustled through crowded branches and skimmed over Lilian's bare arms, carrying with it the scent of honeysuckle.

And the sound of her son's laughter.

She stopped mere feet from the trickling creek that wound around the far western edge of their property. Wilder's houseboat rested in shallow water, surrounded by tall grass that fluttered around Lilian's legs. Of course she'd known this was where she'd find her absentee husband and son. Where else would Wilder have whisked their two-and-a-half-year-old off to when they were supposed to be setting up tables in the backyard?

Wilder stood on the houseboat's deck, little Harry at his side, both their backs to Lilian. In the narrow space between them, sunlight glinted off the object Wilder now pulled from a tall cardboard box. A parcel service had delivered the thing half an hour ago, which had apparently been Wilder's cue to abandon preparations for tonight's festivities.

"What is it?" Harry's high-pitched voice glided on the cool evening air. His mop of dark hair was a perfect match for Wilder's.

"This would be a metal detector, son. Also known as your mom's anniversary gift. Which means you have to keep your lips sealed for another five weeks, okay?"

"What's a metal detector?"

Lilian grinned—at Harry's lisping pronunciation, at the delight in Wilder's voice.

At the gift itself. It was hilarious. It was perfect. After all, they had a track record to keep up—three anniversaries and counting spent hunting for Alec Muir's treasure. Evidently, her husband was already planning for their fourth, coming up at the beginning of August.

Oh, she never could've seen this coming—this marriage, this life.

She'd married him—Wilder Monroe, of all people—at the chapel in a small, candlelit ceremony, exactly one month after they'd finally had that second date in the same location. One of the best days of her life.

Followed by so many more best days. Today, she had a feeling, would be another. Her entire family would be gathering tonight to welcome Maggie and Ray home from their anniversary trip to Scotland. Actually, they were probably descending on Wilder and Lilian's farmhouse even now, with half the items on her party to-do list still unchecked.

No matter. Neil would take charge of firing up the grill and setting up tables under the swooping patio lights in the backyard. Indi knew where everything was in the kitchen.

Tonight's party was also a late celebration of Mariana's law school graduation. And an early birthday gathering for Indi's one-year-old. Plus, Neil and Sydney's treehouse Airbnb business had just been featured in a top tourism magazine, which definitely deserved to be commemorated.

And then there was Lilian's reason to celebrate. Another thing she never could've seen coming. Another surprise that had awaited her in the unknown.

That awaited Wilder even now.

"You two are going to be late to our own party," she called from the water's edge.

Wilder and Harry spun in sync, Wilder keeping the metal detector tucked behind him as he faced Lilian, his expression the perfect mix of charm and chagrin. "I do believe we've been caught, Harry."

A fact that didn't do a thing to faze Harry. He waved at Lilian. "Hi, Mom."

Soon they were tromping through the grove, toward the farmhouse they'd been slowly fixing up over the past few years. Wilder had hidden her gift away inside the boat, but she knew he knew she'd seen it. Because Wilder *always* knew. Him and his gut instincts.

Him and his ability to see straight into her heart, time and again.

She reached for his hand as Harry ran on ahead of them and glanced up to take in his profile, then grinned all over again. Because his gut didn't always pick up on everything, and oh, how she couldn't wait to see him flabbergasted and speechless in front of her family tonight.

"You're just going to have to pretend, Lil."

"Hmm?" The farmhouse came into view ahead and, yep, she'd been correct. That was Neil's old truck parked in the gravel driveway and Indi's little car behind it. She would've picked up Mariana in town before heading this way. Philip was on airport duty, tasked with picking up Maggie and Ray. Their flight had landed two hours ago, so they should be coming down the lane any minute.

"You saw your anniversary gift, but you'll just have to pretend you didn't and act surprised when you unwrap it."

"Lucky for you, I am a very good actress. Lucky for me, you are a very good gift giver."

His fingers laced through hers. "I really am, aren't I?"

"But you're terrible at following a list. Almost everyone's here and we aren't at all ready."

"Excuse me, but who's the one who stayed at the office two hours later than planned today? What happened to coming home midafternoon?"

"It was an important case, Wild."

"They're all important cases."

She flashed one of those mock glares he loved. "Yes, they are."

He tugged her to a halt a few feet from their front porch, Harry already on his way around the house toward the backyard, probably in search of his cousins—Neil and Sydney's three daughters, their youngest still a newborn, and Indi and Philip's son. Wilder's dark eyes danced as he looked down at her. "Have I ever told you how much I like your scowls, Lil?"

"Many, many times." She reached into her pocket. "Did you see what came in the mail?" She held up the letter.

Wilder's brows lifted. "He finally wrote back?"

She nodded. She'd already read Peyton's letter twice. It was brief, not at all flowery or full of feeling. But after all this time, it was a start. Made her think maybe her biological brother hadn't ignored all the notes she'd sent him throughout the years. Maybe one of these days he'd even let her visit him at the state penitentiary.

Wilder kissed her hair, then peered into her eyes. "How are you feeling?"

"About the letter?"

"Yes, but also . . ." His gaze turned earnest as it swept over her. "In general."

"I'm good." She squeezed his hand so he'd know she was serious. "No, I'm great."

"Hmm."

"You don't believe me?"

"I do. It's just that you've been wearing this sneaky sort of grin off and on for a few days now. I need to know what it means."

She shook her head. "Calls for speculation."

"Exactly. I'm speculating. Fill me in."

"No time. We've got burgers to grill and pies to get in the oven." She tried to turn away, but he kept hold of her hand, reached for the other one.

"You're keeping secrets from your husband, Lil, and your husband objects."

Secrets. Plural. He didn't know how right he was.

When she only smirked in response, he pulled her closer and kissed her cheek. Then her lips.

"Badgering the witness," she murmured.

"Is it working?"

They were interrupted by the rumble of an engine. She laughed at Wilder's groan, but he let her pull away this time. Moments later, she was wrapped in Maggie's hug and they were rounding the house, the rest of her family members spilling all around them, welcoming Maggie and Ray home, talking over each other like they always did.

"Did anyone stop to think that these two might be too jet-lagged to enjoy a party on their first night home?" Neil's voice was half-grumble, half-amusement from his spot near the grill.

"That's why we're doing it here instead of Muir Farm, silly." Indi handed him a plate of burgers. "They can leave the moment they get tired."

The evening's golden sunlight was no match for Maggie's beaming expression. "Really wish you wouldn't talk about us like we're old-timers. We have all the energy in the world. I just hope you all have enough energy to look at our thousand Scotland pics."

The grill's charcoal smell, the sound of the kids running

around and laughing, dusk's first inklings rimming feathery clouds with pastel colors—it was just all so perfect. So . . .

"Remarkable," she whispered.

"What was that, dear?" Maggie's voice was soft at her side. Neil had turned back to the grill with Sydney at his side, their newborn now cradled in Mariana's arms. Ray was swinging Philip and Indi's one-year-old onto his shoulders as the pair looked on.

Lilian leaned toward Maggie. "Do you ever just stop to think, wow, I, Maggie Muir, made all of this possible?"

Maggie's hazel eyes skimmed over their boisterous family. "I don't think I can take all the credit."

"Well, okay, God made it happen. But every time He asked you to open your heart to another person, you said yes. You changed every one of our lives. And now . . . just look at all of us."

But Maggie wasn't looking at the rest of them anymore. Her attention was on Lilian. "How are you feeling, Lil?"

"Wilder just asked me the same—" She broke off, following the downward tilt of Maggie's focus. She flattened one palm against her stomach. "You can't possibly know."

"Wilder isn't the only one who gets a gut instinct every now and then." Her eyes twinkled. "When are you due?"

Lilian shook her head in disbelief. "Seven months. An eternity."

"I take it Wilder's beside himself with happiness?"

"Oh yeah. But he's about to be beside himself with shock, too."

"Why's that?"

Lilian bent closer, impatience to spill her secret finally getting the best of her. "We're having twins."

Thankfully, Maggie's gasp was lost to the commotion all around them.

"I haven't told him yet. He had to miss my appointment

earlier this week—Harry was still getting over a cold. Figured I'd surprise him tonight when I tell everyone else."

Maggie's grin was pure delight. Her embrace, pure motherly love. "I am beyond excited for you. And for myself—two more grandbabies. And for poor Wilder, who just might keel over when you tell him."

"I know. I can't wait."

Maggie laughed and stepped back.

"What's so amusing over here?"

Lilian turned to Wilder, to the man who'd filled her world with curiosity and adventure. They'd healed together and learned to hope together. Created a family and a home and a life together, with so much more story still to be told.

She stretched one arm around his waist and leaned her head on his shoulder. From somewhere nearby, Harry's voice floated above the others. A dog barked. Captain, maybe, or Flannel. She still hadn't gotten those pies in the oven.

Later. For right now, this was the only place she wanted to be.

Wilder brushed his thumb over her cheek. "You didn't answer my question, Lil. And there's that smile again."

Yes. "Just thinking about what's next."

THE END

AUTHOR NOTE & ACKNOWLEDGEMENTS

Dear treasured readers,

I've been looking forward to writing *Wedding at Sea* literally since the first page of the first book in this series . . . when P.I. Wilder Monroe first appeared. I loved him from the start!

And Lil—she accidentally became a reflection of me. I don't know why I was surprised by that because it happens with almost every heroine I write! Our circumstances aren't the same, but our hurts and hopes, fears and desires overlap.

And like always, somewhere along the way, instead of me burrowing into this story, it burrowed into me.

One of the things that was really important to me in this novel was leaving some uncertainty on the table for Wilder and Lil even at The End. Lilian doesn't get a concrete diagnosis, Wilder doesn't get an answer to every question about his father's death. I'll confess, I was tempted to tie up those loose ends with a nice little bow—just like I'd looooove to see the loose ends in my own life all tied up and tidy.

But I realized, no, part of the beauty of their story—and certainly my own, too—is learning to live with questions . . .

And learning to ask new questions, too. Questions born of intentional curiosity and determined hope. Hope that's possible when we remember God can write a better story with our lives than we ever could on our own. It's that kind of hope, that kind of trust that allows us to ask *"What's next?"* with a twinkle in our eyes and a soul-stirring sort of exhilaration.

It's that kind of hope I found filling me up as I wrote this novel. And I pray it did the same for you!

Thank you so much for coming along on this seaside journey with me! I've loved writing these books . . . and I don't think I've said goodbye to Muir Harbor for good. ;)

My deepest thanks to:

Mom and Dad—always at the top. Always the most loving and encouraging influences in my life.

Grandma—thank you so much for all the letters and prayers. I'm so grateful for you.

My siblings, nieces, and nephews—as always, for being a) awesome and b) the reason families feature so prominently in my books.

Charlene Patterson—thank you, thank you, thank you for your editing expertise and feedback that's been such a huge part of not only this book, but this whole series and nearly every book I've written.

Denise Harmer—I so appreciate your keen proofreading eye. Thank you for polishing this manuscript.

Nicole Schwieger and Hillary Manton Lodge—every cover in this series has been gorgeous. Thank you!

Joanne Bischof, Lindsay Harrel, Liz Johnson, Alena Tauriainen, and Courtney Walsh—I am blessed beyond measure by so many author friends, but you five in particular uplifted me more than you know throughout the writing of this story. Thank you for all the texts and voxes . . . and Joanne and Liz, that weekend last October was the BEST. Thank you for coming all the way to Iowa!

Finally, of course and as always, thank you to God—for the joy and surprise and yes, even the challenges, that were waiting for me in this series. It's all a gift. And I can't wait to see what's next.

ABOUT THE AUTHOR

MELISSA TAGG is the *USA Today* bestselling, Christy Award-winning author of swoony and hope-filled small-town contemporary romances. She's also a former reporter, current nonprofit marketing strategist, and total Iowa girl. Melissa has taught at multiple national writing conferences, as well as workshops and women's retreats. When she's not happily lost in someone else's book or plugging away her own, she can be found spoiling her nieces and nephews, watching old movies, and daydreaming about her next fictional hero. Connect with Melissa at melissatagg.com.

instagram.com/melissatagg
amazon.com/author/melissatagg
bookbub.com/authors/melissatagg
goodreads.com/melissatagg

Made in United States
Troutdale, OR
12/07/2024

25984055R00239